UNDERWINTER

VOLUME ONE
SYMPHONY

RAY FAWKES
Creator, Writer, Artist

STEVE WANDS
Letterer

DANI V.
Costume Consultant

> *"The trumpet shall be heard on high*
> *The dead shall live, the living die,*
> *And Music shall untune the sky!"*

- John Dryden, *A Song for Saint Cecilia's Day*

IMAGE COMICS, INC.
Robert Kirkman—Chief Operating Officer
Erik Larsen—Chief Financial Officer
Todd McFarlane—President
Marc Silvestri—Chief Executive Officer
Jim Valentino—Vice President

Eric Stephenson—Publisher
Corey Murphy—Director of Sales
Jeff Boison—Director of Publishing Planning & Book Trade Sales
Chris Ross—Director of Digital Sales
Jeff Stang—Director of Specialty Sales
Kat Salazar—Director of PR & Marketing
Branwyn Bigglestone—Controller
Kali Dugan—Senior Accounting Manager
Sue Korpela—Accounting & HR Manager
Drew Gill—Art Director
Heather Doornink—Production Director
Leigh Thomas—Print Manager
Tricia Ramos—Traffic Manager
Briah Skelly—Publicist
Aly Hoffman—Events & Conventions Coordinator
Sasha Head—Sales & Marketing Production Designer
David Brothers—Branding Manager
Melissa Gifford—Content Manager
Drew Fitzgerald—Publicity Assistant
Vincent Kukua—Production Artist
Erika Schnatz—Production Artist
Shanna Matuszak—Production Artist
Carey Hall—Production Artist
Ryan Brewer—Production Artist
Esther Kim—Direct Market Sales Representative
Emilio Bautista—Digital Sales Representative
Leanna Caunter—Accounting Analyst
Chloe Ramos-Peterson—Library Market Sales Representative
Marla Eizik—Administrative Assistant
IMAGECOMICS.COM

UNDERWINTER: SYMPHONY, VOL. 1. First printing. October 2017. Published by Image Comics, Inc. Office of publication: 2701 NW Vaughn St., Suite 780, Portland, OR 97210. Copyright © 2017 Ray Fawkes & Piper Snow Productions Ltd. All rights reserved. Contains material originally published in single magazine form as UNDERWINTER: SYMPHONY #1-6. "UNDERWINTER," its logos, and the likenesses of all characters herein are trademarks of Ray Fawkes & Piper Snow Productions Ltd, unless otherwise noted. "Image" and the Image Comics logos are registered trademarks of Image Comics, Inc. No part of this publication may be reproduced or transmitted, in any form or by any means (except for short excerpts for journalistic or review purposes), without the express written permission of Ray Fawkes & Piper Snow Productions Ltd, or Image Comics, Inc. All names, characters, events, and locales in this publication are entirely fictional. Any resemblance to actual persons (living or dead), events, or places, without satiric intent, is coincidental. Printed in the USA. For information regarding the CPSIA on this printed material call: 203-595-3636 and provide reference #RICH–764790. For international rights, contact: foreignlicensing@imagecomics.com. ISBN: 978-1-5343-0332-4.

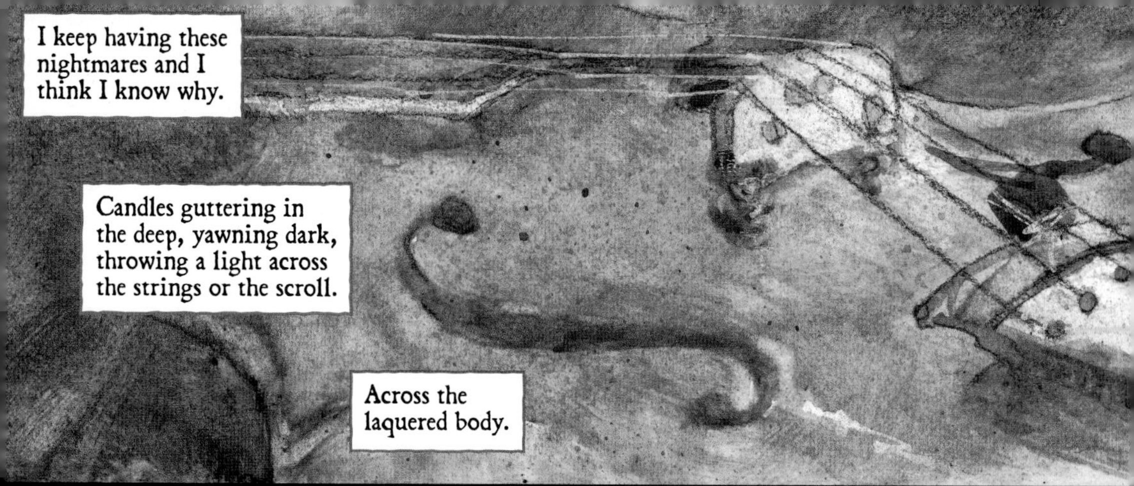
I keep having these nightmares and I think I know why.
Candles guttering in the deep, yawning dark, throwing a light across the strings or the scroll.
Across the laquered body.

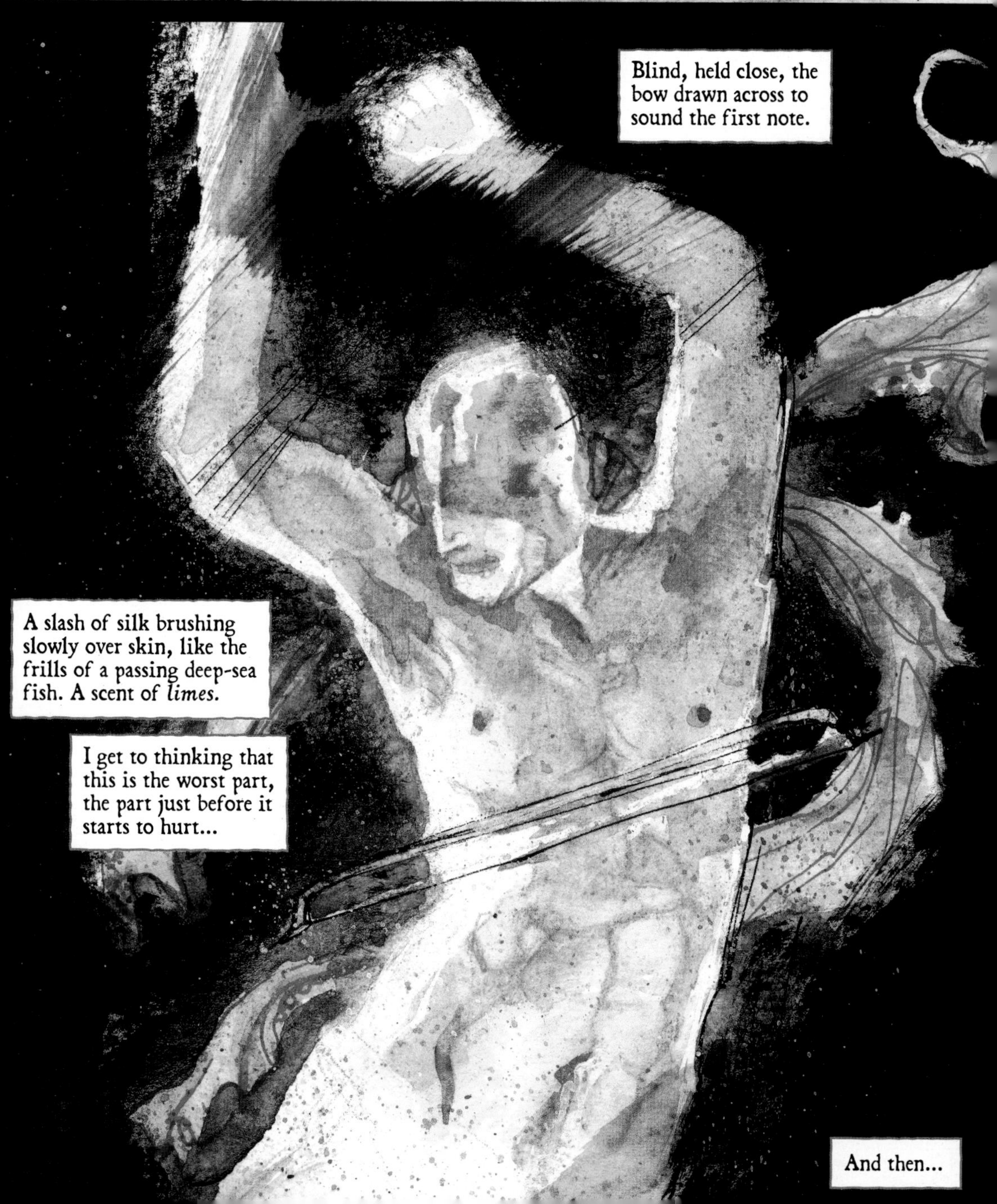
Blind, held close, the bow drawn across to sound the first note.
A slash of silk brushing slowly over skin, like the frills of a passing deep-sea fish. A scent of *limes.*
I get to thinking that this is the worst part, the part just before it starts to hurt...
And then...

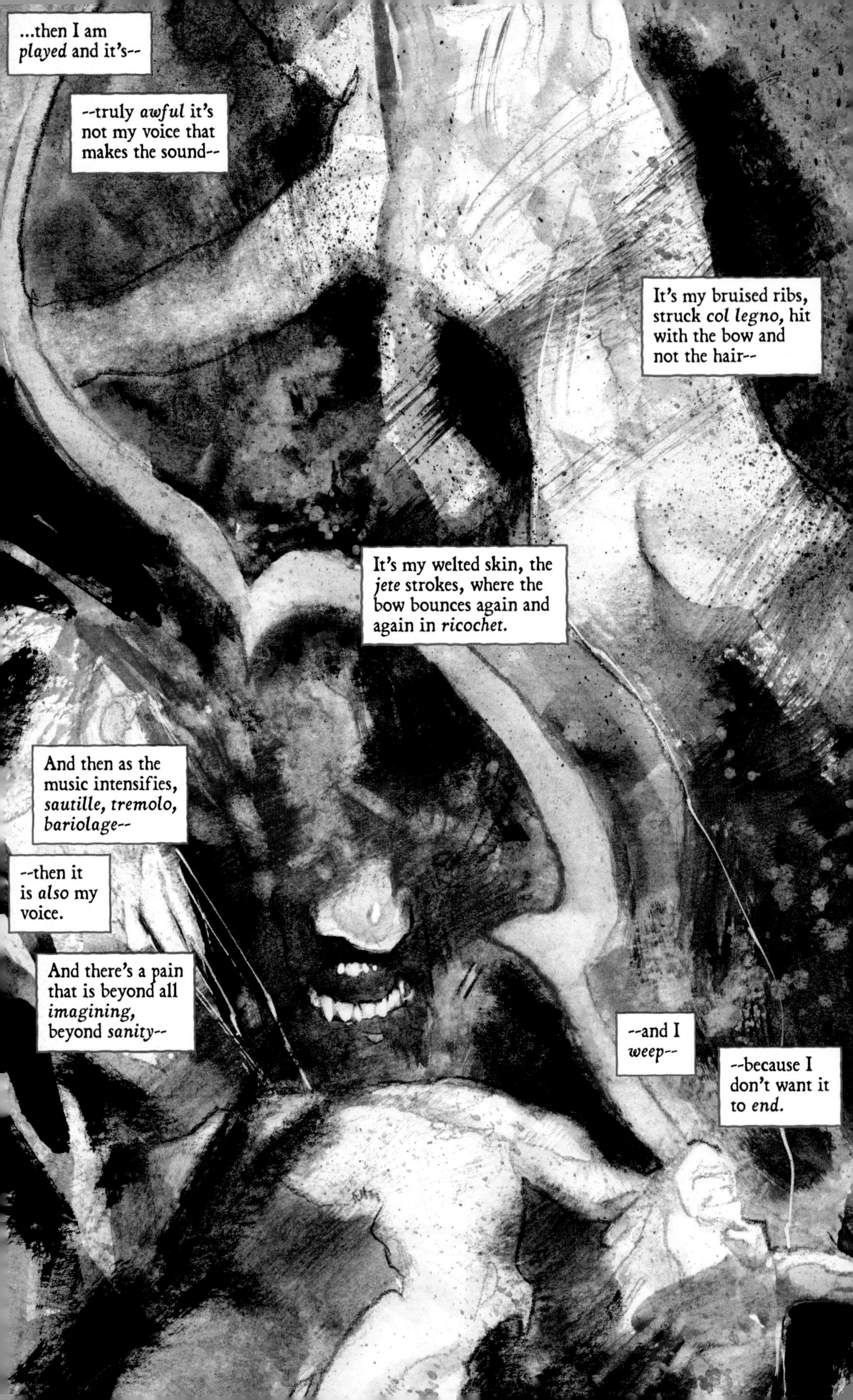
...then I am *played* and it's--
--truly *awful* it's not my voice that makes the sound--
It's my bruised ribs, struck *col legno,* hit with the bow and not the hair--
It's my welted skin, the *jete* strokes, where the bow bounces again and again in *ricochet.*
And then as the music intensifies, *sautille, tremolo, bariolage*--
--then it is *also* my voice.
And there's a pain that is beyond all *imagining,* beyond *sanity*--
--and I *weep*--
--because I don't want it to *end.*

SYMPHONY

PART ONE:
NOVEMBER

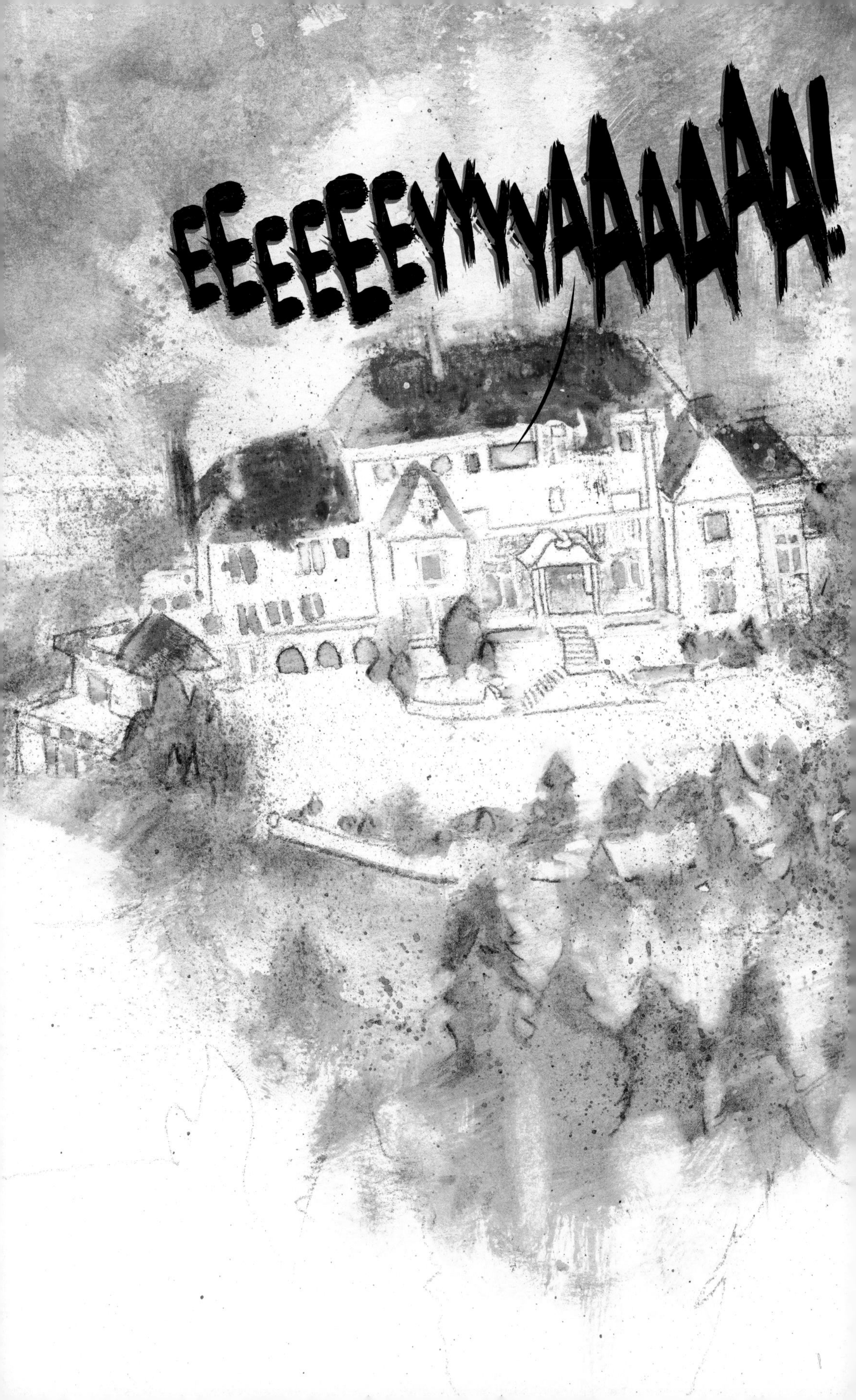
EEEEEEYYYYAAAAAA!

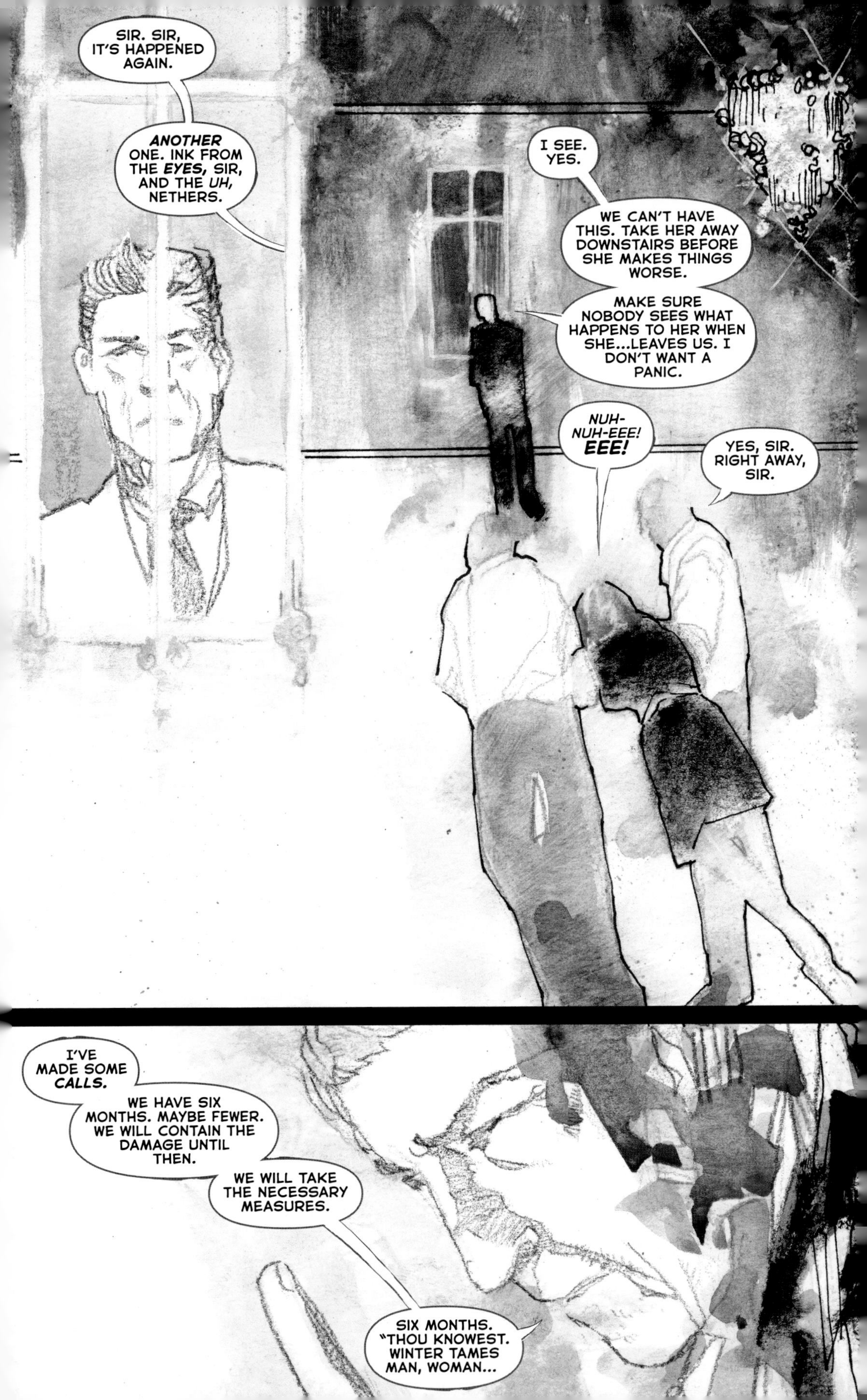
SIR. SIR, IT'S HAPPENED AGAIN.
ANOTHER ONE. INK FROM THE *EYES*, SIR, AND THE *UH*, NETHERS.
I SEE. YES.
WE CAN'T HAVE THIS. TAKE HER AWAY DOWNSTAIRS BEFORE SHE MAKES THINGS WORSE.
MAKE SURE NOBODY SEES WHAT HAPPENS TO HER WHEN SHE...LEAVES US. I DON'T WANT A PANIC.
NUH-NUH-EEE! ***EEE!***
YES, SIR. RIGHT AWAY, SIR.
I'VE MADE SOME *CALLS.*
WE HAVE SIX MONTHS. MAYBE FEWER. WE WILL CONTAIN THE DAMAGE UNTIL THEN.
WE WILL TAKE THE NECESSARY MEASURES.
SIX MONTHS. "THOU KNOWEST. WINTER TAMES MAN, WOMAN...

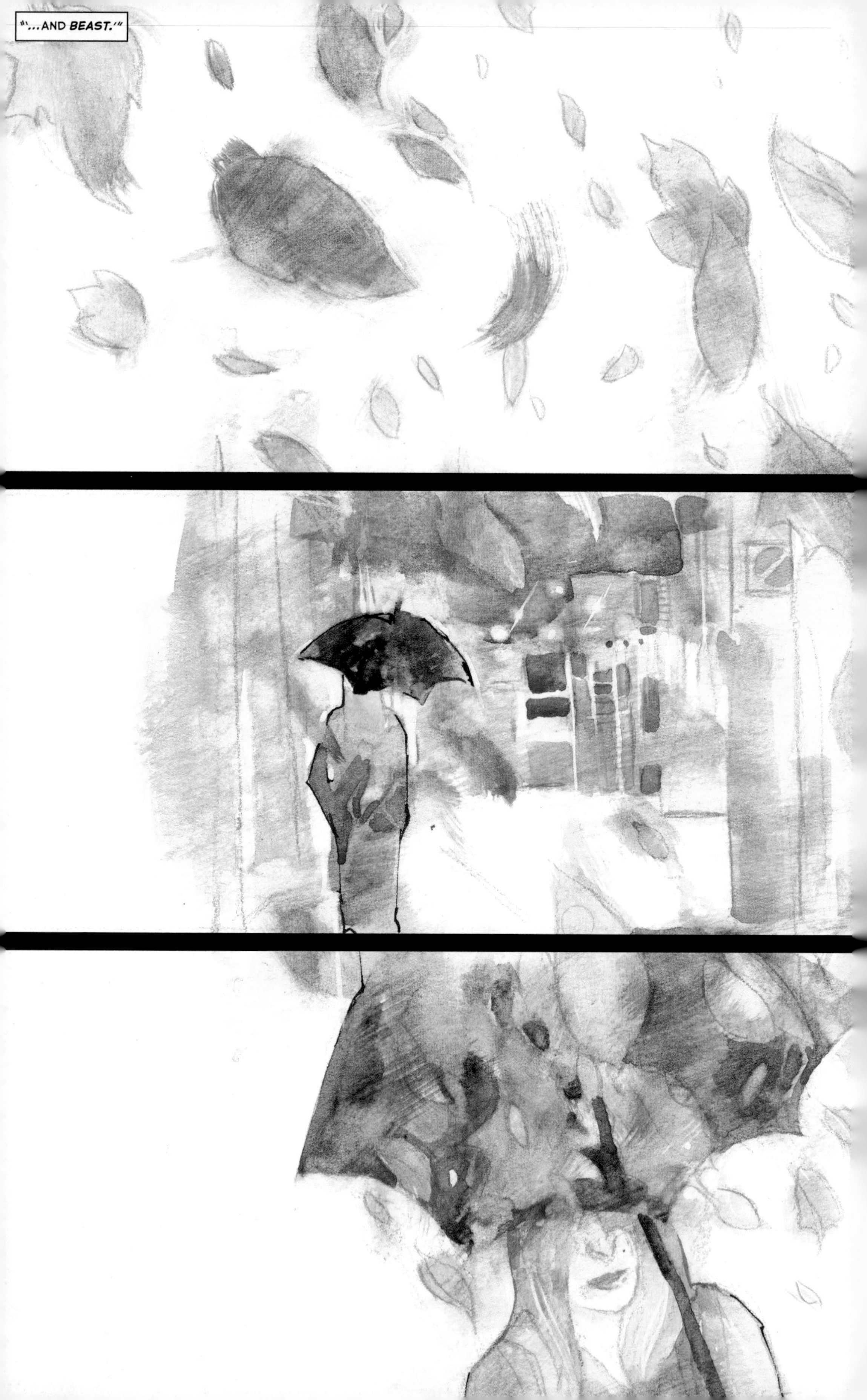
"'...AND BEAST.'"

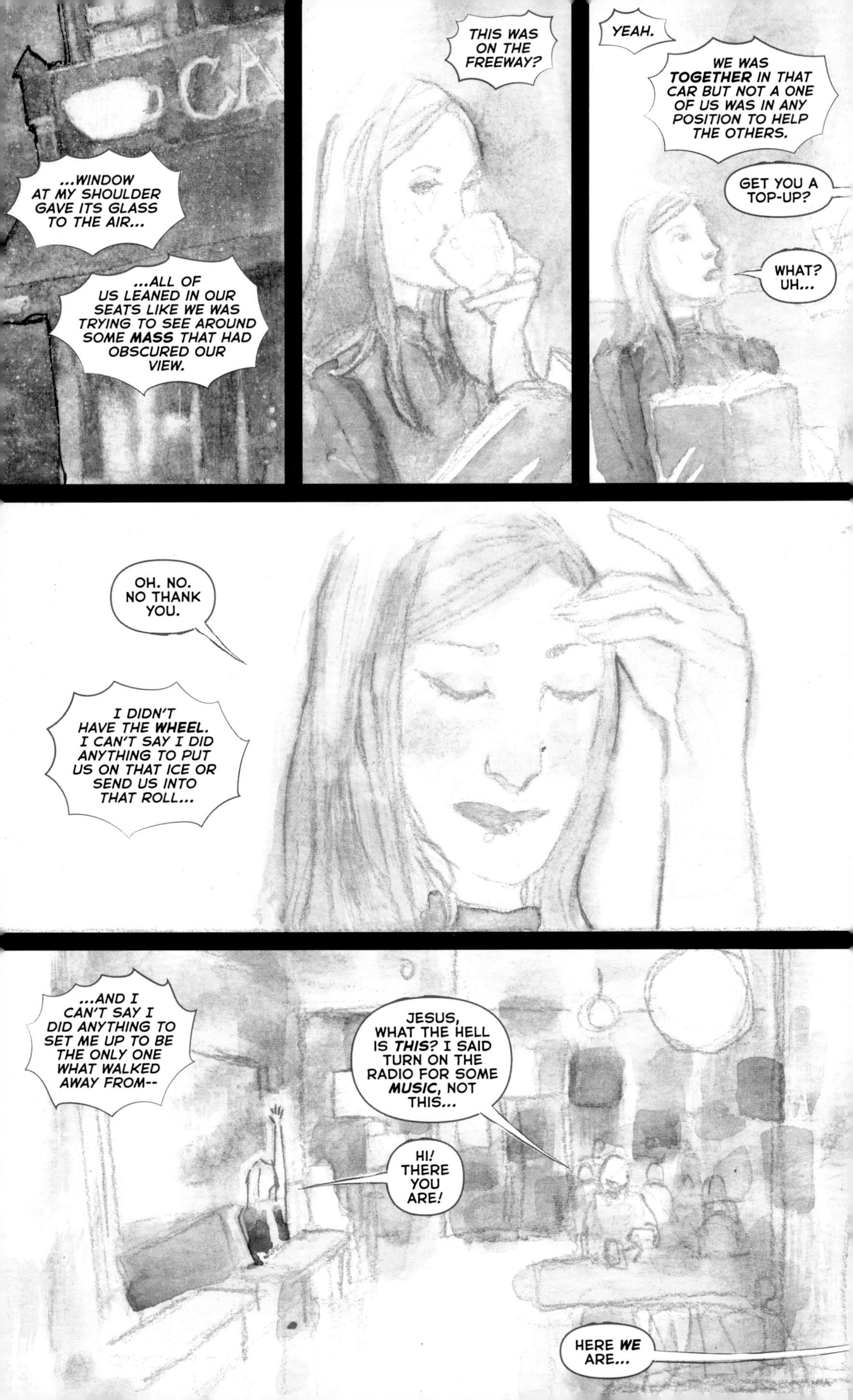
...WINDOW AT MY SHOULDER GAVE ITS GLASS TO THE AIR...
...ALL OF US LEANED IN OUR SEATS LIKE WE WAS TRYING TO SEE AROUND SOME **MASS** THAT HAD OBSCURED OUR VIEW.
THIS WAS ON THE FREEWAY?
YEAH.
WE WAS **TOGETHER** IN THAT CAR BUT NOT A ONE OF US WAS IN ANY POSITION TO HELP THE OTHERS.
GET YOU A TOP-UP?
WHAT? UH...
OH. NO. NO THANK YOU.
I DIDN'T HAVE THE **WHEEL**. I CAN'T SAY I DID ANYTHING TO PUT US ON THAT ICE OR SEND US INTO THAT ROLL...
...AND I CAN'T SAY I DID ANYTHING TO SET ME UP TO BE THE ONLY ONE WHAT WALKED AWAY FROM--
JESUS, WHAT THE HELL IS ***THIS?*** I SAID TURN ON THE RADIO FOR SOME ***MUSIC***, NOT THIS...
HI! THERE YOU ARE!
HERE ***WE*** ARE...

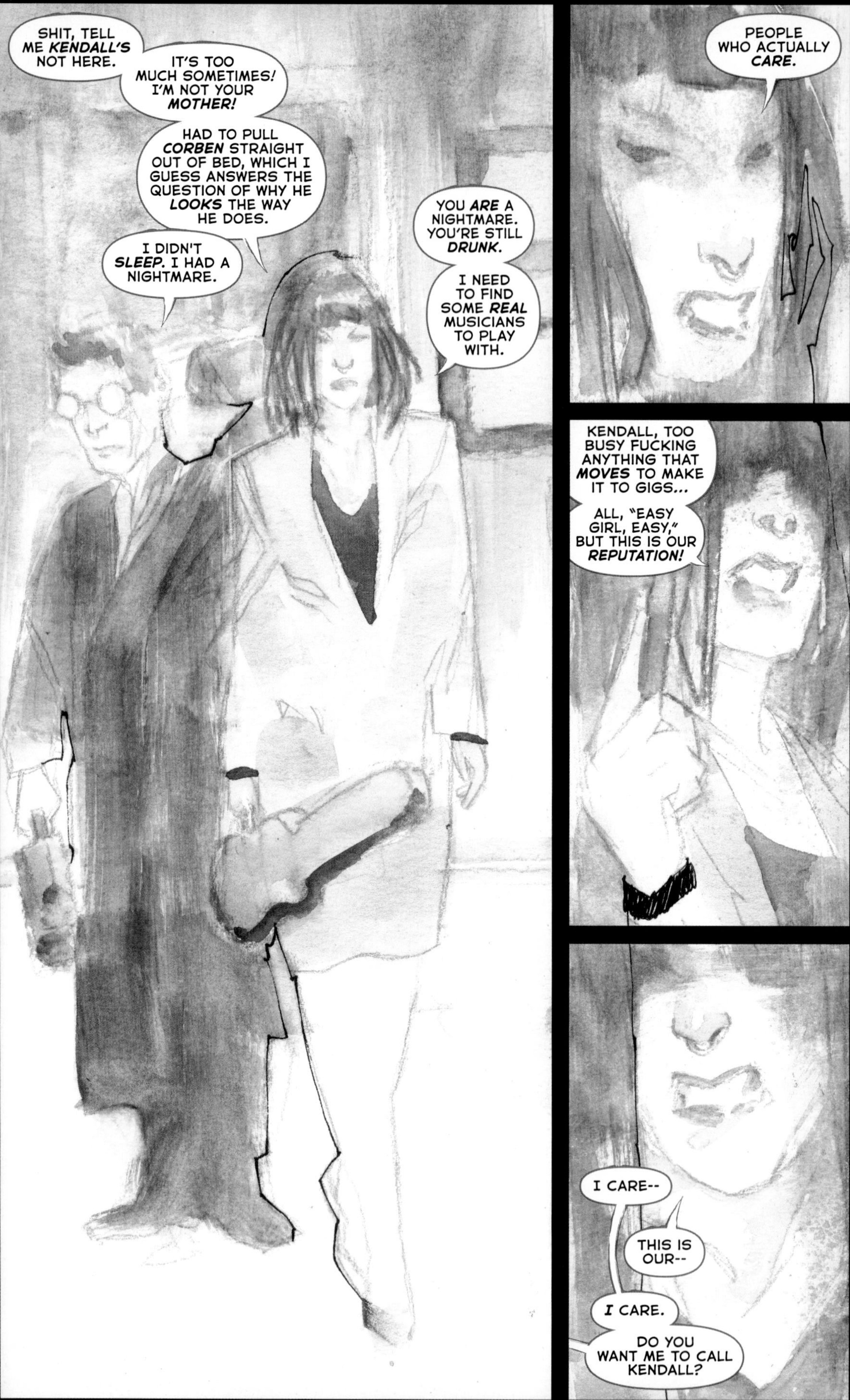

SHIT, TELL ME KENDALL'S NOT HERE.
IT'S TOO MUCH SOMETIMES! I'M NOT YOUR MOTHER!
HAD TO PULL CORBEN STRAIGHT OUT OF BED, WHICH I GUESS ANSWERS THE QUESTION OF WHY HE LOOKS THE WAY HE DOES.
I DIDN'T SLEEP. I HAD A NIGHTMARE.
YOU ARE A NIGHTMARE. YOU'RE STILL DRUNK.
I NEED TO FIND SOME REAL MUSICIANS TO PLAY WITH.
PEOPLE WHO ACTUALLY CARE.
KENDALL, TOO BUSY FUCKING ANYTHING THAT MOVES TO MAKE IT TO GIGS...
ALL, "EASY GIRL, EASY," BUT THIS IS OUR REPUTATION!
I CARE--
THIS IS OUR--
I CARE.
DO YOU WANT ME TO CALL KENDALL?

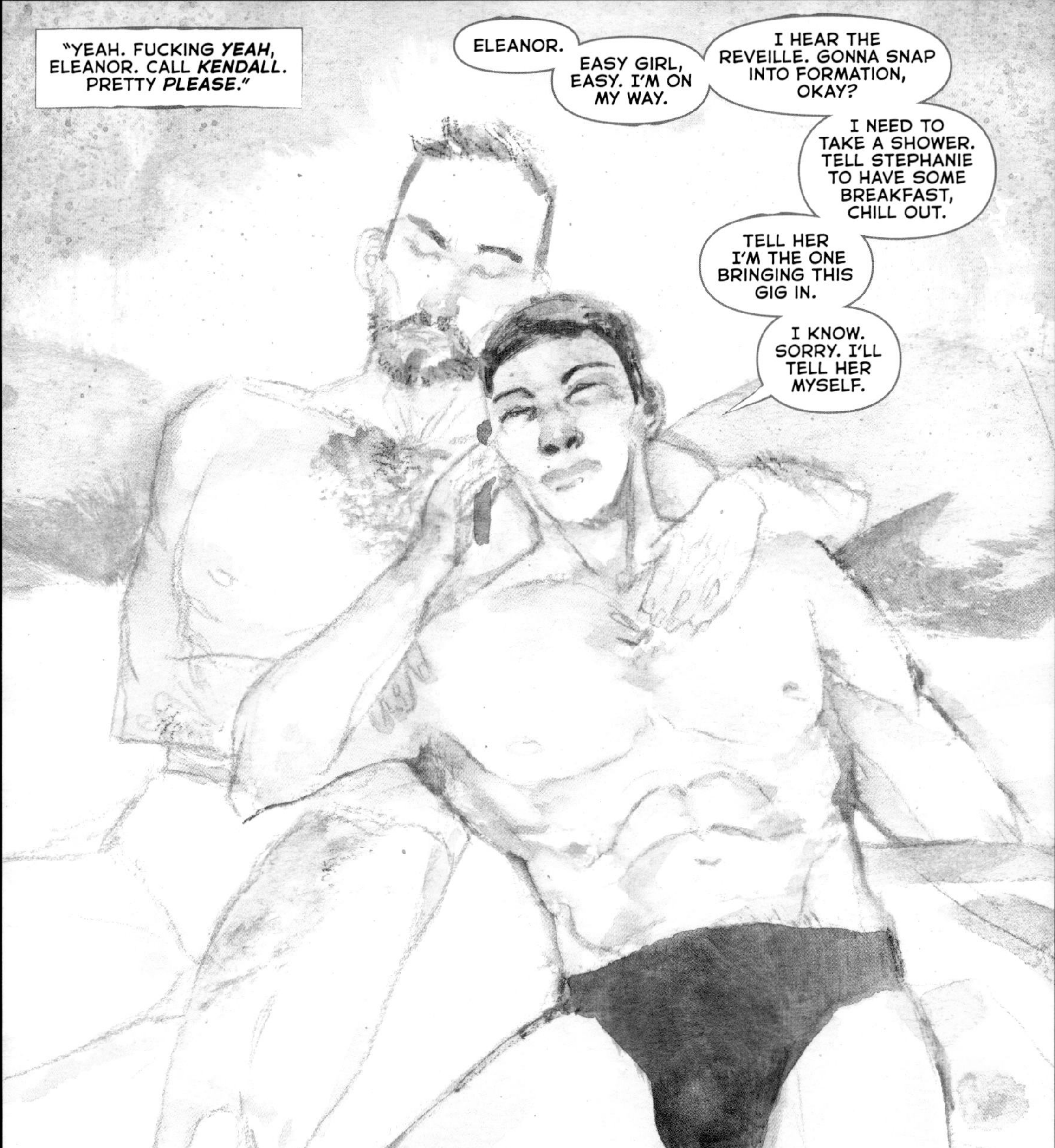
"YEAH. FUCKING *YEAH*, ELEANOR. CALL *KENDALL*. PRETTY *PLEASE*."
ELEANOR.
EASY GIRL, EASY. I'M ON MY WAY.
I HEAR THE REVEILLE. GONNA SNAP INTO FORMATION, OKAY?
I NEED TO TAKE A SHOWER. TELL STEPHANIE TO HAVE SOME BREAKFAST, CHILL OUT.
TELL HER I'M THE ONE BRINGING THIS GIG IN.
I KNOW. SORRY. I'LL TELL HER MYSELF.

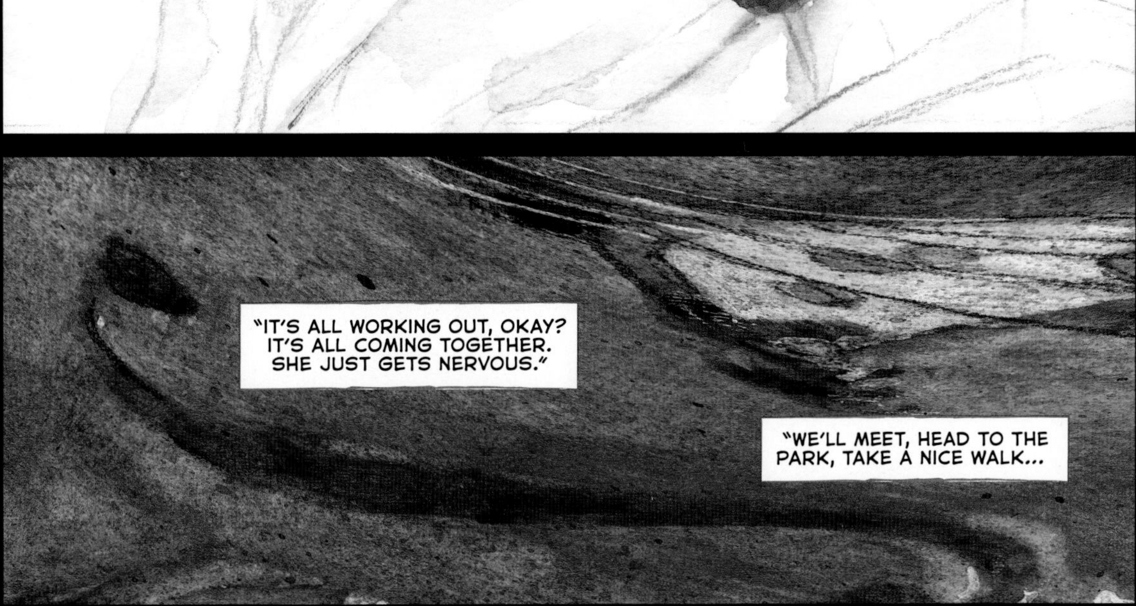
"IT'S ALL WORKING OUT, OKAY? IT'S ALL COMING TOGETHER. SHE JUST GETS NERVOUS."
"WE'LL MEET, HEAD TO THE PARK, TAKE A NICE WALK...

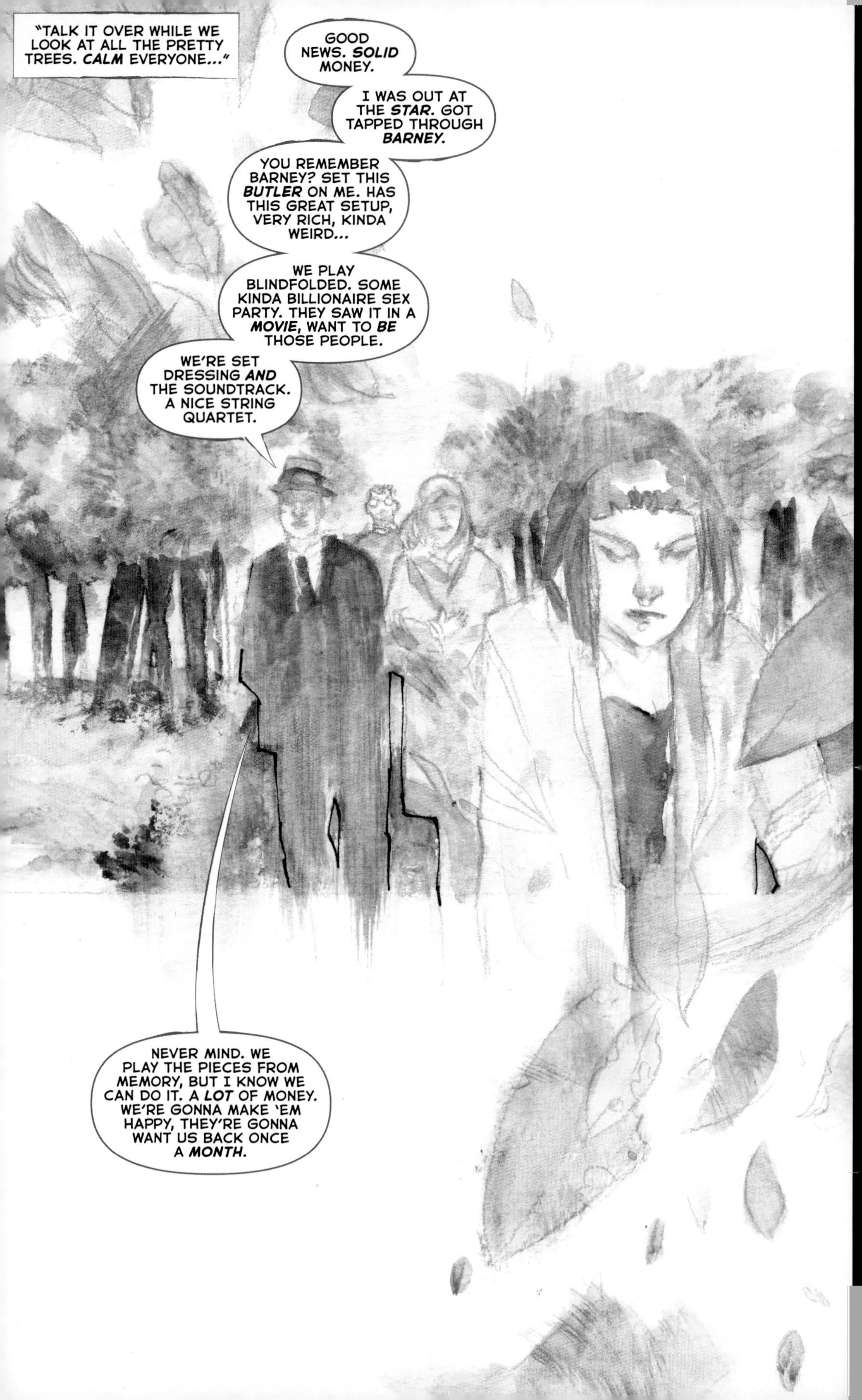
"TALK IT OVER WHILE WE LOOK AT ALL THE PRETTY TREES. CALM EVERYONE..."
GOOD NEWS. SOLID MONEY.
I WAS OUT AT THE STAR. GOT TAPPED THROUGH BARNEY.
YOU REMEMBER BARNEY? SET THIS BUTLER ON ME. HAS THIS GREAT SETUP, VERY RICH, KINDA WEIRD...
WE PLAY BLINDFOLDED. SOME KINDA BILLIONAIRE SEX PARTY. THEY SAW IT IN A MOVIE, WANT TO BE THOSE PEOPLE.
WE'RE SET DRESSING AND THE SOUNDTRACK. A NICE STRING QUARTET.
NEVER MIND. WE PLAY THE PIECES FROM MEMORY, BUT I KNOW WE CAN DO IT. A LOT OF MONEY. WE'RE GONNA MAKE 'EM HAPPY, THEY'RE GONNA WANT US BACK ONCE A MONTH.

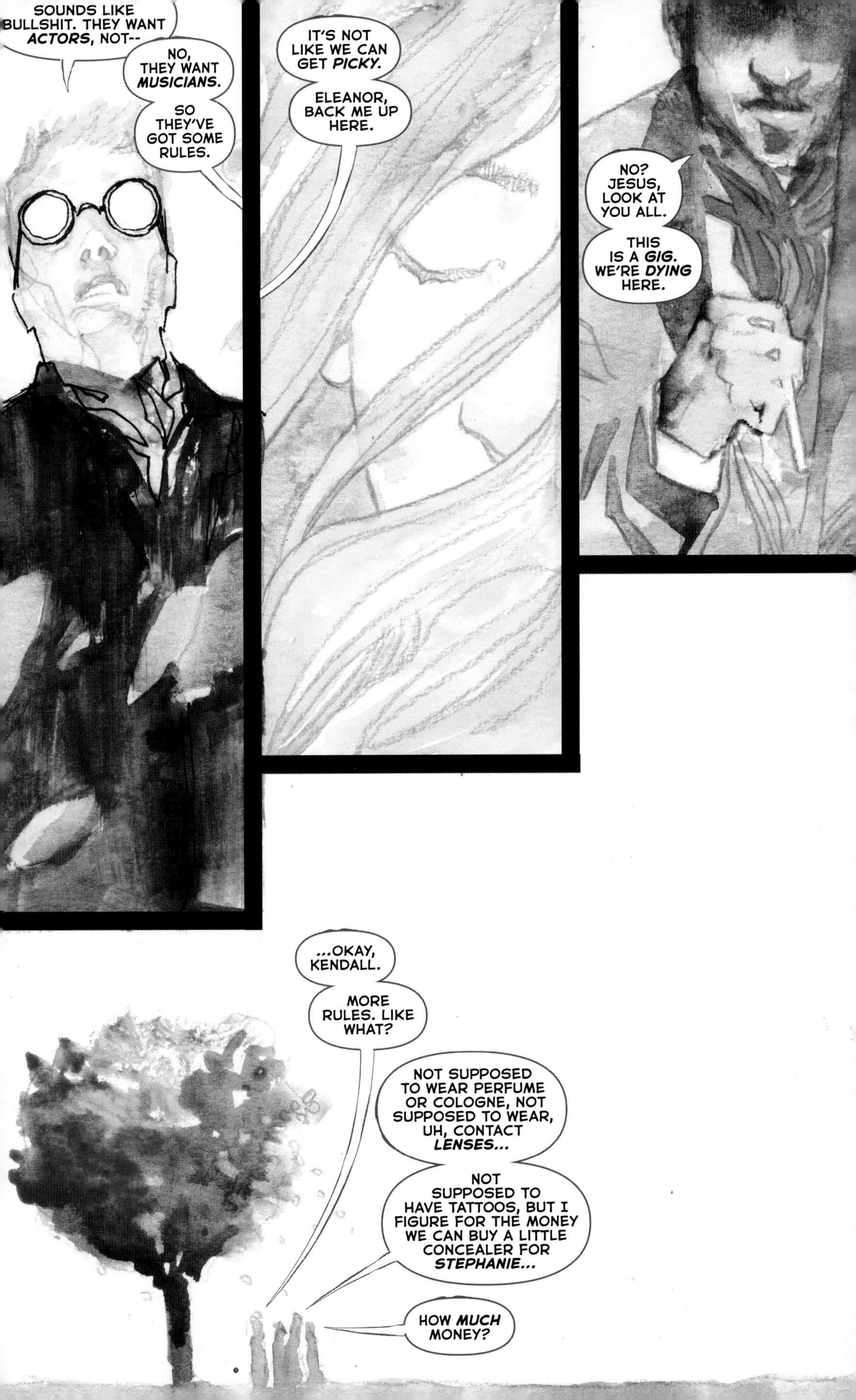
SOUNDS LIKE BULLSHIT. THEY WANT ACTORS, NOT--
NO, THEY WANT MUSICIANS.
SO THEY'VE GOT SOME RULES.
IT'S NOT LIKE WE CAN GET PICKY.
ELEANOR, BACK ME UP HERE.
NO? JESUS, LOOK AT YOU ALL.
THIS IS A GIG. WE'RE DYING HERE.
...OKAY, KENDALL.
MORE RULES. LIKE WHAT?
NOT SUPPOSED TO WEAR PERFUME OR COLOGNE, NOT SUPPOSED TO WEAR, UH, CONTACT LENSES...
NOT SUPPOSED TO HAVE TATTOOS, BUT I FIGURE FOR THE MONEY WE CAN BUY A LITTLE CONCEALER FOR STEPHANIE...
HOW MUCH MONEY?

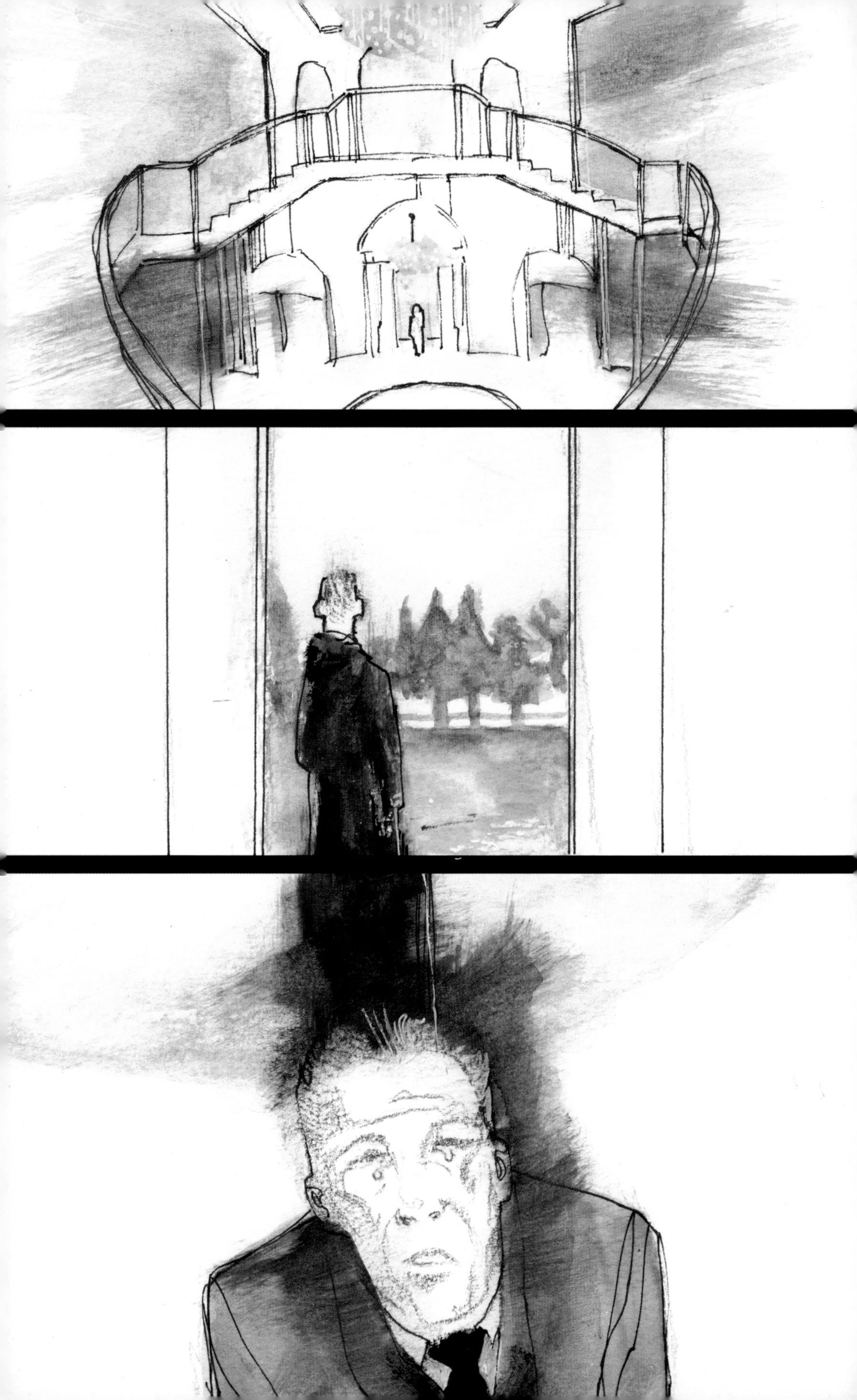

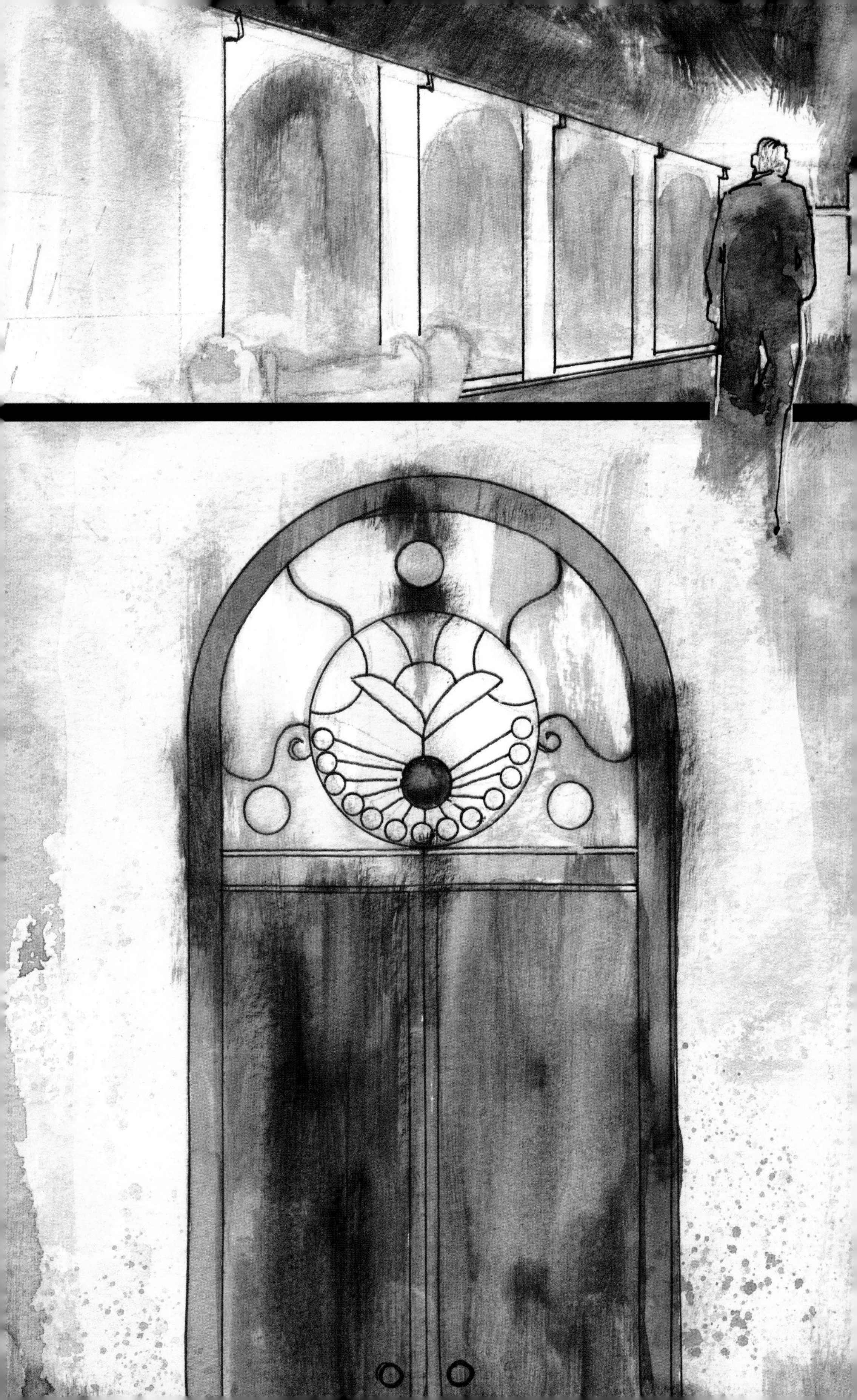

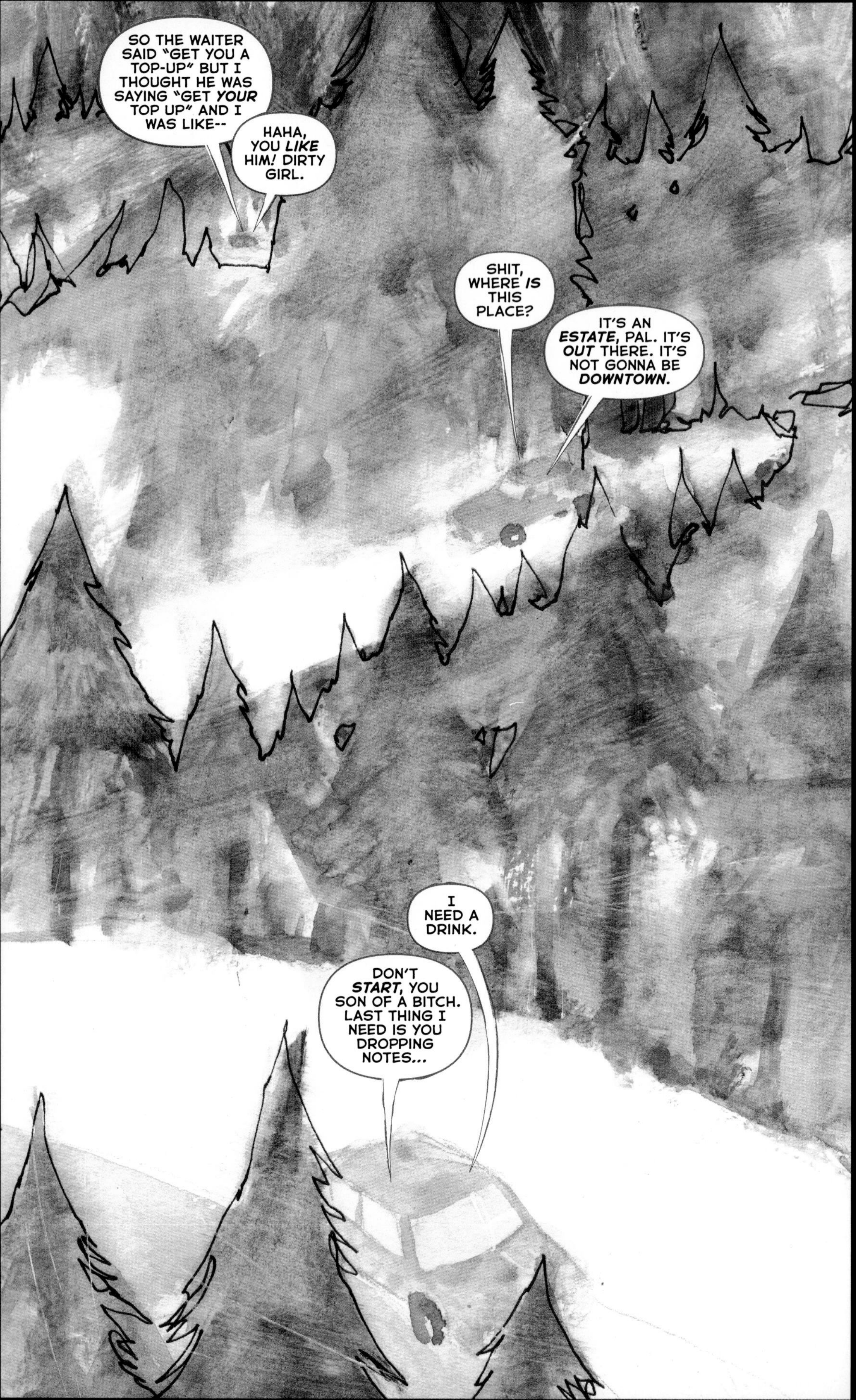
SO THE WAITER SAID "GET YOU A TOP-UP" BUT I THOUGHT HE WAS SAYING "GET *YOUR* TOP UP" AND I WAS LIKE--
HAHA, YOU *LIKE* HIM! DIRTY GIRL.
SHIT, WHERE *IS* THIS PLACE?
IT'S AN *ESTATE*, PAL. IT'S *OUT* THERE. IT'S NOT GONNA BE *DOWNTOWN.*
I NEED A DRINK.
DON'T *START*, YOU SON OF A BITCH. LAST THING I NEED IS YOU DROPPING NOTES...

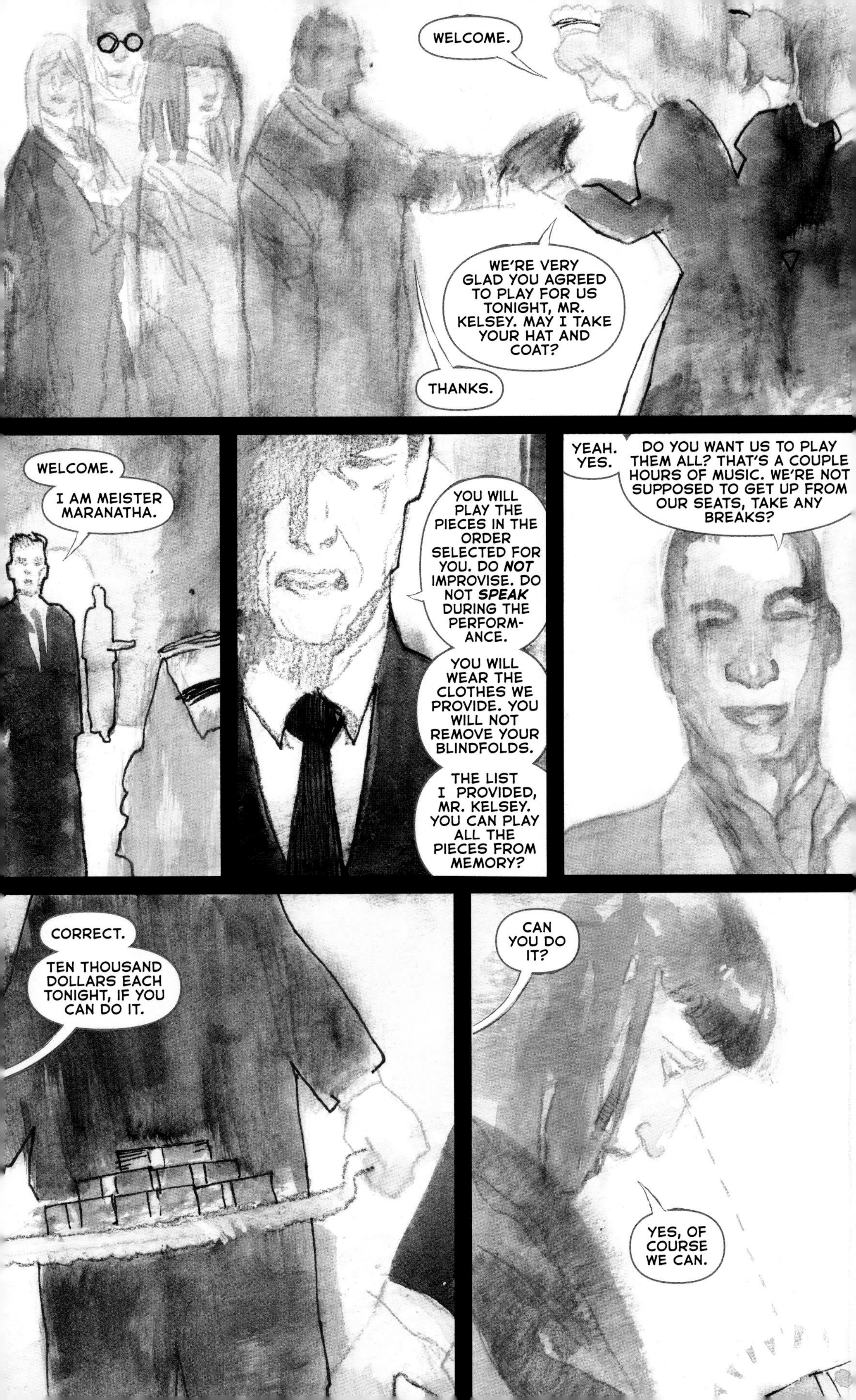
WELCOME.
WE'RE VERY GLAD YOU AGREED TO PLAY FOR US TONIGHT, MR. KELSEY. MAY I TAKE YOUR HAT AND COAT?
THANKS.
WELCOME.
I AM MEISTER MARANATHA.
YOU WILL PLAY THE PIECES IN THE ORDER SELECTED FOR YOU. DO *NOT* IMPROVISE. DO NOT *SPEAK* DURING THE PERFORMANCE.
YOU WILL WEAR THE CLOTHES WE PROVIDE. YOU WILL NOT REMOVE YOUR BLINDFOLDS.
THE LIST I PROVIDED, MR. KELSEY. YOU CAN PLAY ALL THE PIECES FROM MEMORY?
YEAH. YES.
DO YOU WANT US TO PLAY THEM ALL? THAT'S A COUPLE HOURS OF MUSIC. WE'RE NOT SUPPOSED TO GET UP FROM OUR SEATS, TAKE ANY BREAKS?
CORRECT.
TEN THOUSAND DOLLARS EACH TONIGHT, IF YOU CAN DO IT.
CAN YOU DO IT?
YES, OF COURSE WE CAN.

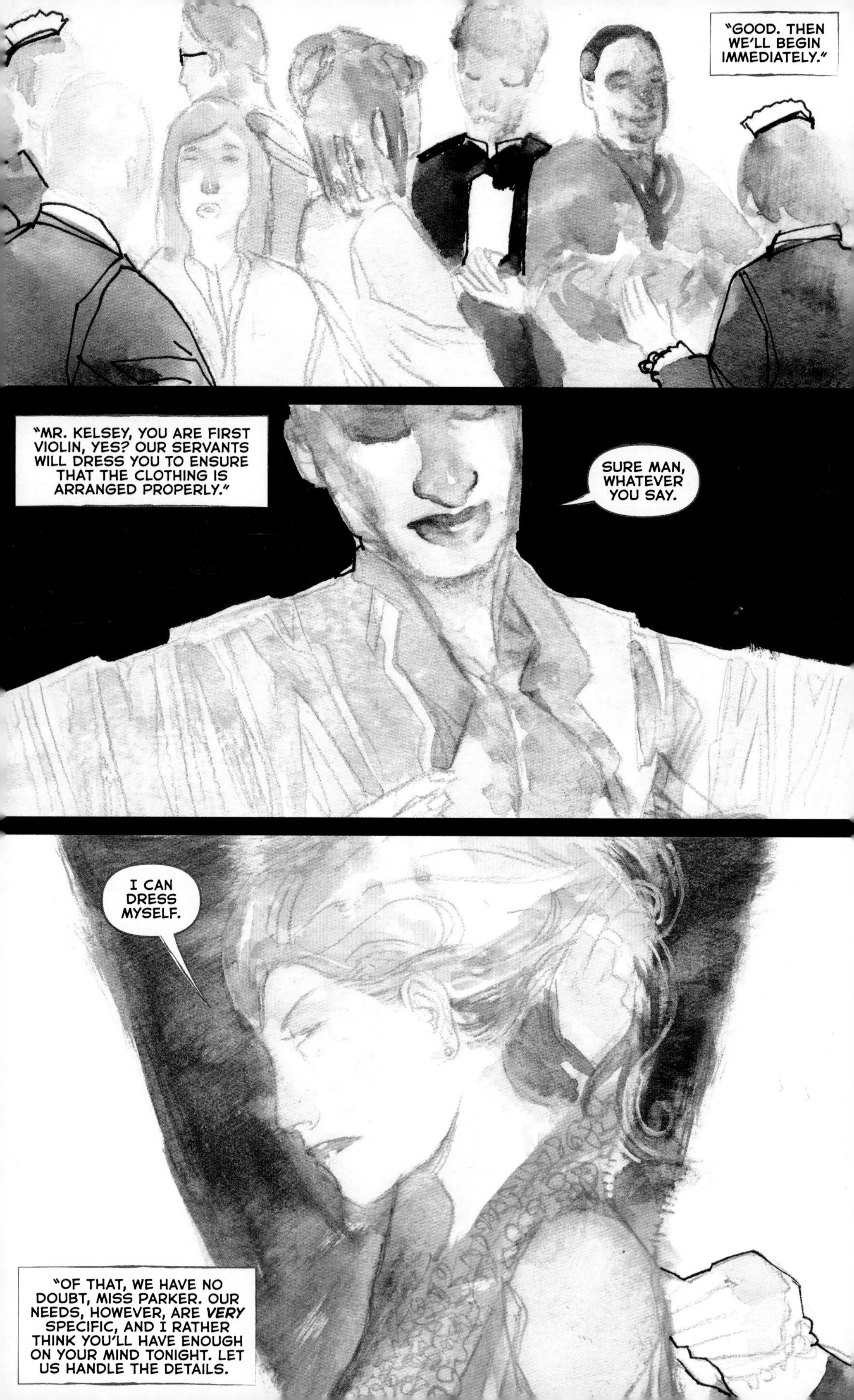
"GOOD. THEN WE'LL BEGIN IMMEDIATELY."
"MR. KELSEY, YOU ARE FIRST VIOLIN, YES? OUR SERVANTS WILL DRESS YOU TO ENSURE THAT THE CLOTHING IS ARRANGED PROPERLY."
SURE MAN, WHATEVER YOU SAY.
I CAN DRESS MYSELF.
"OF THAT, WE HAVE NO DOUBT, MISS PARKER. OUR NEEDS, HOWEVER, ARE *VERY* SPECIFIC, AND I RATHER THINK YOU'LL HAVE ENOUGH ON YOUR MIND TONIGHT. LET US HANDLE THE DETAILS.

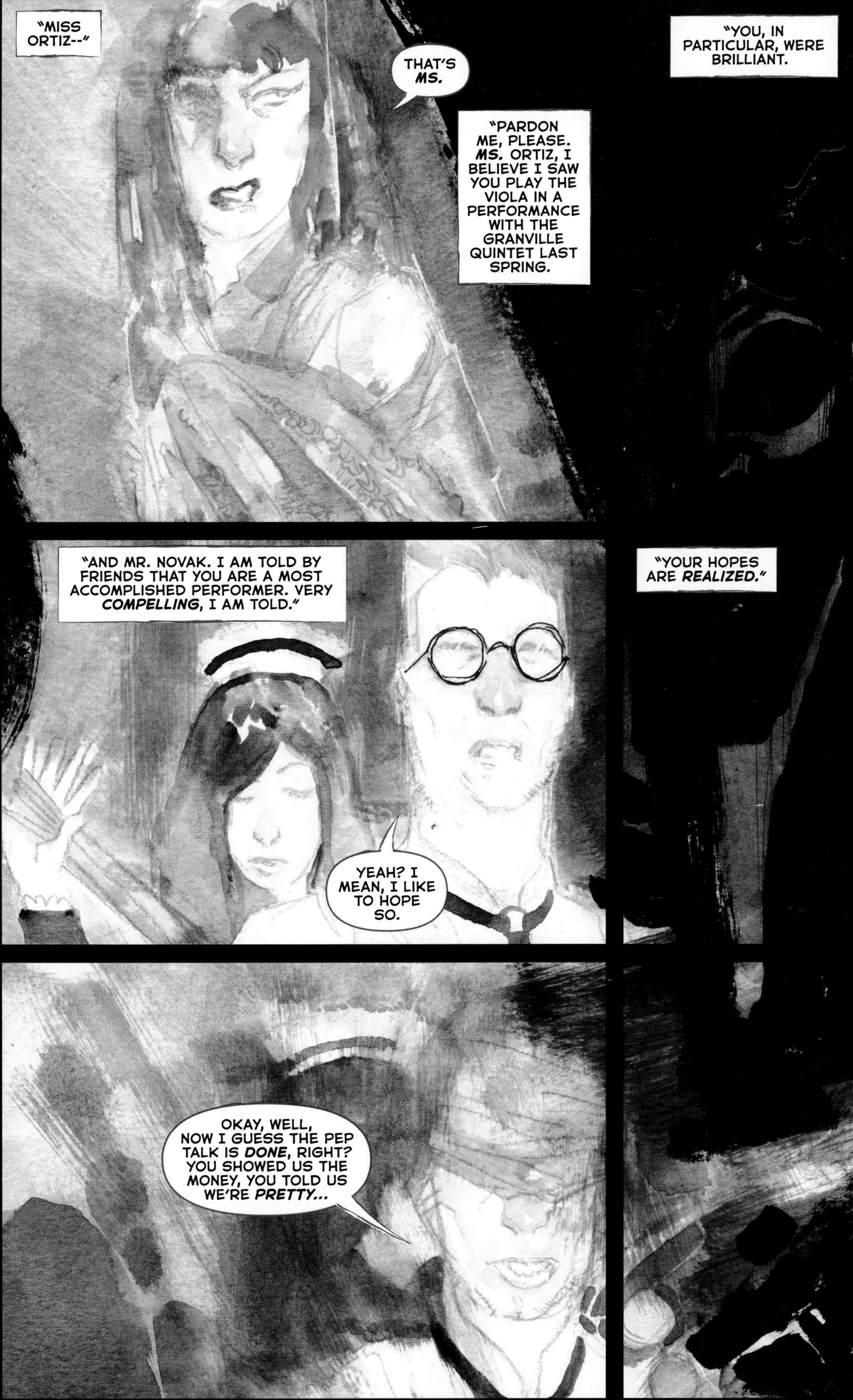
"MISS ORTIZ--"
THAT'S MS.
"PARDON ME, PLEASE. MS. ORTIZ, I BELIEVE I SAW YOU PLAY THE VIOLA IN A PERFORMANCE WITH THE GRANVILLE QUINTET LAST SPRING.
"YOU, IN PARTICULAR, WERE BRILLIANT.
"AND MR. NOVAK. I AM TOLD BY FRIENDS THAT YOU ARE A MOST ACCOMPLISHED PERFORMER. VERY COMPELLING, I AM TOLD."
YEAH? I MEAN, I LIKE TO HOPE SO.
"YOUR HOPES ARE REALIZED."
OKAY, WELL, NOW I GUESS THE PEP TALK IS DONE, RIGHT? YOU SHOWED US THE MONEY, YOU TOLD US WE'RE PRETTY...

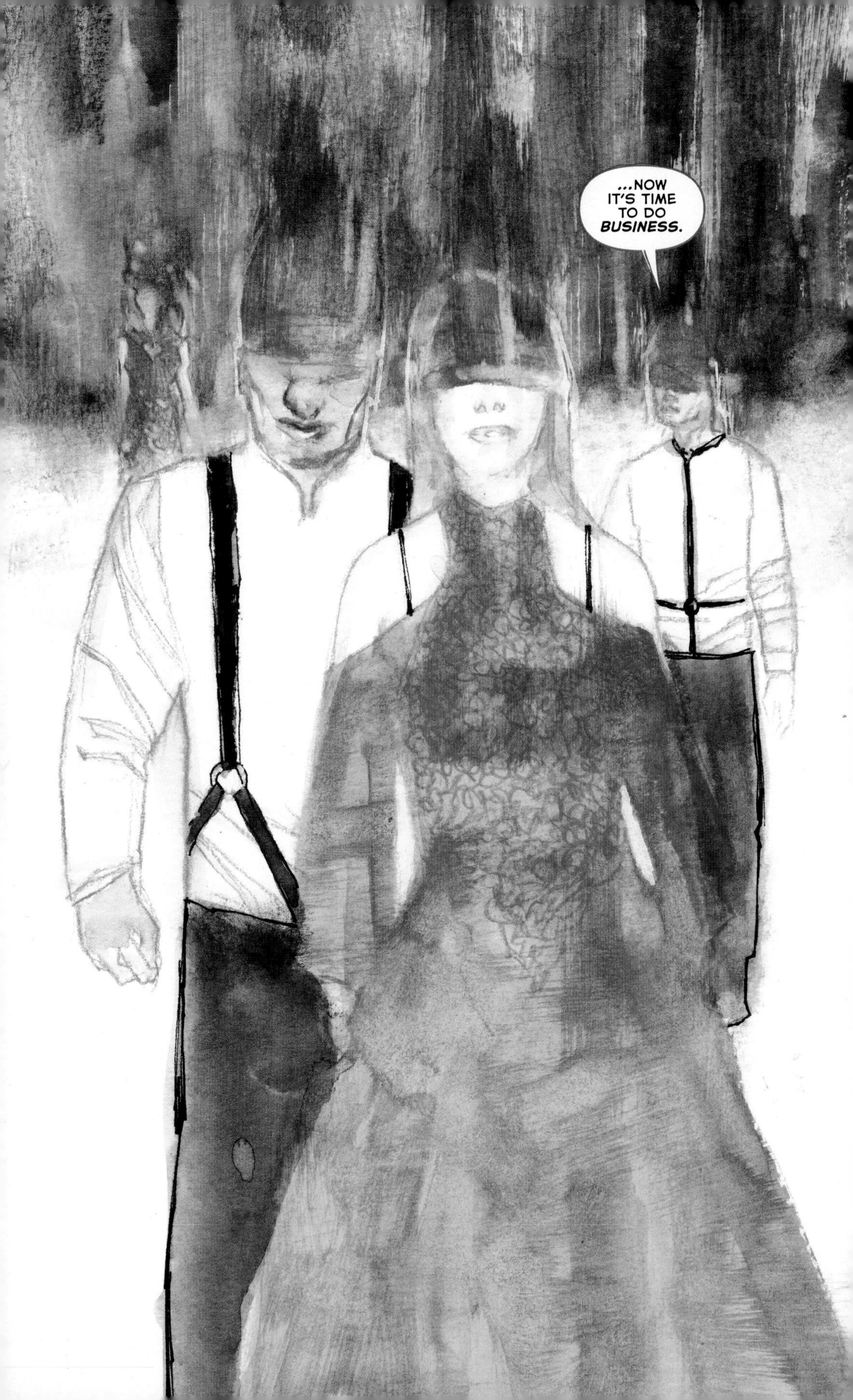
...NOW IT'S TIME TO DO *BUSINESS.*

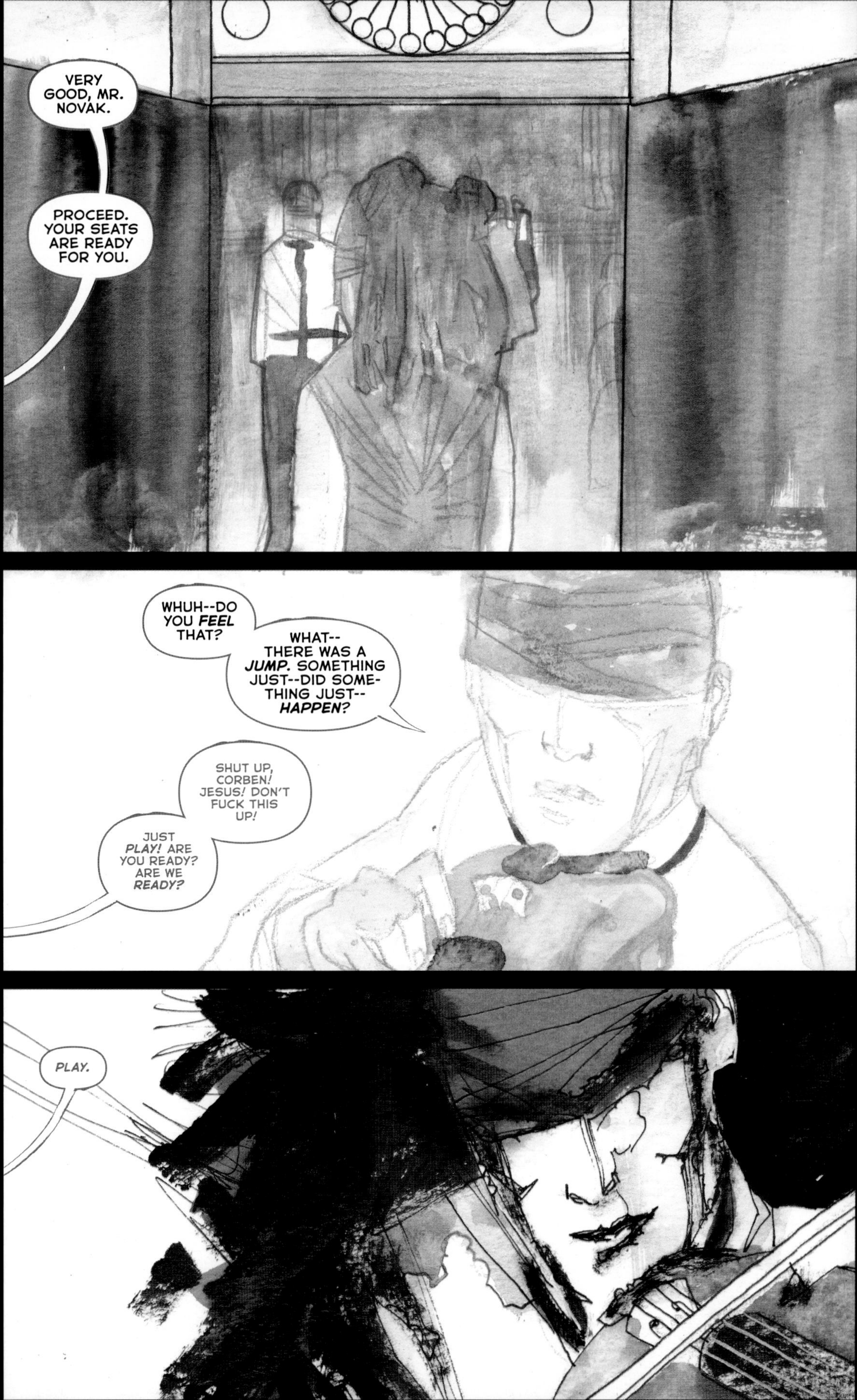
VERY GOOD, MR. NOVAK.
PROCEED. YOUR SEATS ARE READY FOR YOU.
WHUH--DO YOU *FEEL* THAT?
WHAT-- THERE WAS A *JUMP.* SOMETHING JUST--DID SOME-THING JUST-- *HAPPEN?*
SHUT UP, CORBEN! JESUS! DON'T FUCK THIS UP!
JUST *PLAY!* ARE YOU READY? ARE WE *READY?*
PLAY.

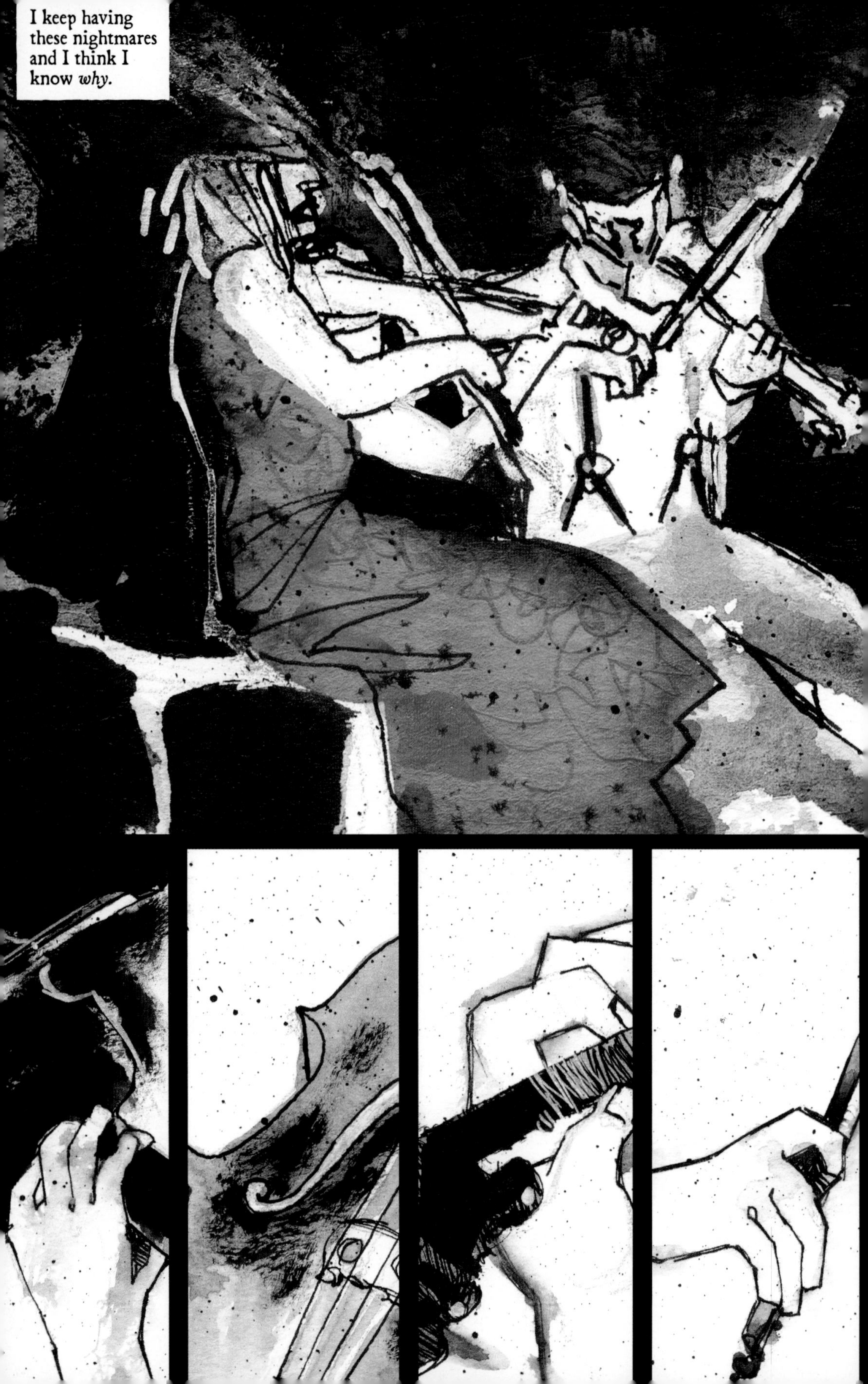
I keep having these nightmares and I think I know *why*.

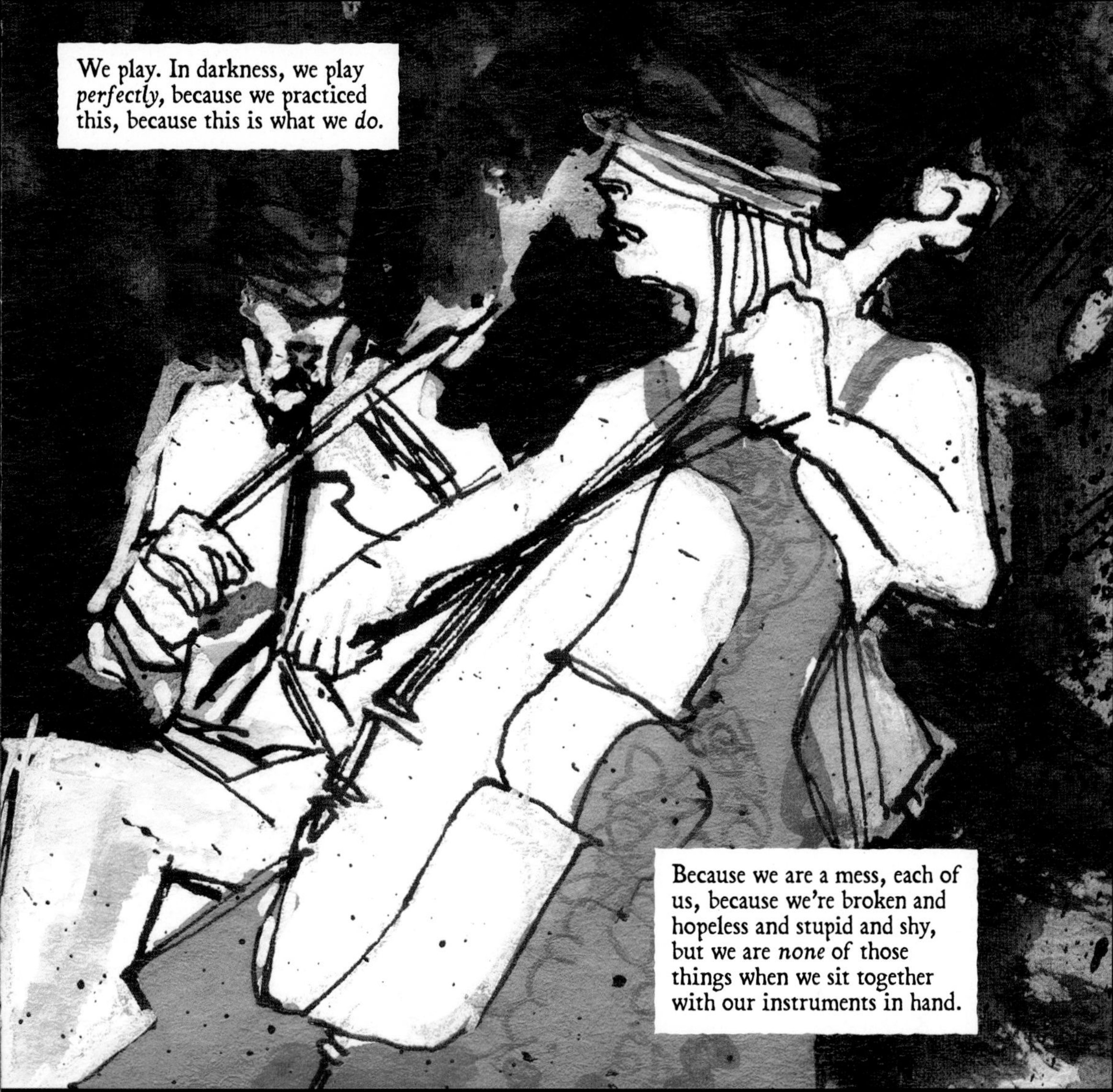
We play. In darkness, we play *perfectly,* because we practiced this, because this is what we *do.*
Because we are a mess, each of us, because we're broken and hopeless and stupid and shy, but we are *none* of those things when we sit together with our instruments in hand.

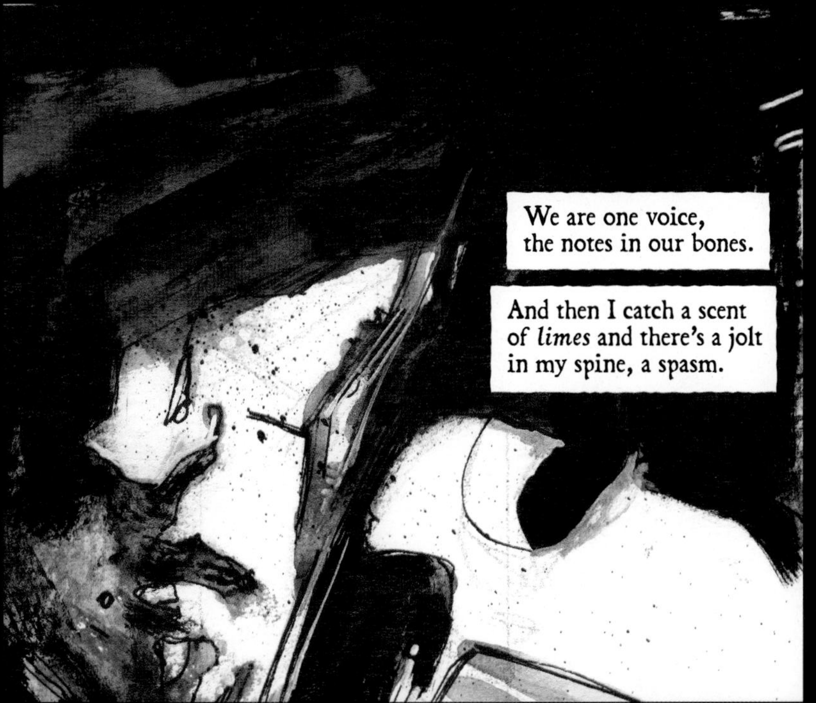
We are one voice, the notes in our bones.
And then I catch a scent of *limes* and there's a jolt in my spine, a spasm.

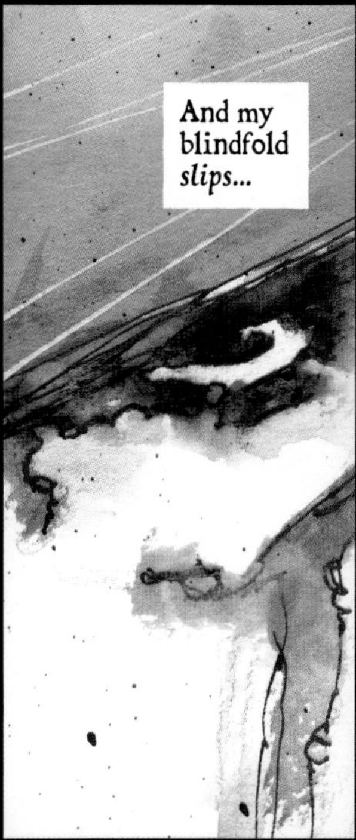
And my blindfold *slips...*

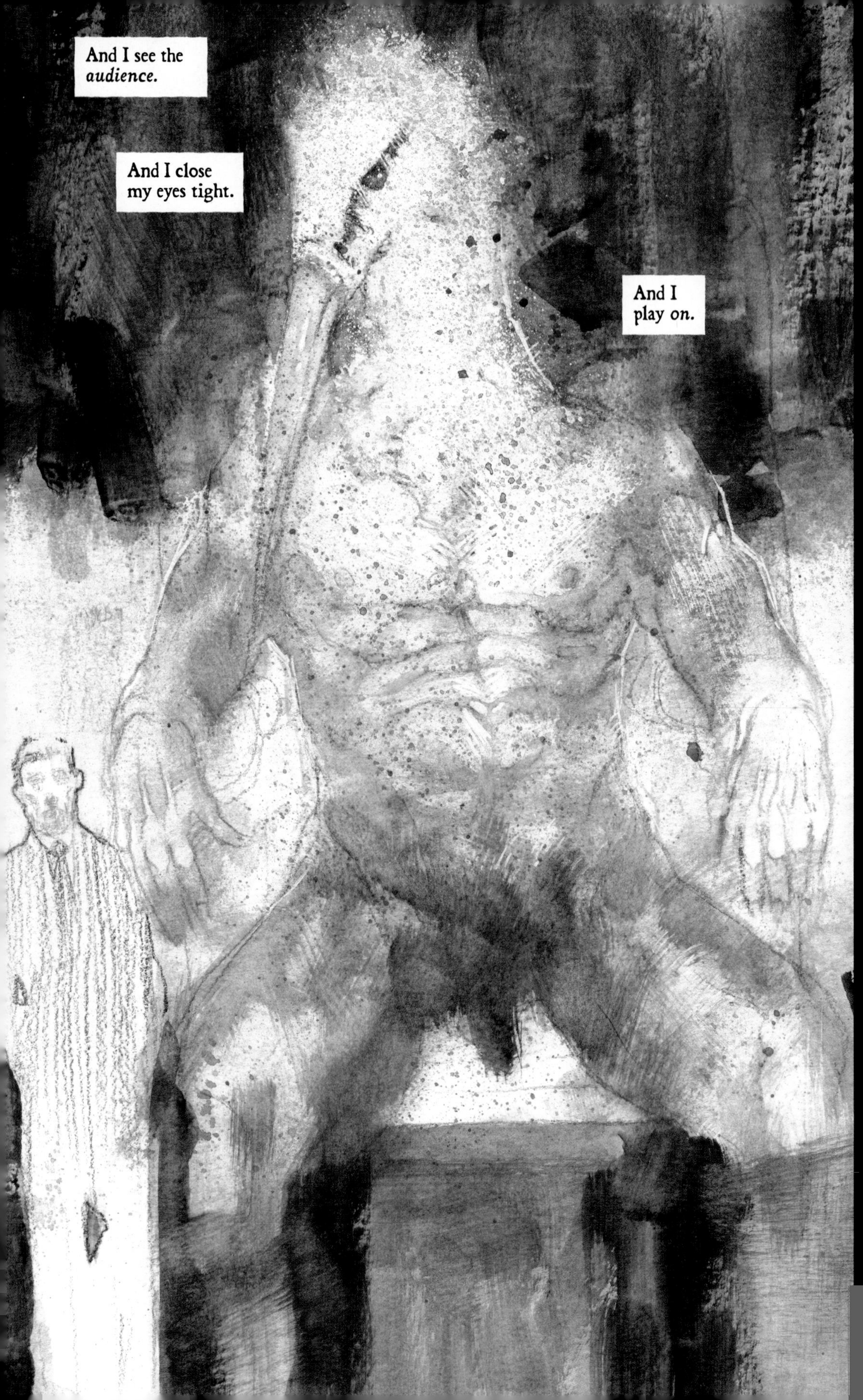
And I see the *audience.*
And I close my eyes tight.
And I play *on.*

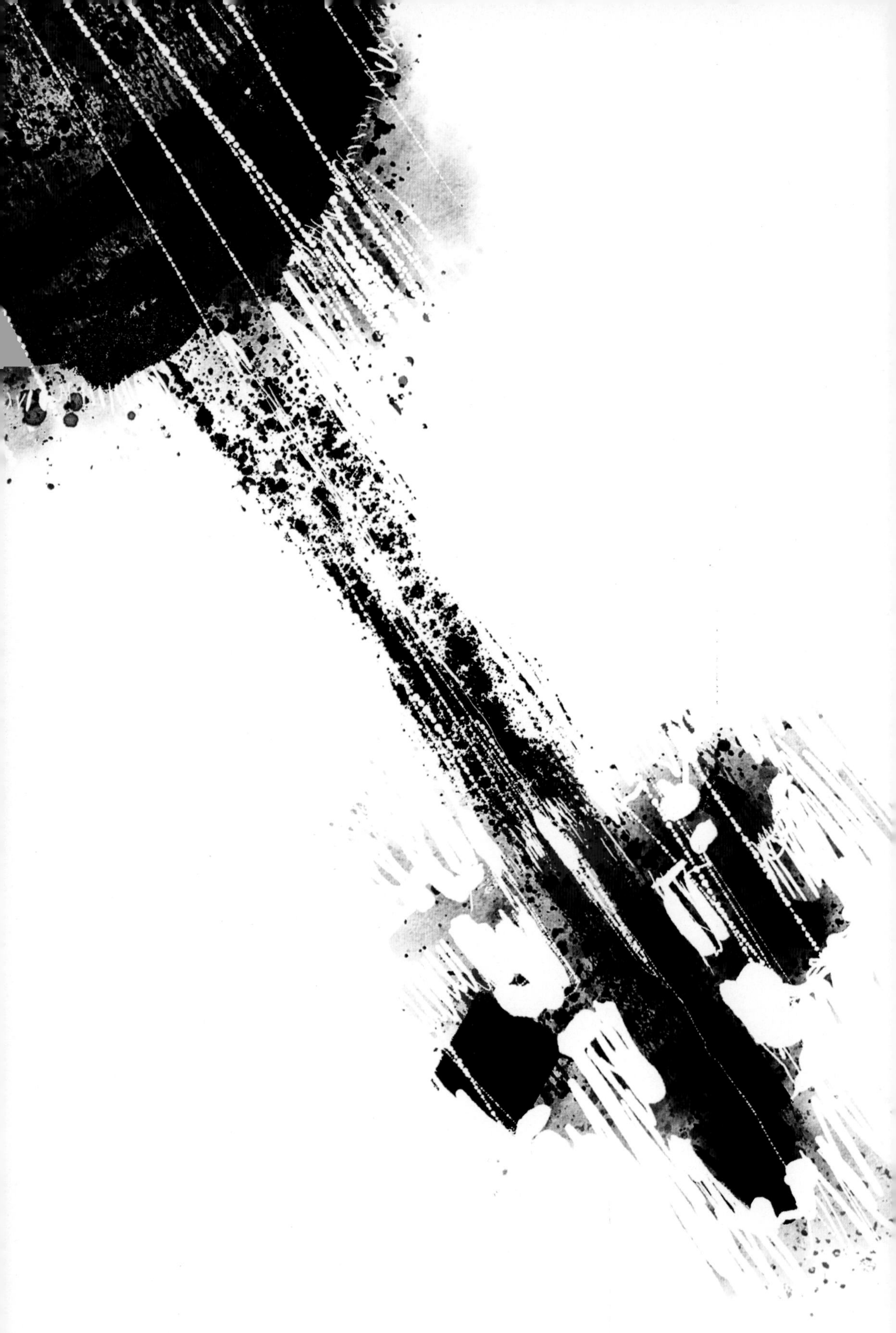

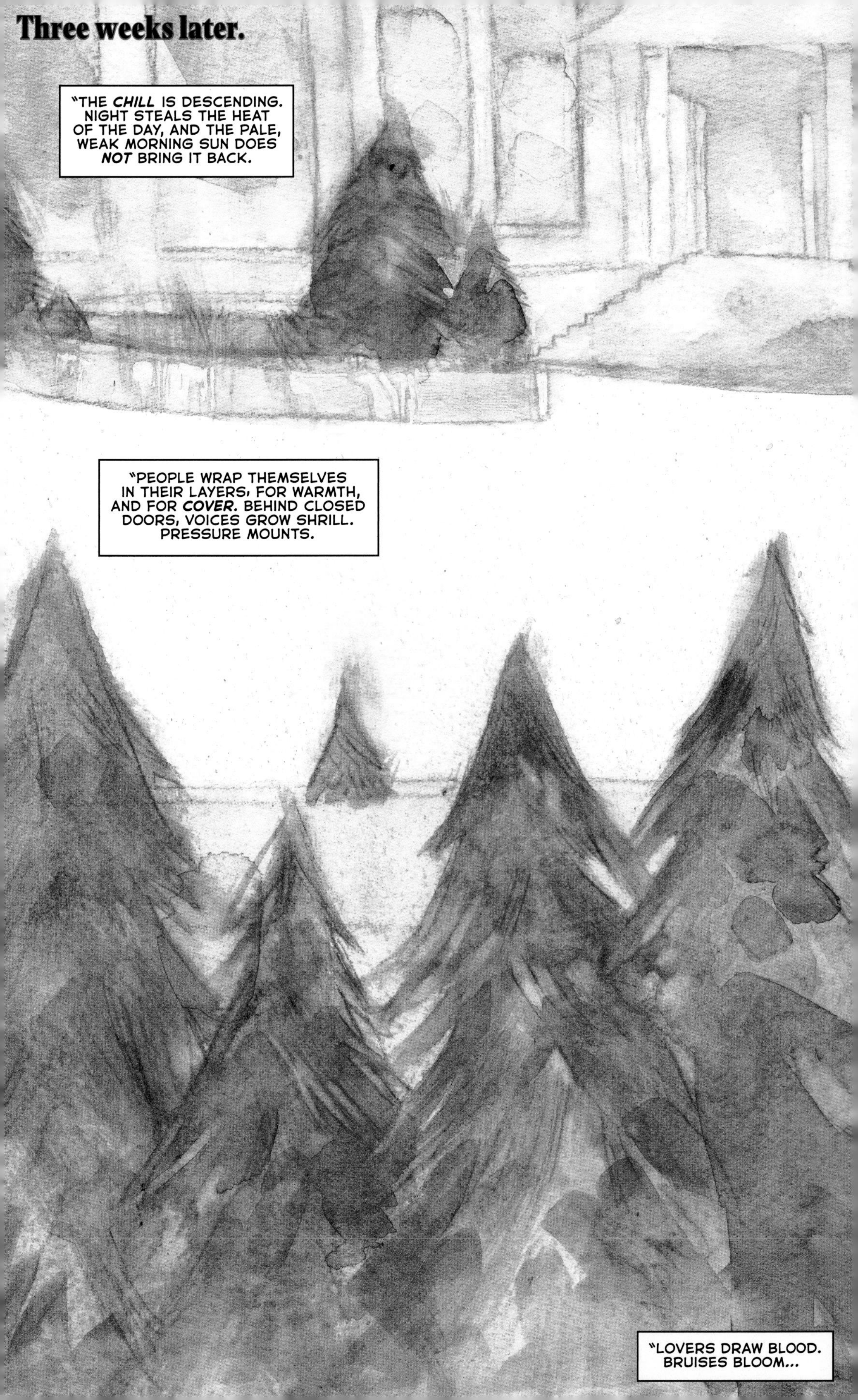
Three weeks later.
"THE CHILL IS DESCENDING. NIGHT STEALS THE HEAT OF THE DAY, AND THE PALE, WEAK MORNING SUN DOES NOT BRING IT BACK.
"PEOPLE WRAP THEMSELVES IN THEIR LAYERS, FOR WARMTH, AND FOR COVER. BEHIND CLOSED DOORS, VOICES GROW SHRILL. PRESSURE MOUNTS.
"LOVERS DRAW BLOOD. BRUISES BLOOM...

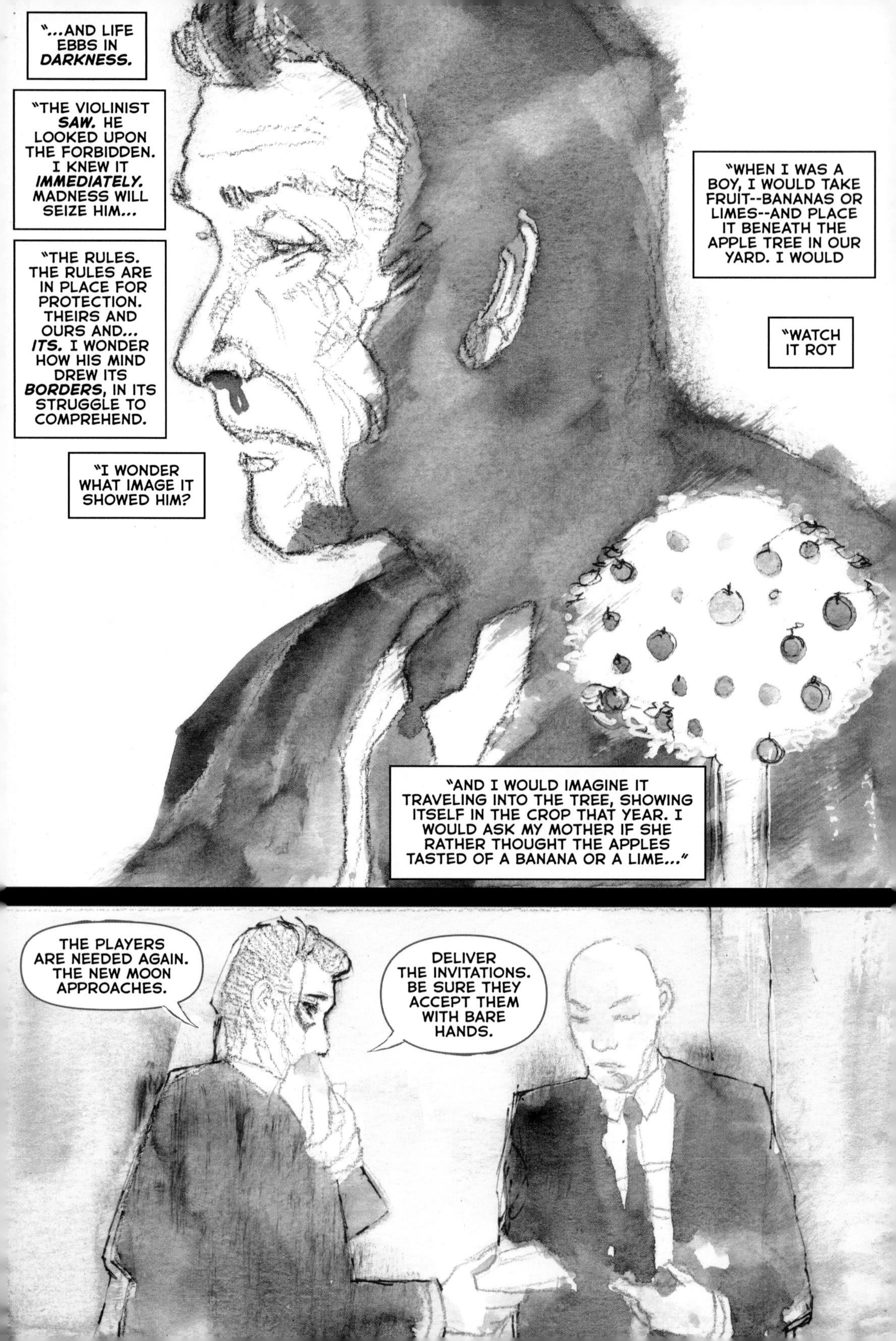
"...AND LIFE EBBS IN DARKNESS.
"THE VIOLINIST SAW. HE LOOKED UPON THE FORBIDDEN. I KNEW IT IMMEDIATELY. MADNESS WILL SEIZE HIM...
"THE RULES. THE RULES ARE IN PLACE FOR PROTECTION. THEIRS AND OURS AND... ITS. I WONDER HOW HIS MIND DREW ITS BORDERS, IN ITS STRUGGLE TO COMPREHEND.
"I WONDER WHAT IMAGE IT SHOWED HIM?
"WHEN I WAS A BOY, I WOULD TAKE FRUIT--BANANAS OR LIMES--AND PLACE IT BENEATH THE APPLE TREE IN OUR YARD. I WOULD
"WATCH IT ROT
"AND I WOULD IMAGINE IT TRAVELING INTO THE TREE, SHOWING ITSELF IN THE CROP THAT YEAR. I WOULD ASK MY MOTHER IF SHE RATHER THOUGHT THE APPLES TASTED OF A BANANA OR A LIME..."
THE PLAYERS ARE NEEDED AGAIN. THE NEW MOON APPROACHES.
DELIVER THE INVITATIONS. BE SURE THEY ACCEPT THEM WITH BARE HANDS.

SYMPHONY

PART TWO:
DECEMBER

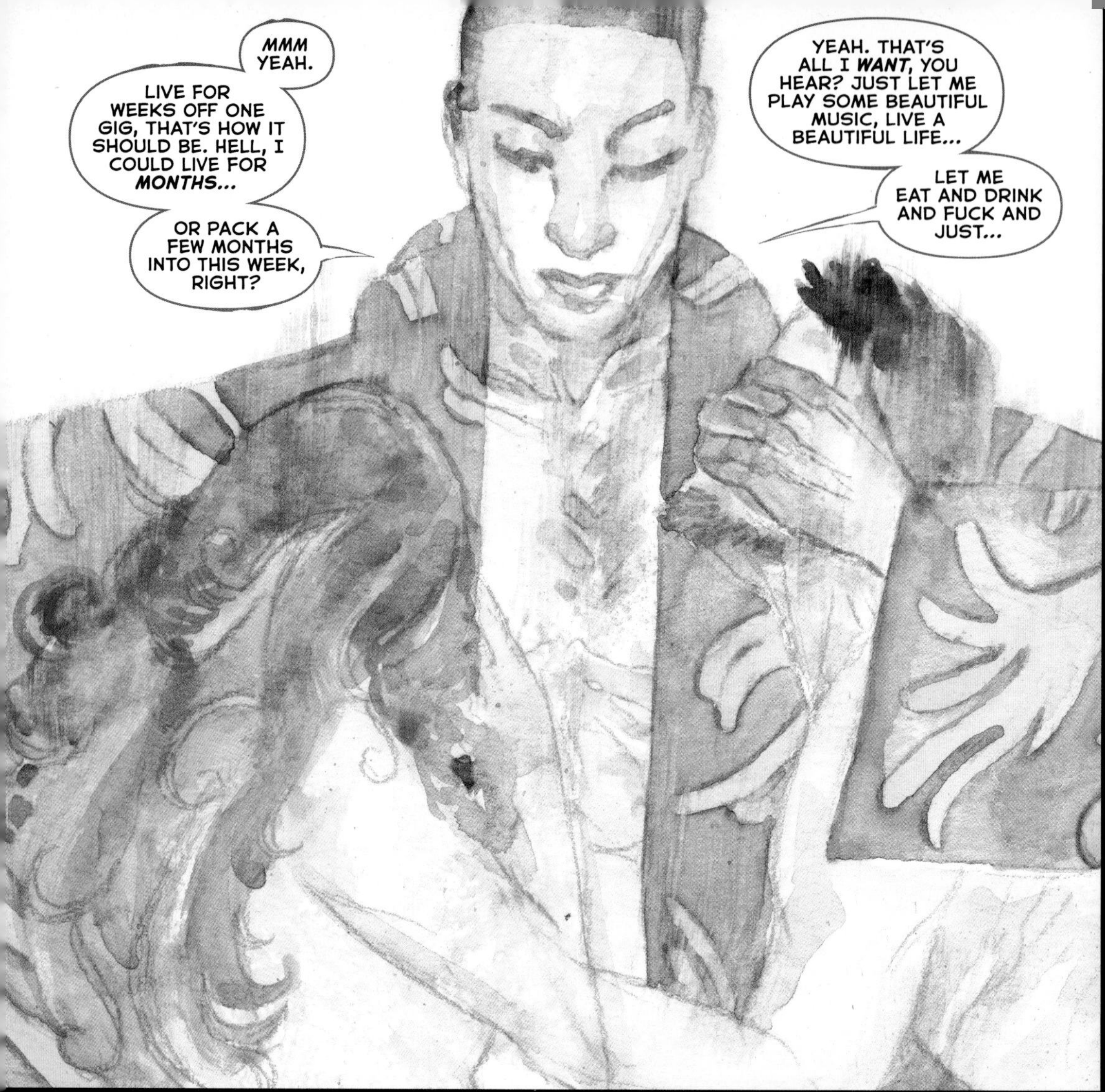
MMM YEAH.
LIVE FOR WEEKS OFF ONE GIG, THAT'S HOW IT SHOULD BE. HELL, I COULD LIVE FOR MONTHS...
OR PACK A FEW MONTHS INTO THIS WEEK, RIGHT?
YEAH. THAT'S ALL I WANT, YOU HEAR? JUST LET ME PLAY SOME BEAUTIFUL MUSIC, LIVE A BEAUTIFUL LIFE...
LET ME EAT AND DRINK AND FUCK AND JUST...

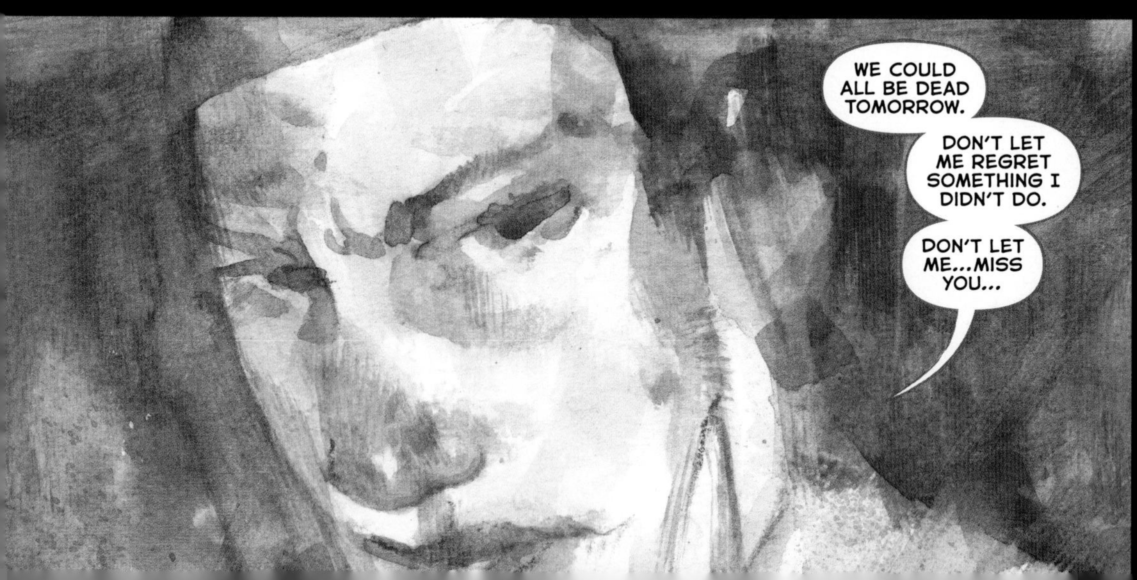
WE COULD ALL BE DEAD TOMORROW.
DON'T LET ME REGRET SOMETHING I DIDN'T DO.
DON'T LET ME...MISS YOU...

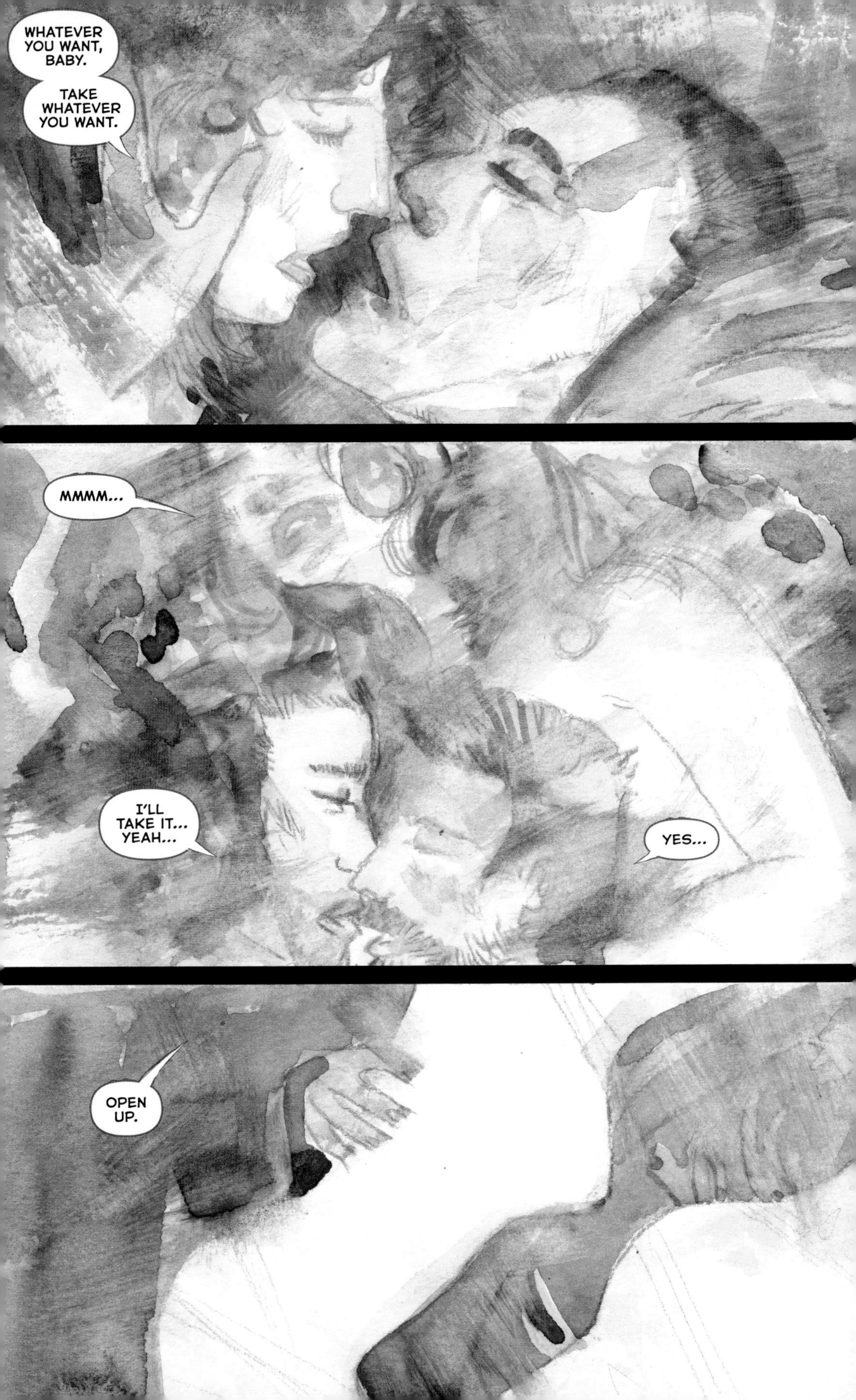
WHATEVER YOU WANT, BABY.
TAKE WHATEVER YOU WANT.
MMMM...
I'LL TAKE IT... YEAH...
YES...
OPEN UP.

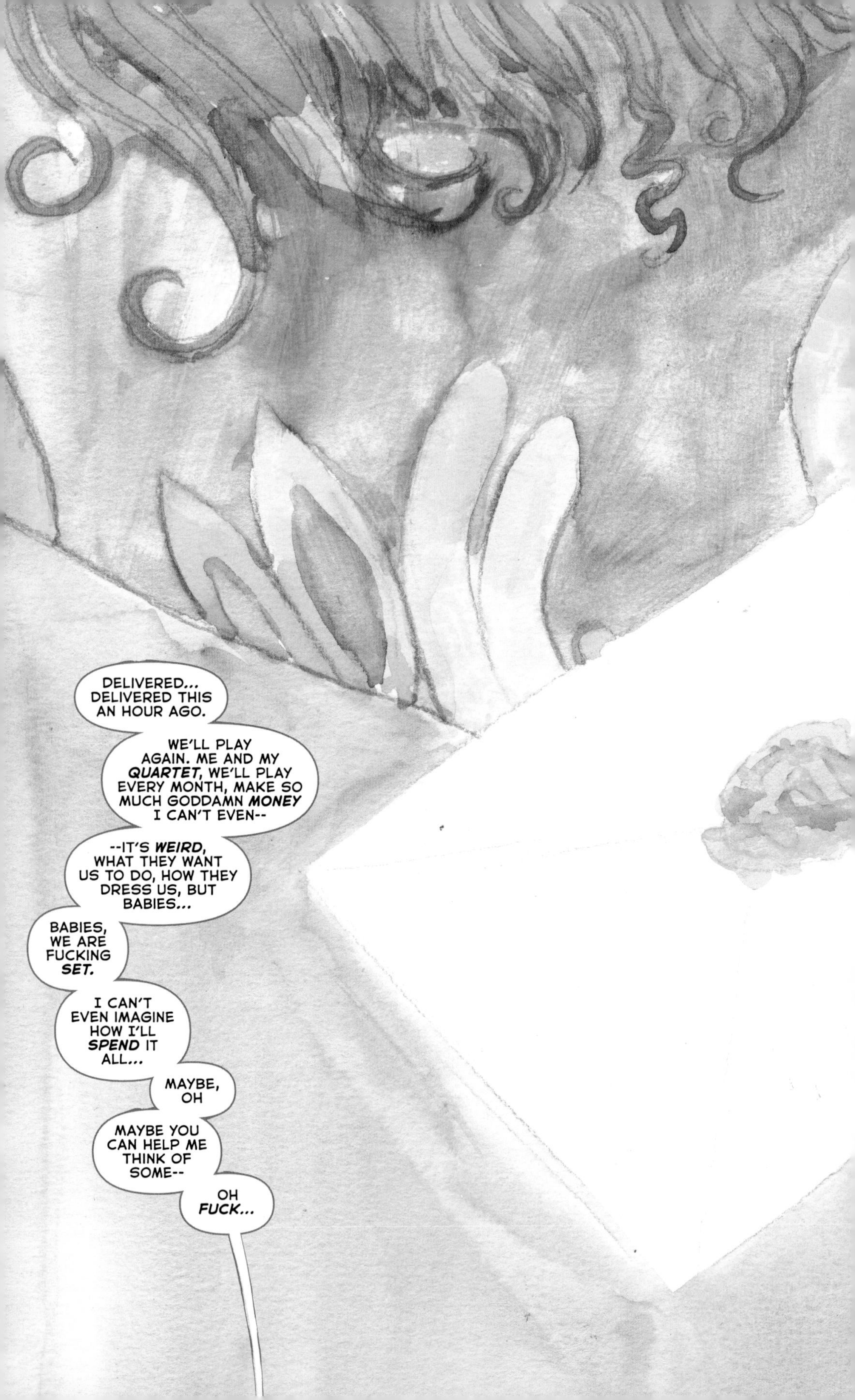
DELIVERED... DELIVERED THIS AN HOUR AGO.
WE'LL PLAY AGAIN. ME AND MY *QUARTET*, WE'LL PLAY EVERY MONTH, MAKE SO MUCH GODDAMN *MONEY* I CAN'T EVEN--
--IT'S *WEIRD*, WHAT THEY WANT US TO DO, HOW THEY DRESS US, BUT BABIES...
BABIES, WE ARE FUCKING *SET.*
I CAN'T EVEN IMAGINE HOW I'LL *SPEND* IT ALL...
MAYBE, OH
MAYBE YOU CAN HELP ME THINK OF SOME--
OH *FUCK*...

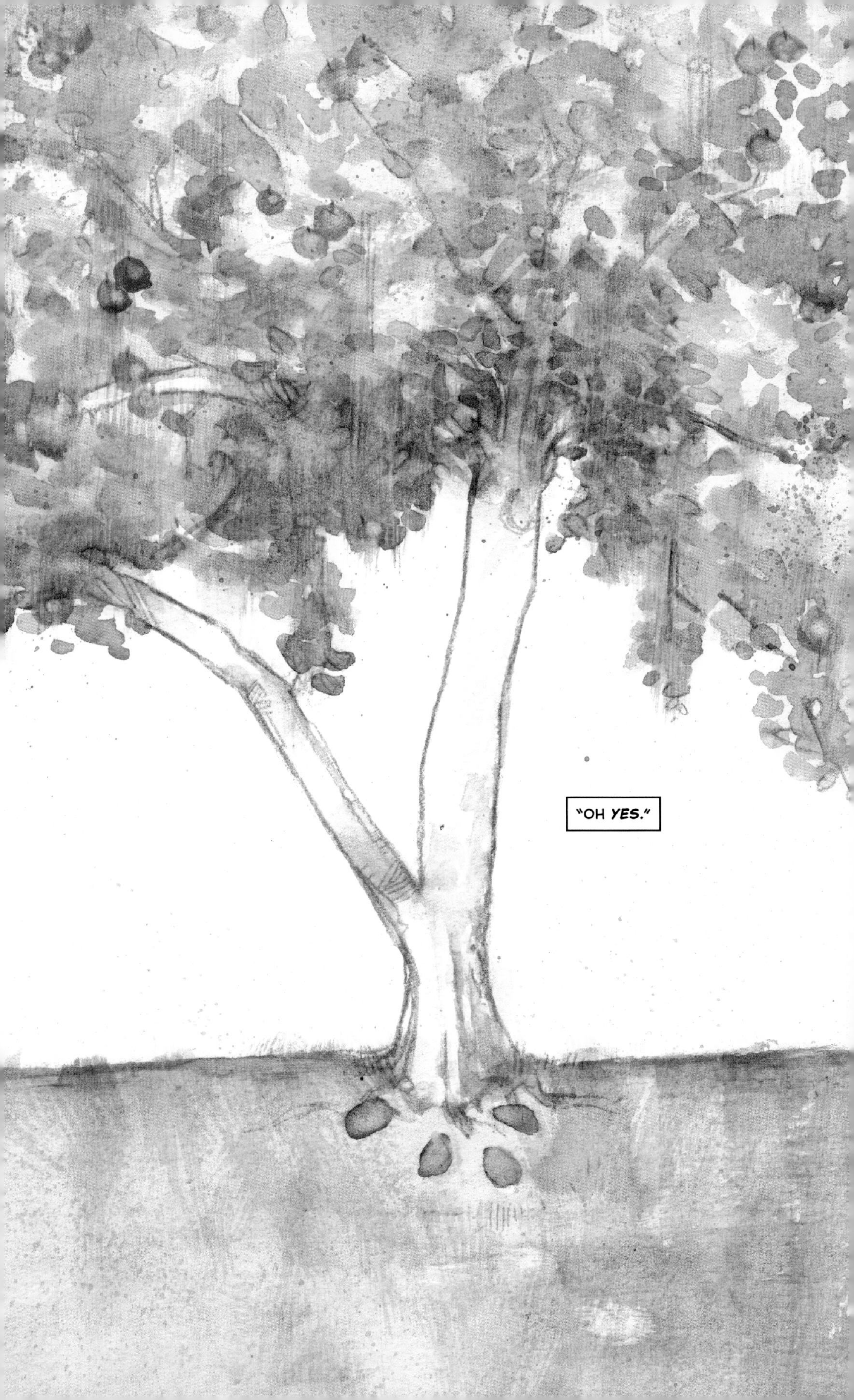
"OH *YES*."

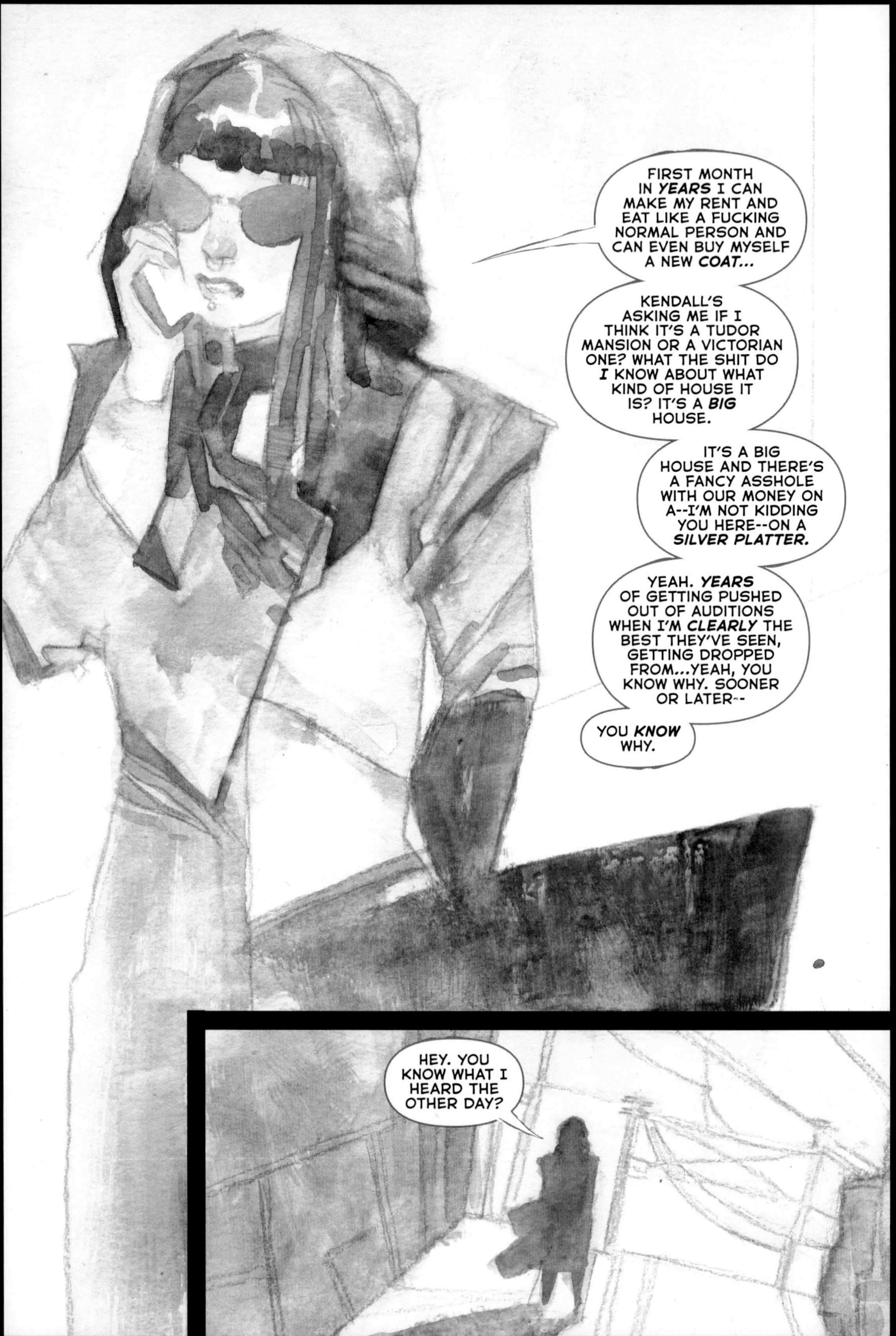
FIRST MONTH IN YEARS I CAN MAKE MY RENT AND EAT LIKE A FUCKING NORMAL PERSON AND CAN EVEN BUY MYSELF A NEW COAT...
KENDALL'S ASKING ME IF I THINK IT'S A TUDOR MANSION OR A VICTORIAN ONE? WHAT THE SHIT DO I KNOW ABOUT WHAT KIND OF HOUSE IT IS? IT'S A BIG HOUSE.
IT'S A BIG HOUSE AND THERE'S A FANCY ASSHOLE WITH OUR MONEY ON A--I'M NOT KIDDING YOU HERE--ON A SILVER PLATTER.
YEAH. YEARS OF GETTING PUSHED OUT OF AUDITIONS WHEN I'M CLEARLY THE BEST THEY'VE SEEN, GETTING DROPPED FROM...YEAH, YOU KNOW WHY. SOONER OR LATER--
YOU KNOW WHY.
HEY. YOU KNOW WHAT I HEARD THE OTHER DAY?

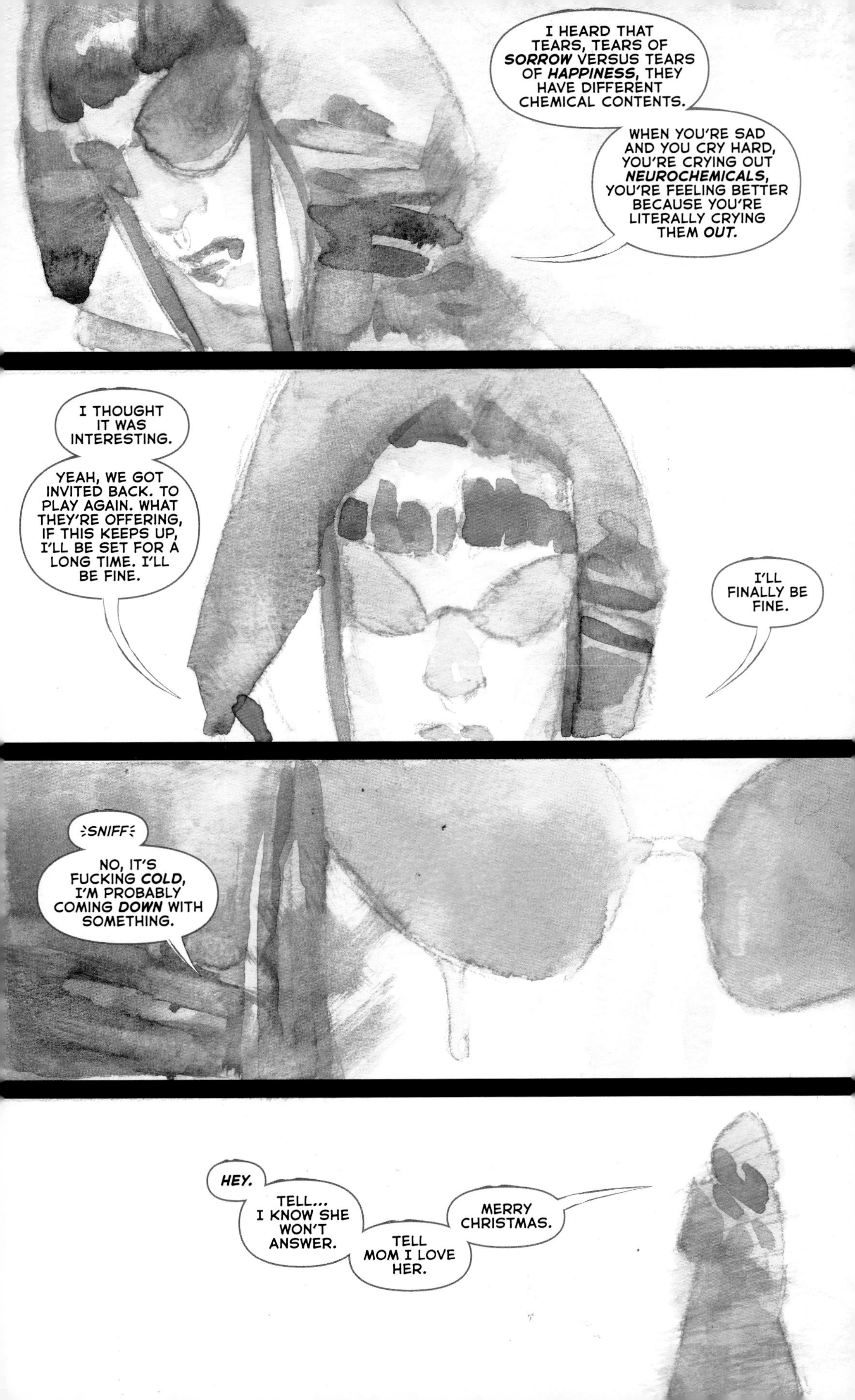
I HEARD THAT TEARS, TEARS OF SORROW VERSUS TEARS OF HAPPINESS, THEY HAVE DIFFERENT CHEMICAL CONTENTS.
WHEN YOU'RE SAD AND YOU CRY HARD, YOU'RE CRYING OUT NEUROCHEMICALS, YOU'RE FEELING BETTER BECAUSE YOU'RE LITERALLY CRYING THEM OUT.
I THOUGHT IT WAS INTERESTING.
YEAH, WE GOT INVITED BACK. TO PLAY AGAIN. WHAT THEY'RE OFFERING, IF THIS KEEPS UP, I'LL BE SET FOR A LONG TIME. I'LL BE FINE.
I'LL FINALLY BE FINE.
SNIFF
NO, IT'S FUCKING COLD, I'M PROBABLY COMING DOWN WITH SOMETHING.
HEY.
TELL... I KNOW SHE WON'T ANSWER.
TELL MOM I LOVE HER.
MERRY CHRISTMAS.

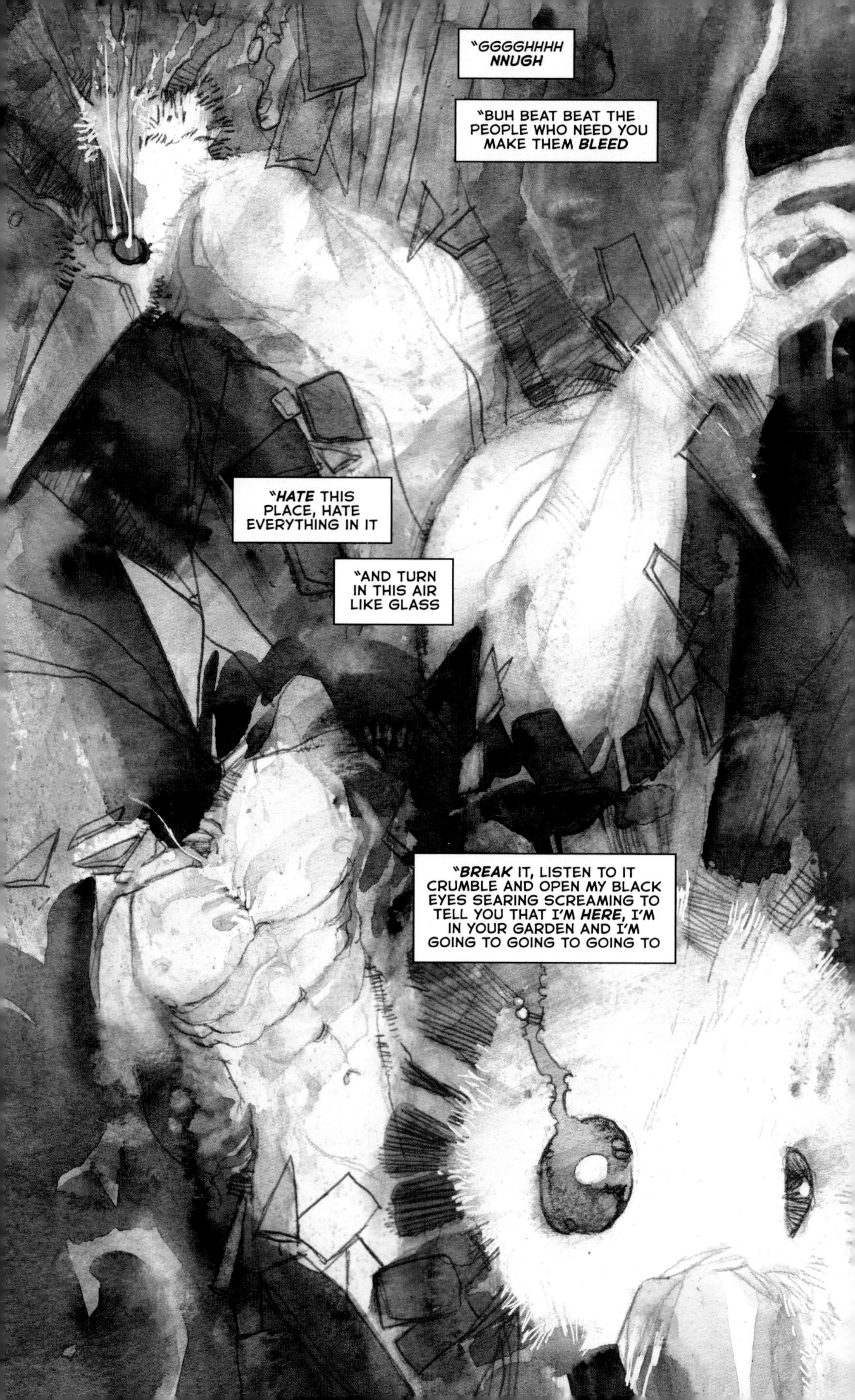
"GGGGHHHH NNUGH
"BUH BEAT BEAT THE PEOPLE WHO NEED YOU MAKE THEM BLEED
"HATE THIS PLACE, HATE EVERYTHING IN IT
"AND TURN IN THIS AIR LIKE GLASS
"BREAK IT, LISTEN TO IT CRUMBLE AND OPEN MY BLACK EYES SEARING SCREAMING TO TELL YOU THAT I'M HERE, I'M IN YOUR GARDEN AND I'M GOING TO GOING TO GOING TO

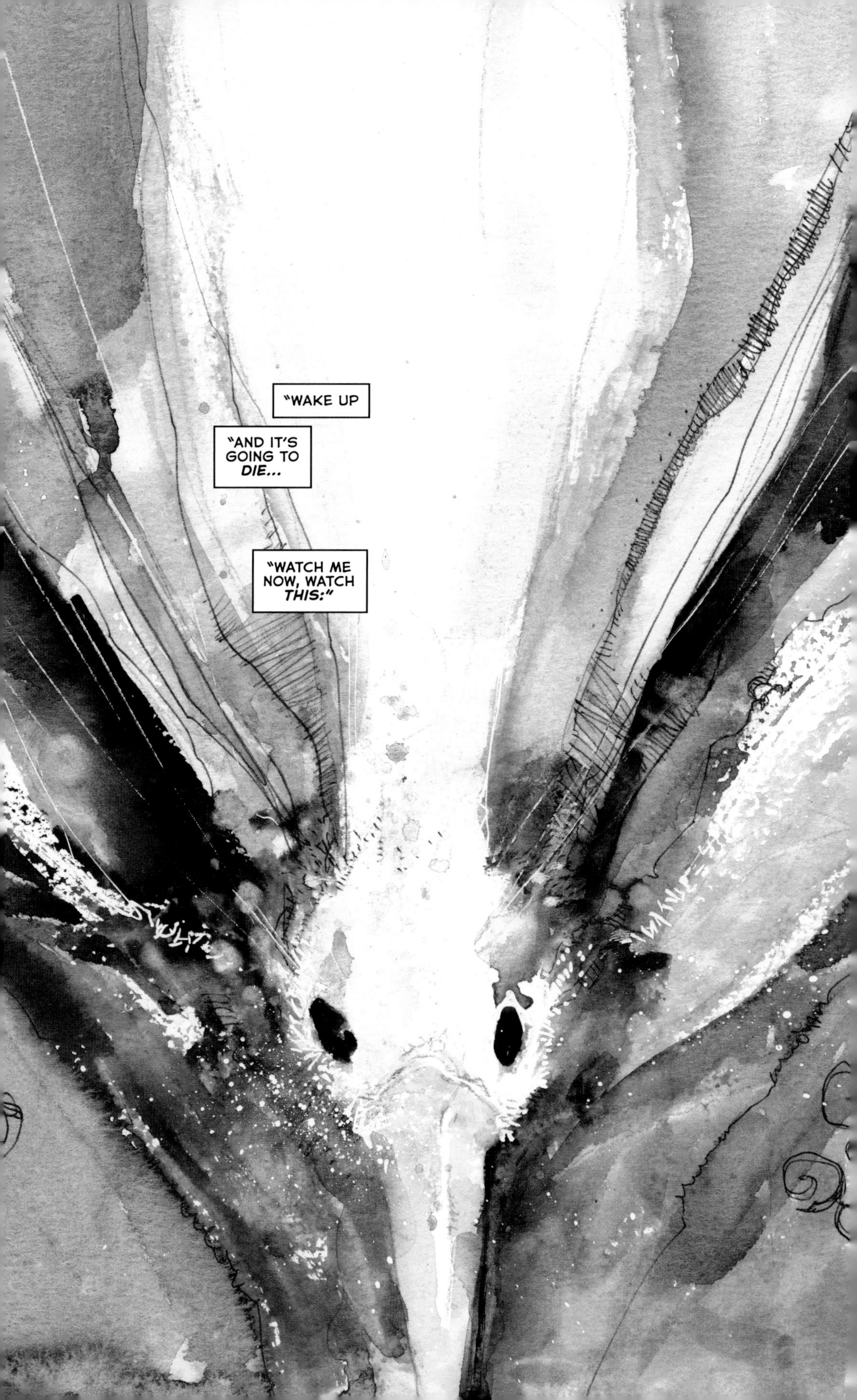
"WAKE UP
"AND IT'S GOING TO *DIE...*
"WATCH ME NOW, WATCH *THIS:"*

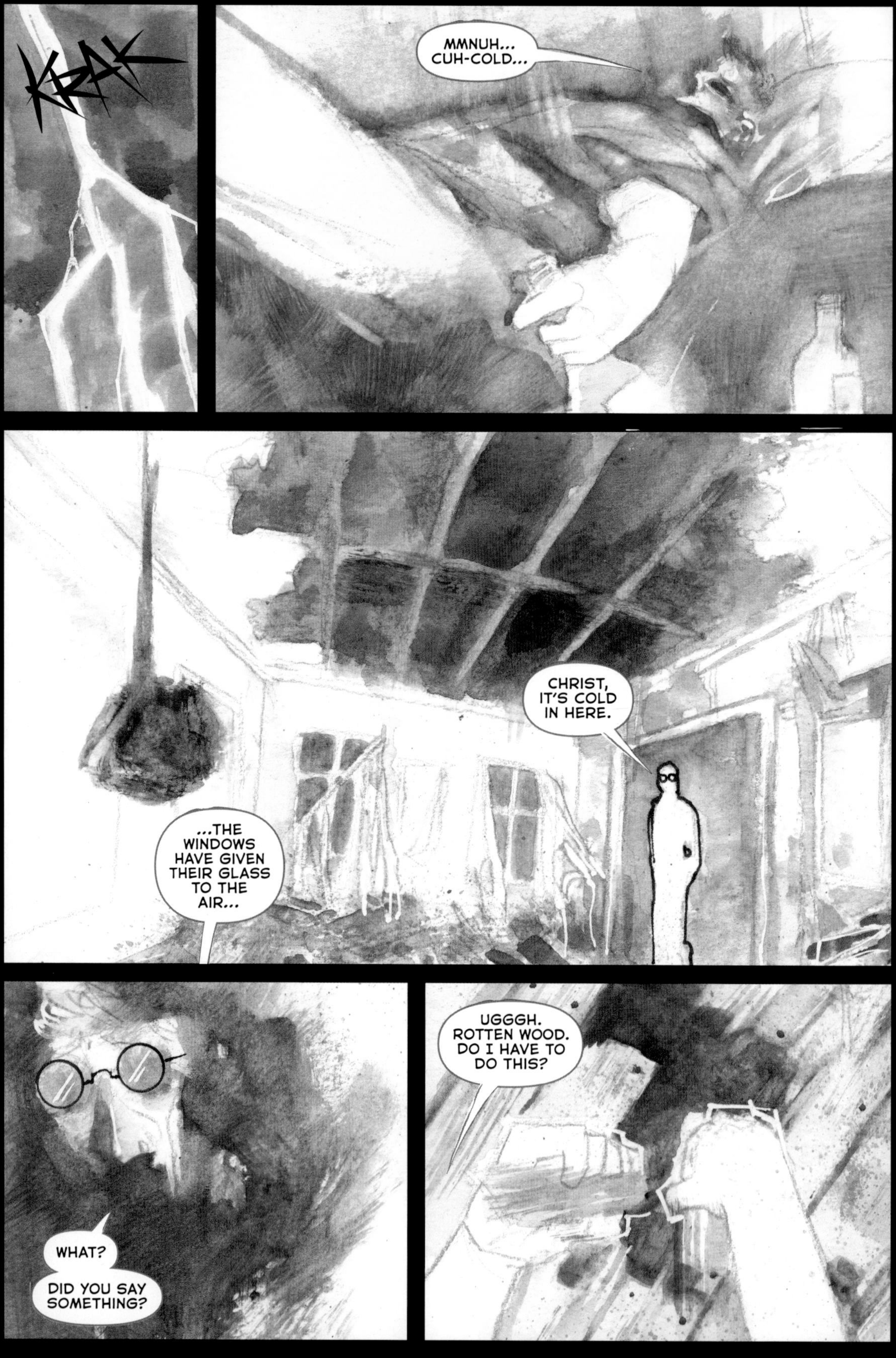
KRAK
MMNUH... CUH-COLD...
CHRIST, IT'S COLD IN HERE.
...THE WINDOWS HAVE GIVEN THEIR GLASS TO THE AIR...
WHAT?
DID YOU SAY SOMETHING?
UGGGH. ROTTEN WOOD. DO I HAVE TO DO THIS?

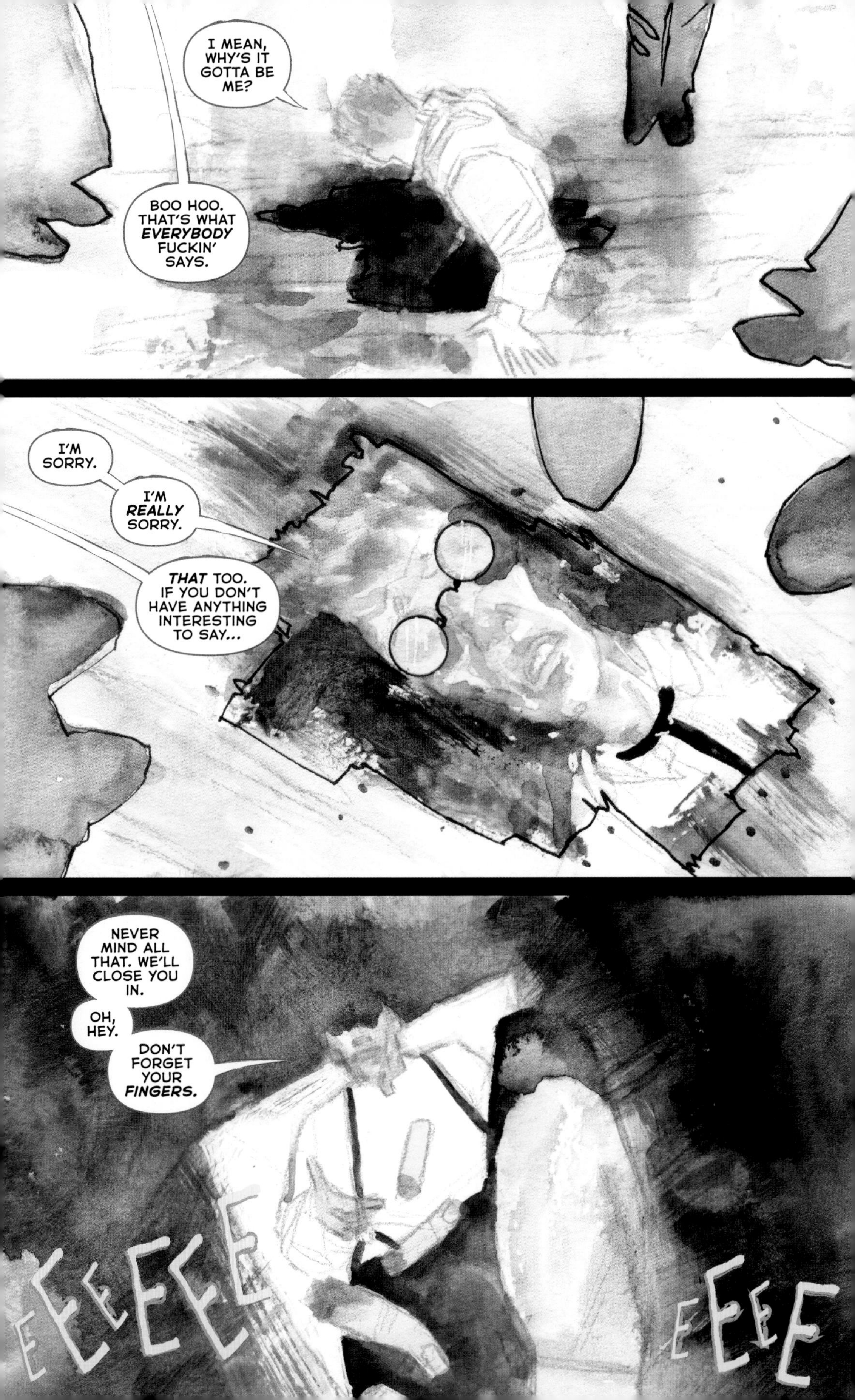
I MEAN, WHY'S IT GOTTA BE ME?
BOO HOO. THAT'S WHAT EVERYBODY FUCKIN' SAYS.
I'M SORRY.
I'M REALLY SORRY.
THAT TOO. IF YOU DON'T HAVE ANYTHING INTERESTING TO SAY...
NEVER MIND ALL THAT. WE'LL CLOSE YOU IN.
OH, HEY.
DON'T FORGET YOUR FINGERS.
EEEEEEE
EEEEE

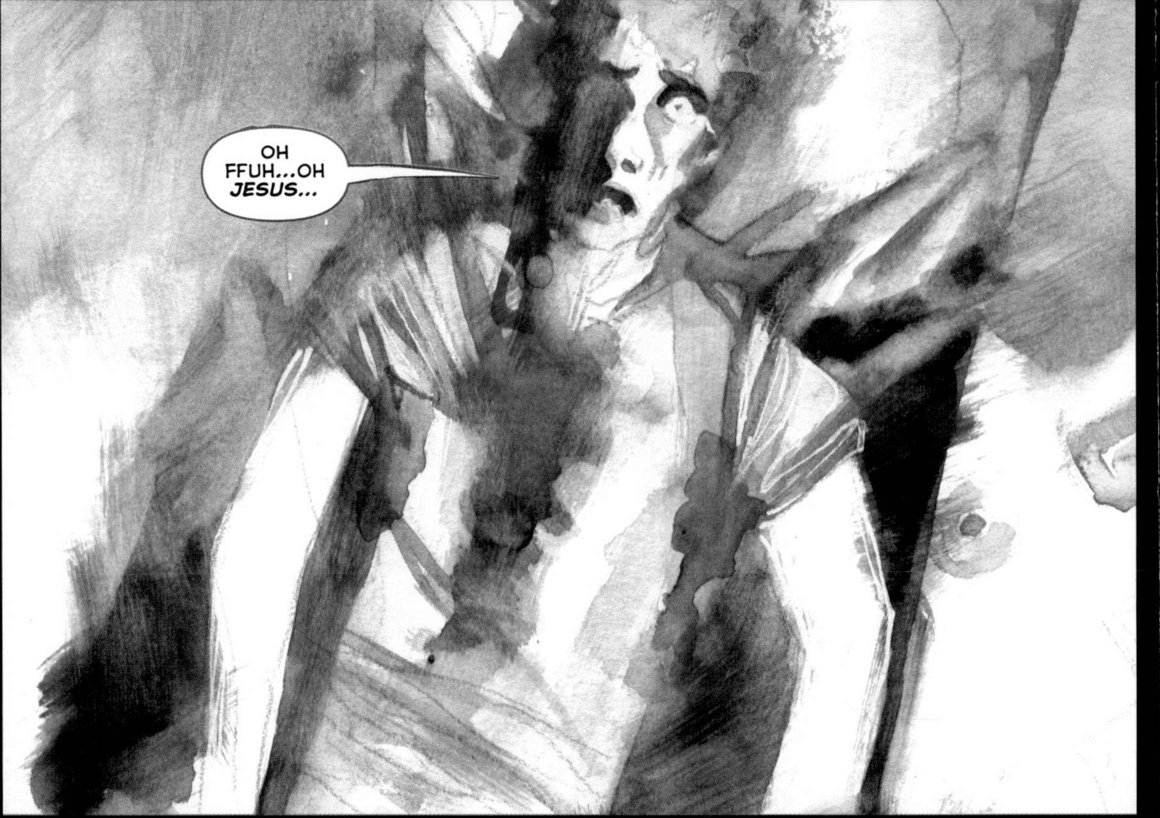
OH FFUH...OH *JESUS...*

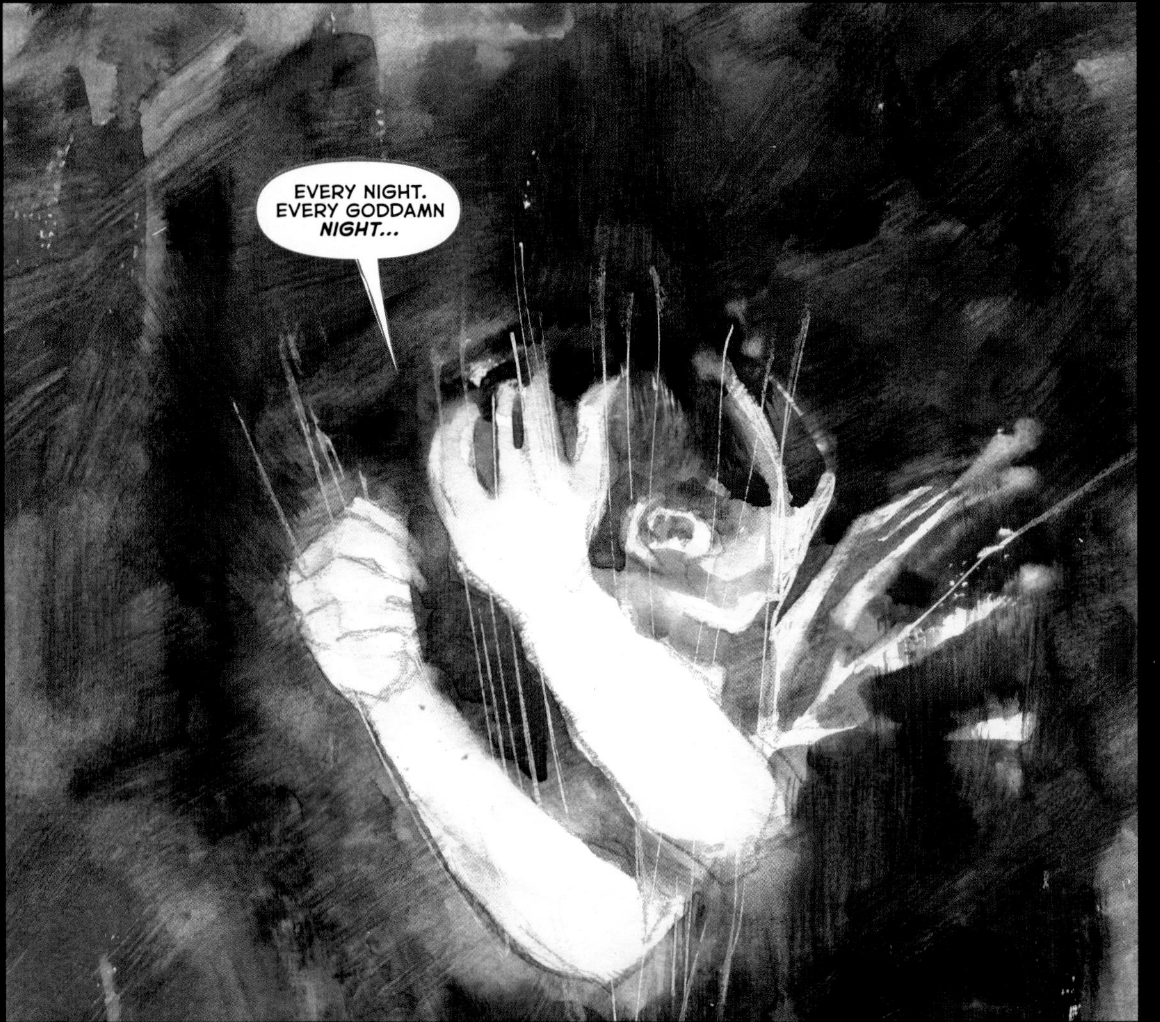
EVERY NIGHT. EVERY GODDAMN *NIGHT...*

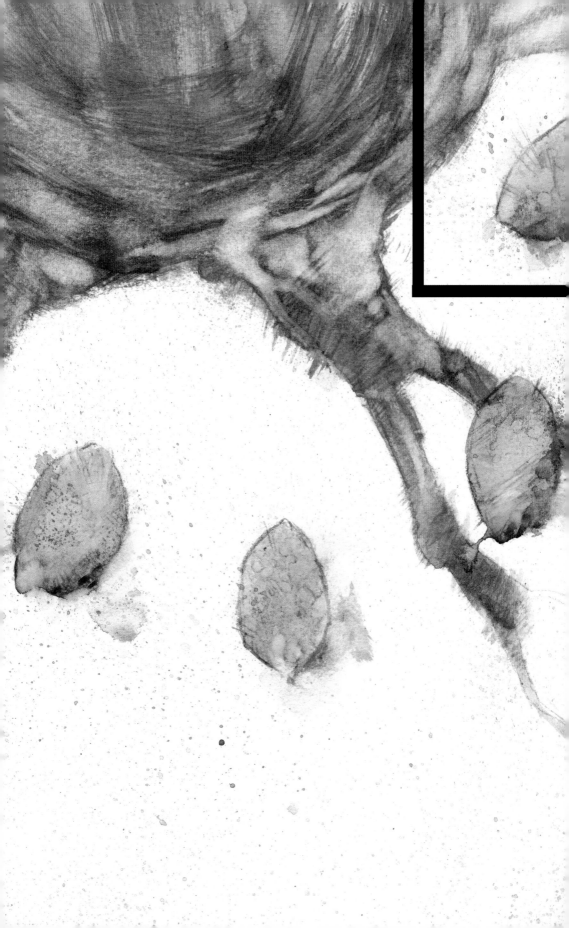

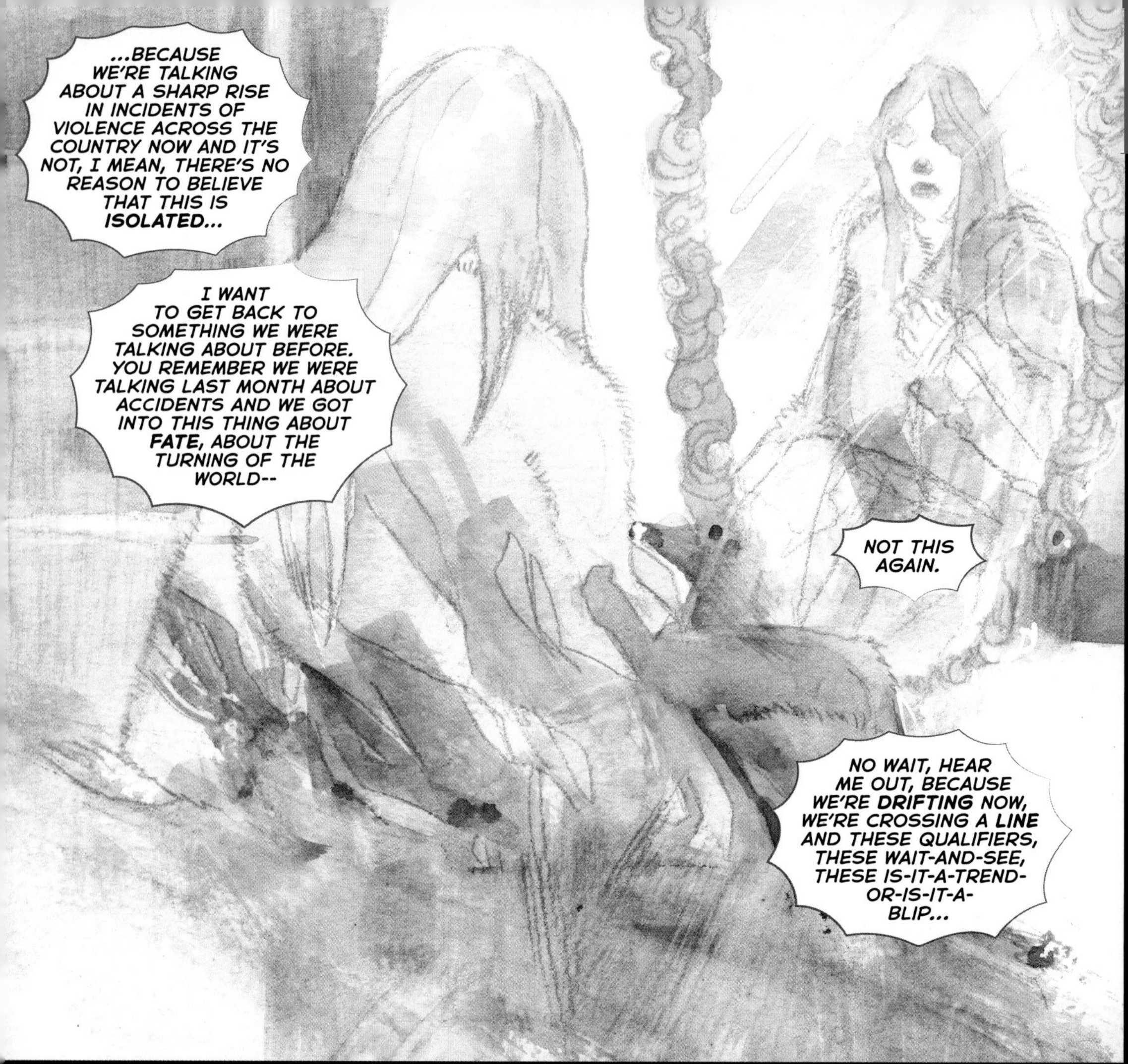
...BECAUSE WE'RE TALKING ABOUT A SHARP RISE IN INCIDENTS OF VIOLENCE ACROSS THE COUNTRY NOW AND IT'S NOT, I MEAN, THERE'S NO REASON TO BELIEVE THAT THIS IS **ISOLATED**...
I WANT TO GET BACK TO SOMETHING WE WERE TALKING ABOUT BEFORE. YOU REMEMBER WE WERE TALKING LAST MONTH ABOUT ACCIDENTS AND WE GOT INTO THIS THING ABOUT **FATE**, ABOUT THE TURNING OF THE WORLD--
NOT THIS AGAIN.
NO WAIT, HEAR ME OUT, BECAUSE WE'RE **DRIFTING** NOW, WE'RE CROSSING A **LINE** AND THESE QUALIFIERS, THESE WAIT-AND-SEE, THESE IS-IT-A-TREND-OR-IS-IT-A-BLIP...

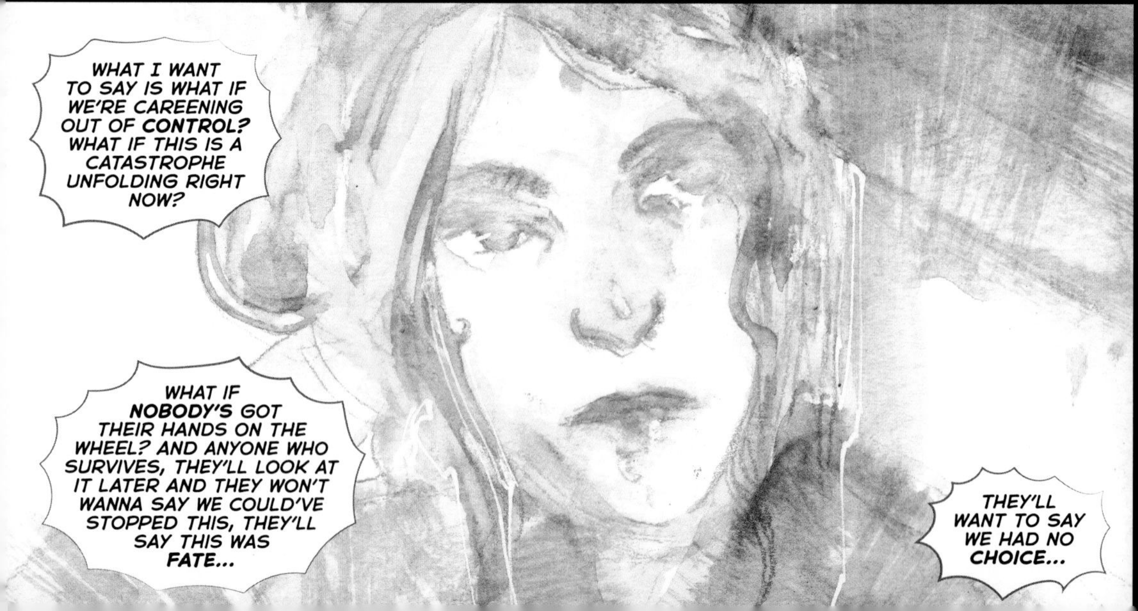
WHAT I WANT TO SAY IS WHAT IF WE'RE CAREENING OUT OF **CONTROL?** WHAT IF THIS IS A CATASTROPHE UNFOLDING RIGHT NOW?
WHAT IF **NOBODY'S** GOT THEIR HANDS ON THE WHEEL? AND ANYONE WHO SURVIVES, THEY'LL LOOK AT IT LATER AND THEY WON'T WANNA SAY WE COULD'VE STOPPED THIS, THEY'LL SAY THIS WAS **FATE**...
THEY'LL WANT TO SAY WE HAD NO **CHOICE**...

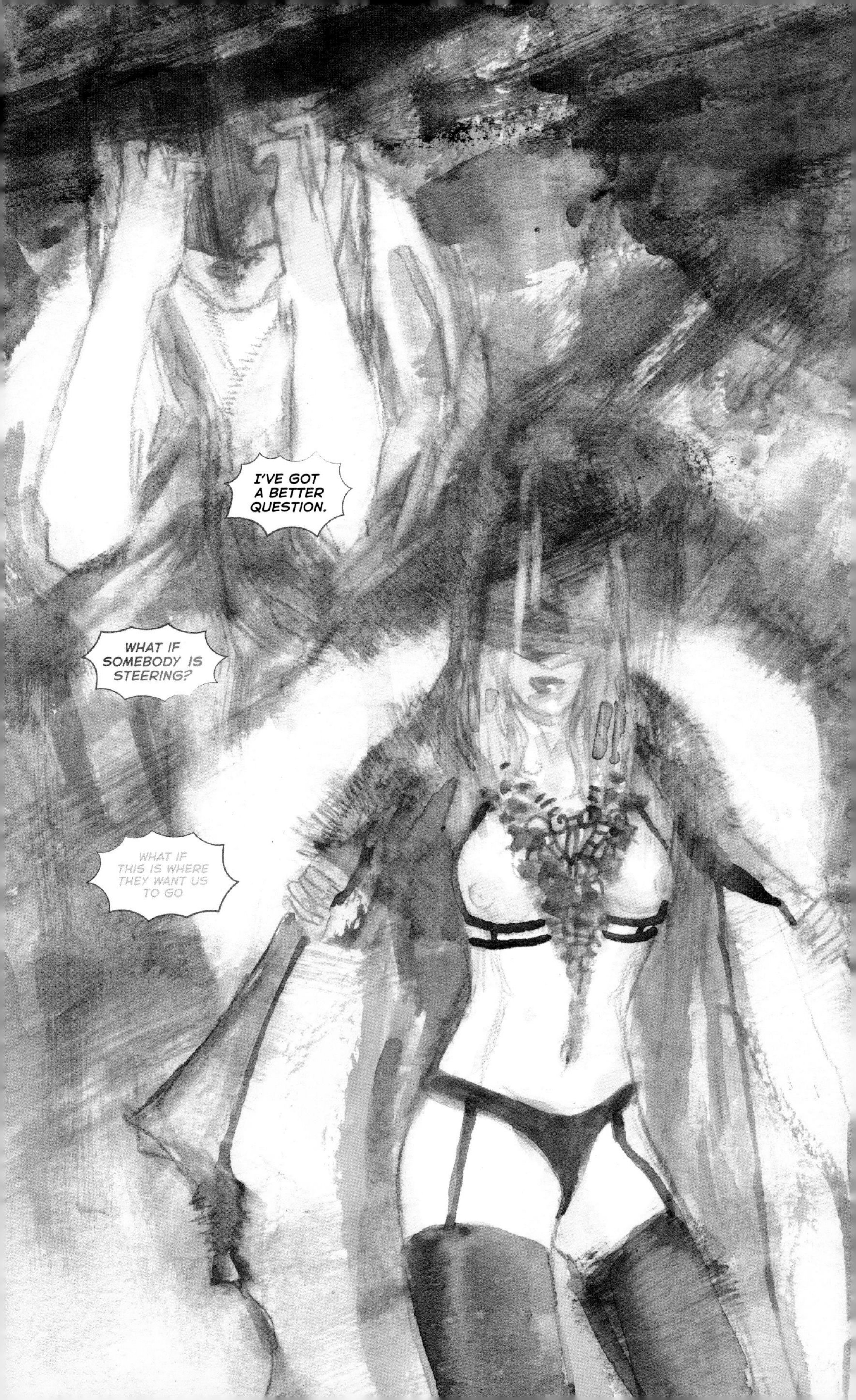
I'VE GOT A BETTER QUESTION.
WHAT IF SOMEBODY IS STEERING?
WHAT IF THIS IS WHERE THEY WANT US TO GO

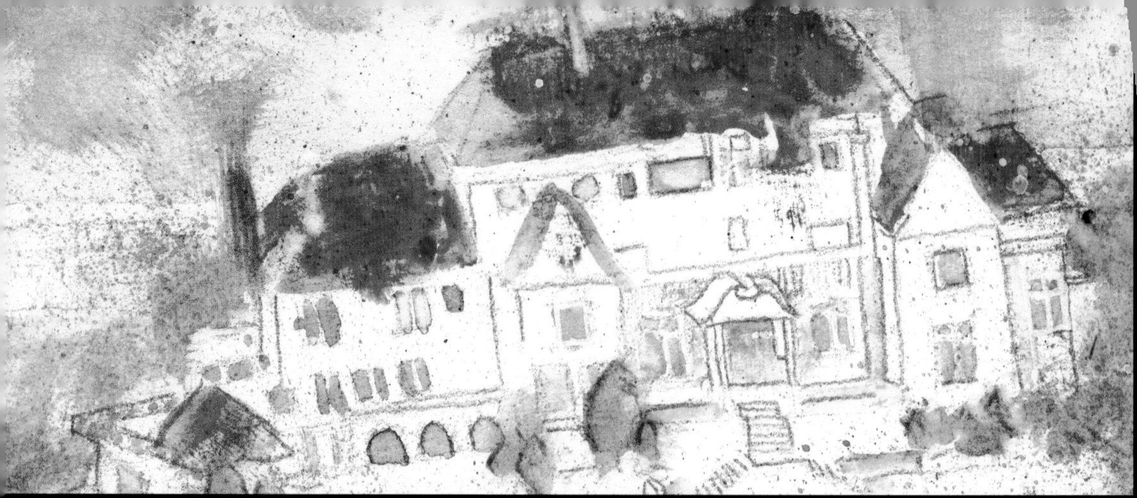

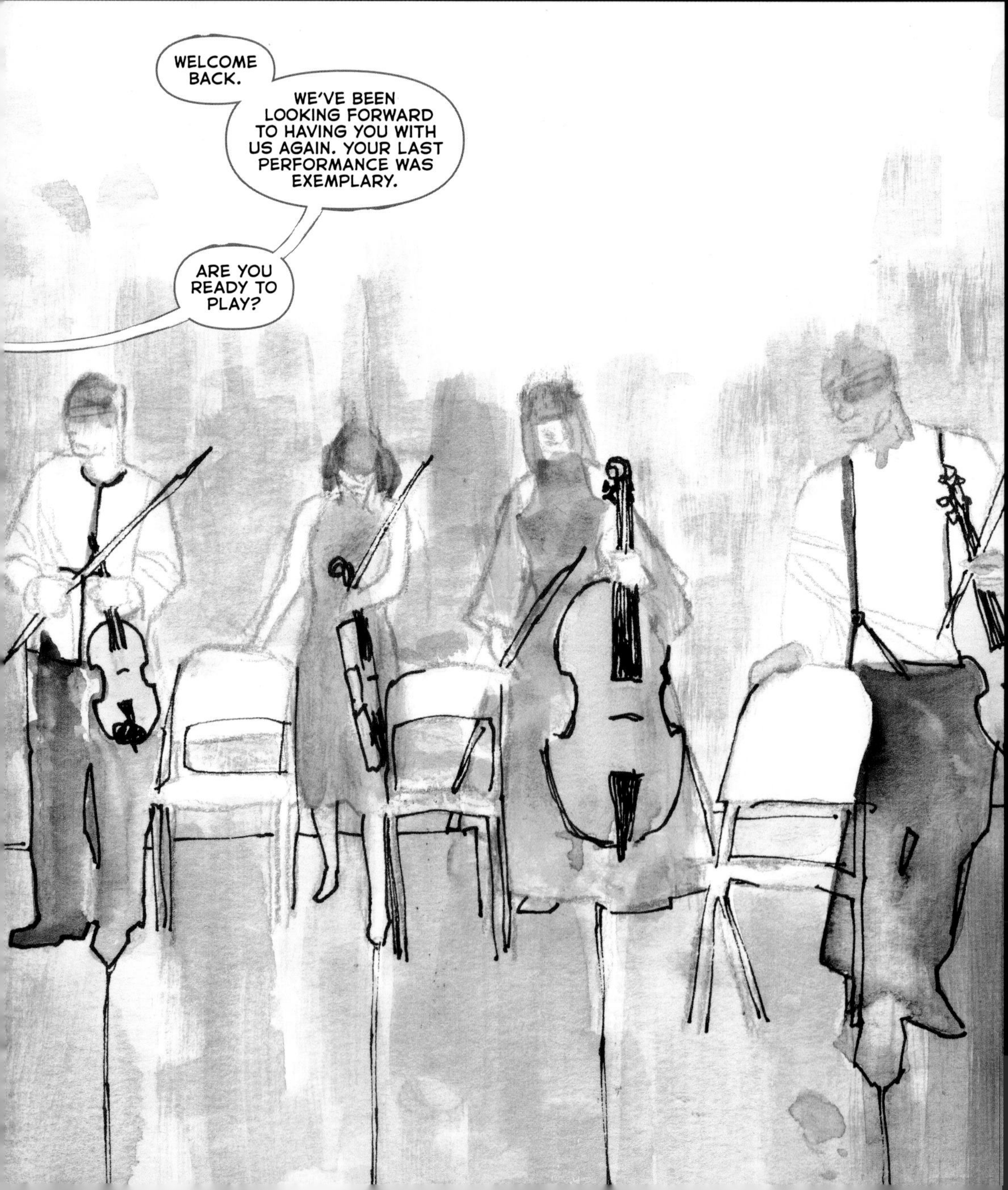
WELCOME BACK.
WE'VE BEEN LOOKING FORWARD TO HAVING YOU WITH US AGAIN. YOUR LAST PERFORMANCE WAS EXEMPLARY.
ARE YOU READY TO PLAY?

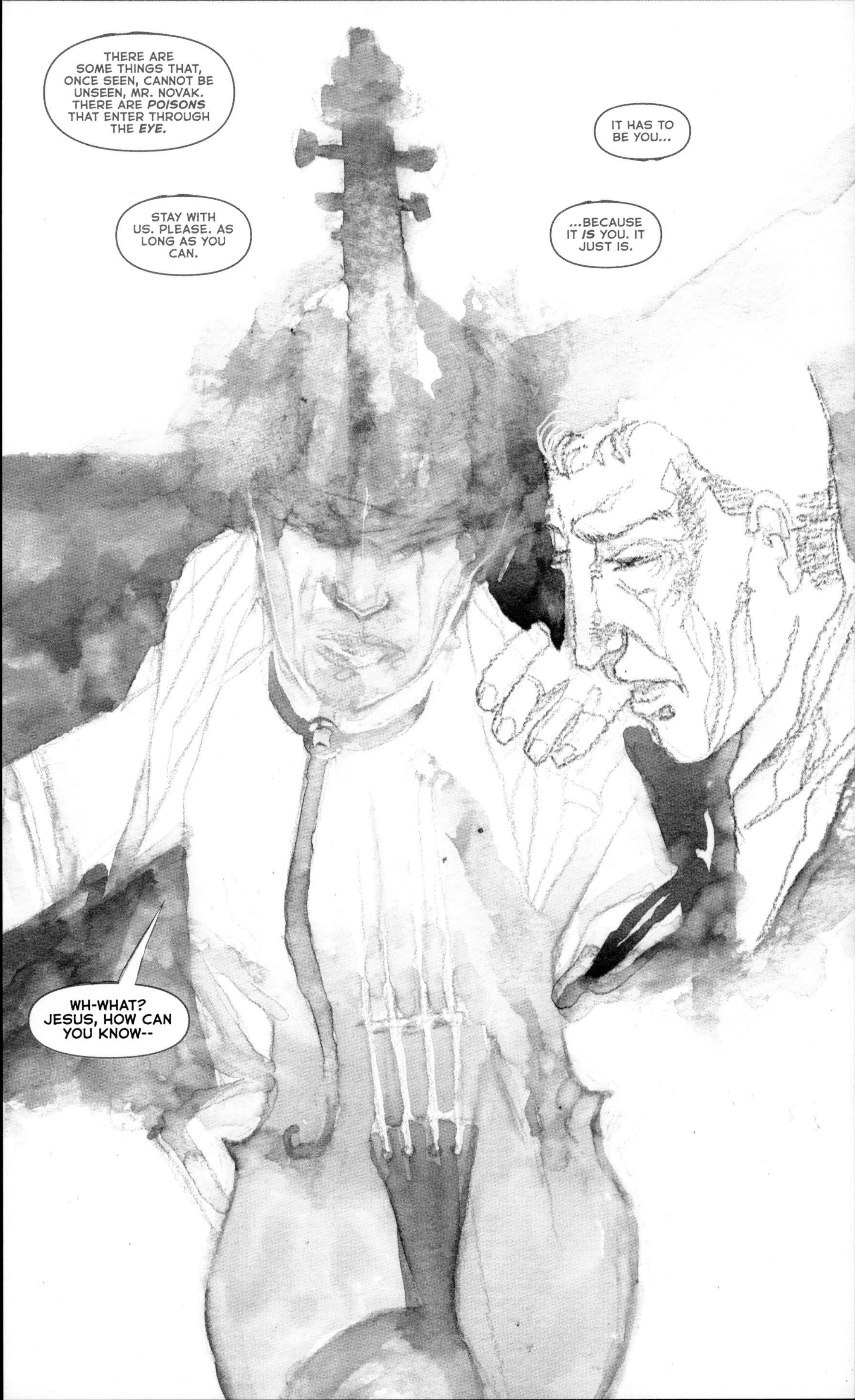
THERE ARE SOME THINGS THAT, ONCE SEEN, CANNOT BE UNSEEN, MR. NOVAK. THERE ARE *POISONS* THAT ENTER THROUGH THE *EYE.*
STAY WITH US. PLEASE. AS LONG AS YOU CAN.
IT HAS TO BE YOU...
...BECAUSE IT *IS* YOU. IT JUST IS.
WH-WHAT? JESUS, HOW CAN YOU KNOW--

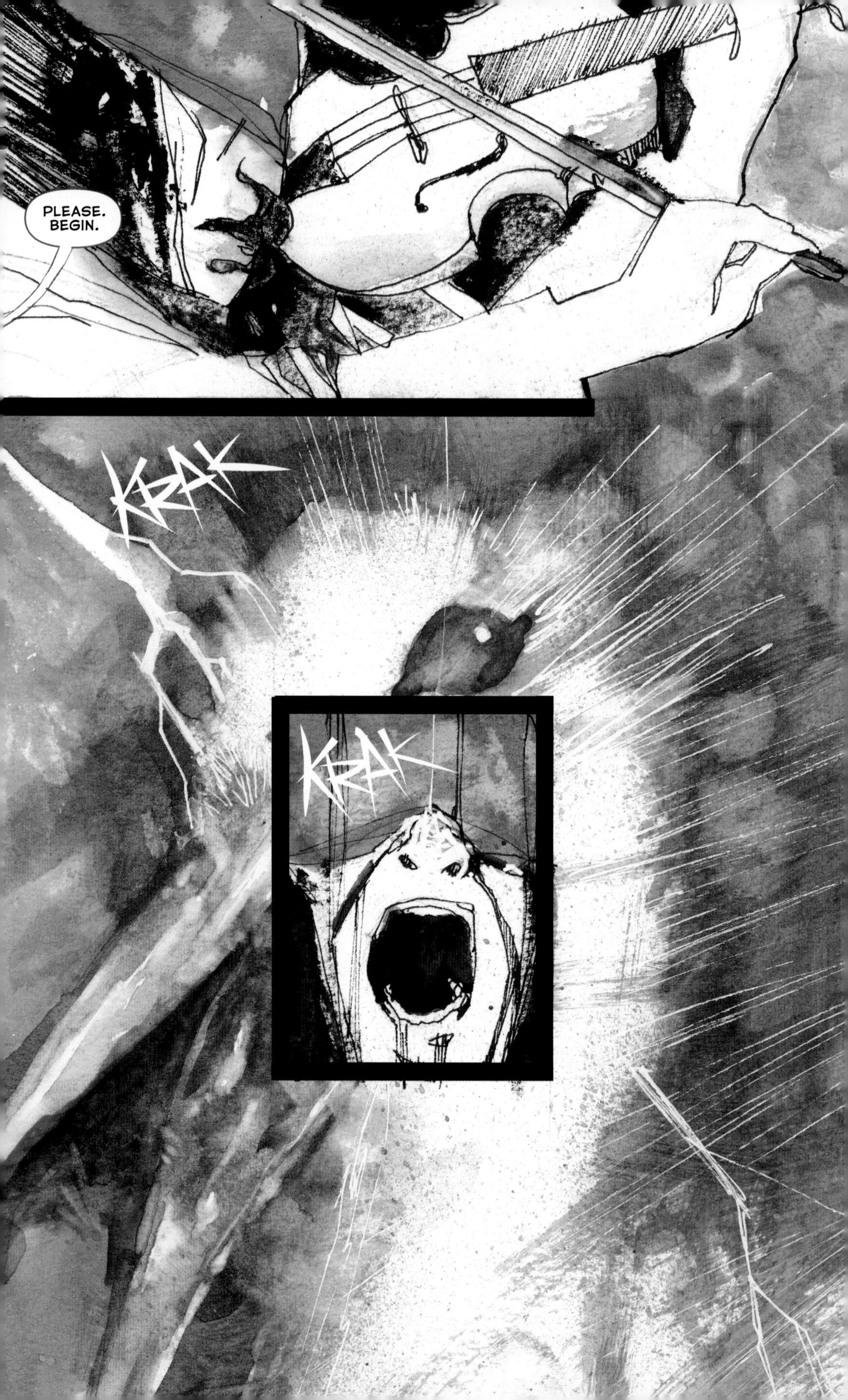
PLEASE. BEGIN.
KRAK
KRAK

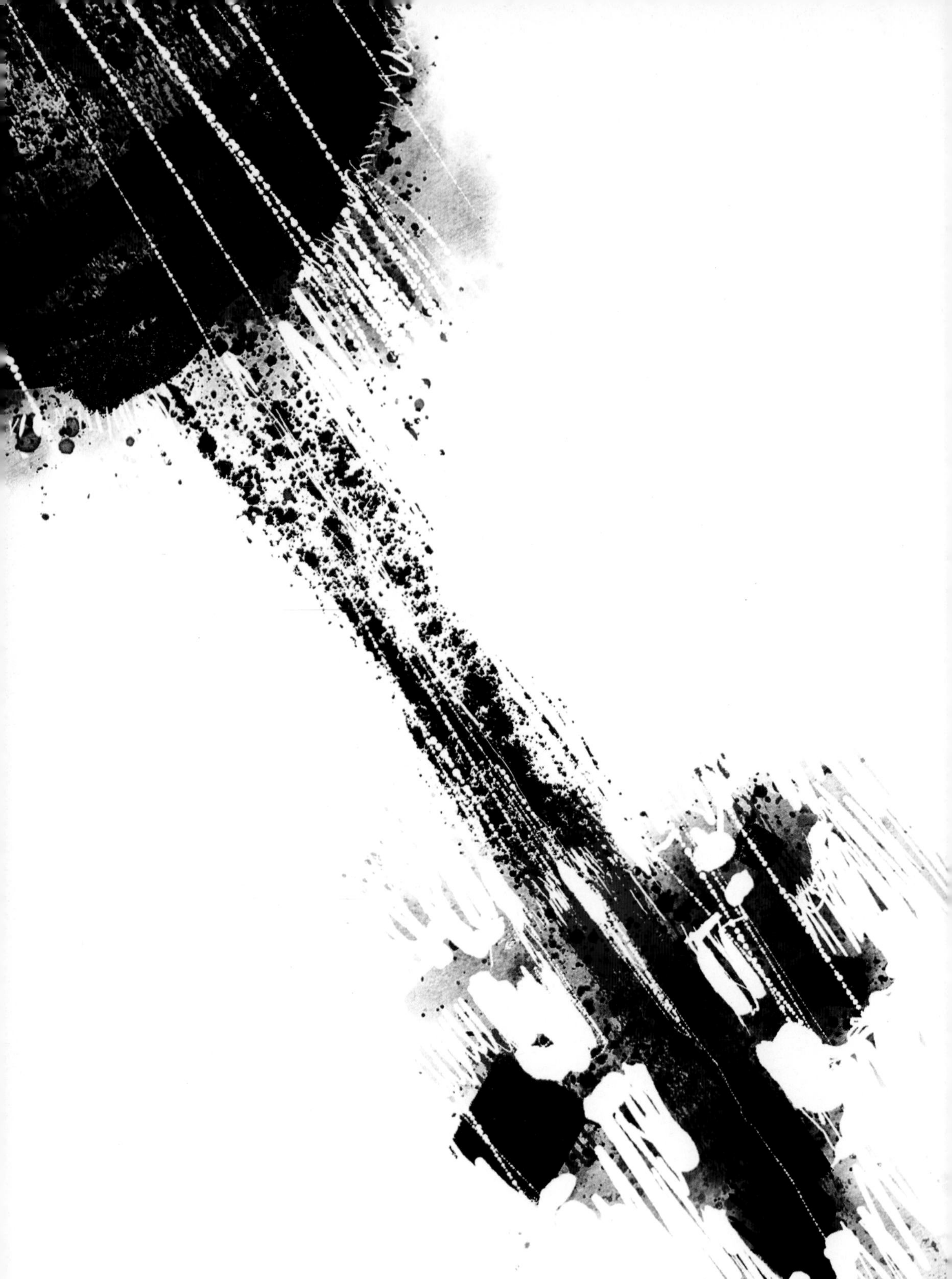

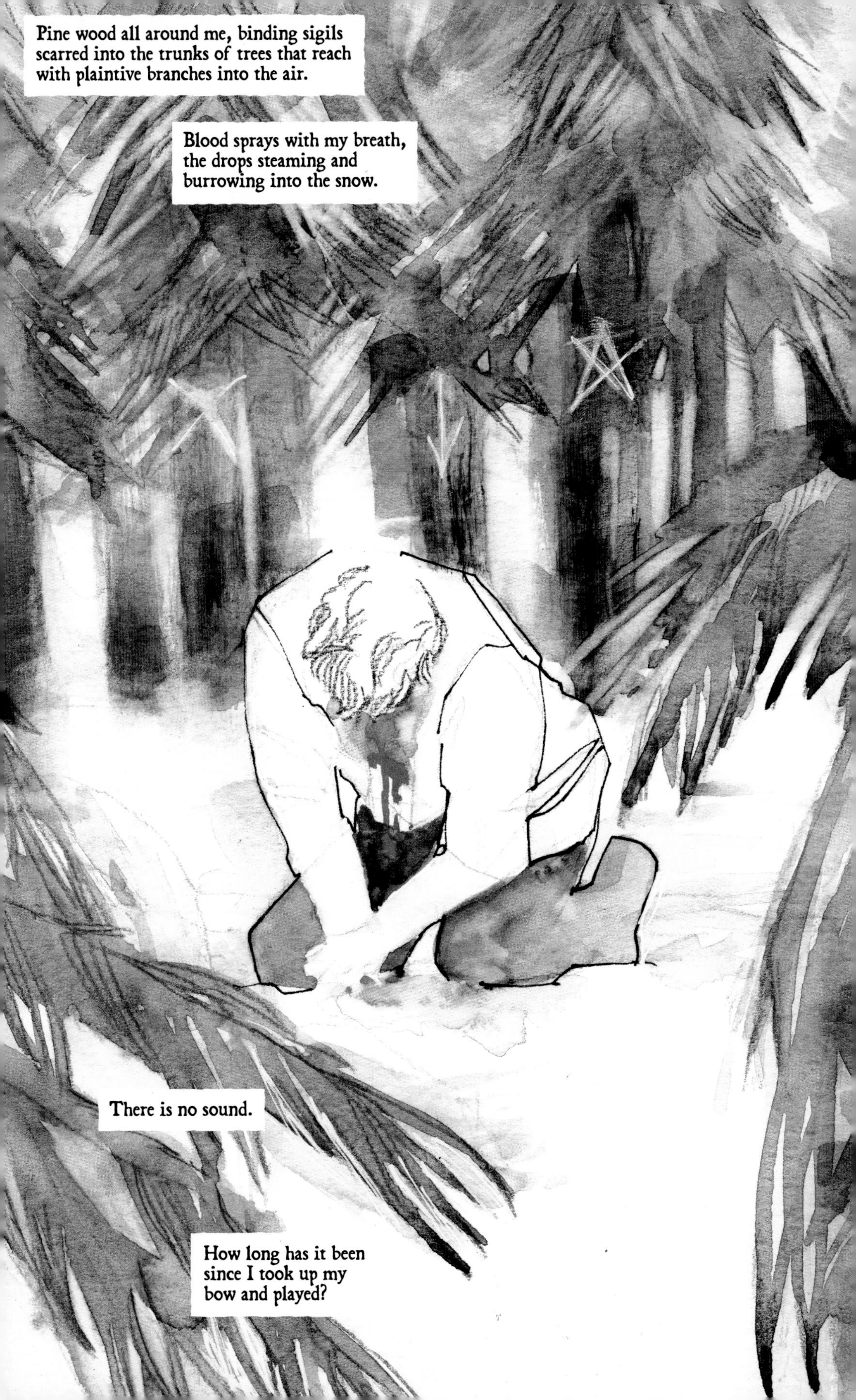
Pine wood all around me, binding sigils scarred into the trunks of trees that reach with plaintive branches into the air.
Blood sprays with my breath, the drops steaming and burrowing into the snow.
There is no sound.
How long has it been since I took up my bow and played?

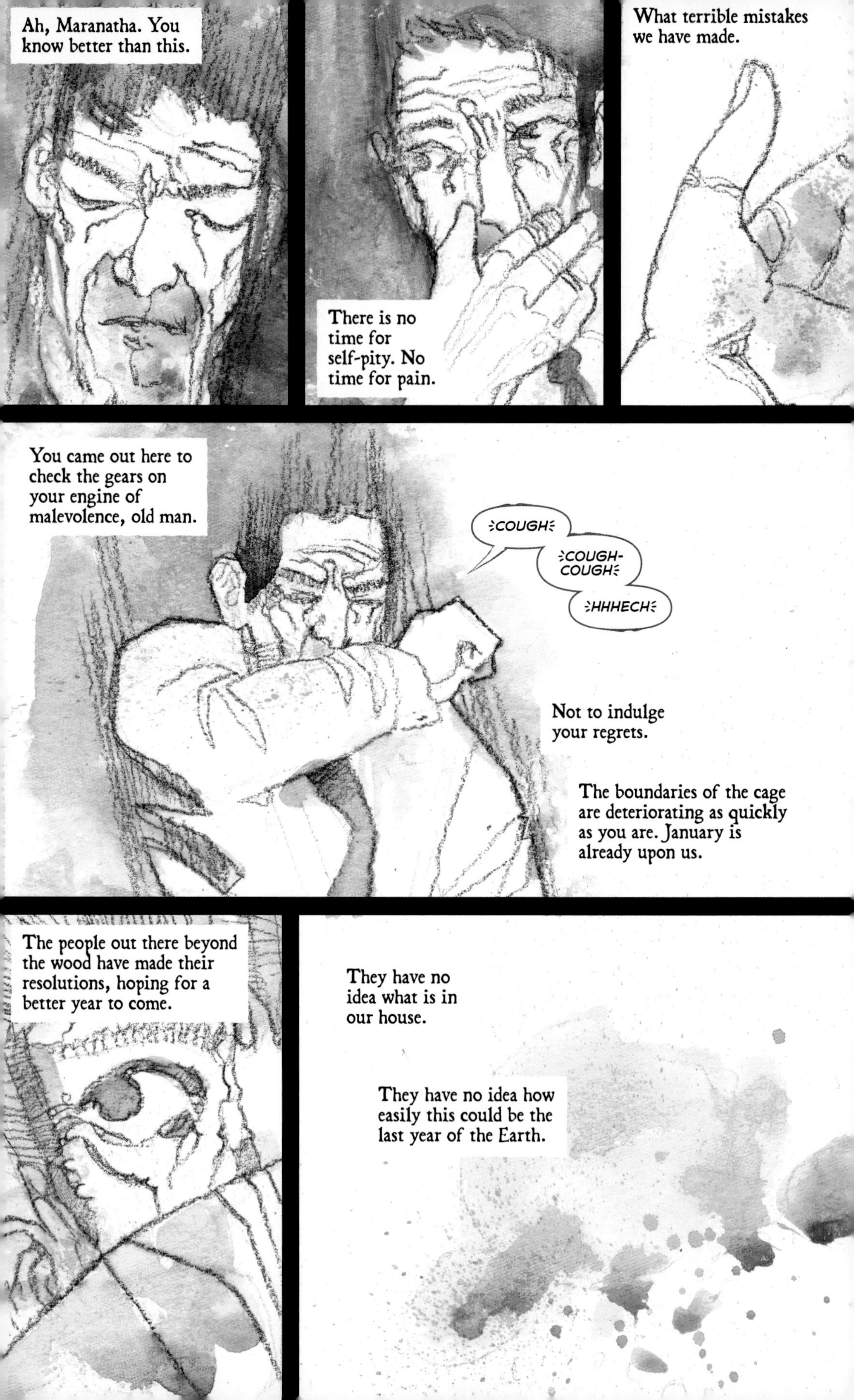
Ah, Maranatha. You know better than this.
There is no time for self-pity. No time for pain.
What terrible mistakes we have made.
You came out here to check the gears on your engine of malevolence, old man.
COUGH
COUGH-COUGH
HHHECH
Not to indulge your regrets.
The boundaries of the cage are deteriorating as quickly as you are. January is already upon us.
The people out there beyond the wood have made their resolutions, hoping for a better year to come.
They have no idea what is in our house.
They have no idea how easily this could be the last year of the Earth.

SYMPHONY

PART THREE:
JANUARY

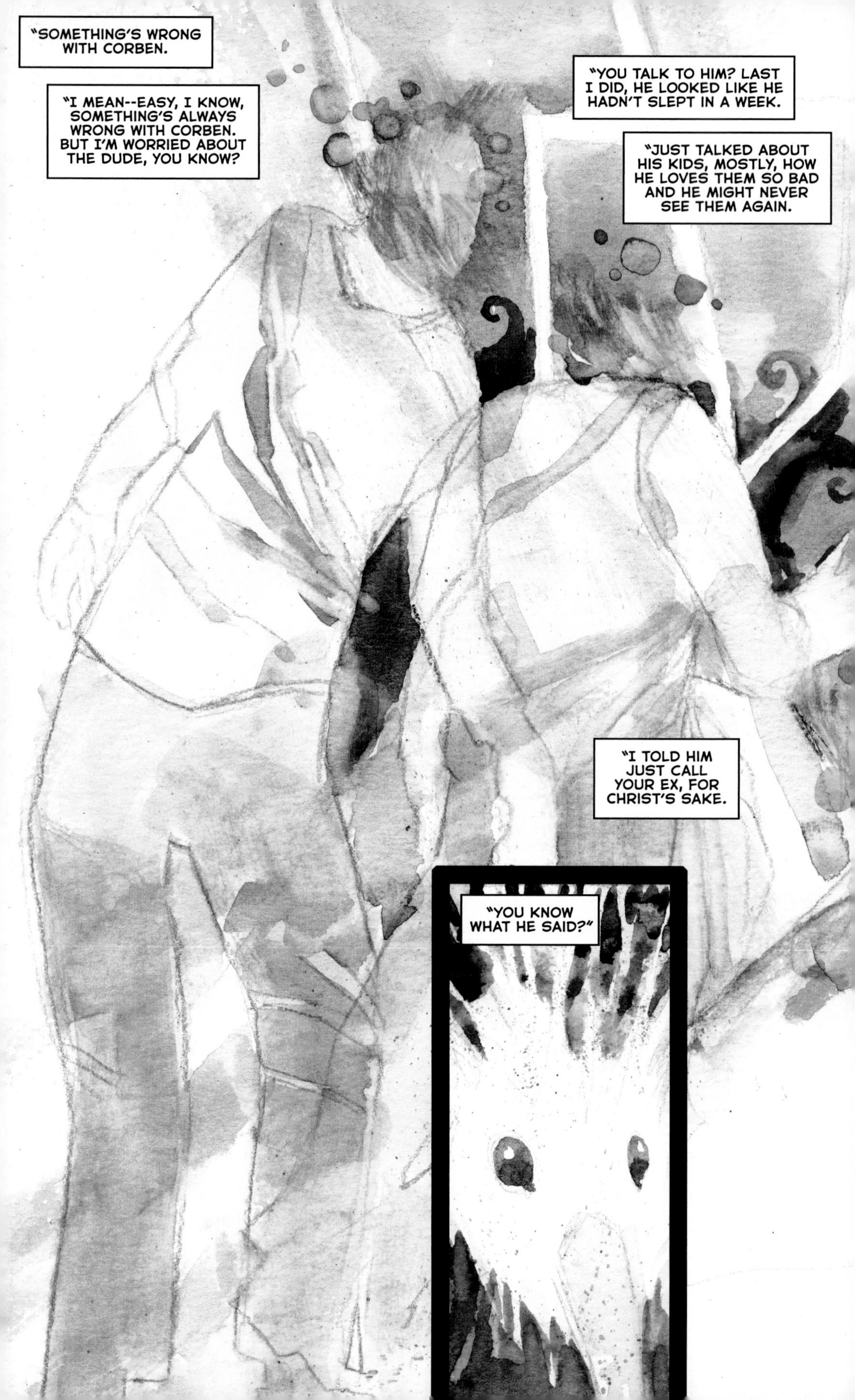
"SOMETHING'S WRONG WITH CORBEN.
"I MEAN--EASY, I KNOW, SOMETHING'S ALWAYS WRONG WITH CORBEN. BUT I'M WORRIED ABOUT THE DUDE, YOU KNOW?
"YOU TALK TO HIM? LAST I DID, HE LOOKED LIKE HE HADN'T SLEPT IN A WEEK.
"JUST TALKED ABOUT HIS KIDS, MOSTLY, HOW HE LOVES THEM SO BAD AND HE MIGHT NEVER SEE THEM AGAIN.
"I TOLD HIM JUST CALL YOUR EX, FOR CHRIST'S SAKE.
"YOU KNOW WHAT HE SAID?"

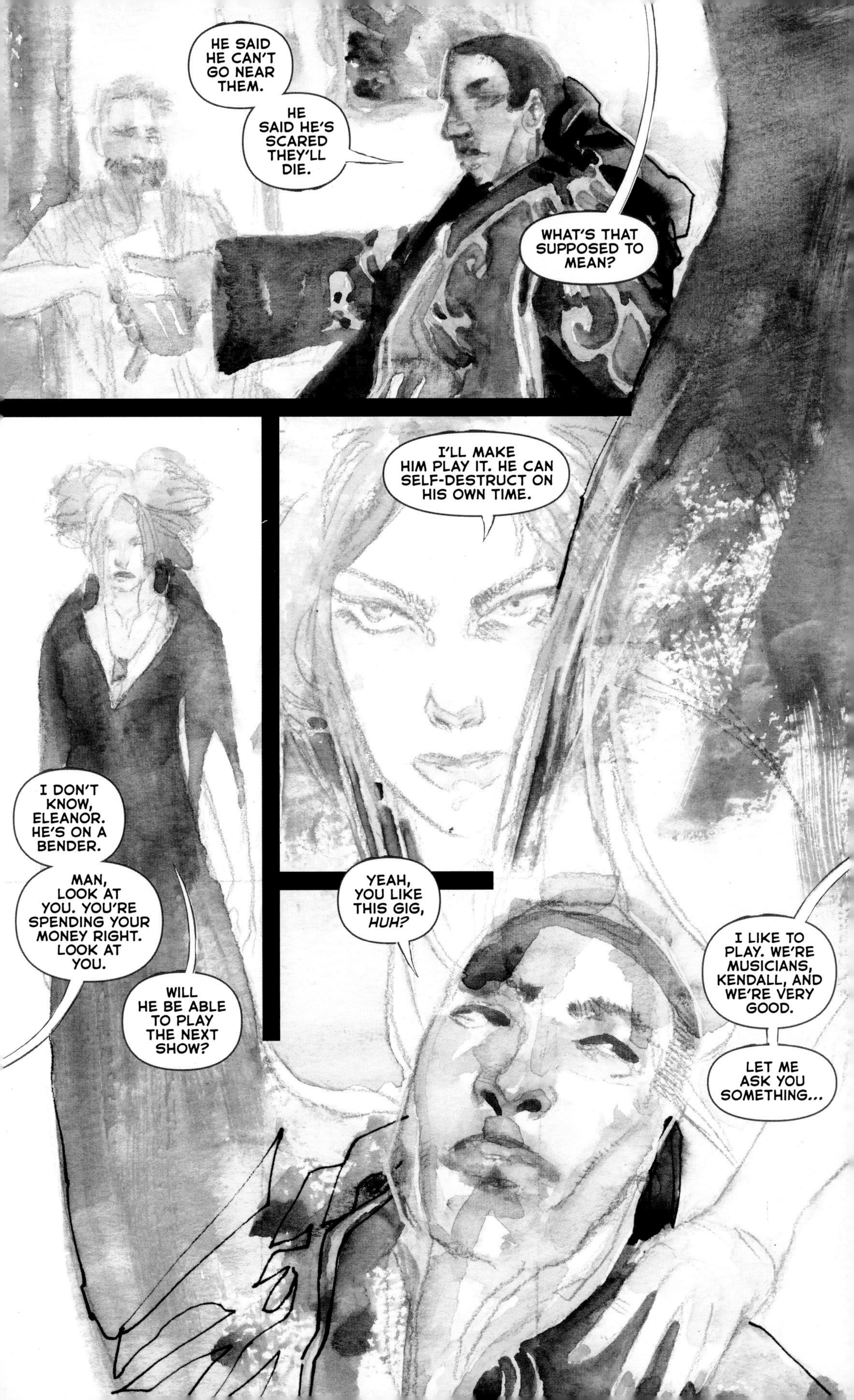

HE SAID HE CAN'T GO NEAR THEM.
HE SAID HE'S SCARED THEY'LL DIE.
WHAT'S THAT SUPPOSED TO MEAN?
I'LL MAKE HIM PLAY IT. HE CAN SELF-DESTRUCT ON HIS OWN TIME.
I DON'T KNOW, ELEANOR. HE'S ON A BENDER.
MAN, LOOK AT YOU. YOU'RE SPENDING YOUR MONEY RIGHT. LOOK AT YOU.
WILL HE BE ABLE TO PLAY THE NEXT SHOW?
YEAH, YOU LIKE THIS GIG, *HUH?*
I LIKE TO PLAY. WE'RE MUSICIANS, KENDALL, AND WE'RE VERY GOOD.
LET ME ASK YOU SOMETHING...

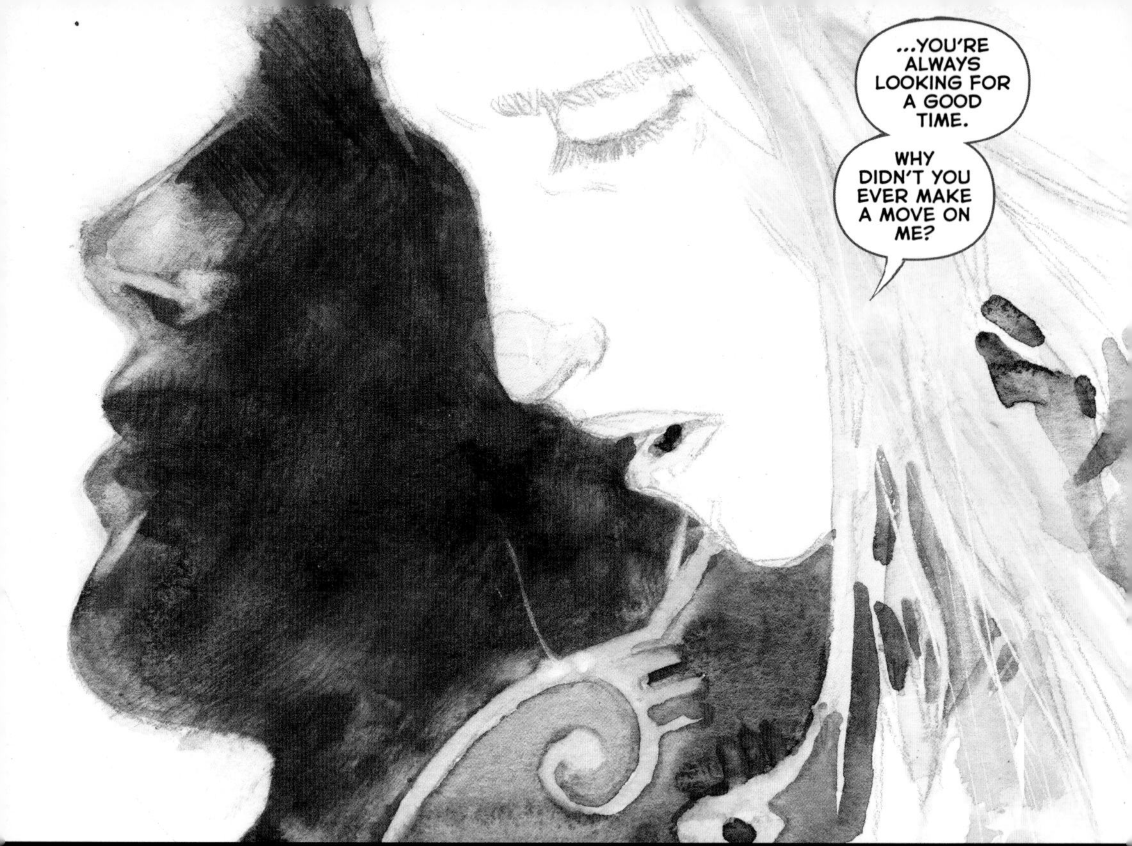
...YOU'RE ALWAYS LOOKING FOR A GOOD TIME.
WHY DIDN'T YOU EVER MAKE A MOVE ON ME?

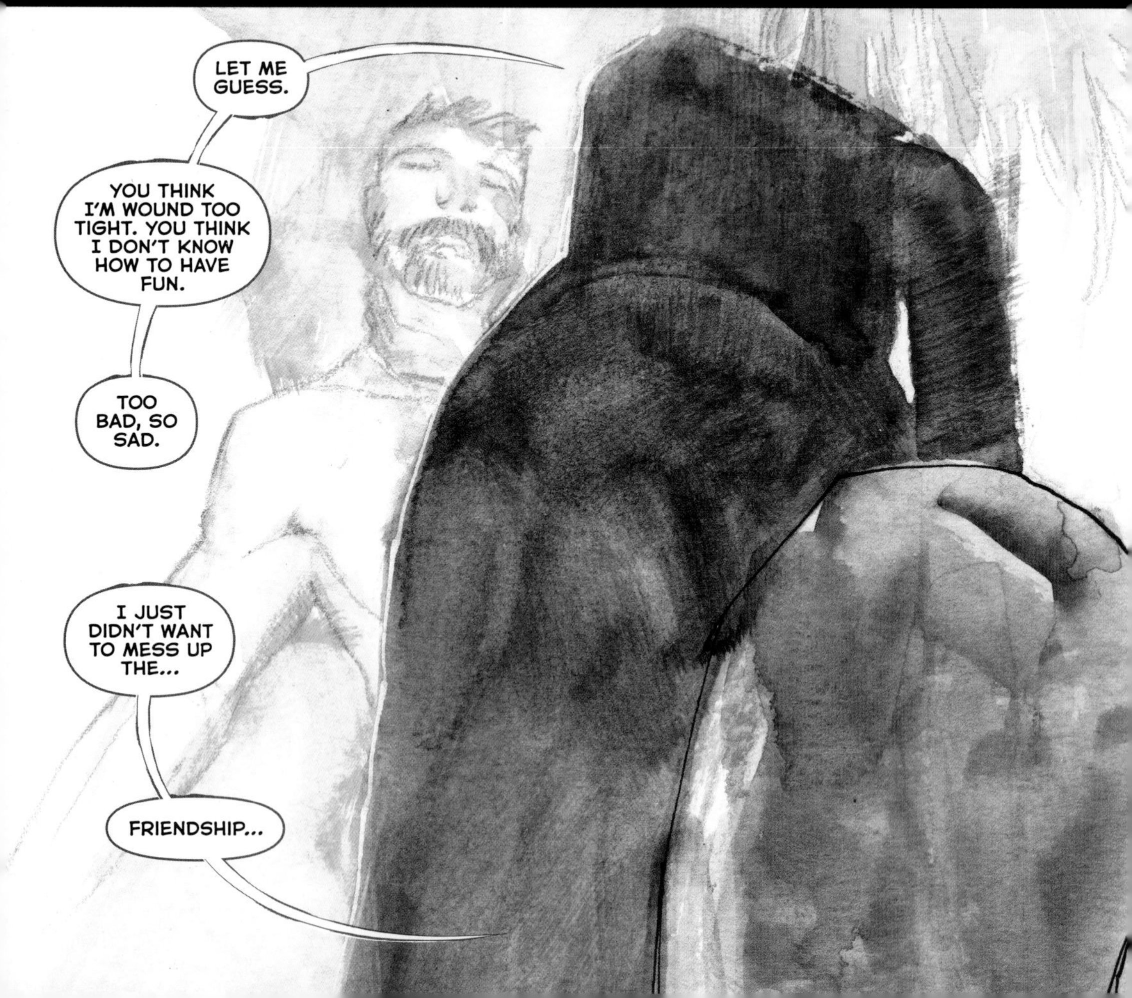
LET ME GUESS.
YOU THINK I'M WOUND TOO TIGHT. YOU THINK I DON'T KNOW HOW TO HAVE FUN.
TOO BAD, SO SAD.
I JUST DIDN'T WANT TO MESS UP THE...
FRIENDSHIP...

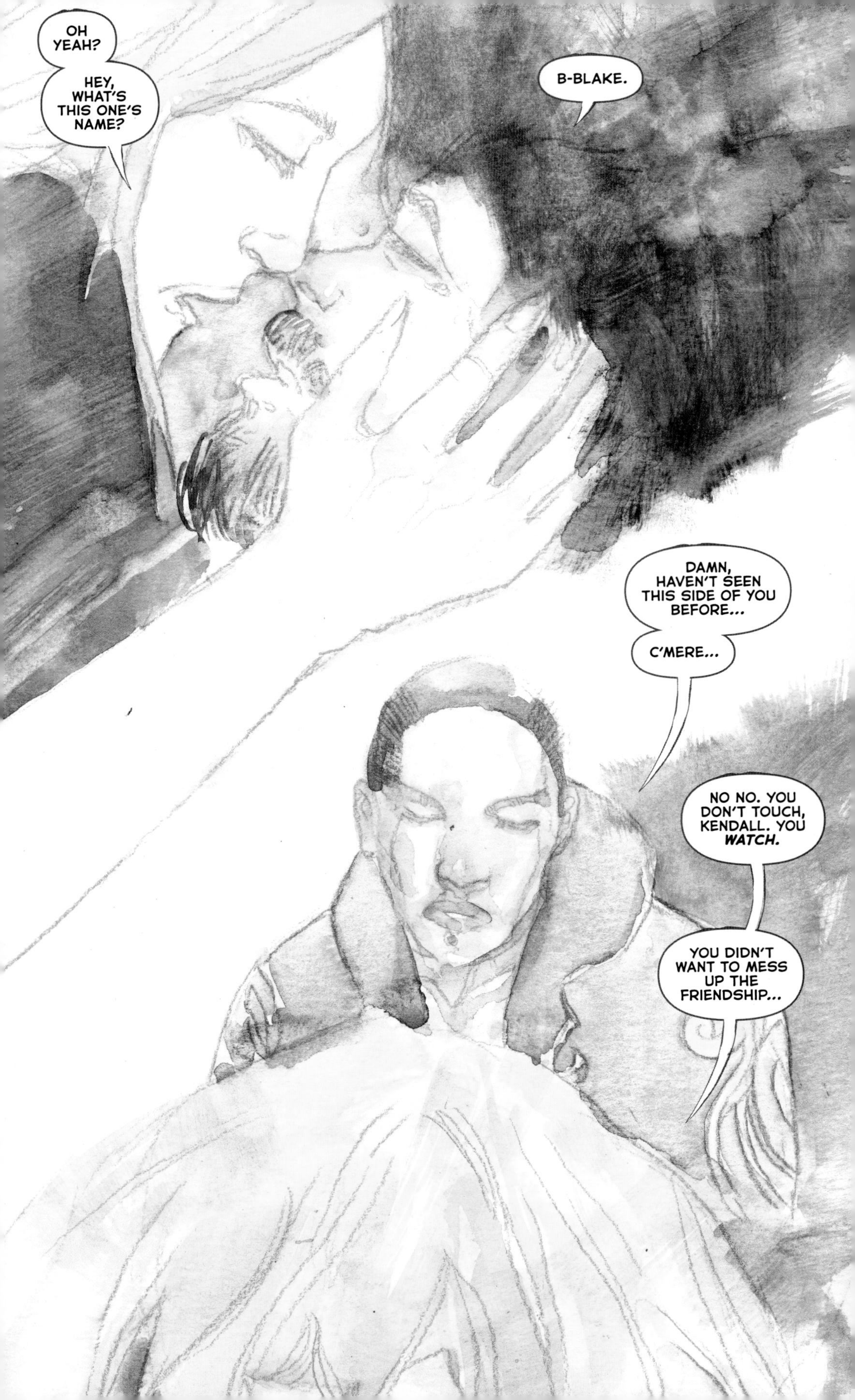
OH YEAH?
HEY, WHAT'S THIS ONE'S NAME?
B-BLAKE.
DAMN, HAVEN'T SEEN THIS SIDE OF YOU BEFORE...
C'MERE...
NO NO. YOU DON'T TOUCH, KENDALL. YOU *WATCH.*
YOU DIDN'T WANT TO MESS UP THE FRIENDSHIP...

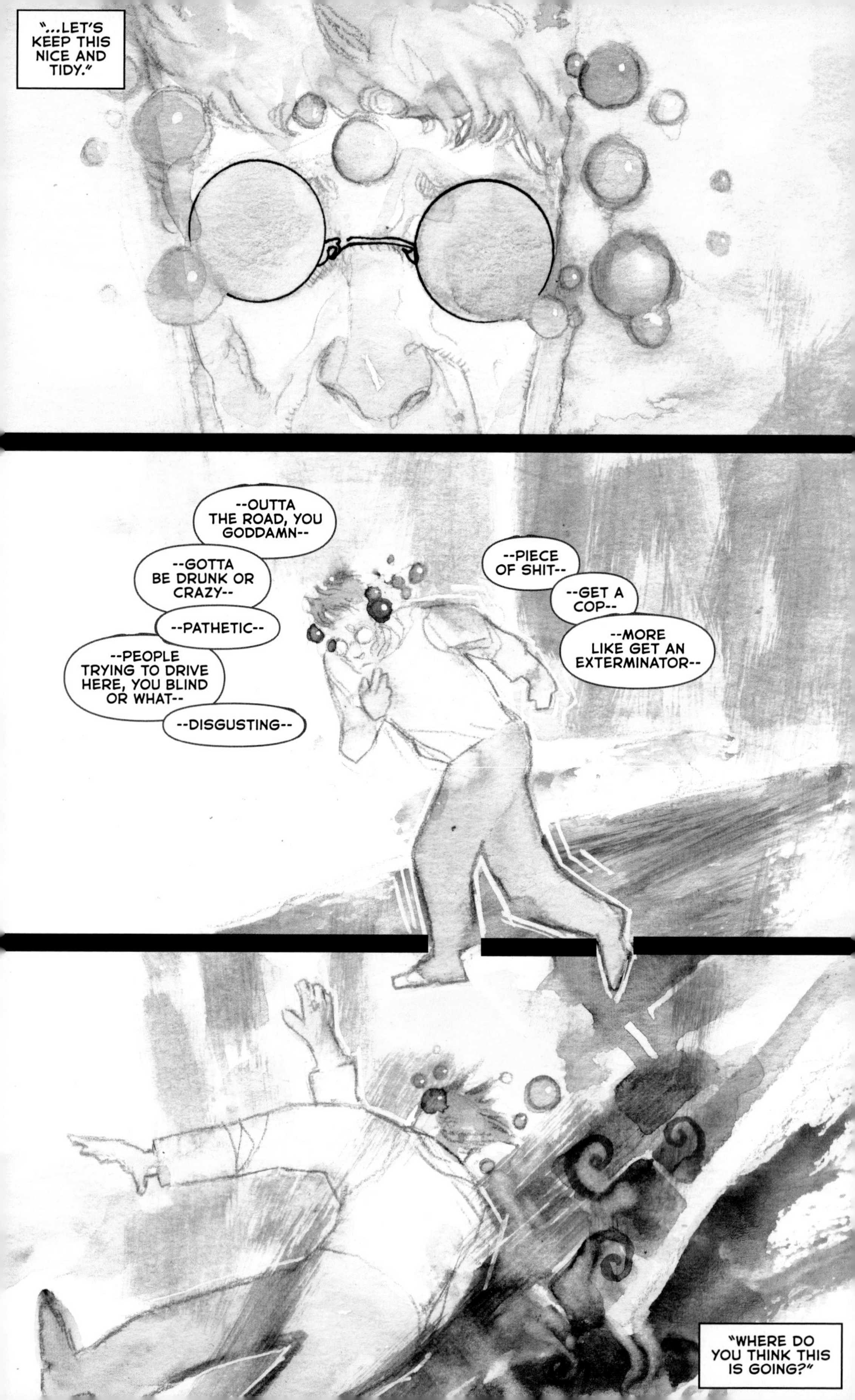
"...LET'S KEEP THIS NICE AND TIDY."
--OUTTA THE ROAD, YOU GODDAMN--
--GOTTA BE DRUNK OR CRAZY--
--PATHETIC--
--PEOPLE TRYING TO DRIVE HERE, YOU BLIND OR WHAT--
--DISGUSTING--
--PIECE OF SHIT--
--GET A COP--
--MORE LIKE GET AN EXTERMINATOR--
"WHERE DO YOU THINK THIS IS GOING?"

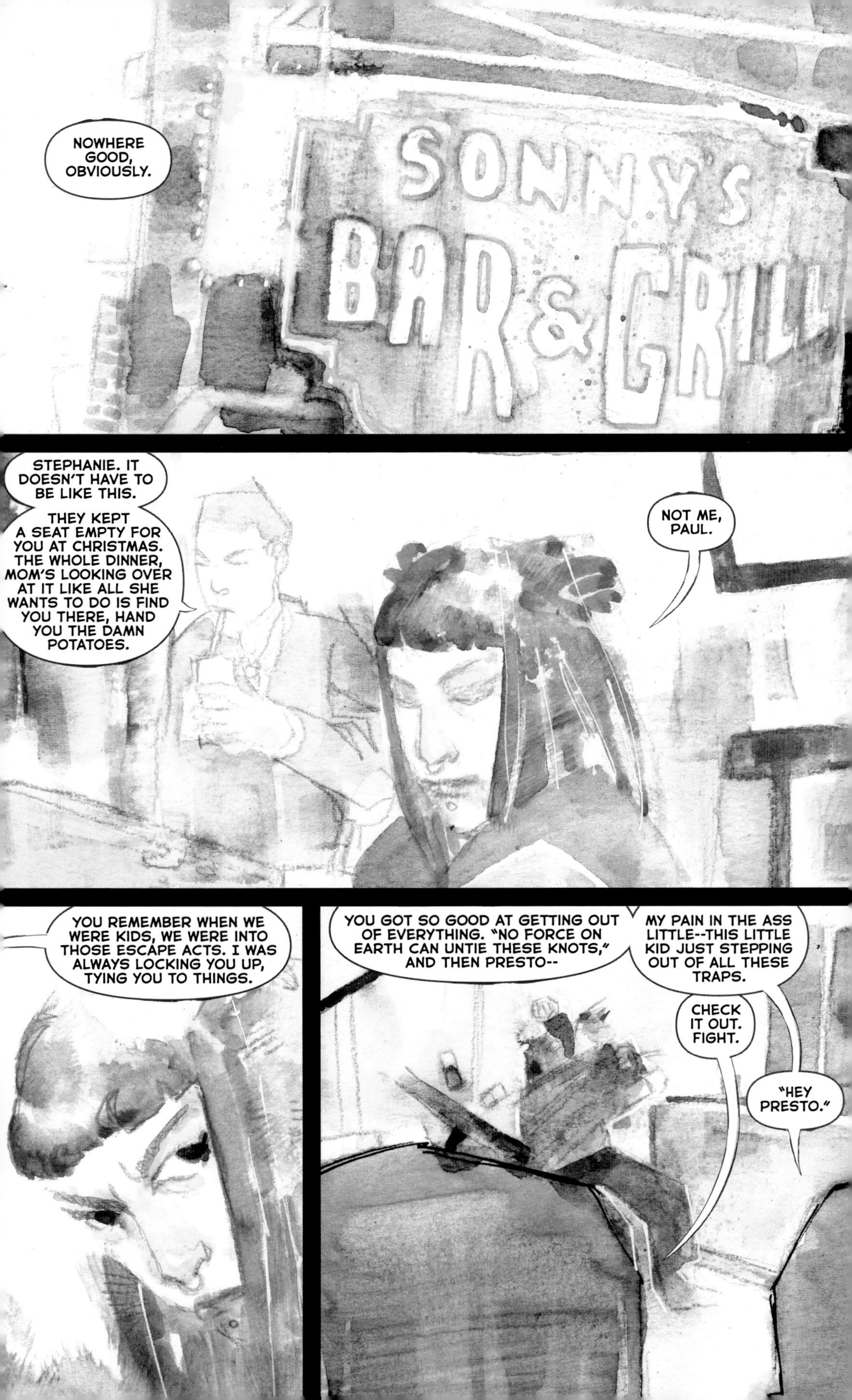
NOWHERE GOOD, OBVIOUSLY.
SONNY'S BAR & GRILL
STEPHANIE. IT DOESN'T HAVE TO BE LIKE THIS.
THEY KEPT A SEAT EMPTY FOR YOU AT CHRISTMAS. THE WHOLE DINNER, MOM'S LOOKING OVER AT IT LIKE ALL SHE WANTS TO DO IS FIND YOU THERE, HAND YOU THE DAMN POTATOES.
NOT ME, PAUL.
YOU REMEMBER WHEN WE WERE KIDS, WE WERE INTO THOSE ESCAPE ACTS. I WAS ALWAYS LOCKING YOU UP, TYING YOU TO THINGS.
YOU GOT SO GOOD AT GETTING OUT OF EVERYTHING. "NO FORCE ON EARTH CAN UNTIE THESE KNOTS," AND THEN PRESTO--
MY PAIN IN THE ASS LITTLE--THIS LITTLE KID JUST STEPPING OUT OF ALL THESE TRAPS.
"HEY PRESTO."
CHECK IT OUT. FIGHT.

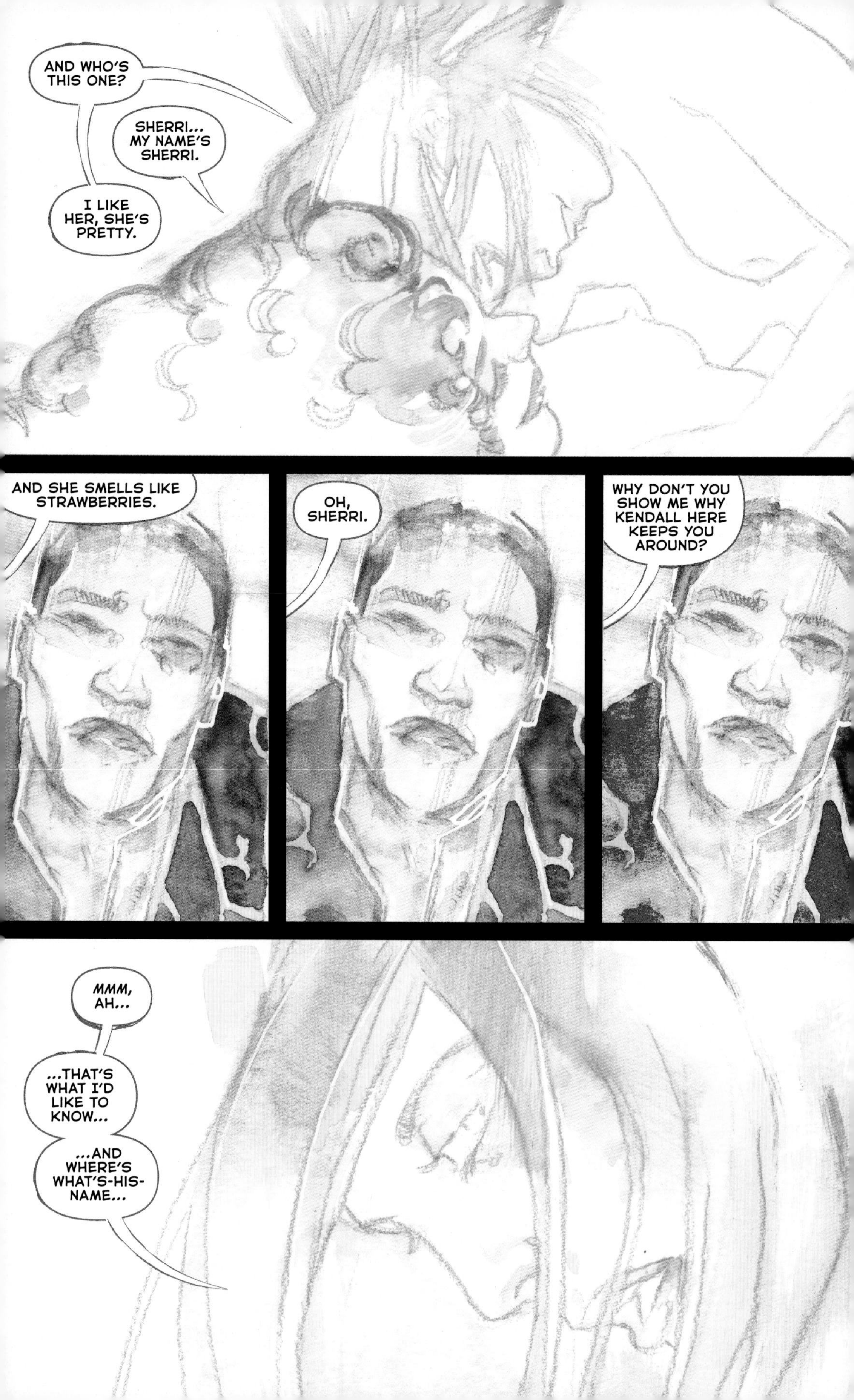
AND WHO'S THIS ONE?
SHERRI... MY NAME'S SHERRI.
I LIKE HER, SHE'S PRETTY.
AND SHE SMELLS LIKE STRAWBERRIES.
OH, SHERRI.
WHY DON'T YOU SHOW ME WHY KENDALL HERE KEEPS YOU AROUND?
MMM, AH...
...THAT'S WHAT I'D LIKE TO KNOW...
...AND WHERE'S WHAT'S-HIS-NAME...

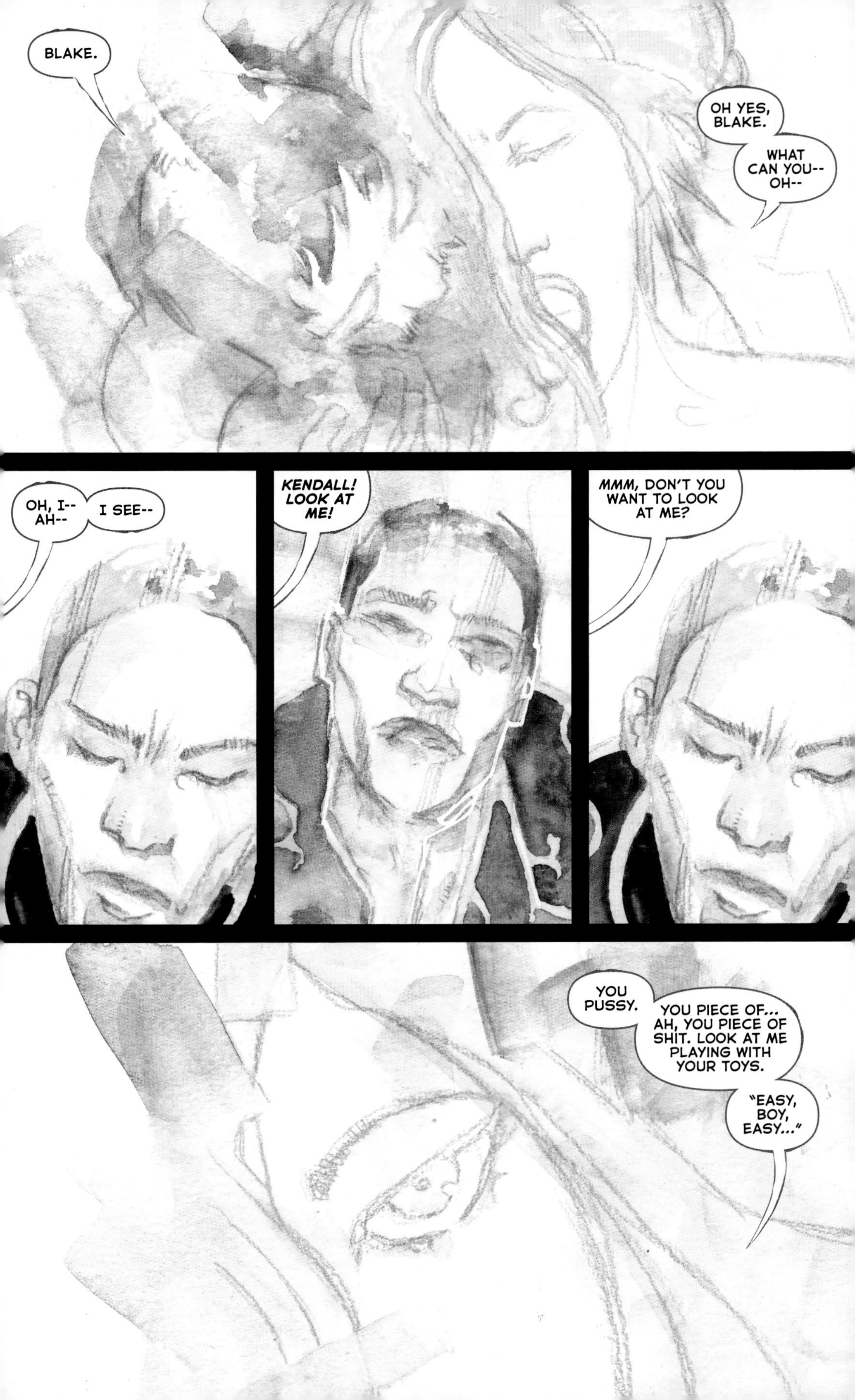
BLAKE.
OH YES, BLAKE.
WHAT CAN YOU-- OH--
OH, I-- AH--
I SEE--
KENDALL! LOOK AT ME!
MMM, DON'T YOU WANT TO LOOK AT ME?
YOU PUSSY.
YOU PIECE OF... AH, YOU PIECE OF SHIT. LOOK AT ME PLAYING WITH YOUR TOYS.
"EASY, BOY, EASY..."

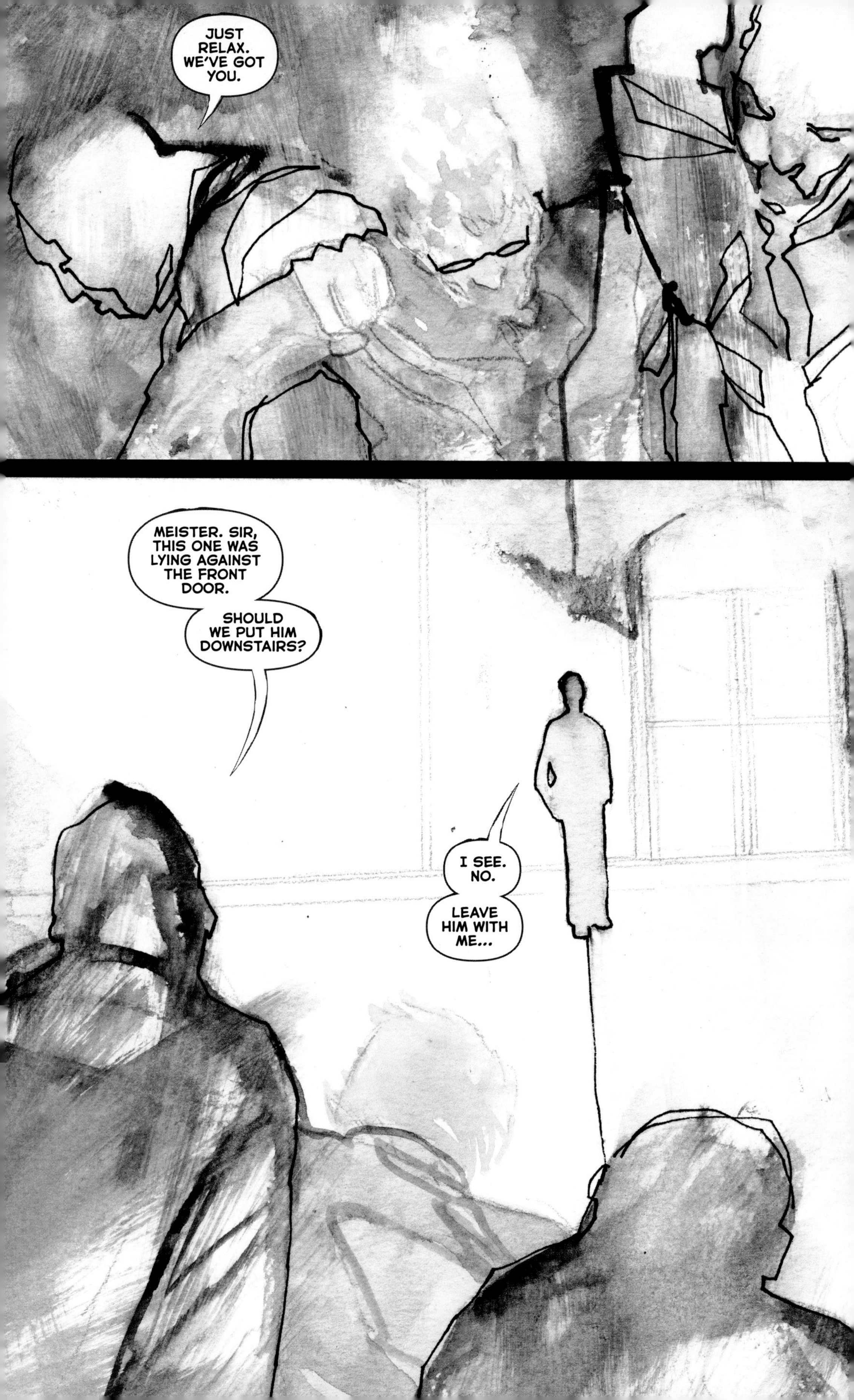
JUST RELAX. WE'VE GOT YOU.
MEISTER. SIR, THIS ONE WAS LYING AGAINST THE FRONT DOOR.
SHOULD WE PUT HIM DOWNSTAIRS?
I SEE. NO.
LEAVE HIM WITH ME...

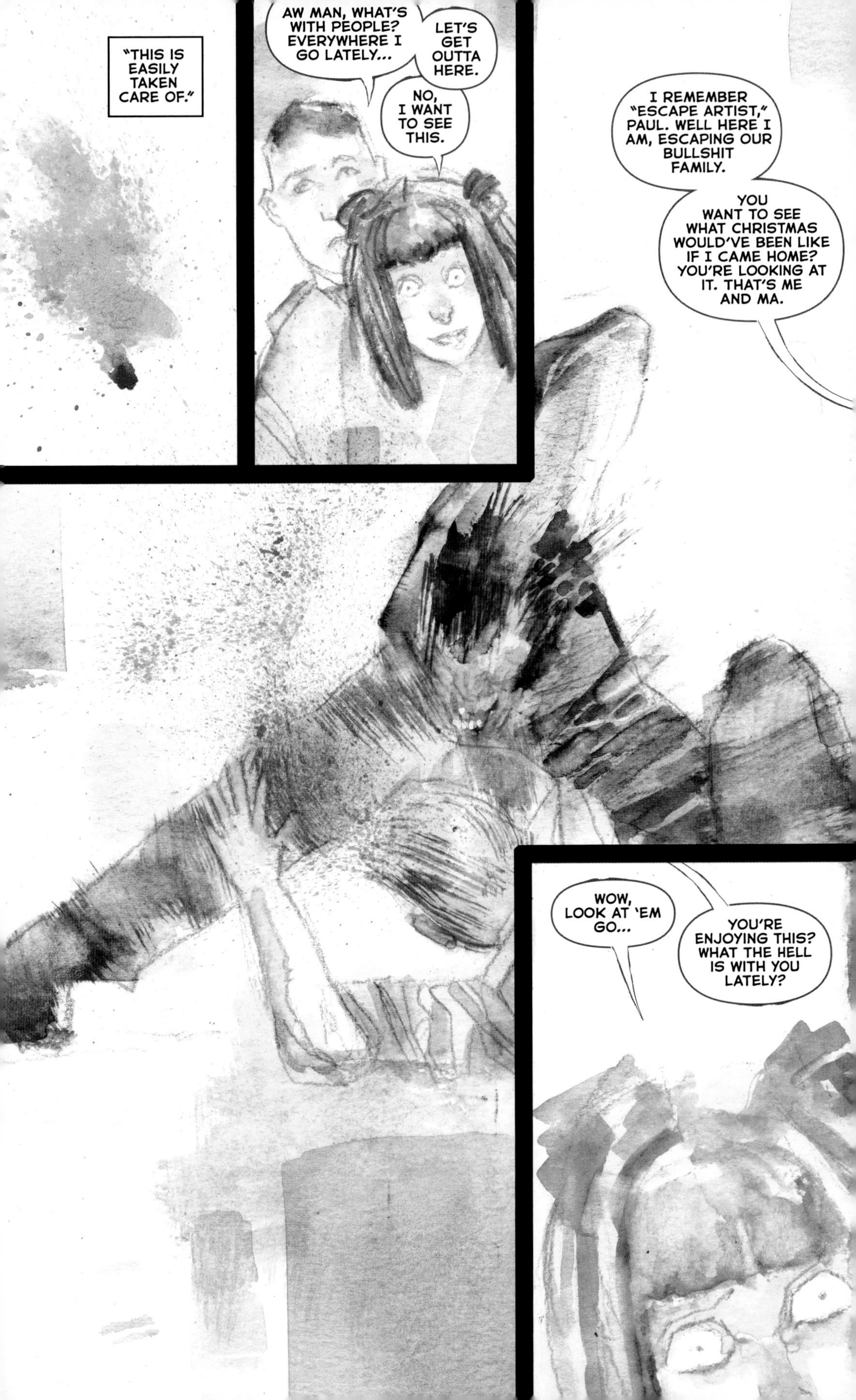
"THIS IS EASILY TAKEN CARE OF."
AW MAN, WHAT'S WITH PEOPLE? EVERYWHERE I GO LATELY...
LET'S GET OUTTA HERE.
NO, I WANT TO SEE THIS.
I REMEMBER "ESCAPE ARTIST," PAUL. WELL HERE I AM, ESCAPING OUR BULLSHIT FAMILY.
YOU WANT TO SEE WHAT CHRISTMAS WOULD'VE BEEN LIKE IF I CAME HOME? YOU'RE LOOKING AT IT. THAT'S ME AND MA.
WOW, LOOK AT 'EM GO...
YOU'RE ENJOYING THIS? WHAT THE HELL IS WITH YOU LATELY?

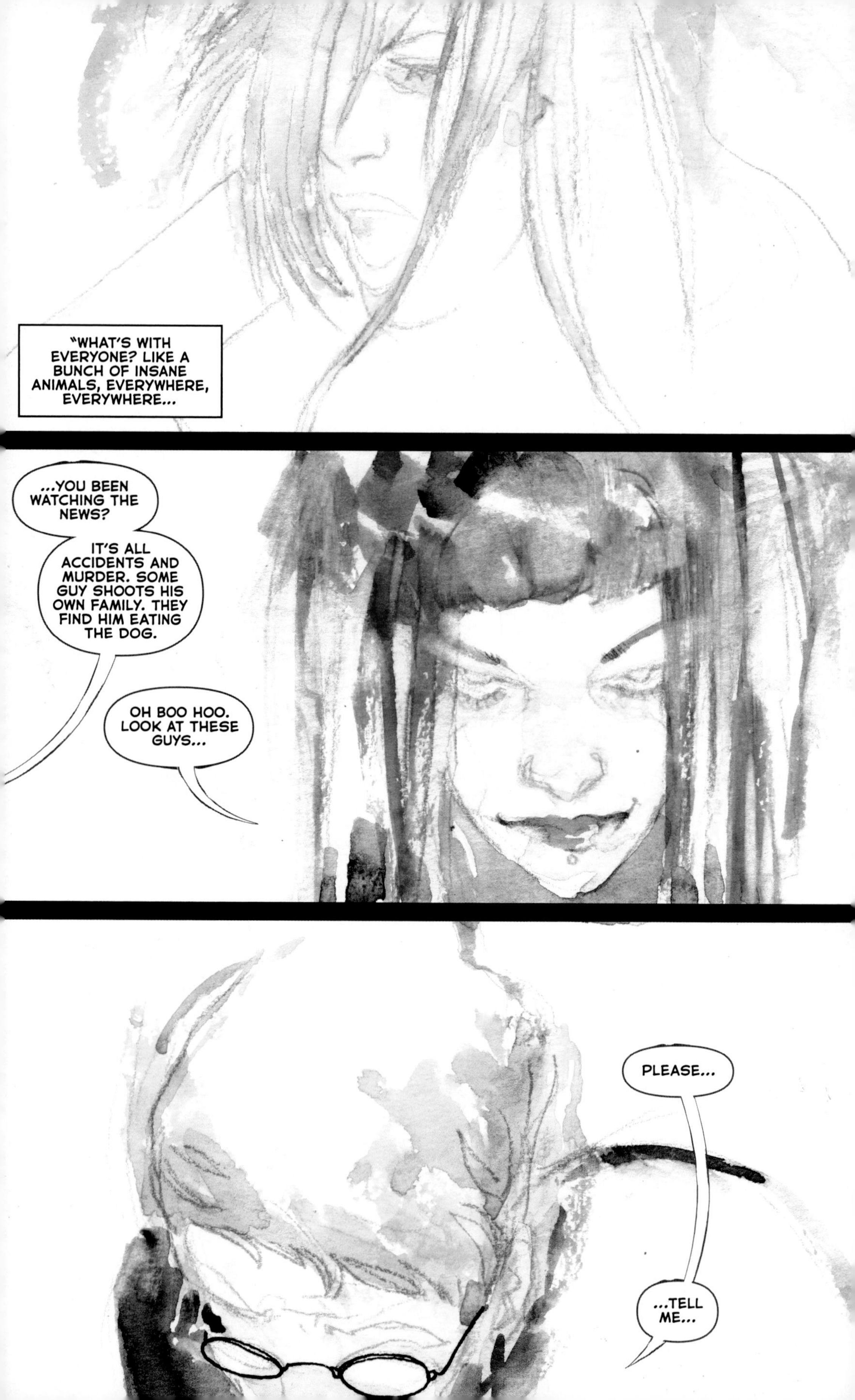
"WHAT'S WITH EVERYONE? LIKE A BUNCH OF INSANE ANIMALS, EVERYWHERE, EVERYWHERE...
...YOU BEEN WATCHING THE NEWS?
IT'S ALL ACCIDENTS AND MURDER. SOME GUY SHOOTS HIS OWN FAMILY. THEY FIND HIM EATING THE DOG.
OH BOO HOO. LOOK AT THESE GUYS...
PLEASE...
...TELL ME...

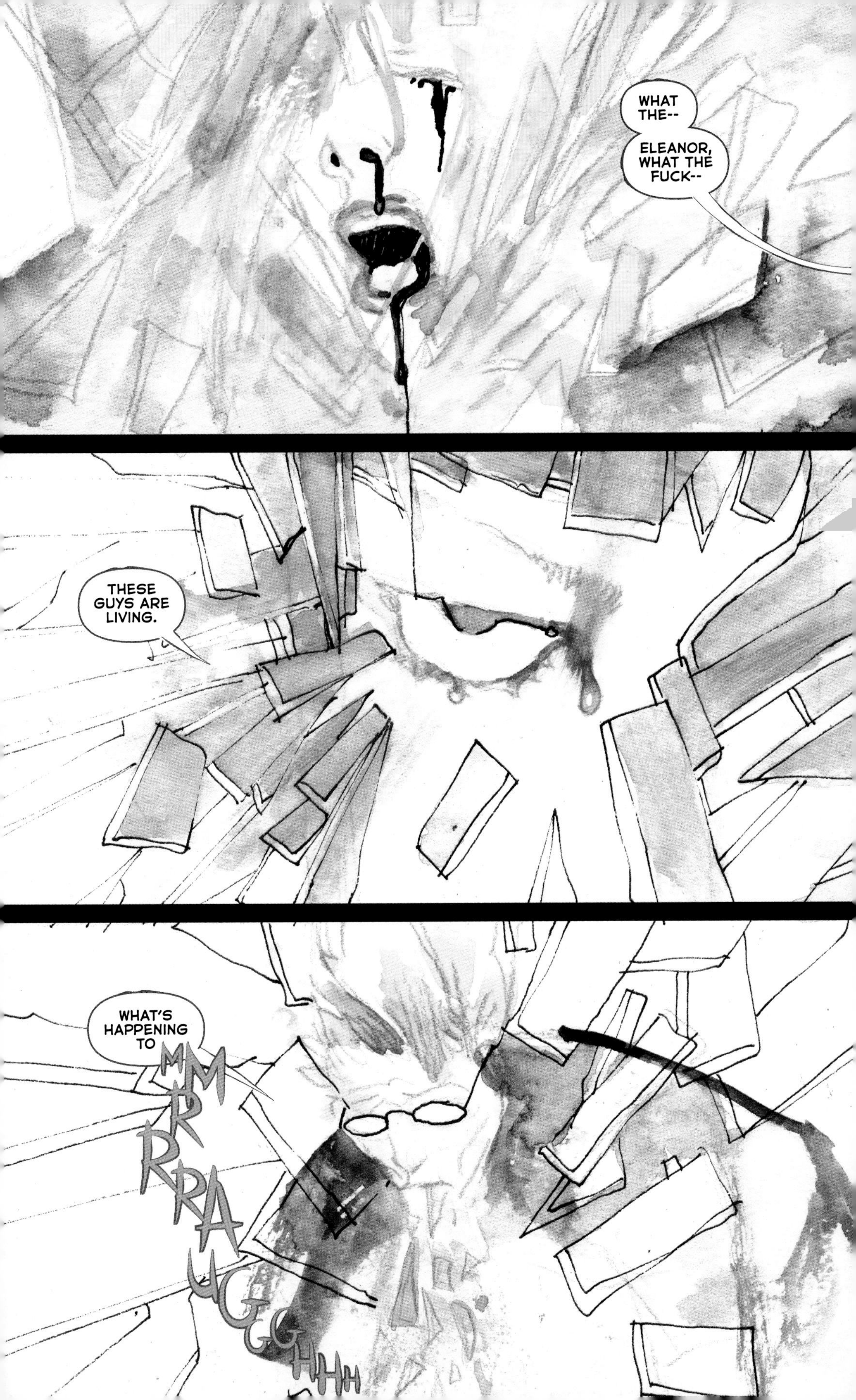
WHAT THE--
ELEANOR, WHAT THE FUCK--
THESE GUYS ARE LIVING.
WHAT'S HAPPENING TO
MMRRRAUGGHHHH

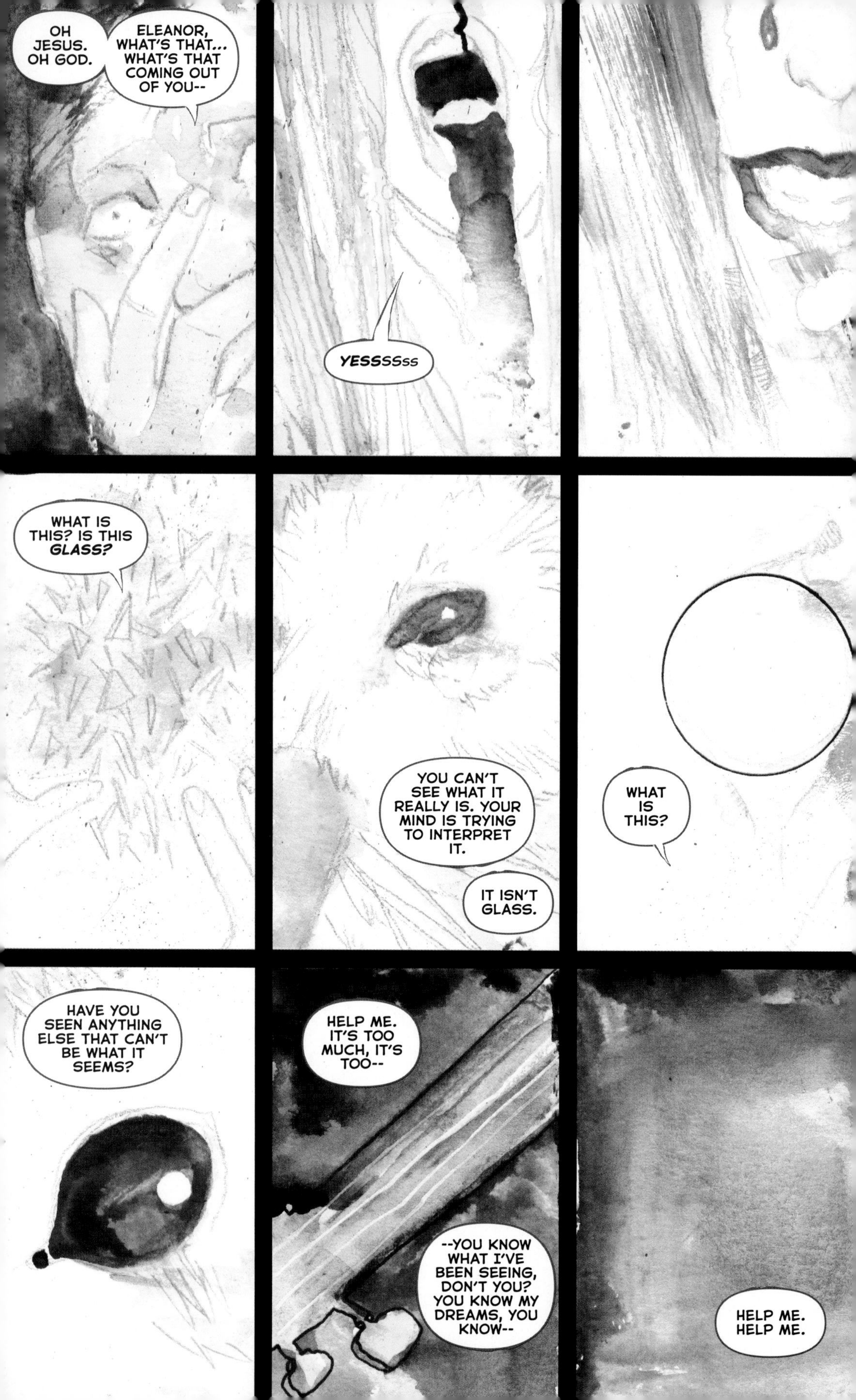
OH JESUS. OH GOD.
ELEANOR, WHAT'S THAT... WHAT'S THAT COMING OUT OF YOU--
YESSSSss
WHAT IS THIS? IS THIS *GLASS?*
YOU CAN'T SEE WHAT IT REALLY IS. YOUR MIND IS TRYING TO INTERPRET IT.
IT ISN'T GLASS.
WHAT IS THIS?
HAVE YOU SEEN ANYTHING ELSE THAT CAN'T BE WHAT IT SEEMS?
HELP ME. IT'S TOO MUCH, IT'S TOO--
--YOU KNOW WHAT I'VE BEEN SEEING, DON'T YOU? YOU KNOW MY DREAMS, YOU KNOW--
HELP ME. HELP ME.

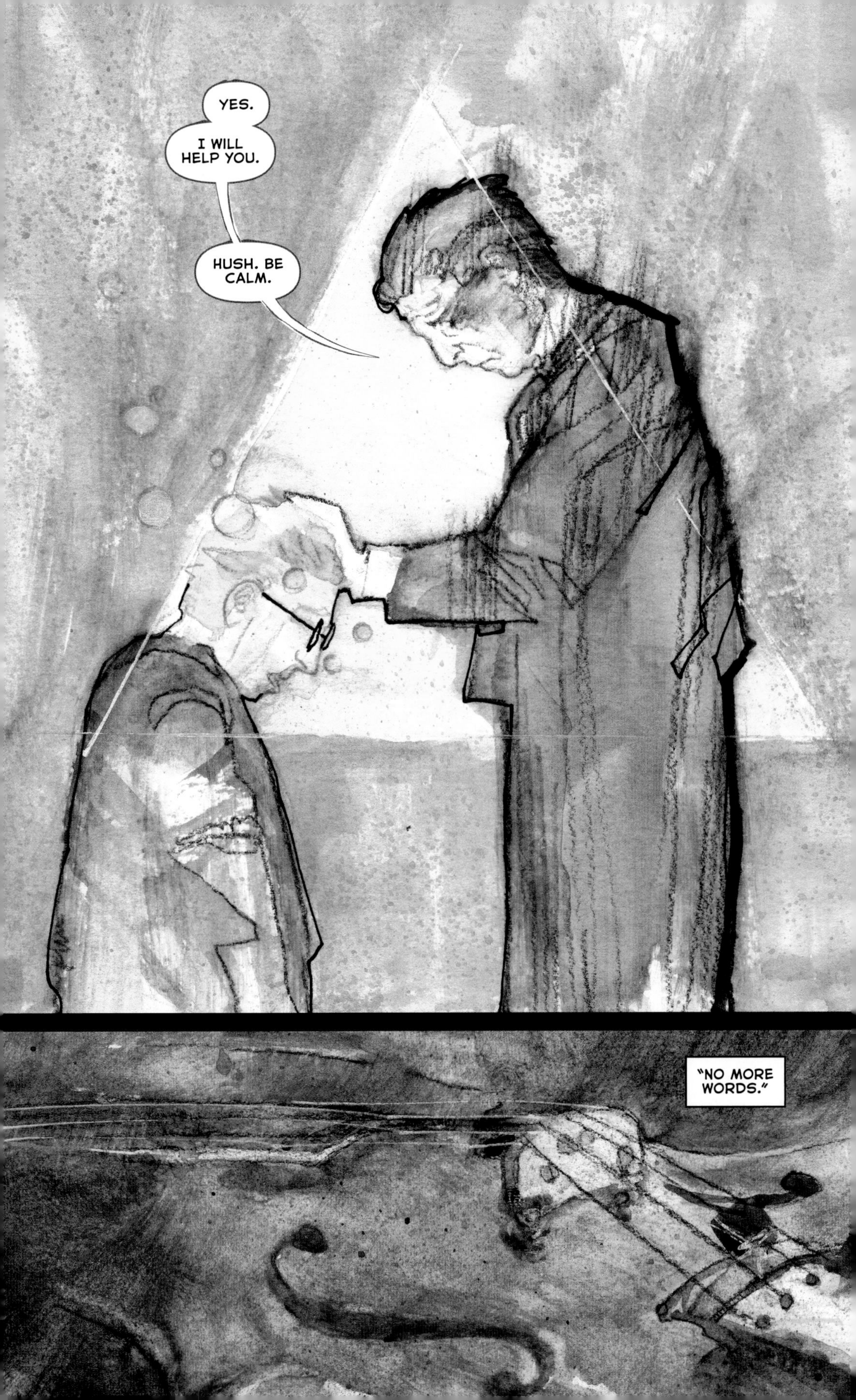
YES.
I WILL HELP YOU.
HUSH. BE CALM.
"NO MORE WORDS."

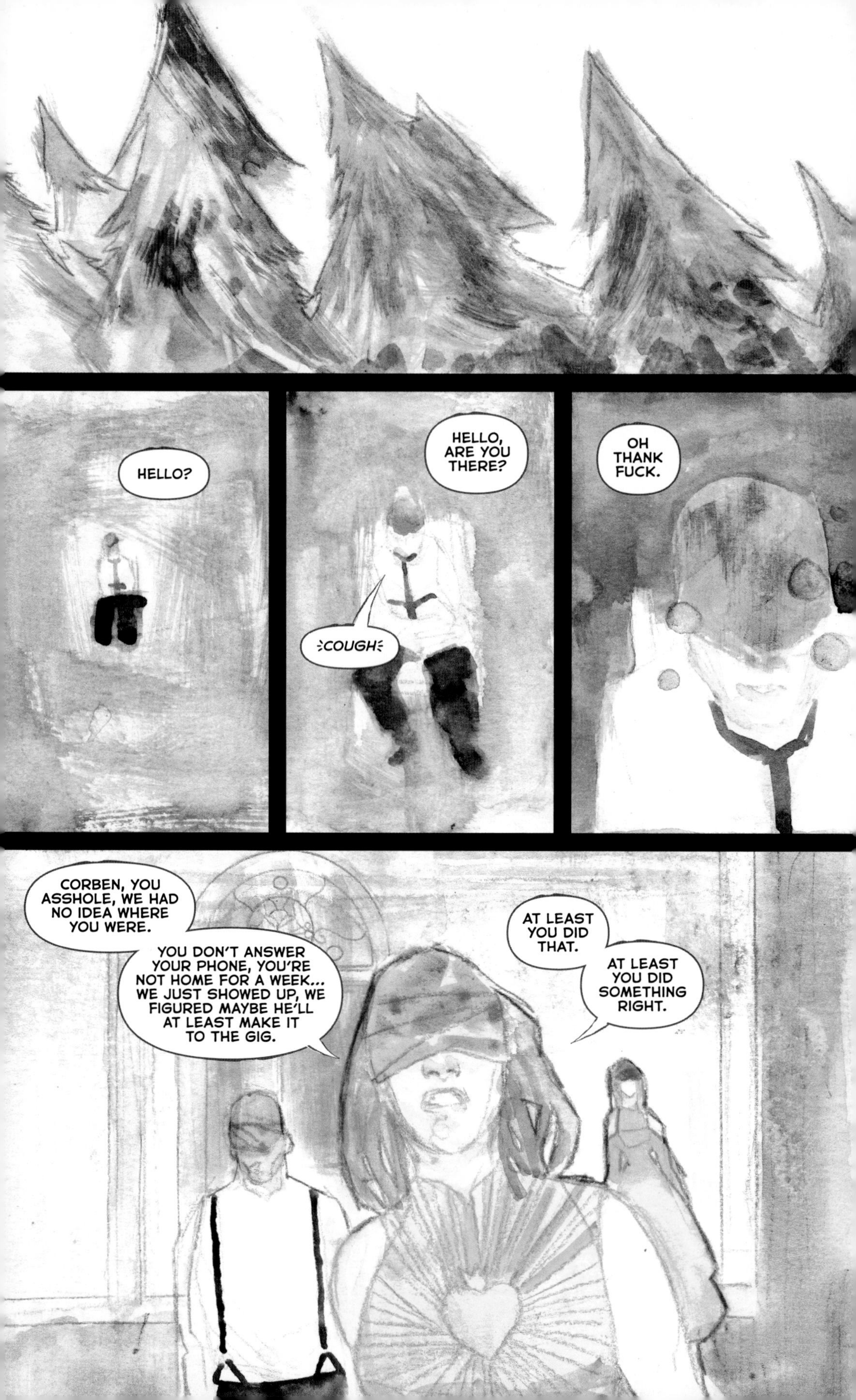
HELLO?
HELLO, ARE YOU THERE?
COUGH
OH THANK FUCK.
CORBEN, YOU ASSHOLE, WE HAD NO IDEA WHERE YOU WERE.
YOU DON'T ANSWER YOUR PHONE, YOU'RE NOT HOME FOR A WEEK... WE JUST SHOWED UP, WE FIGURED MAYBE HE'LL AT LEAST MAKE IT TO THE GIG.
AT LEAST YOU DID THAT.
AT LEAST YOU DID SOMETHING RIGHT.

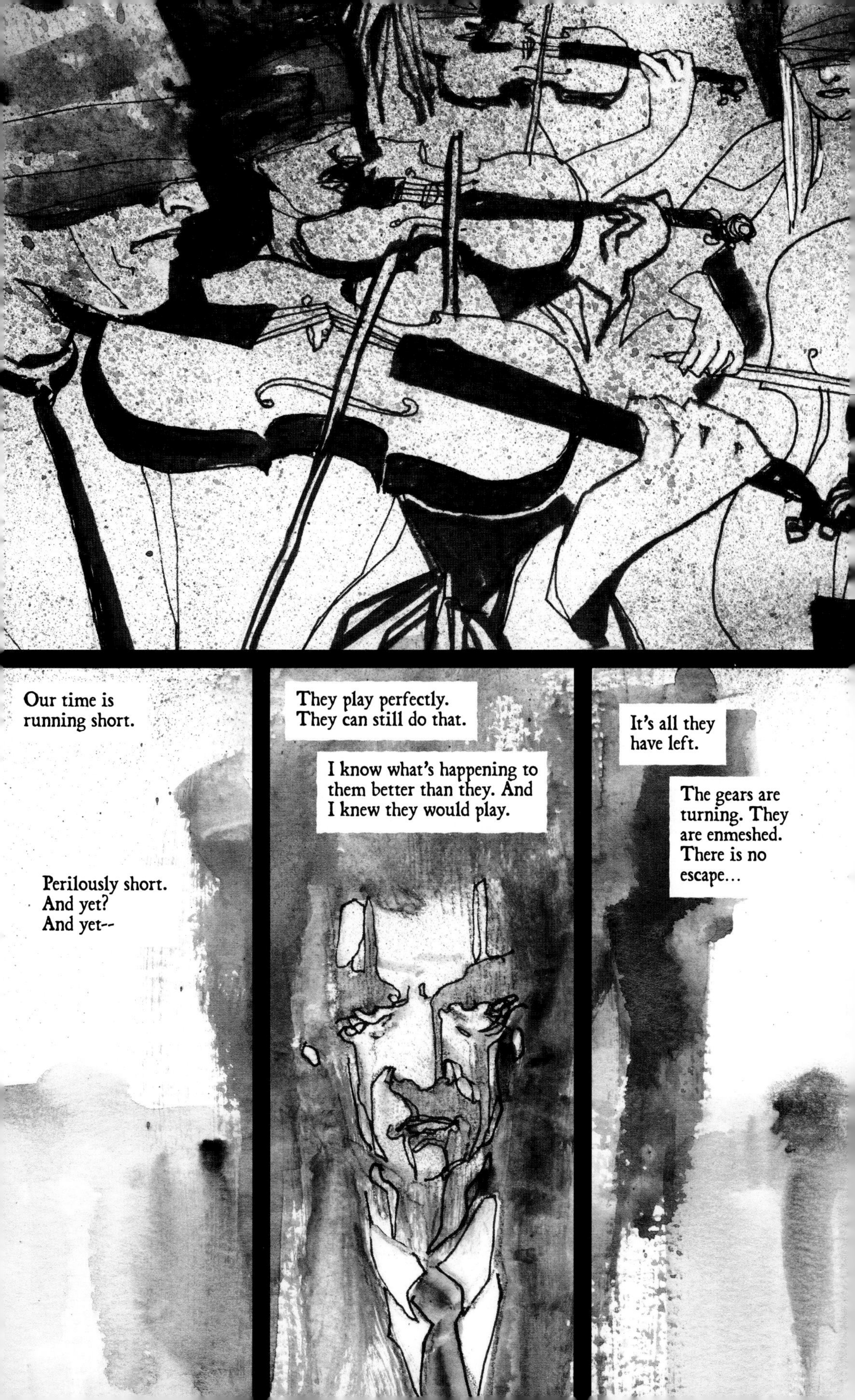
Our time is running short.
Perilously short.
And yet?
And yet--
They play perfectly. They can still do that.
I know what's happening to them better than they. And I knew they would play.
It's all they have left.
The gears are turning. They are enmeshed. There is no escape...

No escape for them.

For us.

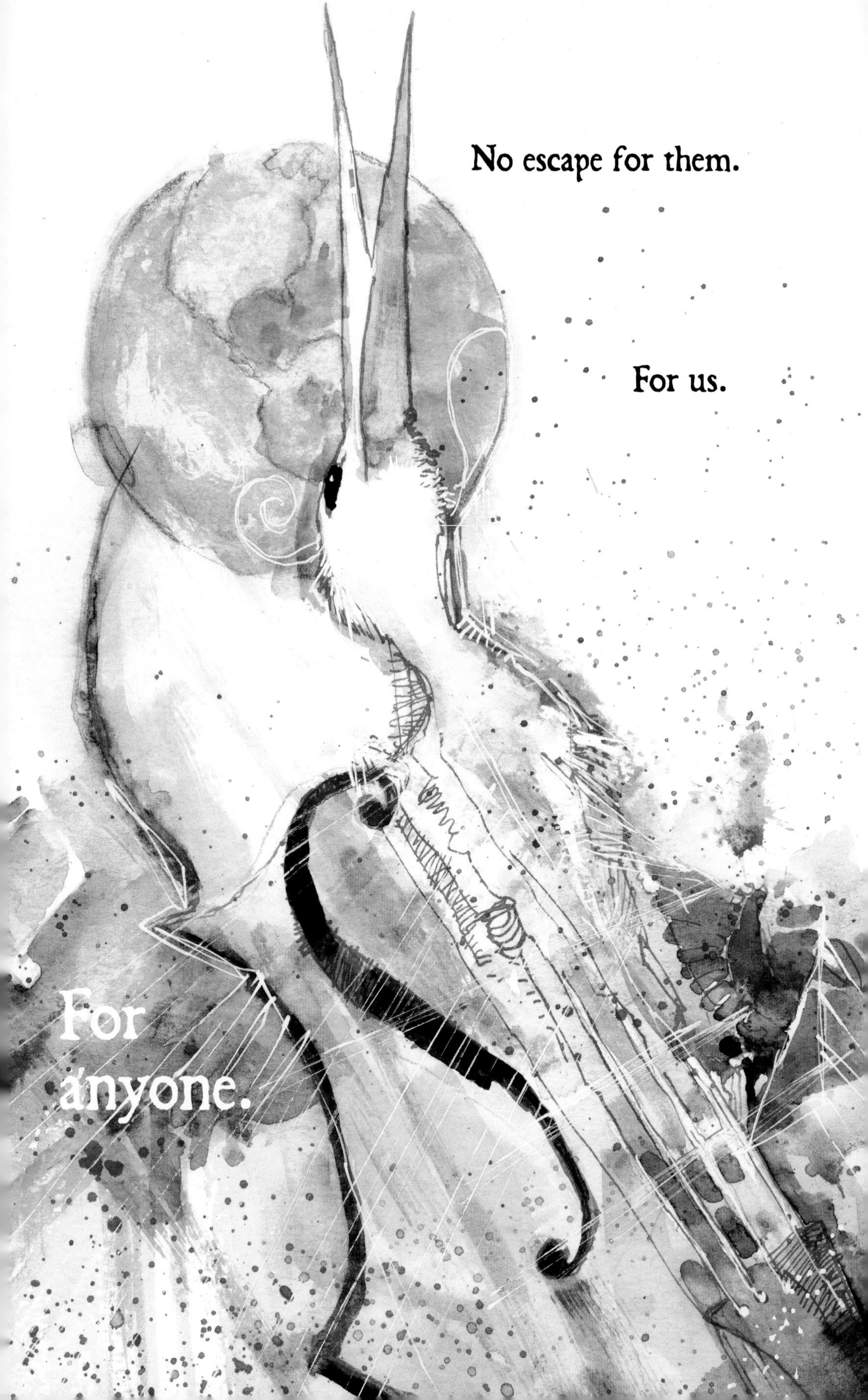

For anyone.

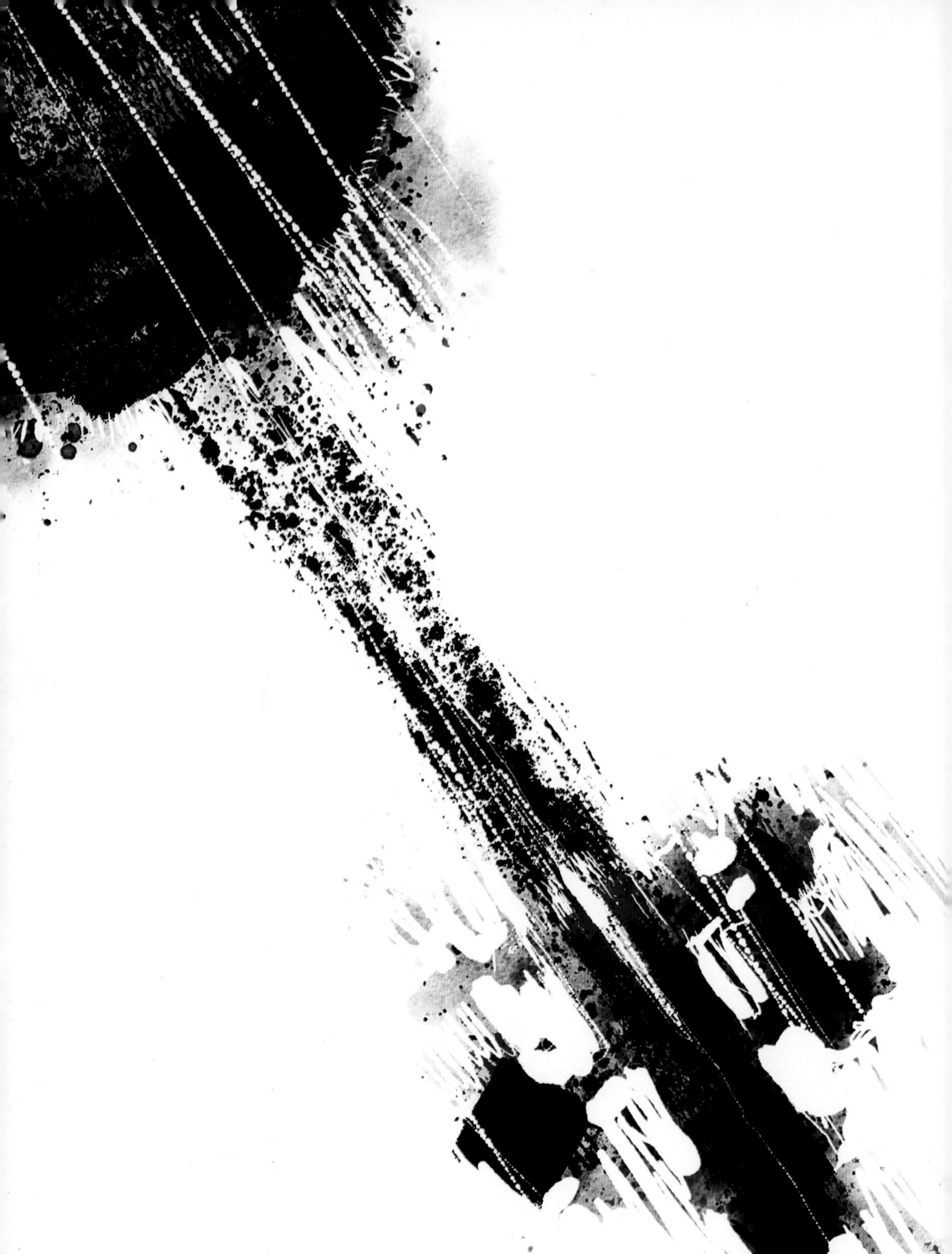

THERE'S SOMETHING WRONG WITH ME. I CAN'T SLEEP, I CAN'T EAT...I FEEL AFRAID ALL THE TIME, *ANXIOUS*. I WANT TO DROWN IT OUT, TO *DRINK*...

I'VE GOT THE *SHAKES.* I'M FALLING *APART.*

I THINK I'M *SICK.*

THAT'S BECAUSE YOU *ARE.*

I *KNOW* THIS SICKNESS, MR. NOVAK. I KNOW IT VERY WELL.

YOU SAID YOU'D HELP ME, MARANATHA. THAT'S WHY I'M STILL HERE.

TELL ME WHAT'S HAPPENING TO ME. TO ALL OF US. TELL ME WHAT I SAW THAT NIGHT WHEN WE PLAYED HERE FOR THE FIRST TIME AND WHY IT MESSED ME UP SO *BAD.*

TELL ME WHAT I CAN DO TO FIX IT.

AH.

WHY DO YOU LOVE *MUSIC*, MR. NOVAK?

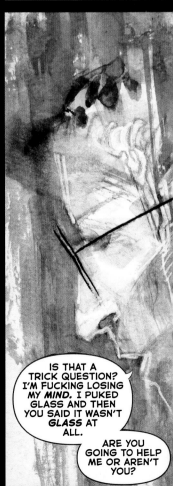

IS THAT A TRICK QUESTION? I'M FUCKING LOSING MY *MIND.* I PUKED GLASS AND THEN YOU SAID IT WASN'T *GLASS* AT ALL.

ARE YOU GOING TO HELP ME OR AREN'T YOU?

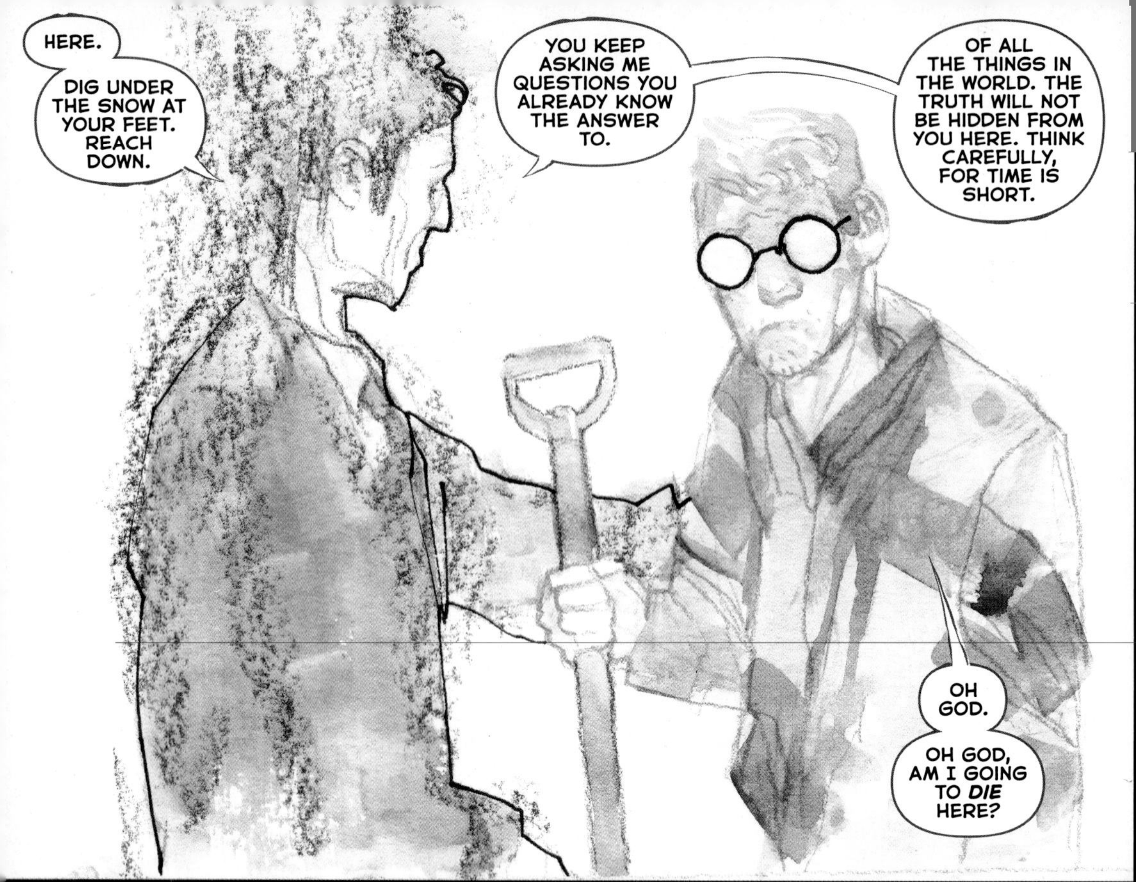
HERE.
DIG UNDER THE SNOW AT YOUR FEET. REACH DOWN.
YOU KEEP ASKING ME QUESTIONS YOU ALREADY KNOW THE ANSWER TO.
OF ALL THE THINGS IN THE WORLD. THE TRUTH WILL NOT BE HIDDEN FROM YOU HERE. THINK CAREFULLY, FOR TIME IS SHORT.
OH GOD.
OH GOD, AM I GOING TO *DIE* HERE?

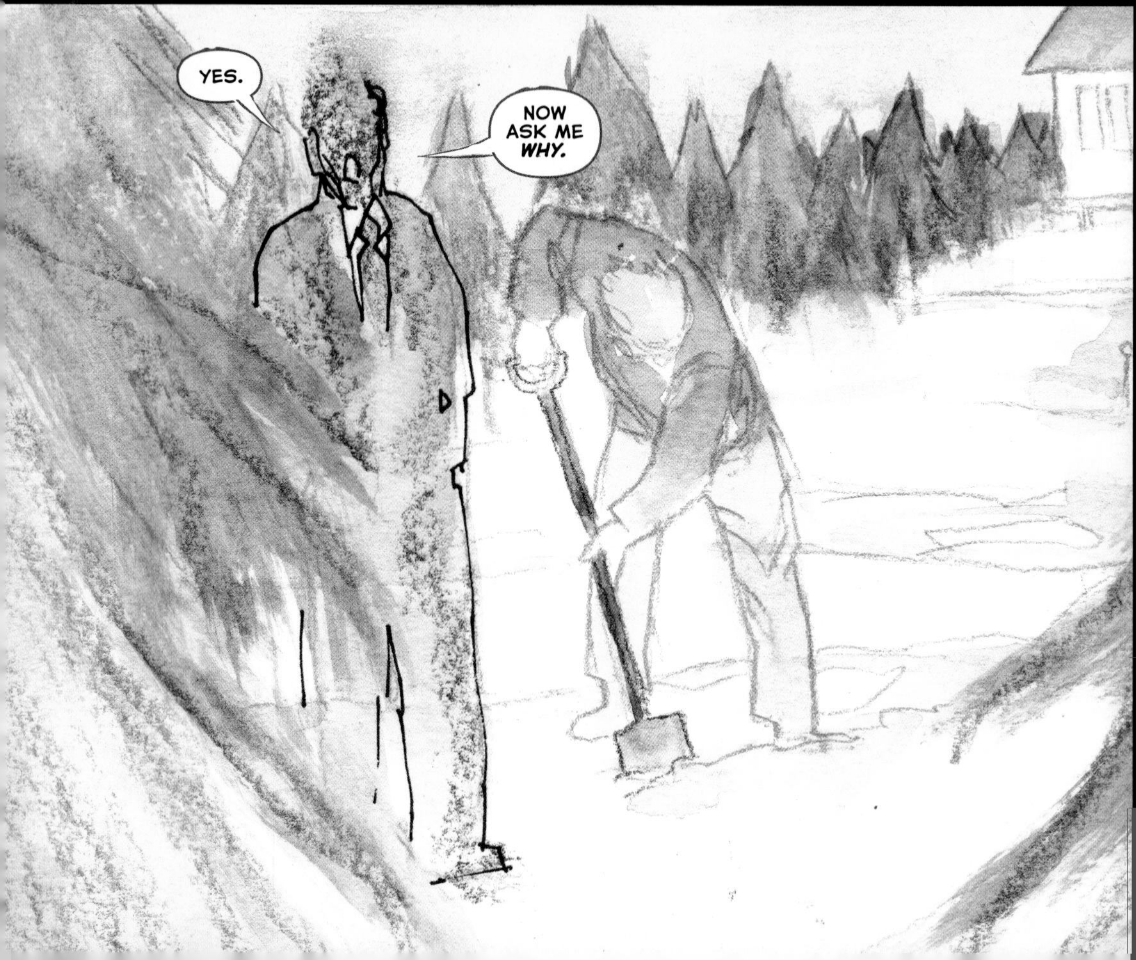
YES.
NOW ASK ME *WHY.*

SYMPHONY

PART FOUR:
FEBRUARY

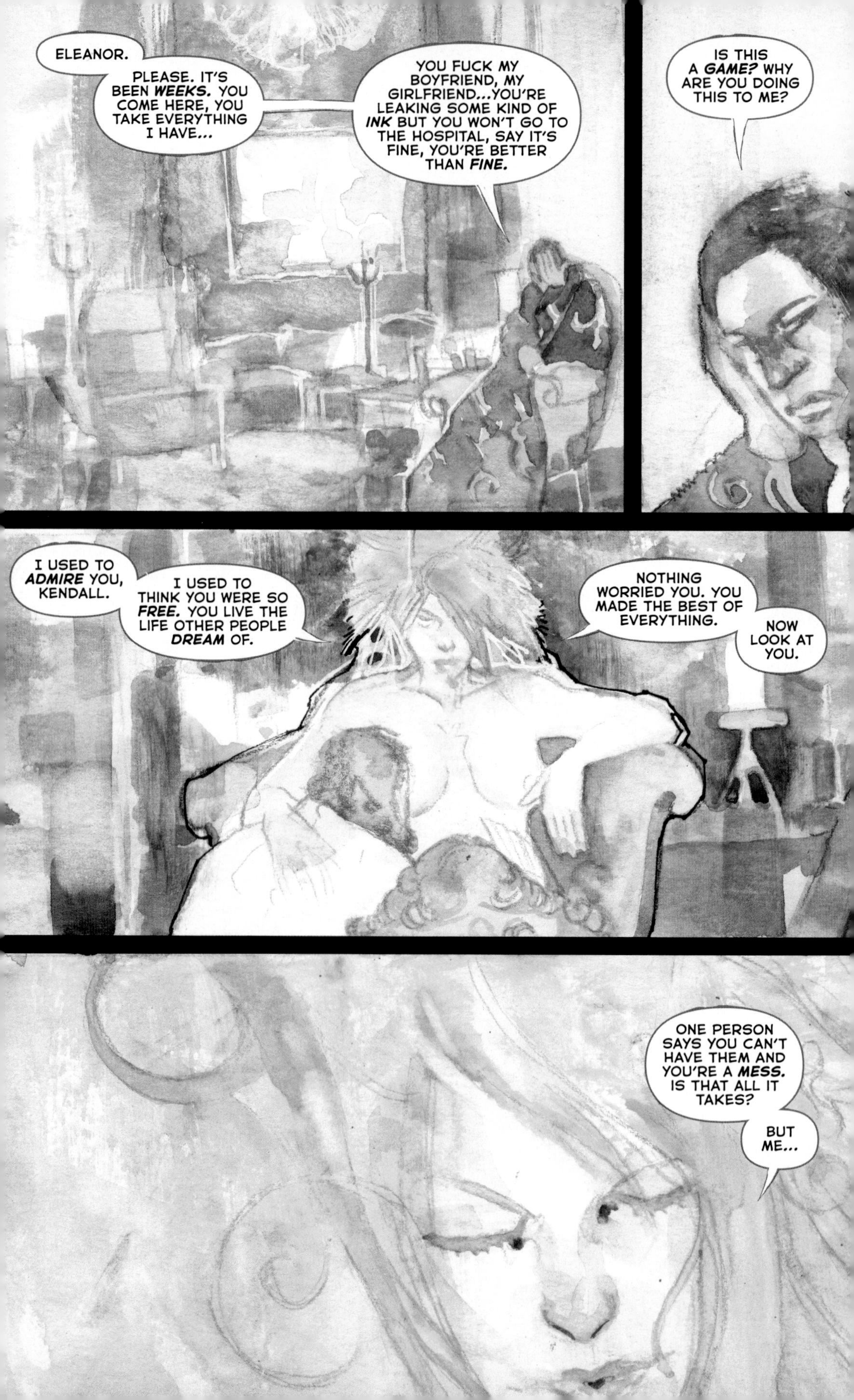
ELEANOR.
PLEASE. IT'S BEEN WEEKS. YOU COME HERE, YOU TAKE EVERYTHING I HAVE...
YOU FUCK MY BOYFRIEND, MY GIRLFRIEND...YOU'RE LEAKING SOME KIND OF INK BUT YOU WON'T GO TO THE HOSPITAL, SAY IT'S FINE, YOU'RE BETTER THAN FINE.
IS THIS A GAME? WHY ARE YOU DOING THIS TO ME?
I USED TO ADMIRE YOU, KENDALL.
I USED TO THINK YOU WERE SO FREE. YOU LIVE THE LIFE OTHER PEOPLE DREAM OF.
NOTHING WORRIED YOU. YOU MADE THE BEST OF EVERYTHING.
NOW LOOK AT YOU.
ONE PERSON SAYS YOU CAN'T HAVE THEM AND YOU'RE A MESS. IS THAT ALL IT TAKES?
BUT ME...

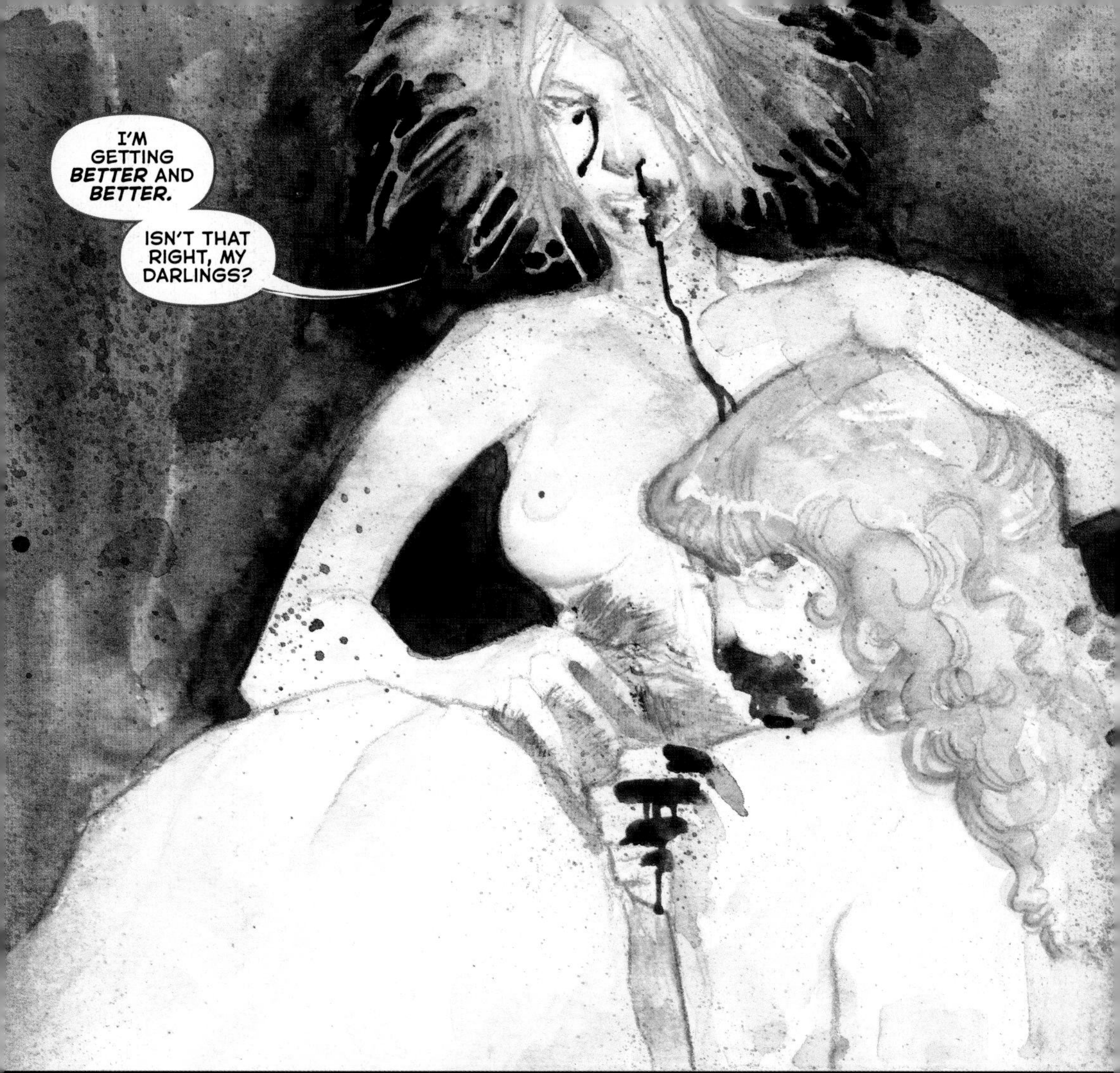
I'M GETTING *BETTER* AND *BETTER.*
ISN'T THAT RIGHT, MY DARLINGS?

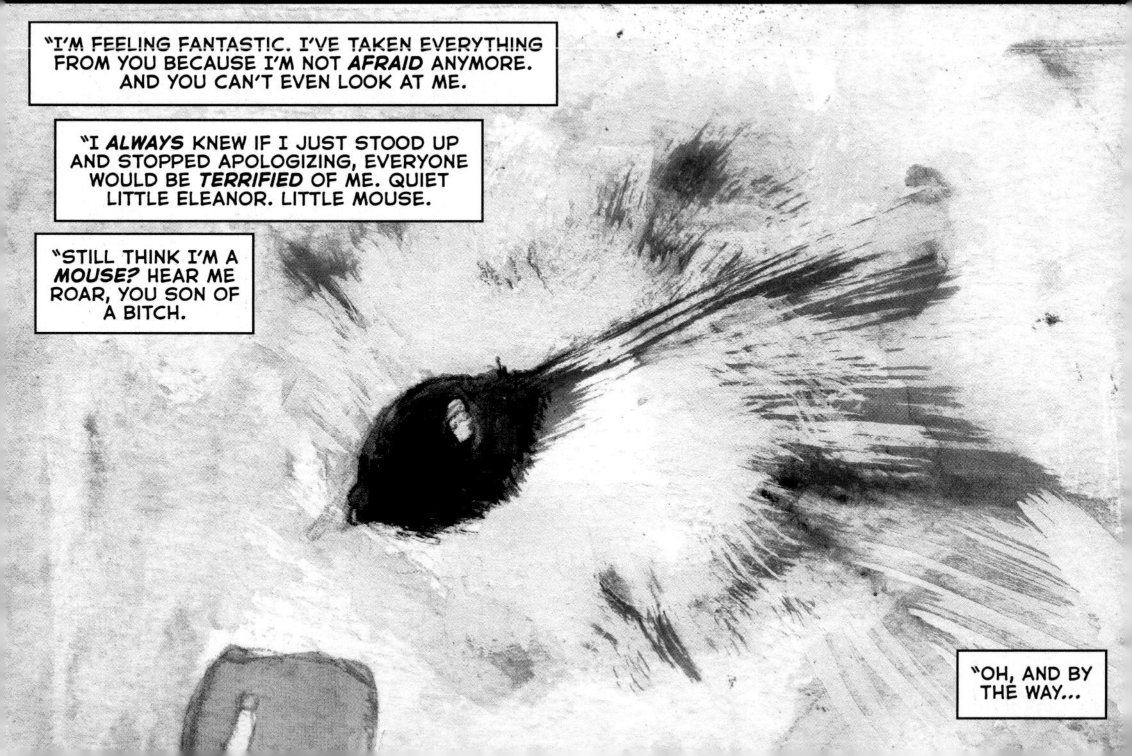
"I'M FEELING FANTASTIC. I'VE TAKEN EVERYTHING FROM YOU BECAUSE I'M NOT *AFRAID* ANYMORE. AND YOU CAN'T EVEN LOOK AT ME.
"I *ALWAYS* KNEW IF I JUST STOOD UP AND STOPPED APOLOGIZING, EVERYONE WOULD BE *TERRIFIED* OF ME. QUIET LITTLE ELEANOR. LITTLE MOUSE.
"STILL THINK I'M A *MOUSE?* HEAR ME ROAR, YOU SON OF A BITCH.
"OH, AND BY THE WAY...

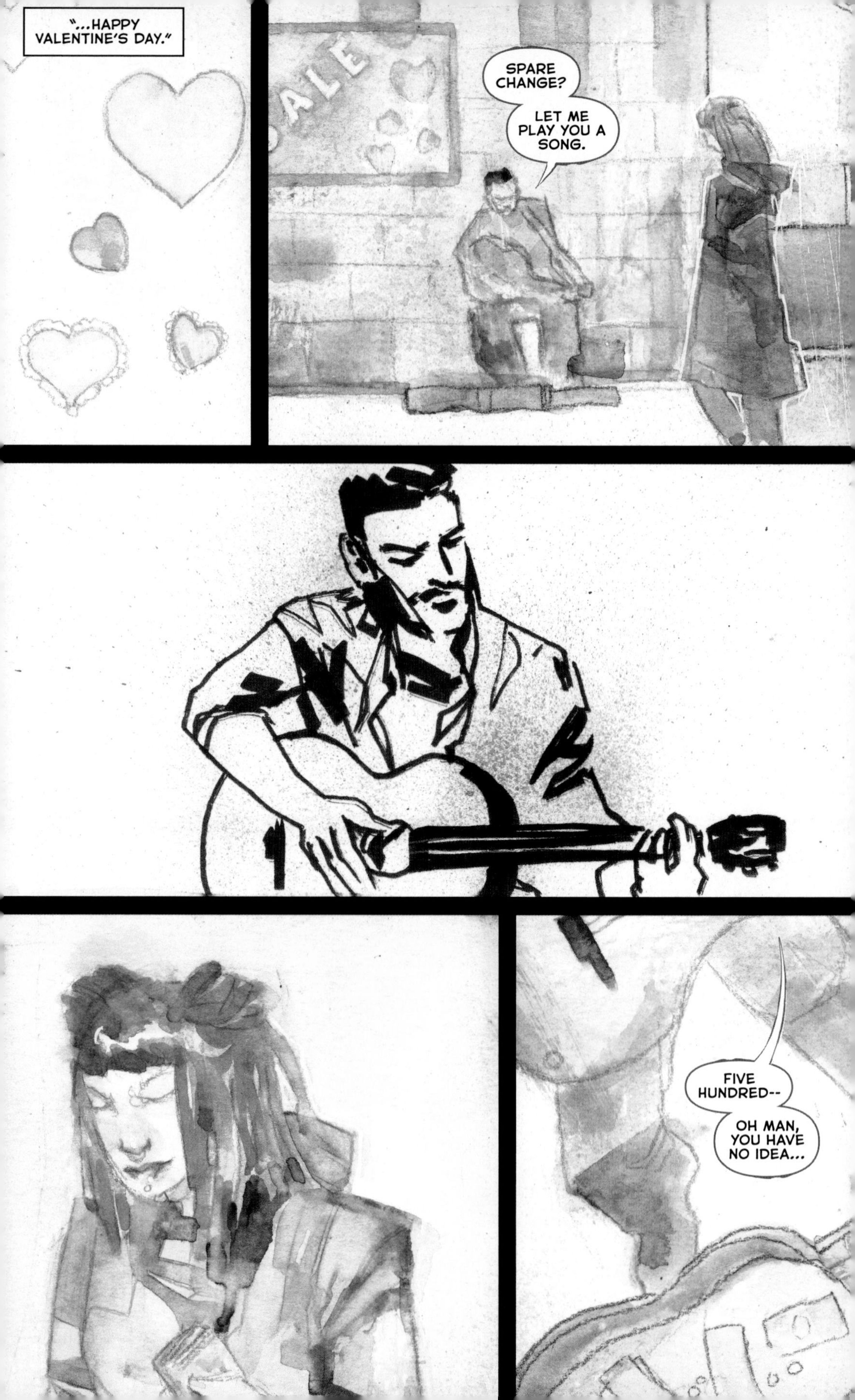
"...HAPPY VALENTINE'S DAY."
SALE
SPARE CHANGE?
LET ME PLAY YOU A SONG.
FIVE HUNDRED--
OH MAN, YOU HAVE NO IDEA...

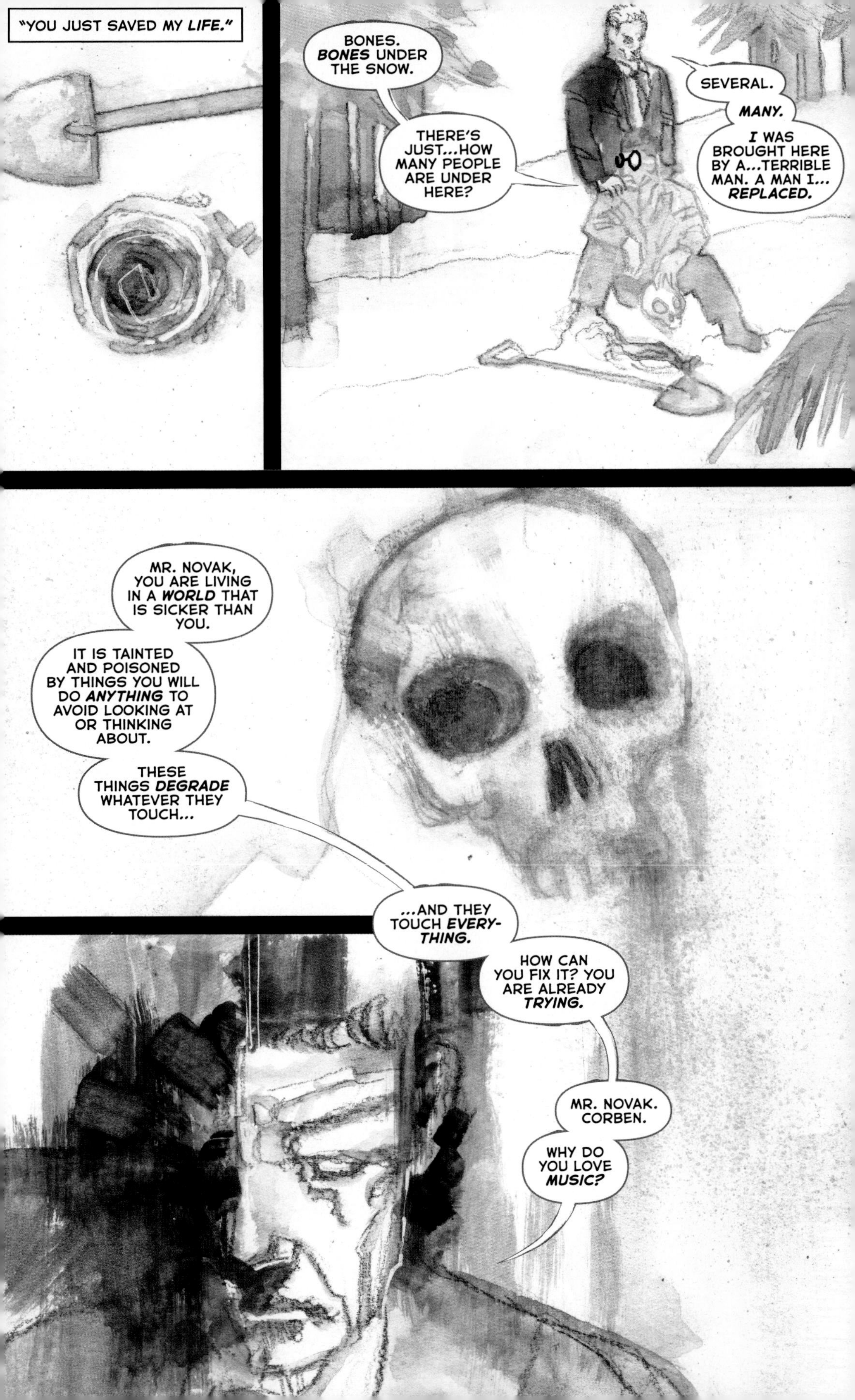
"YOU JUST SAVED MY LIFE."
BONES. BONES UNDER THE SNOW.
THERE'S JUST...HOW MANY PEOPLE ARE UNDER HERE?
SEVERAL.
MANY.
I WAS BROUGHT HERE BY A...TERRIBLE MAN. A MAN I... REPLACED.
MR. NOVAK, YOU ARE LIVING IN A WORLD THAT IS SICKER THAN YOU.
IT IS TAINTED AND POISONED BY THINGS YOU WILL DO ANYTHING TO AVOID LOOKING AT OR THINKING ABOUT.
THESE THINGS DEGRADE WHATEVER THEY TOUCH...
...AND THEY TOUCH EVERY-THING.
HOW CAN YOU FIX IT? YOU ARE ALREADY TRYING.
MR. NOVAK. CORBEN.
WHY DO YOU LOVE MUSIC?

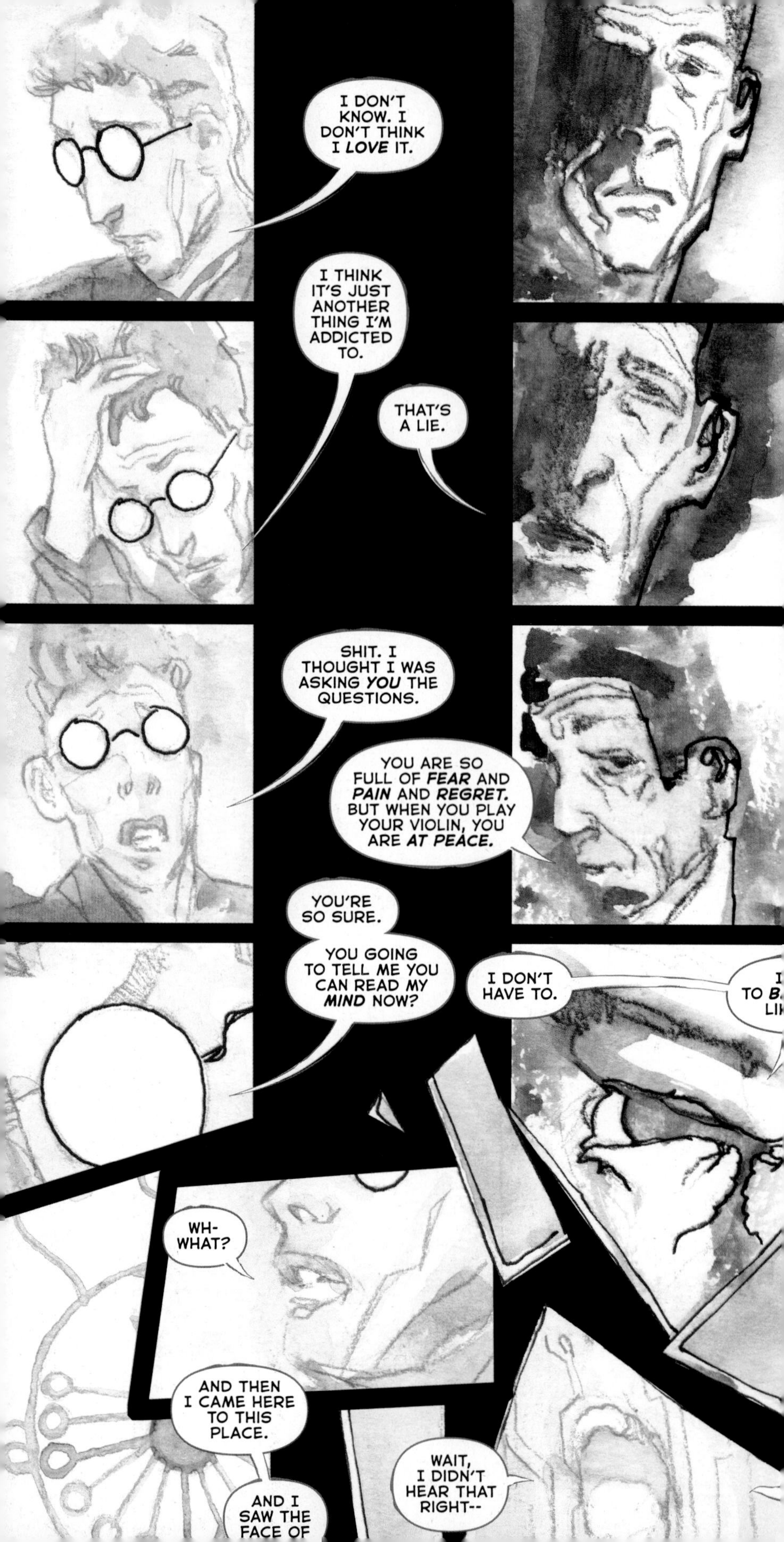
I DON'T KNOW. I DON'T THINK I *LOVE* IT.
I THINK IT'S JUST ANOTHER THING I'M ADDICTED TO.
THAT'S A LIE.
SHIT. I THOUGHT I WAS ASKING *YOU* THE QUESTIONS.
YOU ARE SO FULL OF *FEAR* AND *PAIN* AND *REGRET.* BUT WHEN YOU PLAY YOUR VIOLIN, YOU ARE *AT PEACE.*
YOU'RE SO SURE.
YOU GOING TO TELL ME YOU CAN READ MY *MIND* NOW?
I DON'T HAVE TO.
WH-WHAT?
AND THEN I CAME HERE TO THIS PLACE.
AND I SAW THE FACE OF
WAIT, I DIDN'T HEAR THAT RIGHT--

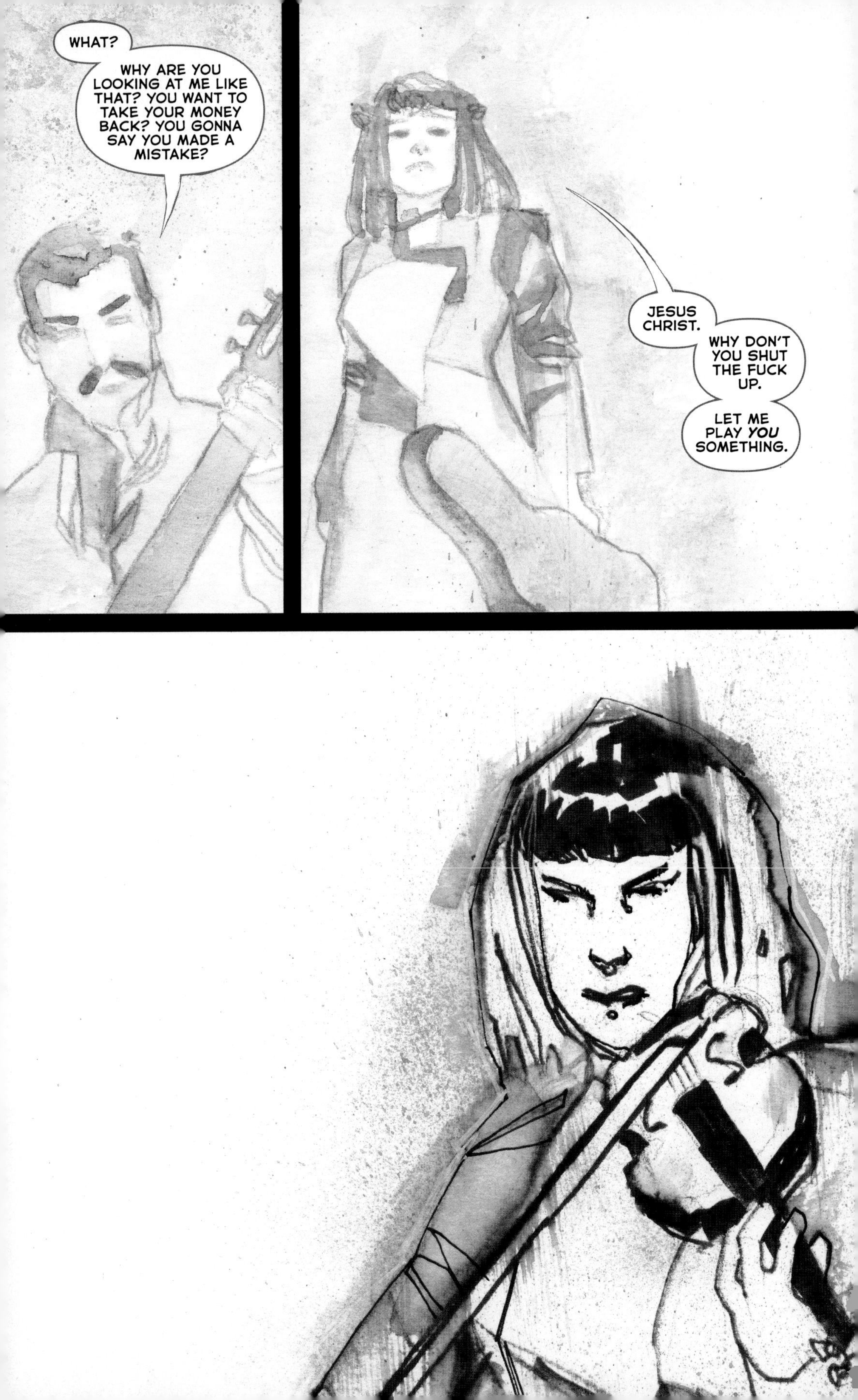
WHAT?
WHY ARE YOU LOOKING AT ME LIKE THAT? YOU WANT TO TAKE YOUR MONEY BACK? YOU GONNA SAY YOU MADE A MISTAKE?
JESUS CHRIST.
WHY DON'T YOU SHUT THE FUCK UP.
LET ME PLAY *YOU* SOMETHING.

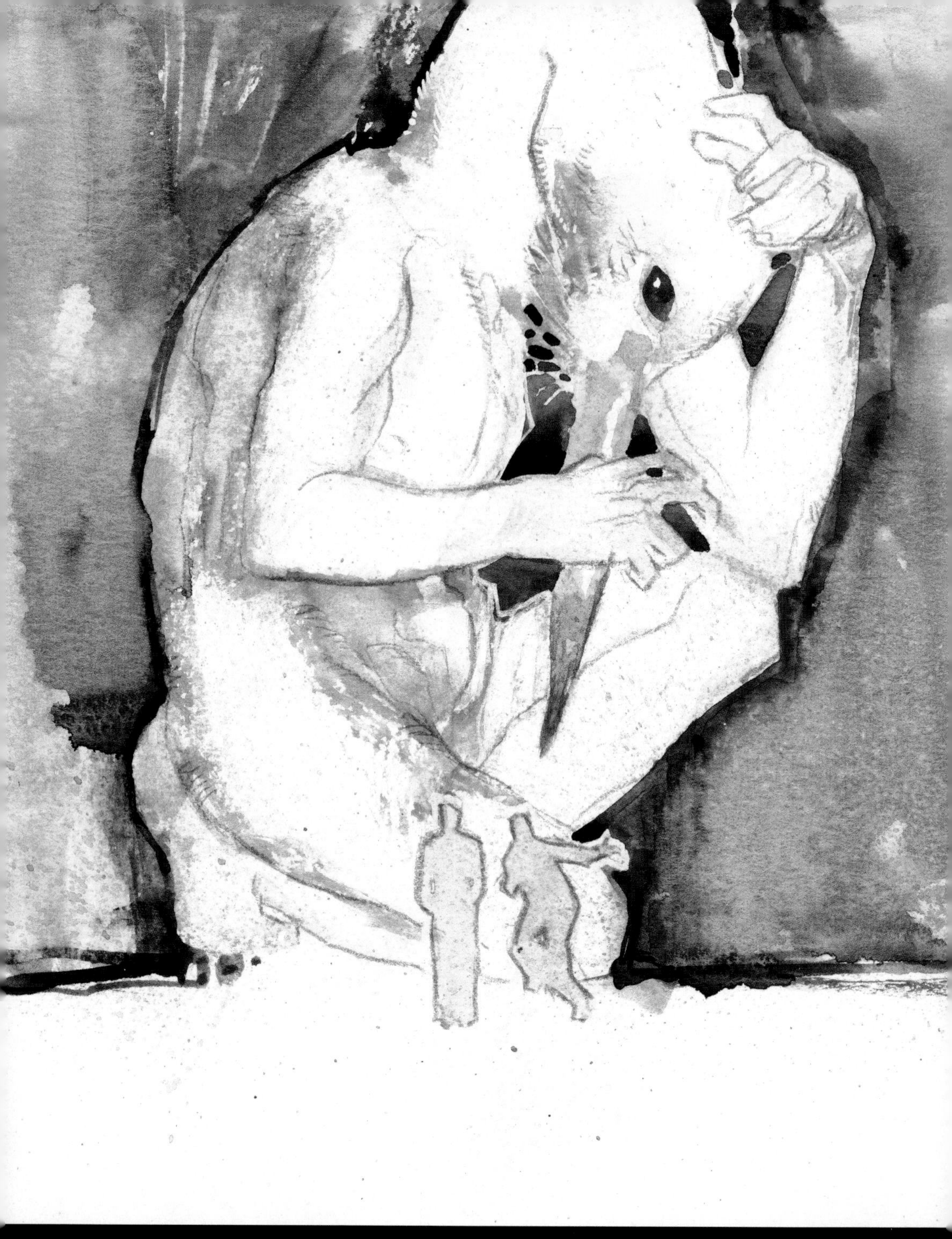

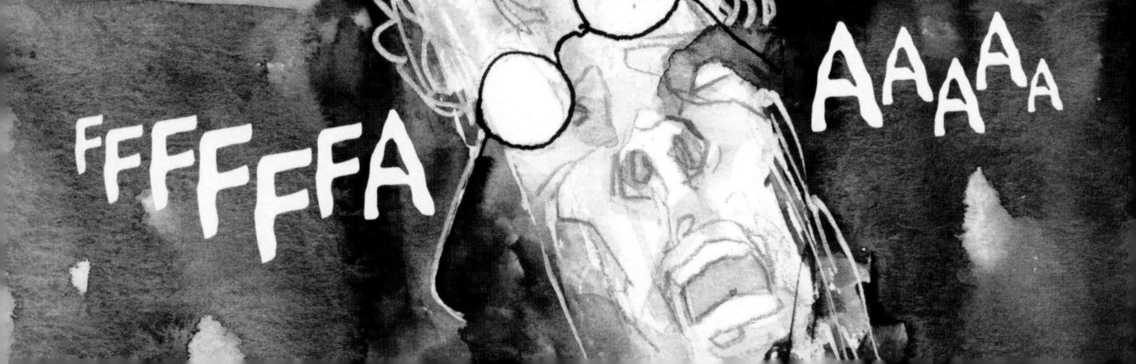
FFFFFFA
AAAAA

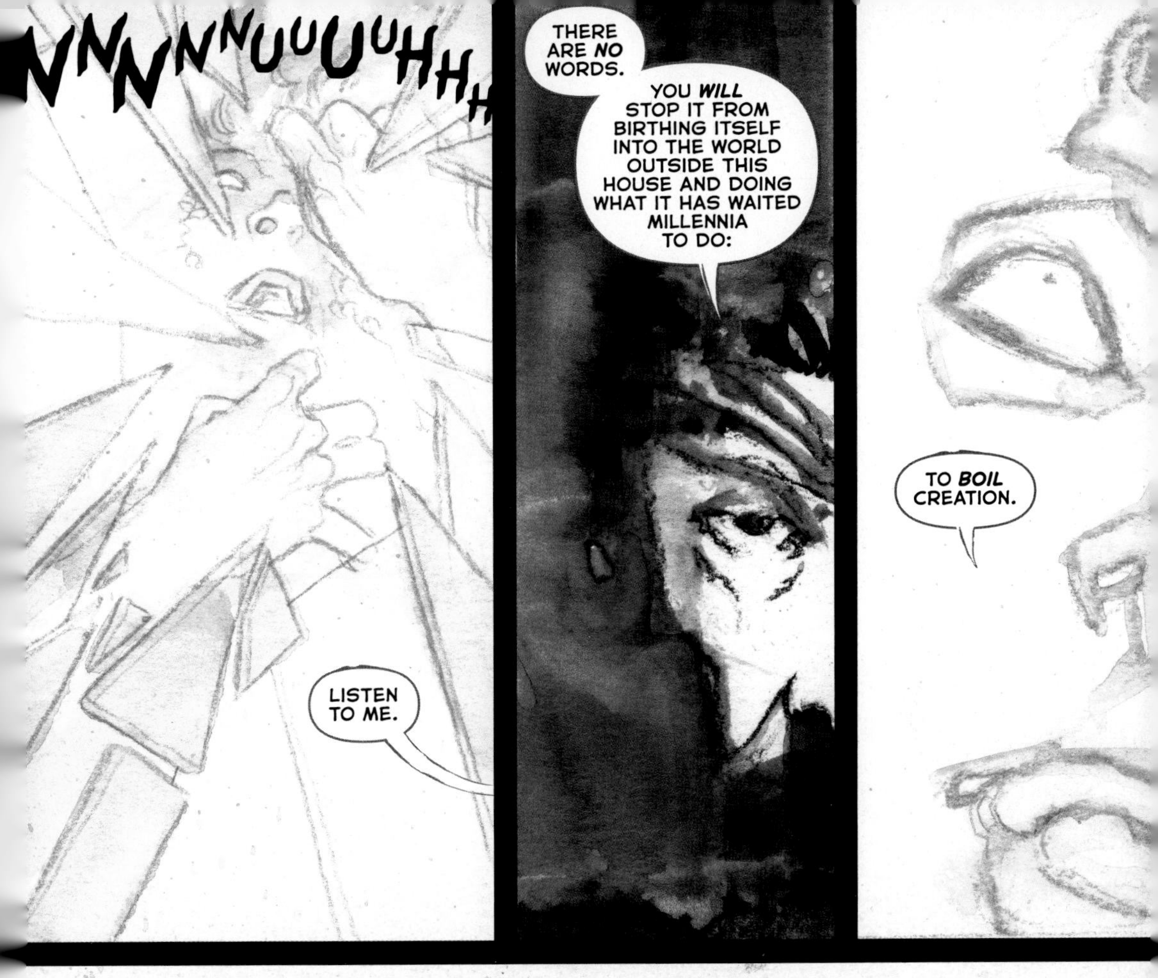
NNNNNUUUUHHH
LISTEN TO ME.
THERE ARE *NO* WORDS.
YOU *WILL* STOP IT FROM BIRTHING ITSELF INTO THE WORLD OUTSIDE THIS HOUSE AND DOING WHAT IT HAS WAITED MILLENNIA TO DO:
TO *BOIL* CREATION.

"BUT TIME, AS I SAID, IS *SHORT.*

"*YOUR* TIME...

"*MY* TIME...

"*EVERYBODY'S* TIME..."

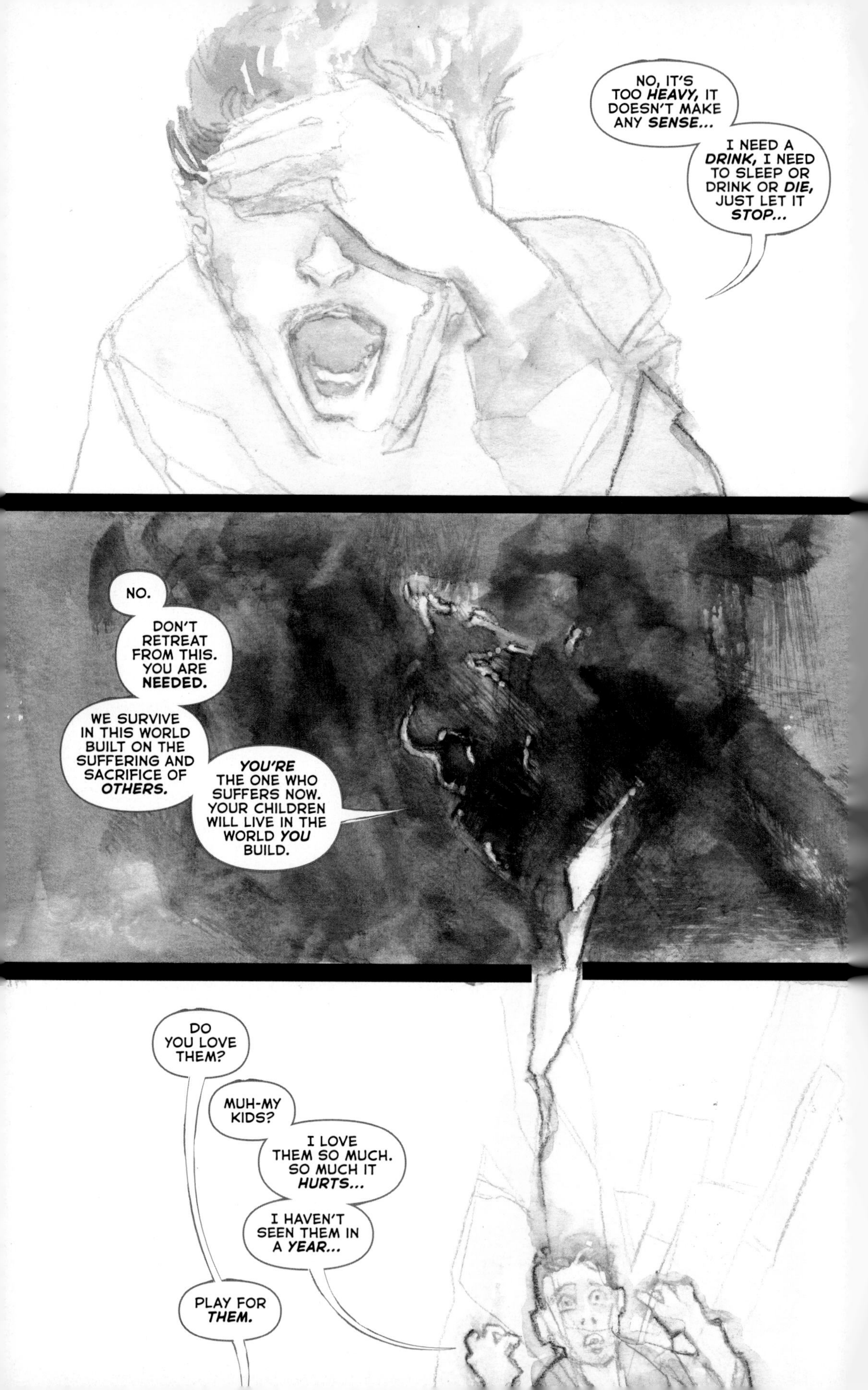
NO, IT'S TOO HEAVY, IT DOESN'T MAKE ANY SENSE...
I NEED A DRINK, I NEED TO SLEEP OR DRINK OR DIE, JUST LET IT STOP...
NO.
DON'T RETREAT FROM THIS. YOU ARE NEEDED.
WE SURVIVE IN THIS WORLD BUILT ON THE SUFFERING AND SACRIFICE OF OTHERS.
YOU'RE THE ONE WHO SUFFERS NOW. YOUR CHILDREN WILL LIVE IN THE WORLD YOU BUILD.
DO YOU LOVE THEM?
MUH-MY KIDS?
I LOVE THEM SO MUCH. SO MUCH IT HURTS...
I HAVEN'T SEEN THEM IN A YEAR...
PLAY FOR THEM.

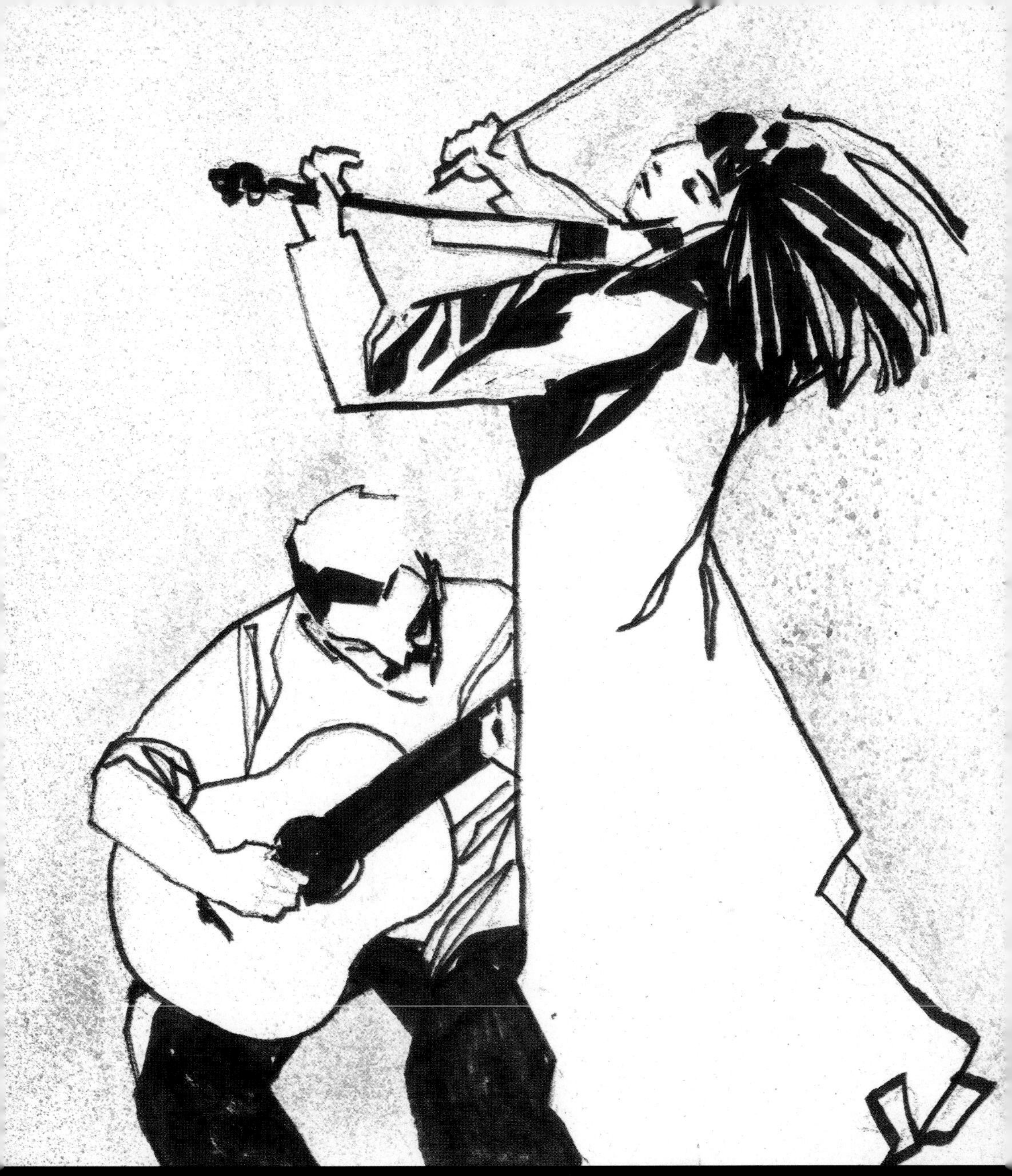

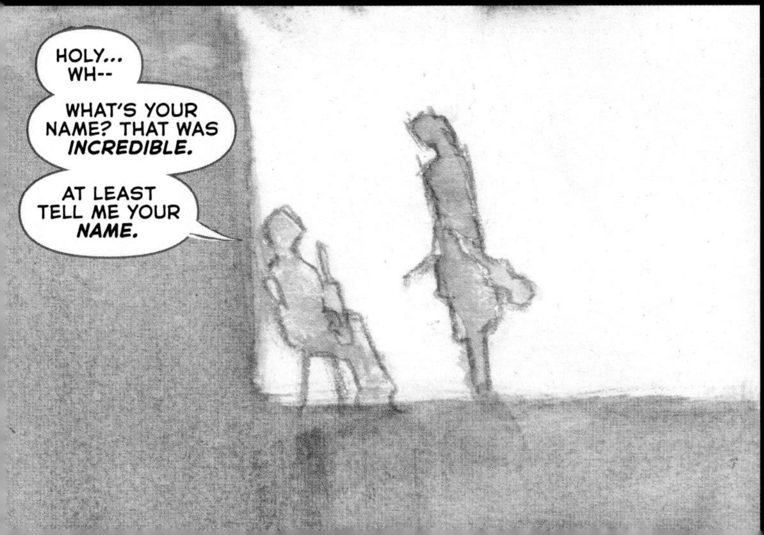
HOLY... WH--
WHAT'S YOUR NAME? THAT WAS *INCREDIBLE.*
AT LEAST TELL ME YOUR *NAME.*

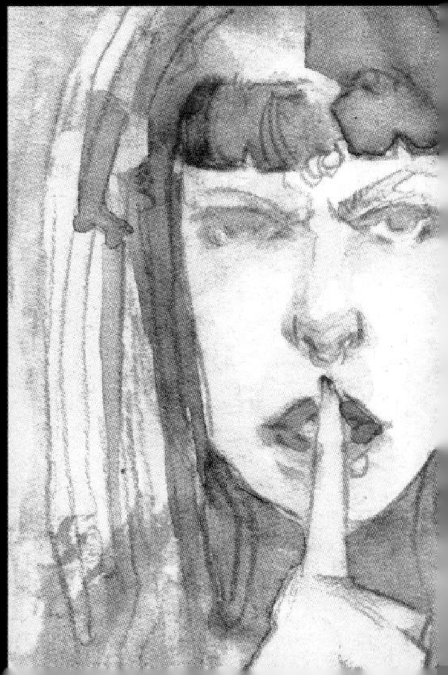

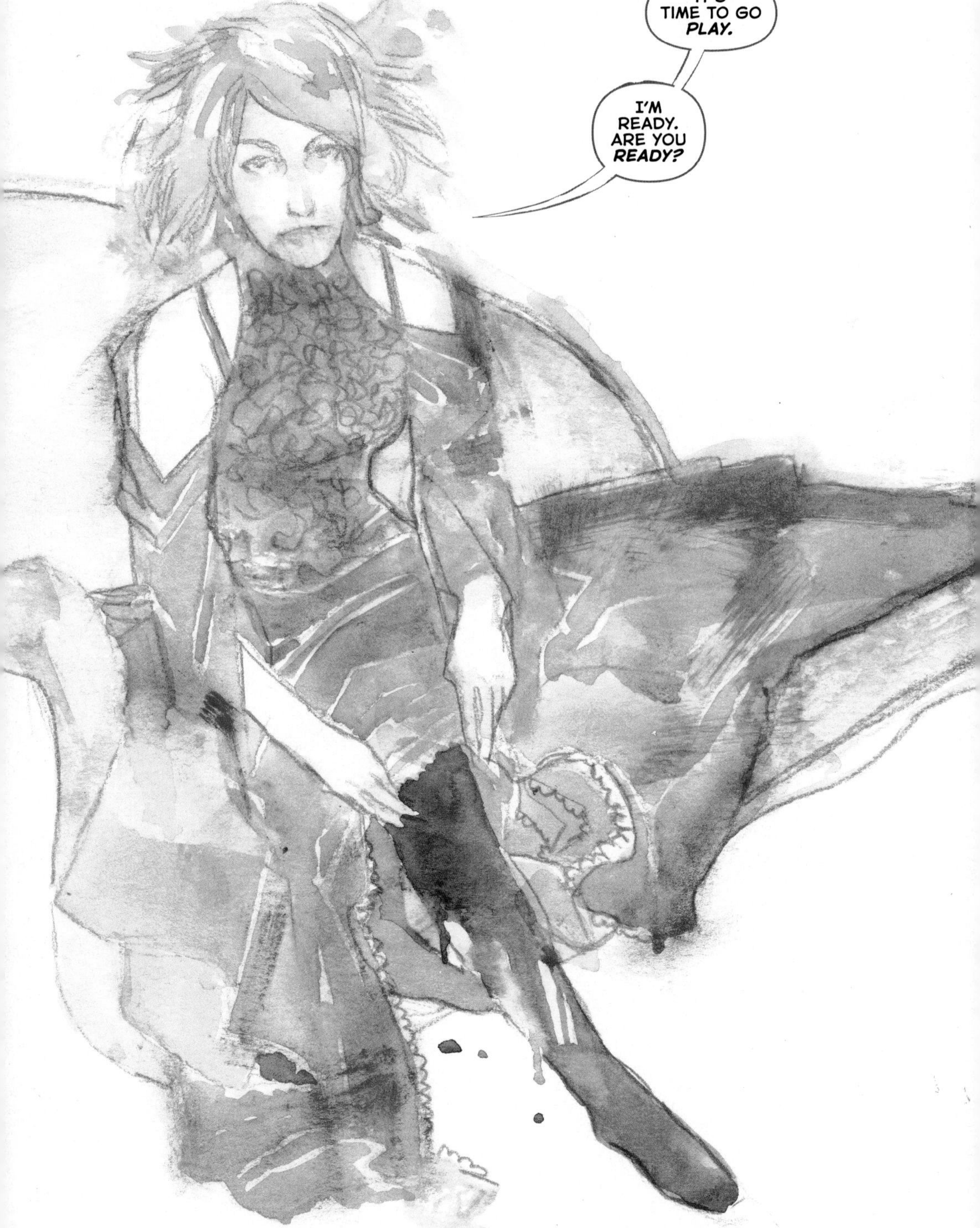
IT'S TIME TO GO *PLAY.*
I'M READY. ARE YOU *READY?*

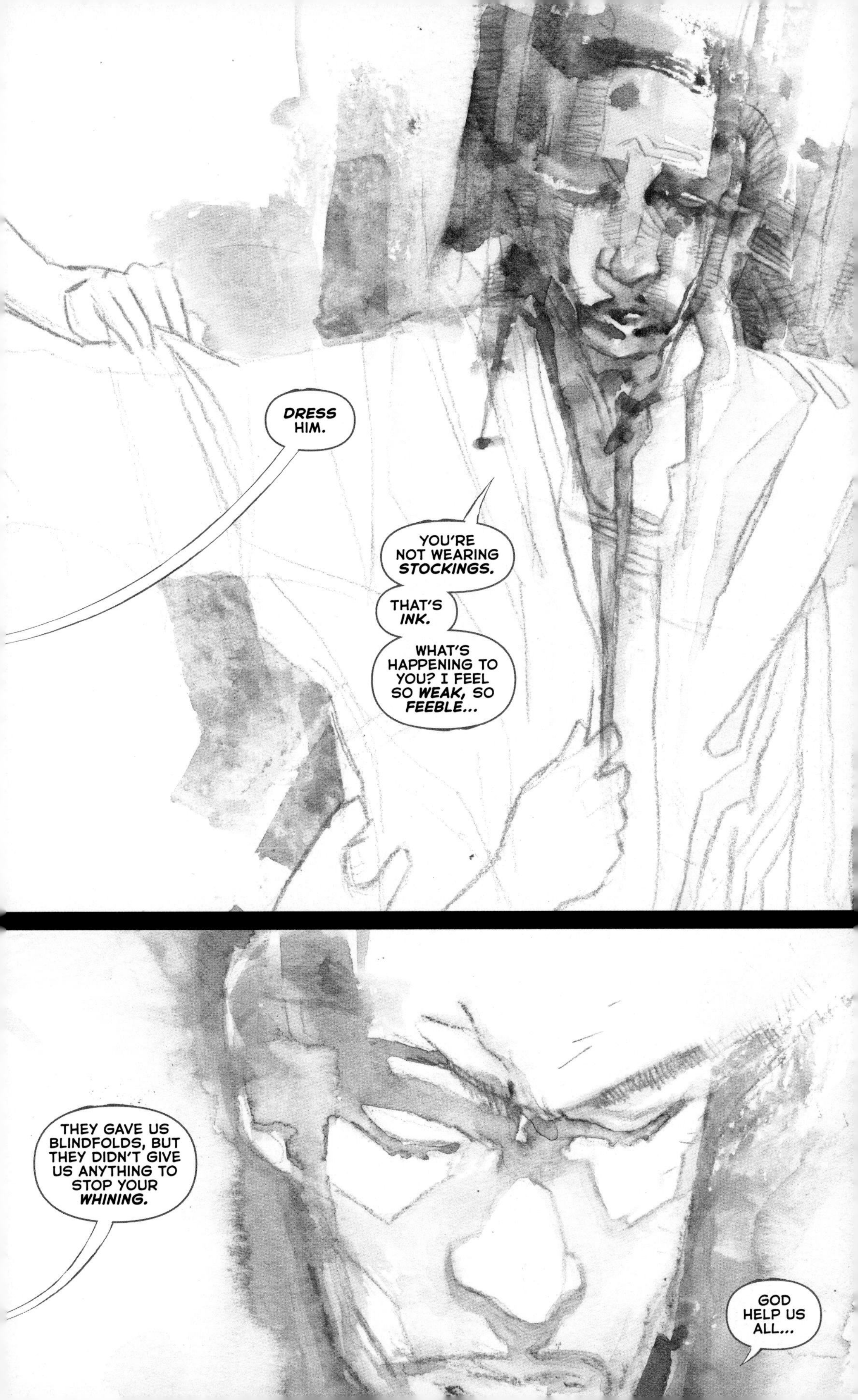
DRESS HIM.
YOU'RE NOT WEARING STOCKINGS.
THAT'S INK.
WHAT'S HAPPENING TO YOU? I FEEL SO WEAK, SO FEEBLE...
THEY GAVE US BLINDFOLDS, BUT THEY DIDN'T GIVE US ANYTHING TO STOP YOUR WHINING.
GOD HELP US ALL...

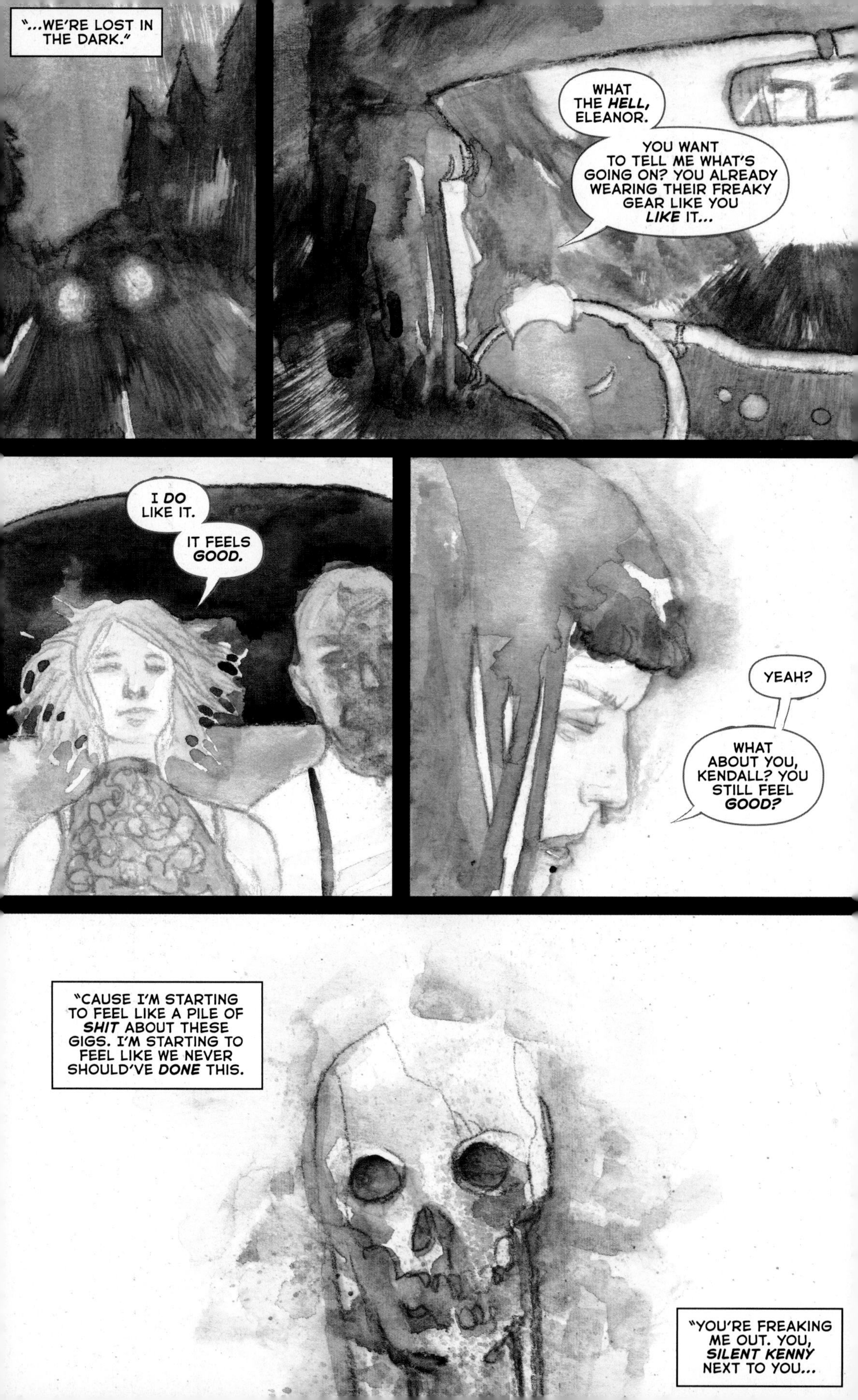
"...WE'RE LOST IN THE DARK."
WHAT THE *HELL,* ELEANOR.
YOU WANT TO TELL ME WHAT'S GOING ON? YOU ALREADY WEARING THEIR FREAKY GEAR LIKE YOU *LIKE* IT...
I *DO* LIKE IT.
IT FEELS *GOOD.*
YEAH?
WHAT ABOUT YOU, KENDALL? YOU STILL FEEL *GOOD?*
"CAUSE I'M STARTING TO FEEL LIKE A PILE OF *SHIT* ABOUT THESE GIGS. I'M STARTING TO FEEL LIKE WE NEVER SHOULD'VE *DONE* THIS.
"YOU'RE FREAKING ME OUT. YOU, *SILENT KENNY* NEXT TO YOU...

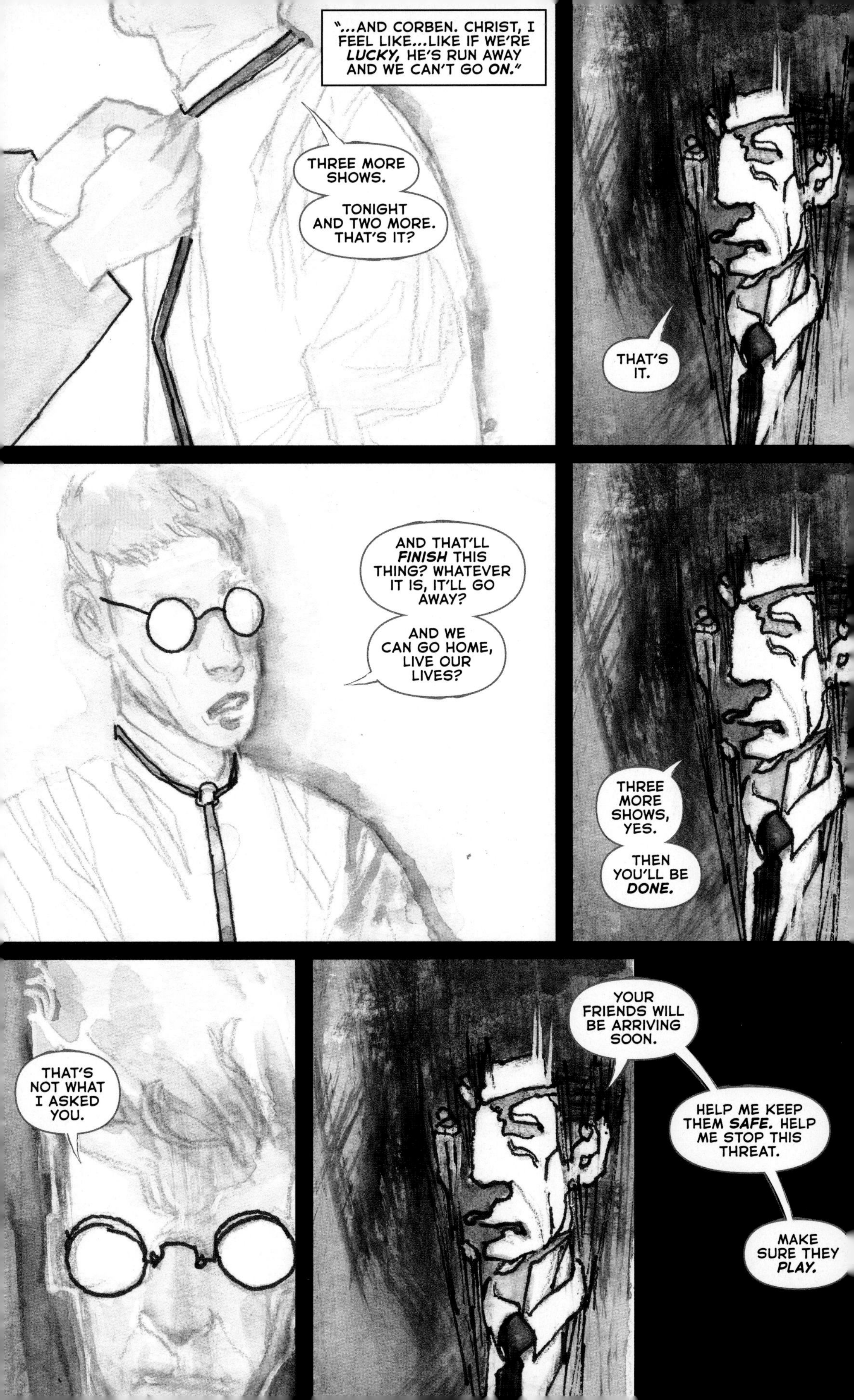
"...AND CORBEN. CHRIST, I FEEL LIKE...LIKE IF WE'RE *LUCKY,* HE'S RUN AWAY AND WE CAN'T GO *ON.*"
THREE MORE SHOWS.
TONIGHT AND TWO MORE. THAT'S IT?
THAT'S IT.
AND THAT'LL *FINISH* THIS THING? WHATEVER IT IS, IT'LL GO AWAY?
AND WE CAN GO HOME, LIVE OUR LIVES?
THREE MORE SHOWS, YES.
THEN YOU'LL BE *DONE.*
THAT'S NOT WHAT I ASKED YOU.
YOUR FRIENDS WILL BE ARRIVING SOON.
HELP ME KEEP THEM *SAFE.* HELP ME STOP THIS THREAT.
MAKE SURE THEY *PLAY.*

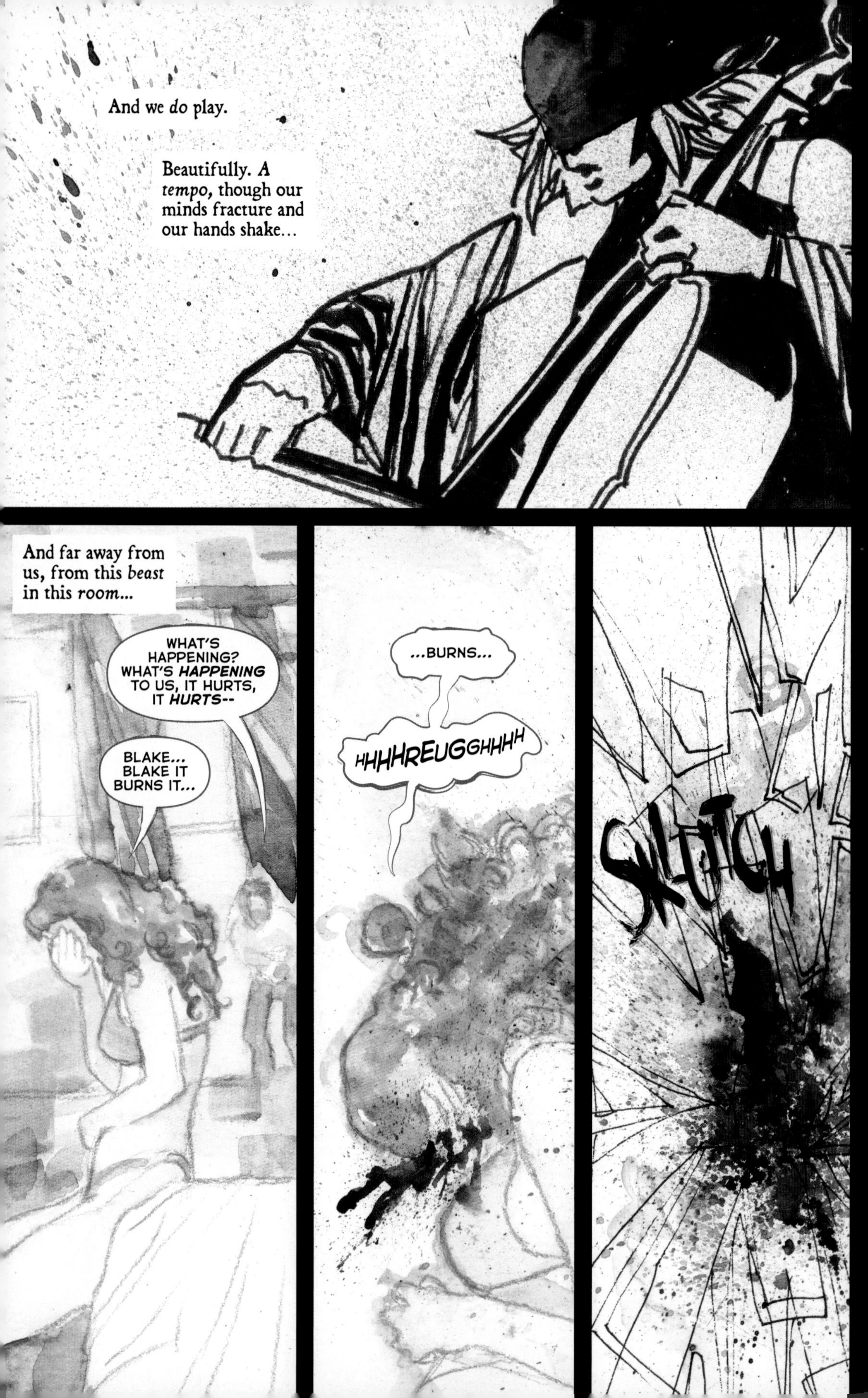
And we *do* play.
Beautifully. *A tempo,* though our minds fracture and our hands shake...
And far away from us, from this *beast* in this *room*...
WHAT'S HAPPENING? WHAT'S *HAPPENING* TO US, IT HURTS, IT *HURTS*--
BLAKE... BLAKE IT BURNS IT...
...BURNS...
HHHHREUGGHHHH
SKLTCH

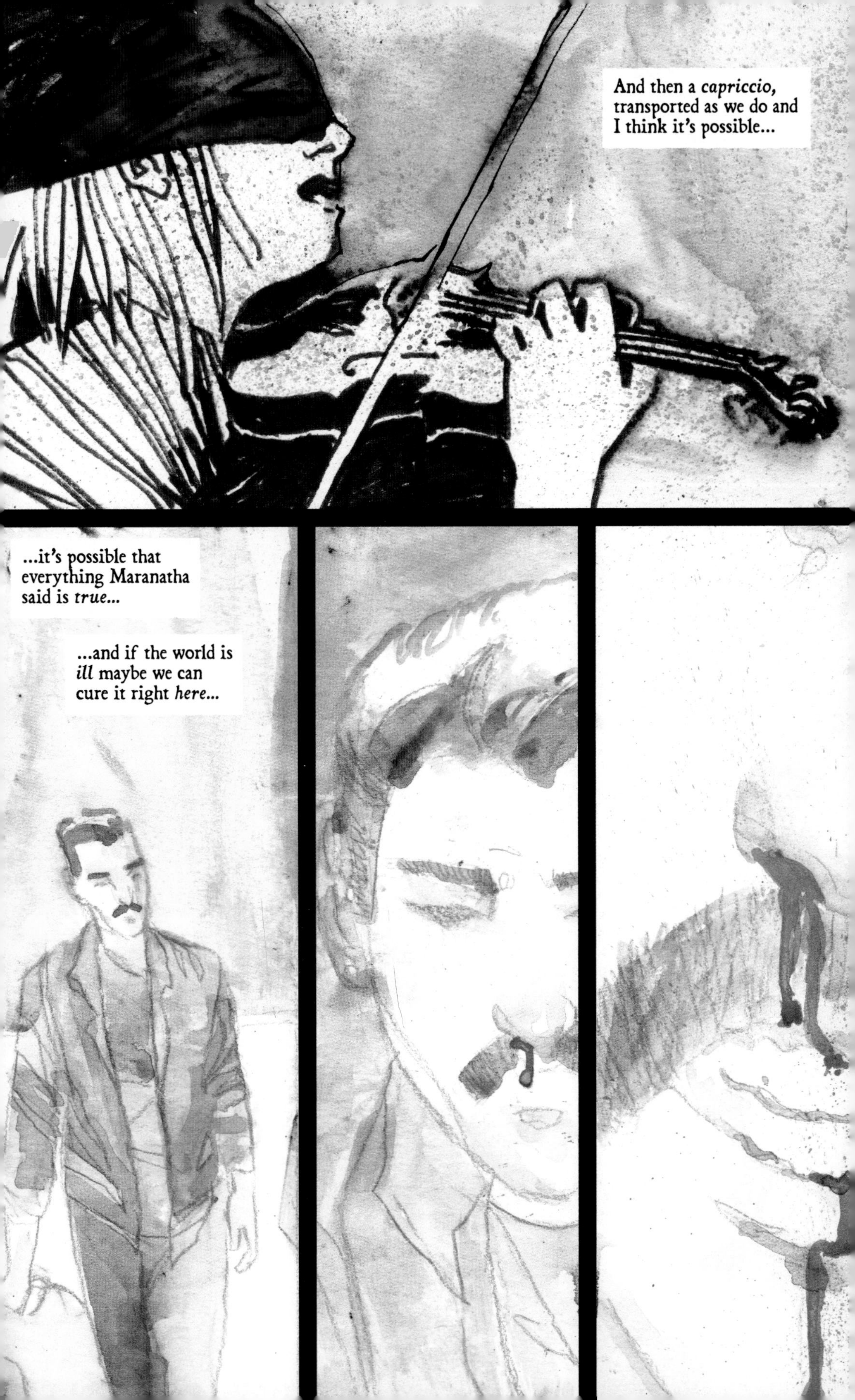
And then a *capriccio*, transported as we do and I think it's possible...
...it's possible that everything Maranatha said is *true*...
...and if the world is *ill* maybe we can cure it right *here*...

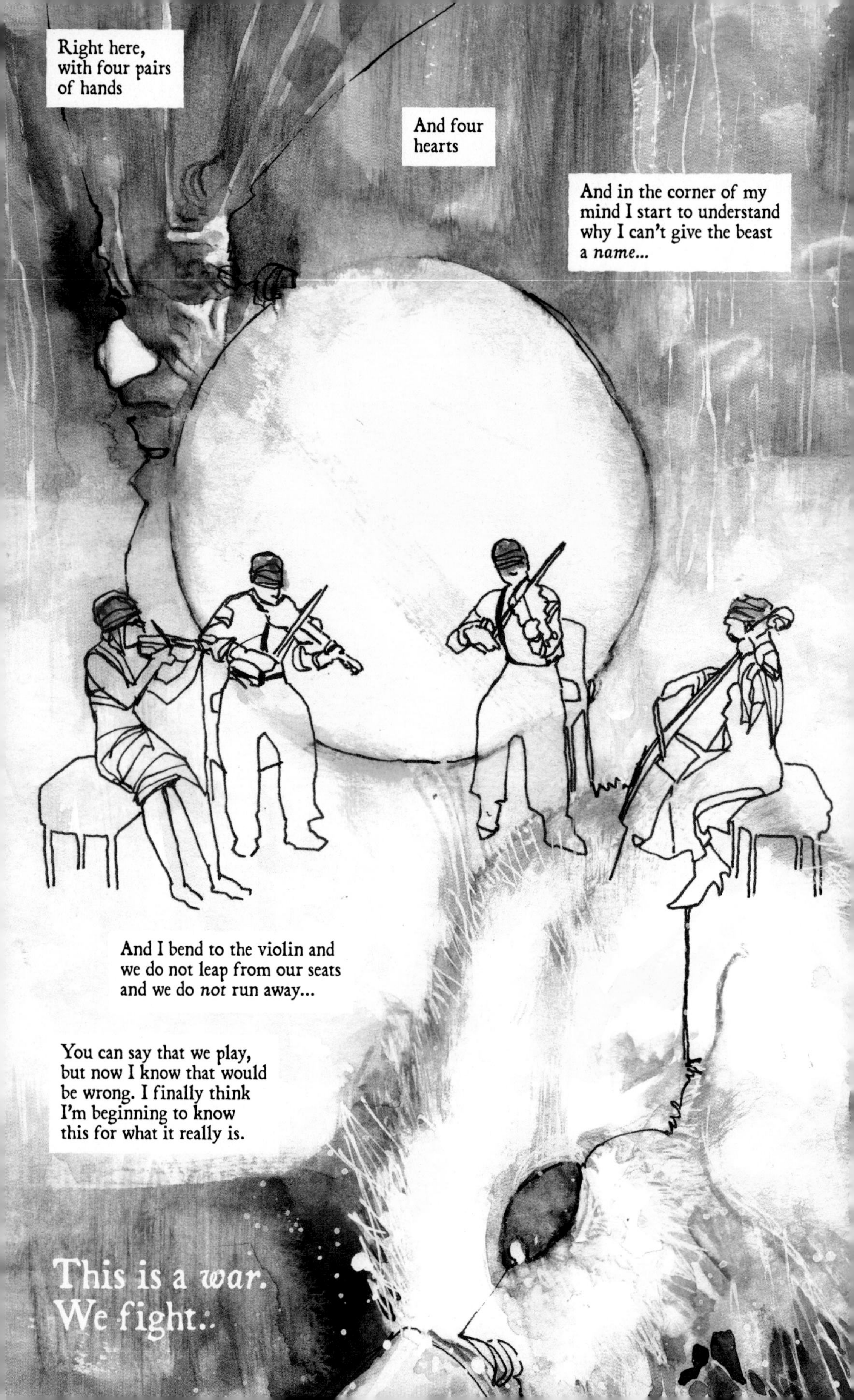
Right here, with four pairs of hands
And four hearts
And in the corner of my mind I start to understand why I can't give the beast a *name...*
And I bend to the violin and we do not leap from our seats and we do *not* run away...
You can say that we play, but now I know that would be wrong. I finally think I'm beginning to know this for what it really is.
This is a *war.* We fight.

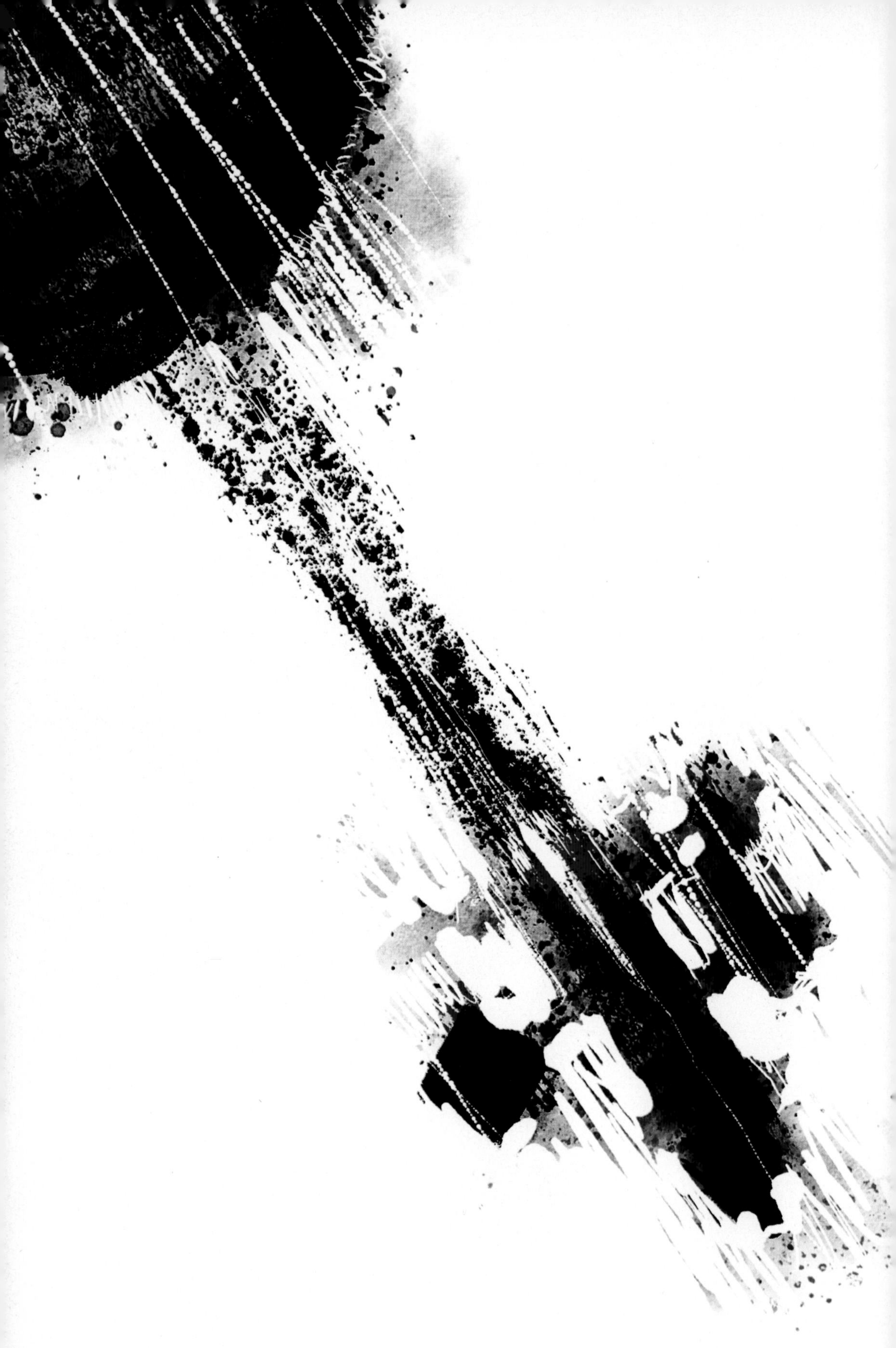

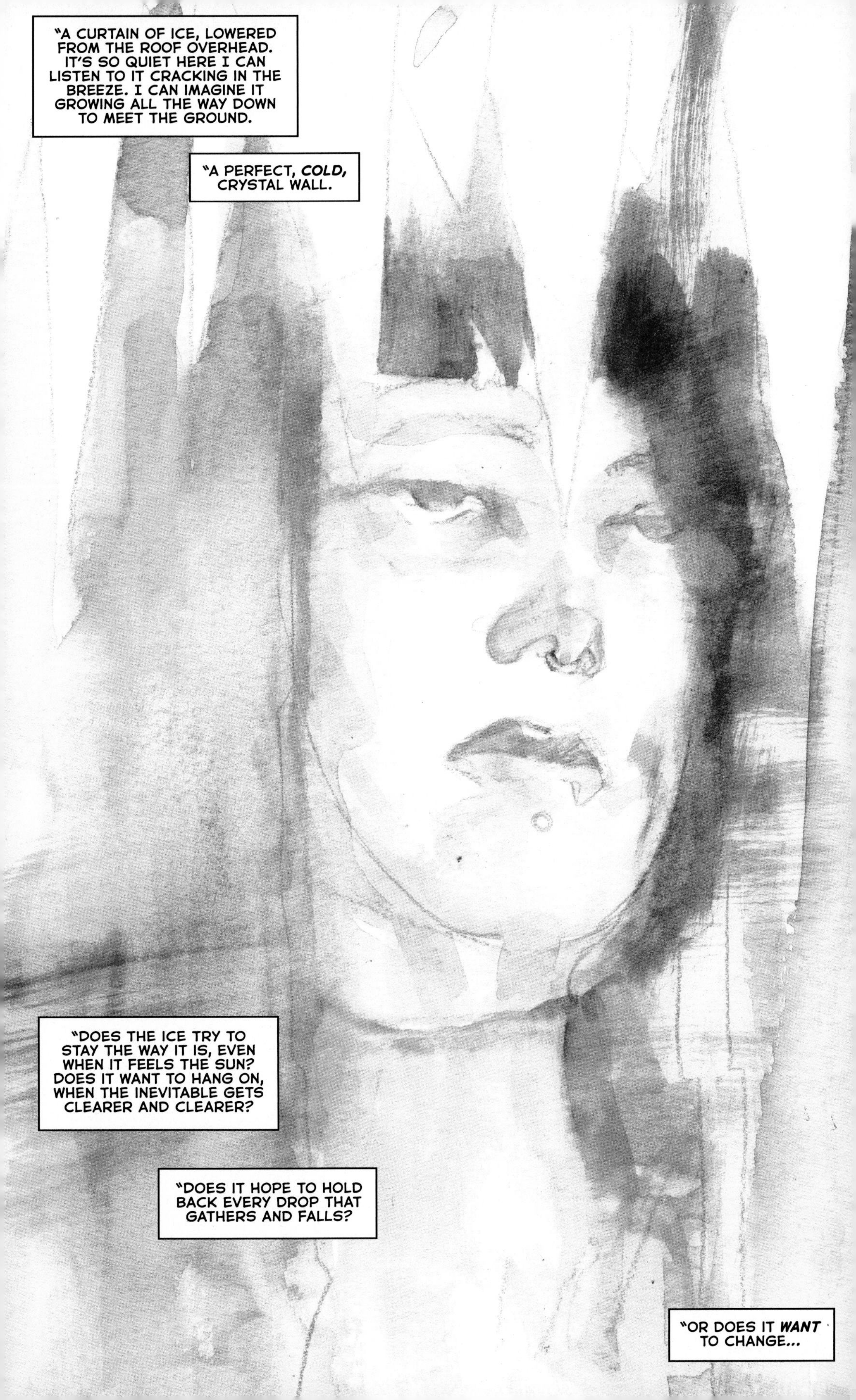
"A CURTAIN OF ICE, LOWERED FROM THE ROOF OVERHEAD. IT'S SO QUIET HERE I CAN LISTEN TO IT CRACKING IN THE BREEZE. I CAN IMAGINE IT GROWING ALL THE WAY DOWN TO MEET THE GROUND.
"A PERFECT, *COLD,* CRYSTAL WALL.
"DOES THE ICE TRY TO STAY THE WAY IT IS, EVEN WHEN IT FEELS THE SUN? DOES IT WANT TO HANG ON, WHEN THE INEVITABLE GETS CLEARER AND CLEARER?
"DOES IT HOPE TO HOLD BACK EVERY DROP THAT GATHERS AND FALLS?
"OR DOES IT *WANT* TO CHANGE...

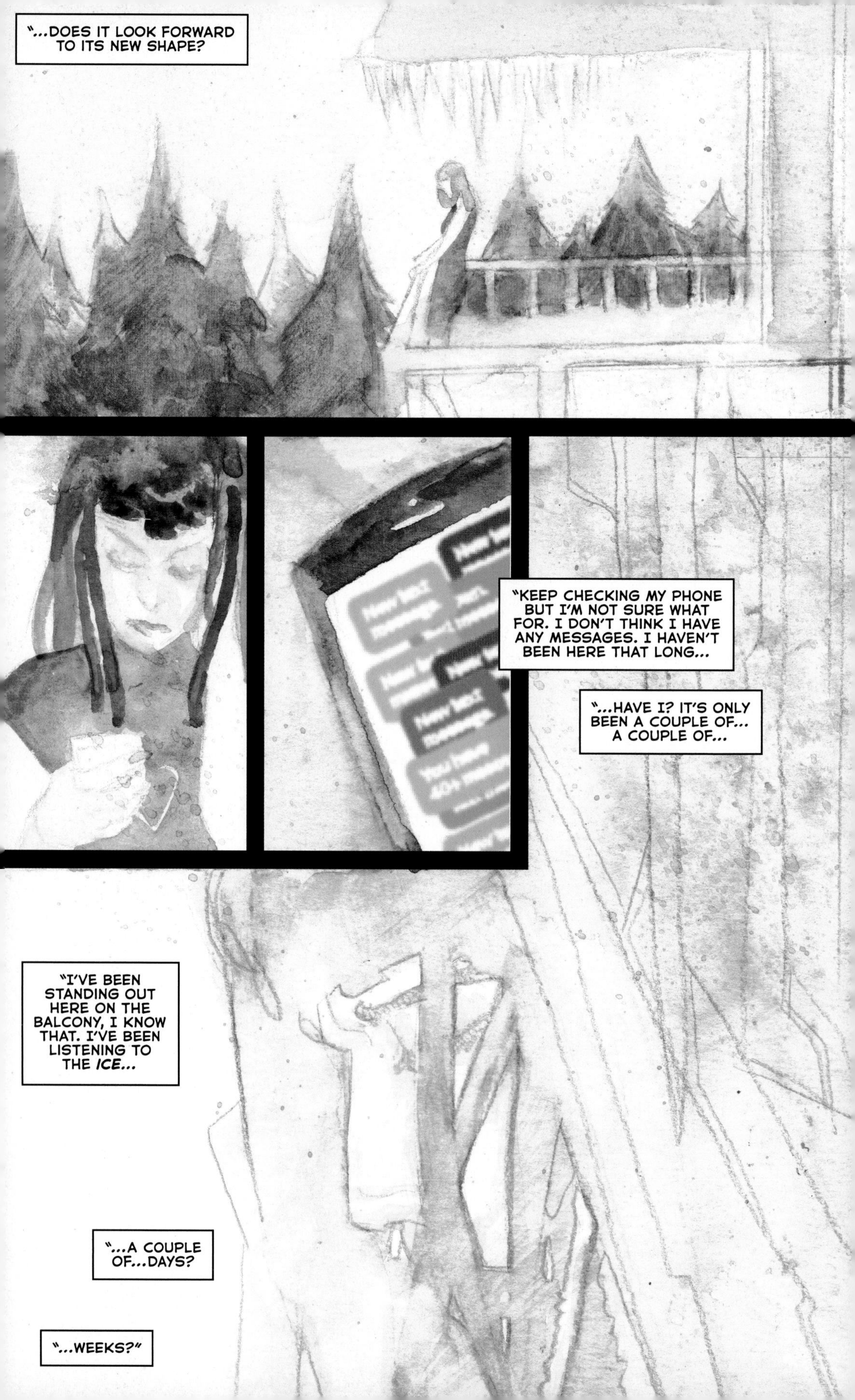
"...DOES IT LOOK FORWARD TO ITS NEW SHAPE?
"KEEP CHECKING MY PHONE BUT I'M NOT SURE WHAT FOR. I DON'T THINK I HAVE ANY MESSAGES. I HAVEN'T BEEN HERE THAT LONG...
"...HAVE I? IT'S ONLY BEEN A COUPLE OF... A COUPLE OF...
"I'VE BEEN STANDING OUT HERE ON THE BALCONY, I KNOW THAT. I'VE BEEN LISTENING TO THE *ICE*...
"...A COUPLE OF...DAYS?
"...WEEKS?"

SYMPHONY

PART FIVE:
MARCH

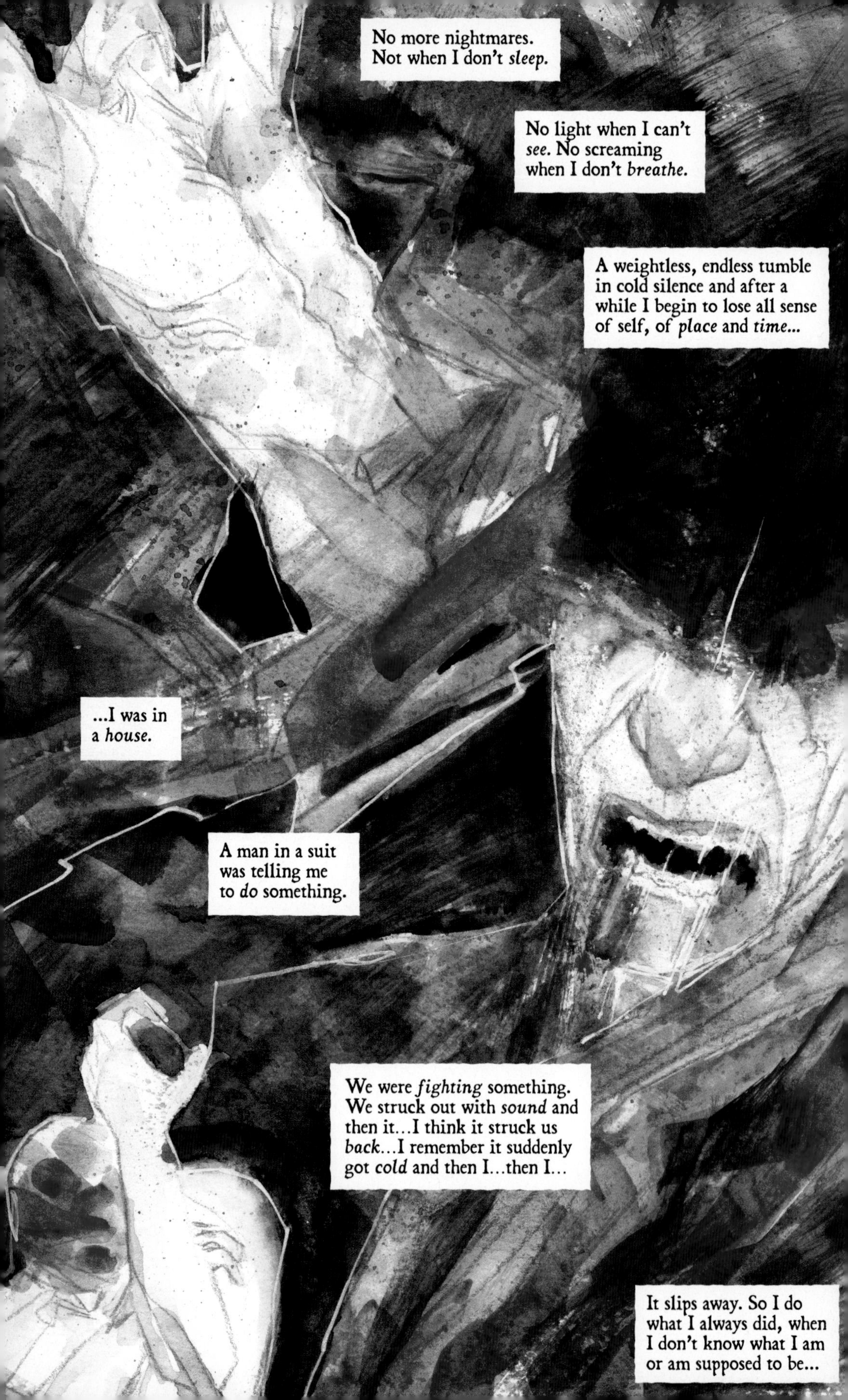
No more nightmares. Not when I don't *sleep.*
No light when I can't *see.* No screaming when I don't *breathe.*
A weightless, endless tumble in cold silence and after a while I begin to lose all sense of self, of *place* and *time...*
...I was in a *house.*
A man in a suit was telling me to *do* something.
We were *fighting* something. We struck out with *sound* and then it...I think it struck us *back*...I remember it suddenly got *cold* and then I...then I...
It slips away. So I do what I always did, when I don't know what I am or am supposed to be...

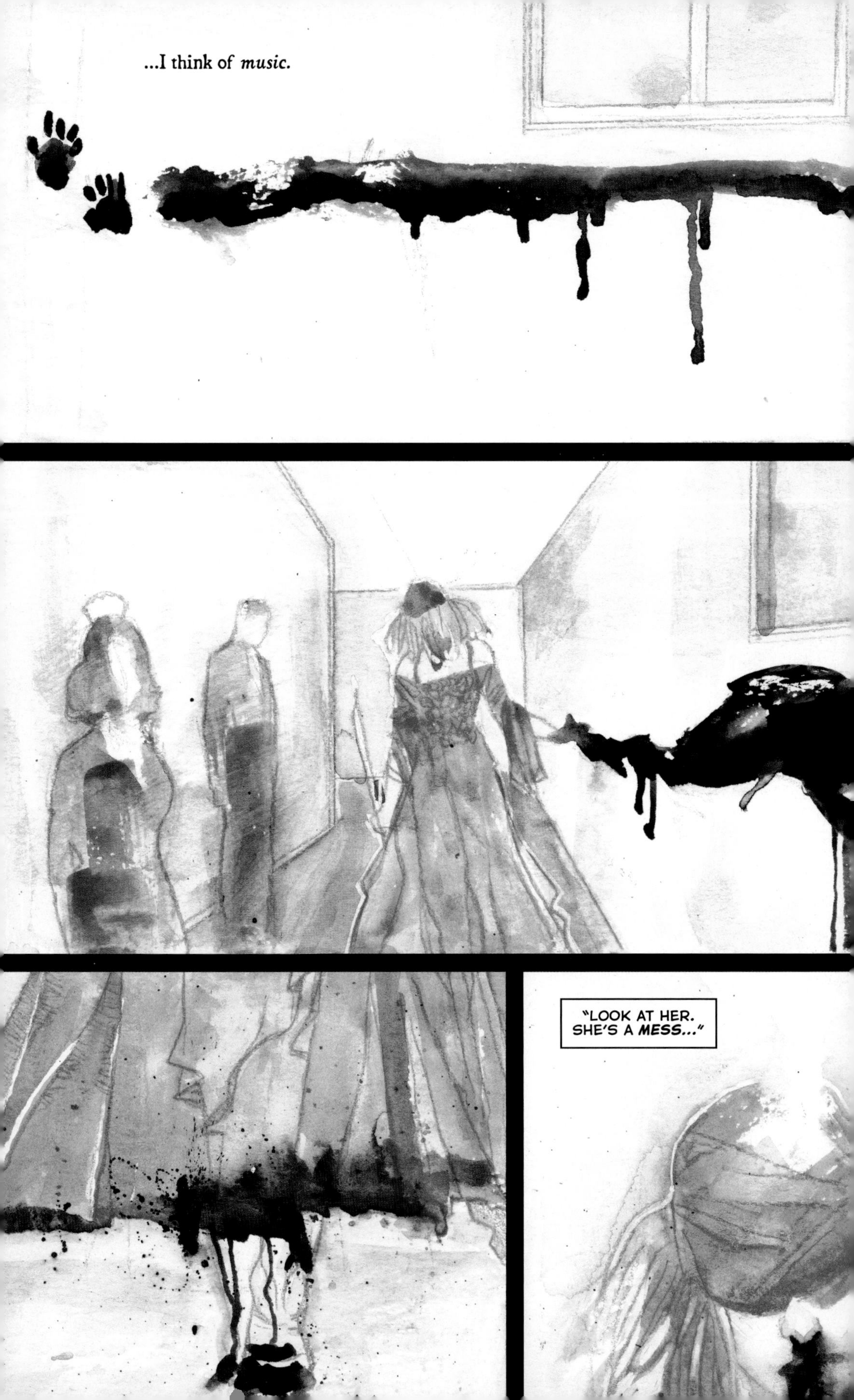
...I think of *music*.
"LOOK AT HER. SHE'S A *MESS*..."

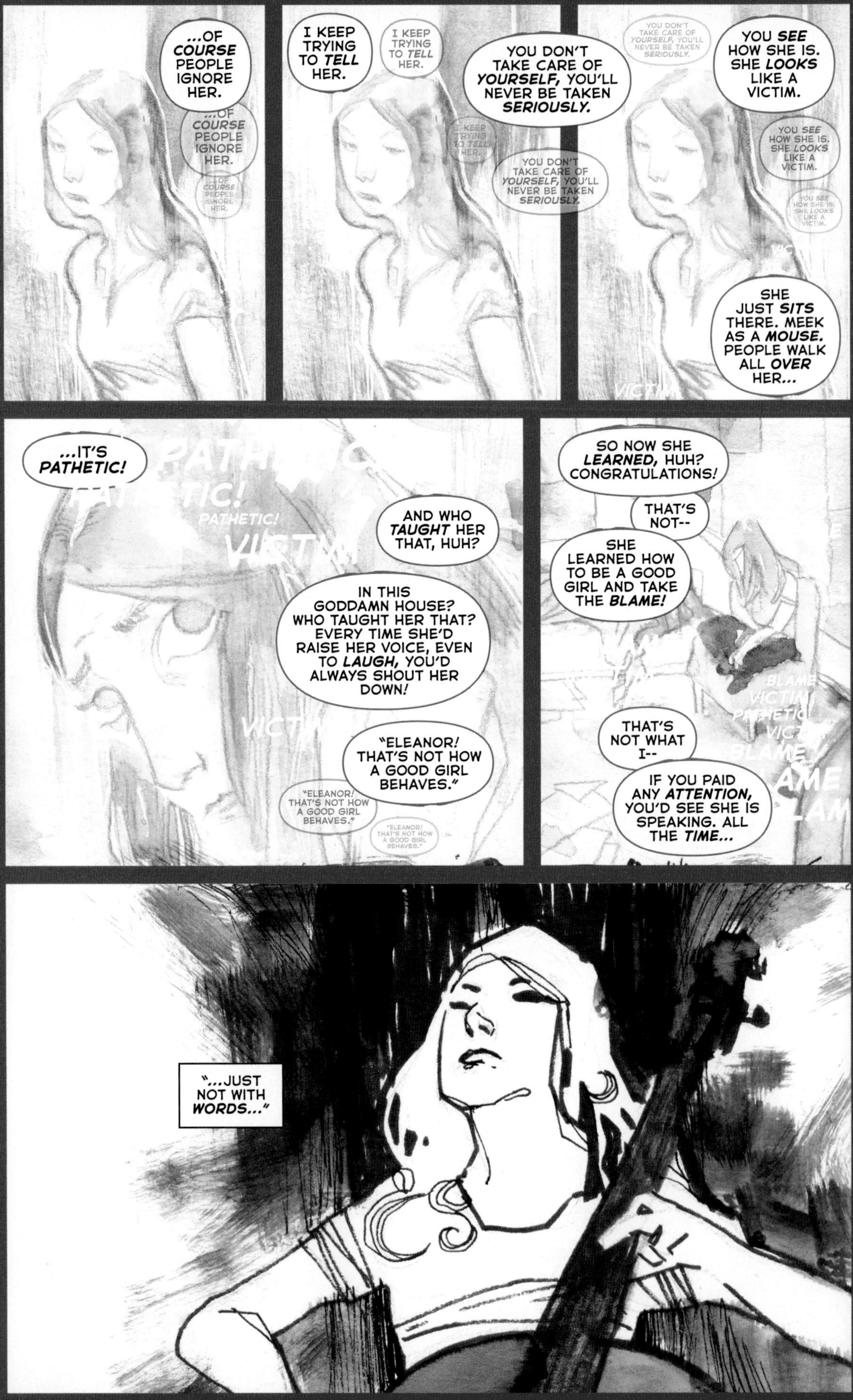
...OF COURSE PEOPLE IGNORE HER.
I KEEP TRYING TO TELL HER.
YOU DON'T TAKE CARE OF YOURSELF, YOU'LL NEVER BE TAKEN SERIOUSLY.
YOU SEE HOW SHE IS. SHE LOOKS LIKE A VICTIM.
SHE JUST SITS THERE. MEEK AS A MOUSE. PEOPLE WALK ALL OVER HER...
...IT'S PATHETIC!
AND WHO TAUGHT HER THAT, HUH?
IN THIS GODDAMN HOUSE? WHO TAUGHT HER THAT? EVERY TIME SHE'D RAISE HER VOICE, EVEN TO LAUGH, YOU'D ALWAYS SHOUT HER DOWN!
"ELEANOR! THAT'S NOT HOW A GOOD GIRL BEHAVES."
SO NOW SHE LEARNED, HUH? CONGRATULATIONS!
THAT'S NOT--
SHE LEARNED HOW TO BE A GOOD GIRL AND TAKE THE BLAME!
THAT'S NOT WHAT I--
IF YOU PAID ANY ATTENTION, YOU'D SEE SHE IS SPEAKING. ALL THE TIME...
"...JUST NOT WITH WORDS..."

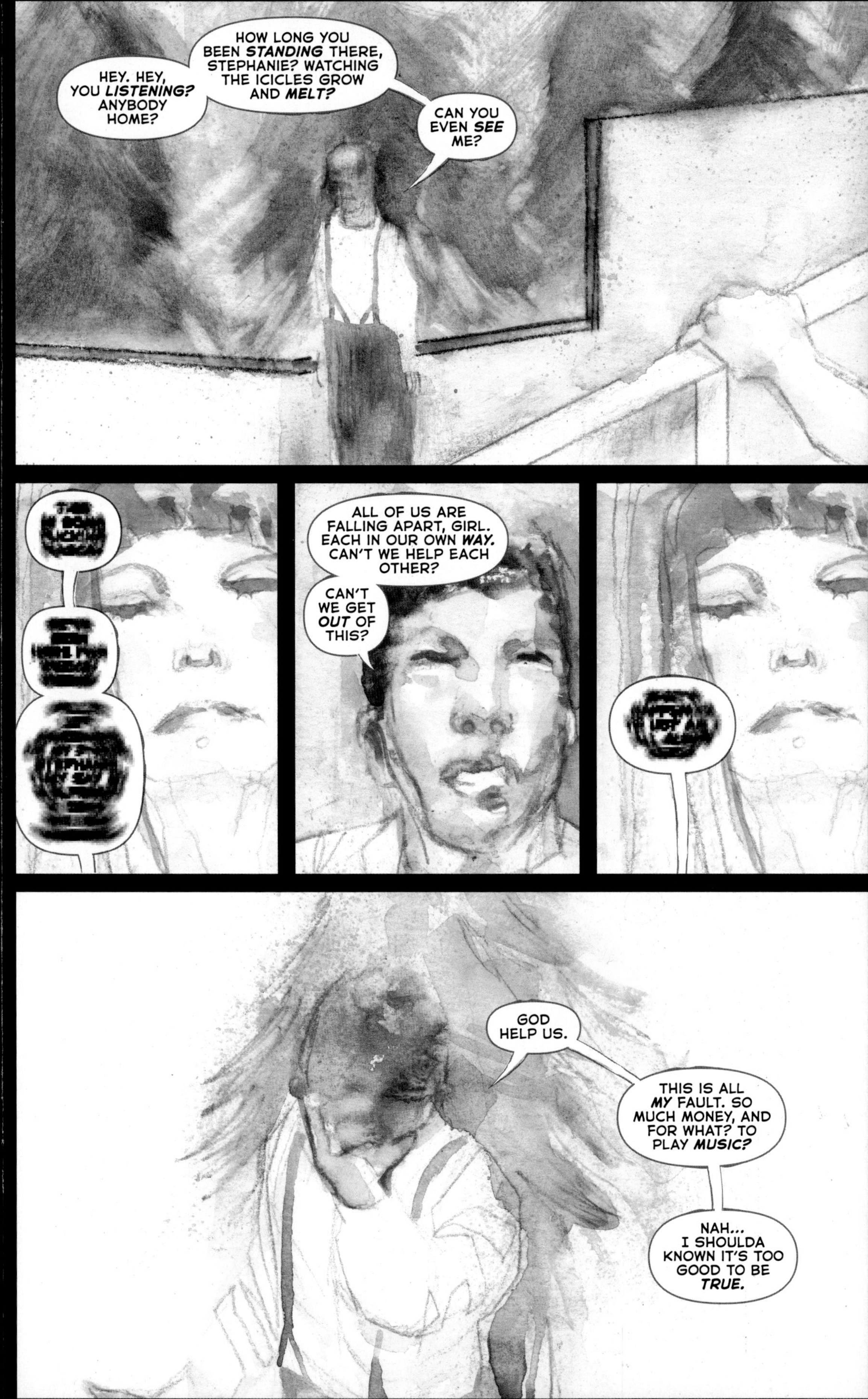
HEY. HEY, YOU LISTENING? ANYBODY HOME?
HOW LONG YOU BEEN STANDING THERE, STEPHANIE? WATCHING THE ICICLES GROW AND MELT?
CAN YOU EVEN SEE ME?
ALL OF US ARE FALLING APART, GIRL. EACH IN OUR OWN WAY. CAN'T WE HELP EACH OTHER?
CAN'T WE GET OUT OF THIS?
GOD HELP US.
THIS IS ALL MY FAULT. SO MUCH MONEY, AND FOR WHAT? TO PLAY MUSIC?
NAH... I SHOULDA KNOWN IT'S TOO GOOD TO BE TRUE.

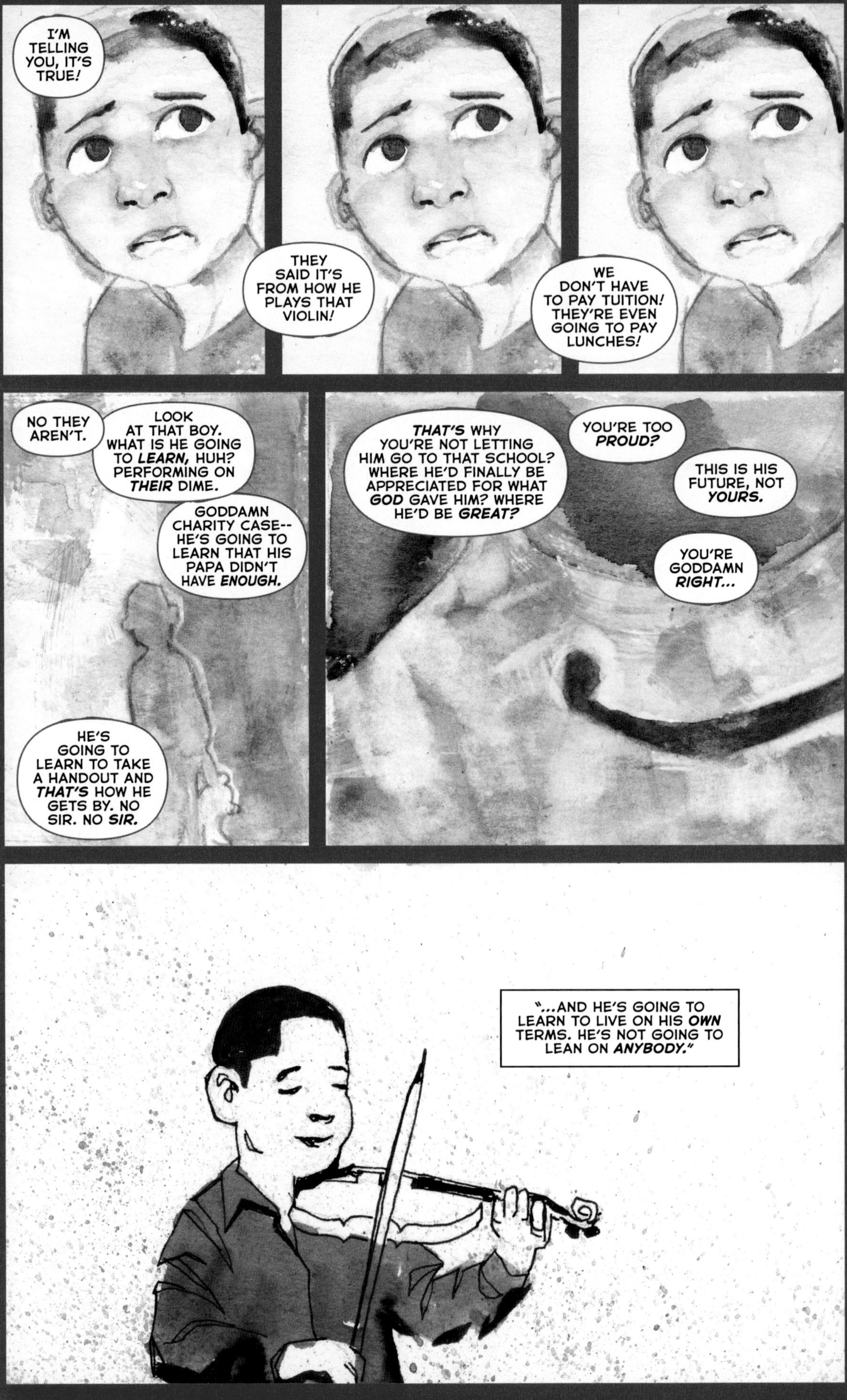

I'M TELLING YOU, IT'S TRUE!
THEY SAID IT'S FROM HOW HE PLAYS THAT VIOLIN!
WE DON'T HAVE TO PAY TUITION! THEY'RE EVEN GOING TO PAY LUNCHES!
NO THEY AREN'T.
LOOK AT THAT BOY. WHAT IS HE GOING TO LEARN, HUH? PERFORMING ON THEIR DIME.
GODDAMN CHARITY CASE-- HE'S GOING TO LEARN THAT HIS PAPA DIDN'T HAVE ENOUGH.
HE'S GOING TO LEARN TO TAKE A HANDOUT AND THAT'S HOW HE GETS BY. NO SIR. NO SIR.
THAT'S WHY YOU'RE NOT LETTING HIM GO TO THAT SCHOOL? WHERE HE'D FINALLY BE APPRECIATED FOR WHAT GOD GAVE HIM? WHERE HE'D BE GREAT?
YOU'RE TOO PROUD?
THIS IS HIS FUTURE, NOT YOURS.
YOU'RE GODDAMN RIGHT...
"...AND HE'S GOING TO LEARN TO LIVE ON HIS OWN TERMS. HE'S NOT GOING TO LEAN ON ANYBODY."

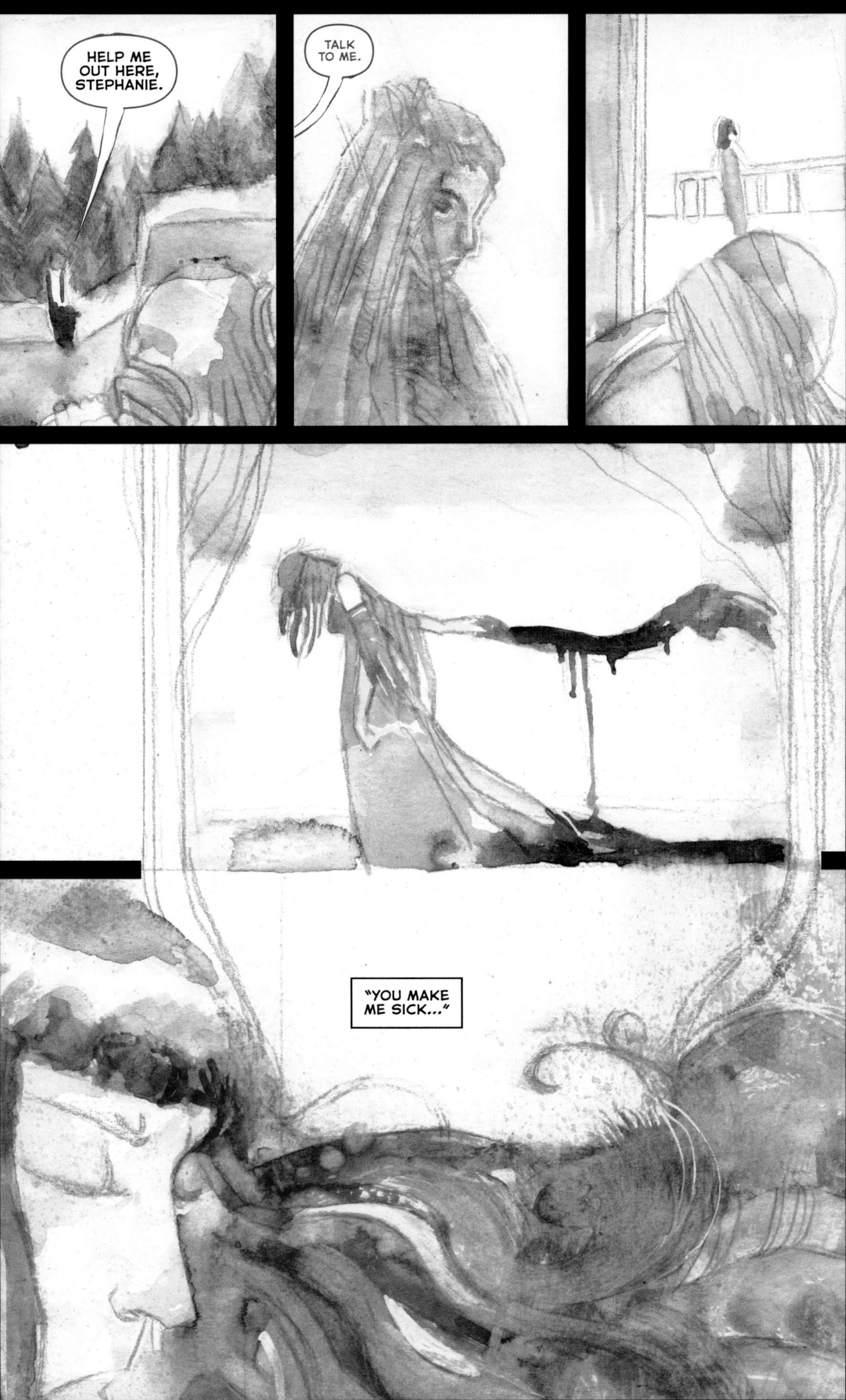
HELP ME OUT HERE, STEPHANIE.
TALK TO ME.
"YOU MAKE ME SICK..."

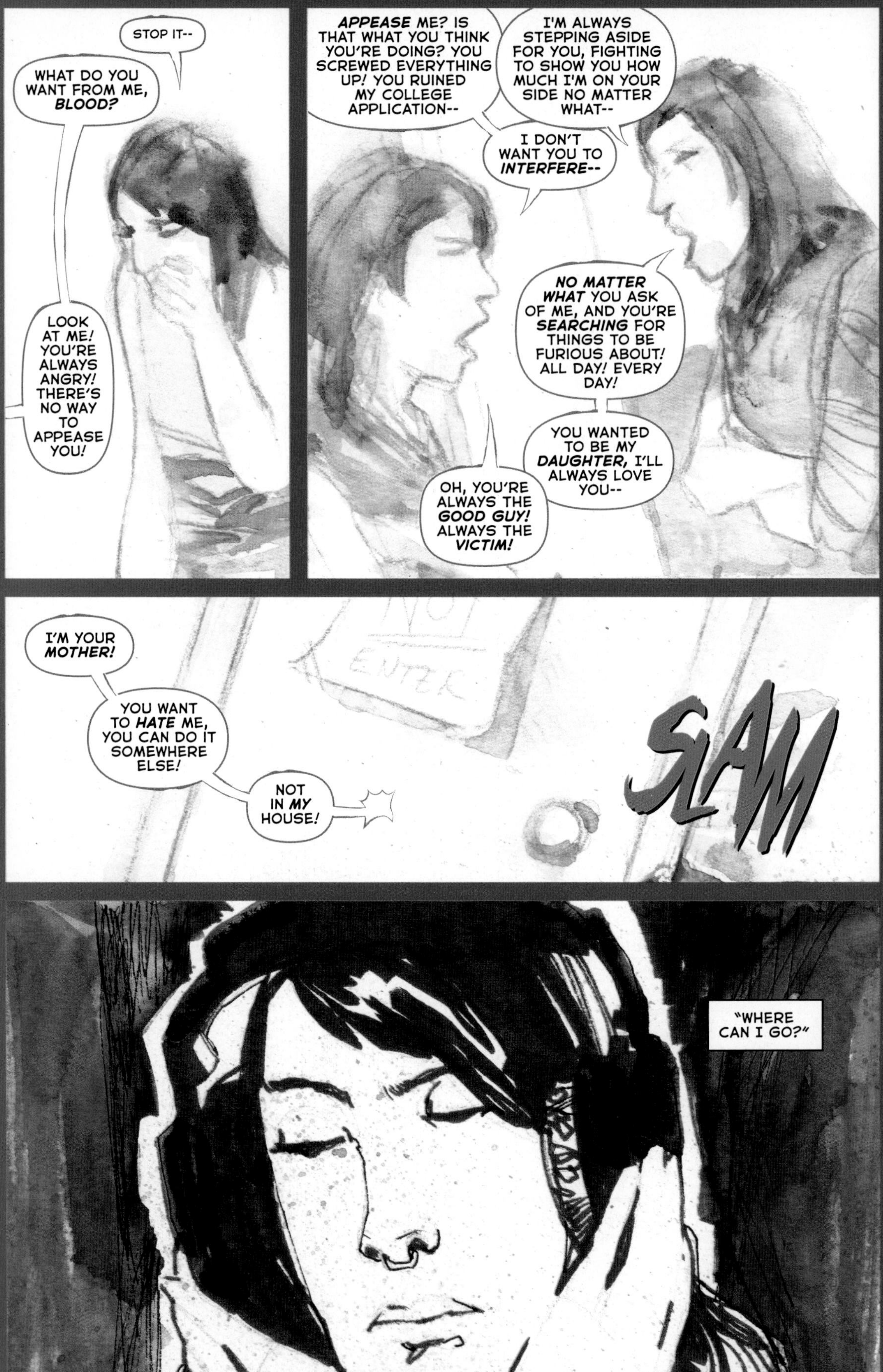

STOP IT--
WHAT DO YOU WANT FROM ME, BLOOD?
LOOK AT ME! YOU'RE ALWAYS ANGRY! THERE'S NO WAY TO APPEASE YOU!
APPEASE ME? IS THAT WHAT YOU THINK YOU'RE DOING? YOU SCREWED EVERYTHING UP! YOU RUINED MY COLLEGE APPLICATION--
I'M ALWAYS STEPPING ASIDE FOR YOU, FIGHTING TO SHOW YOU HOW MUCH I'M ON YOUR SIDE NO MATTER WHAT--
I DON'T WANT YOU TO INTERFERE--
NO MATTER WHAT YOU ASK OF ME, AND YOU'RE SEARCHING FOR THINGS TO BE FURIOUS ABOUT! ALL DAY! EVERY DAY!
YOU WANTED TO BE MY DAUGHTER, I'LL ALWAYS LOVE YOU--
OH, YOU'RE ALWAYS THE GOOD GUY! ALWAYS THE VICTIM!
I'M YOUR MOTHER!
YOU WANT TO HATE ME, YOU CAN DO IT SOMEWHERE ELSE!
NOT IN MY HOUSE!
SLAM
"WHERE CAN I GO?"

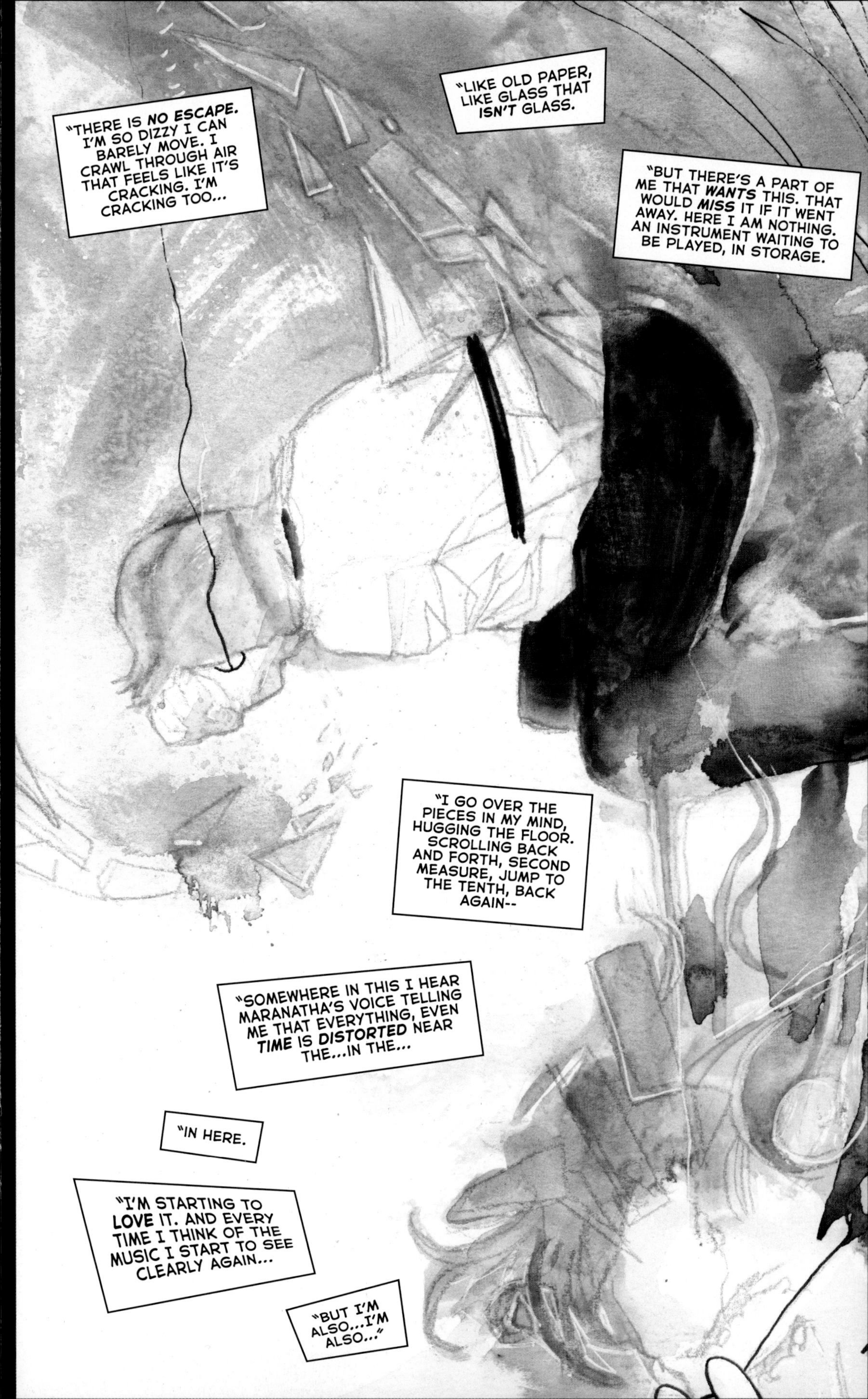
"THERE IS NO ESCAPE. I'M SO DIZZY I CAN BARELY MOVE. I CRAWL THROUGH AIR THAT FEELS LIKE IT'S CRACKING. I'M CRACKING TOO...
"LIKE OLD PAPER, LIKE GLASS THAT ISN'T GLASS.
"BUT THERE'S A PART OF ME THAT WANTS THIS. THAT WOULD MISS IT IF IT WENT AWAY. HERE I AM NOTHING. AN INSTRUMENT WAITING TO BE PLAYED, IN STORAGE.
"I GO OVER THE PIECES IN MY MIND, HUGGING THE FLOOR. SCROLLING BACK AND FORTH, SECOND MEASURE, JUMP TO THE TENTH, BACK AGAIN--
"SOMEWHERE IN THIS I HEAR MARANATHA'S VOICE TELLING ME THAT EVERYTHING, EVEN TIME IS DISTORTED NEAR THE...IN THE...
"IN HERE.
"I'M STARTING TO LOVE IT. AND EVERY TIME I THINK OF THE MUSIC I START TO SEE CLEARLY AGAIN...
"BUT I'M ALSO...I'M ALSO..."

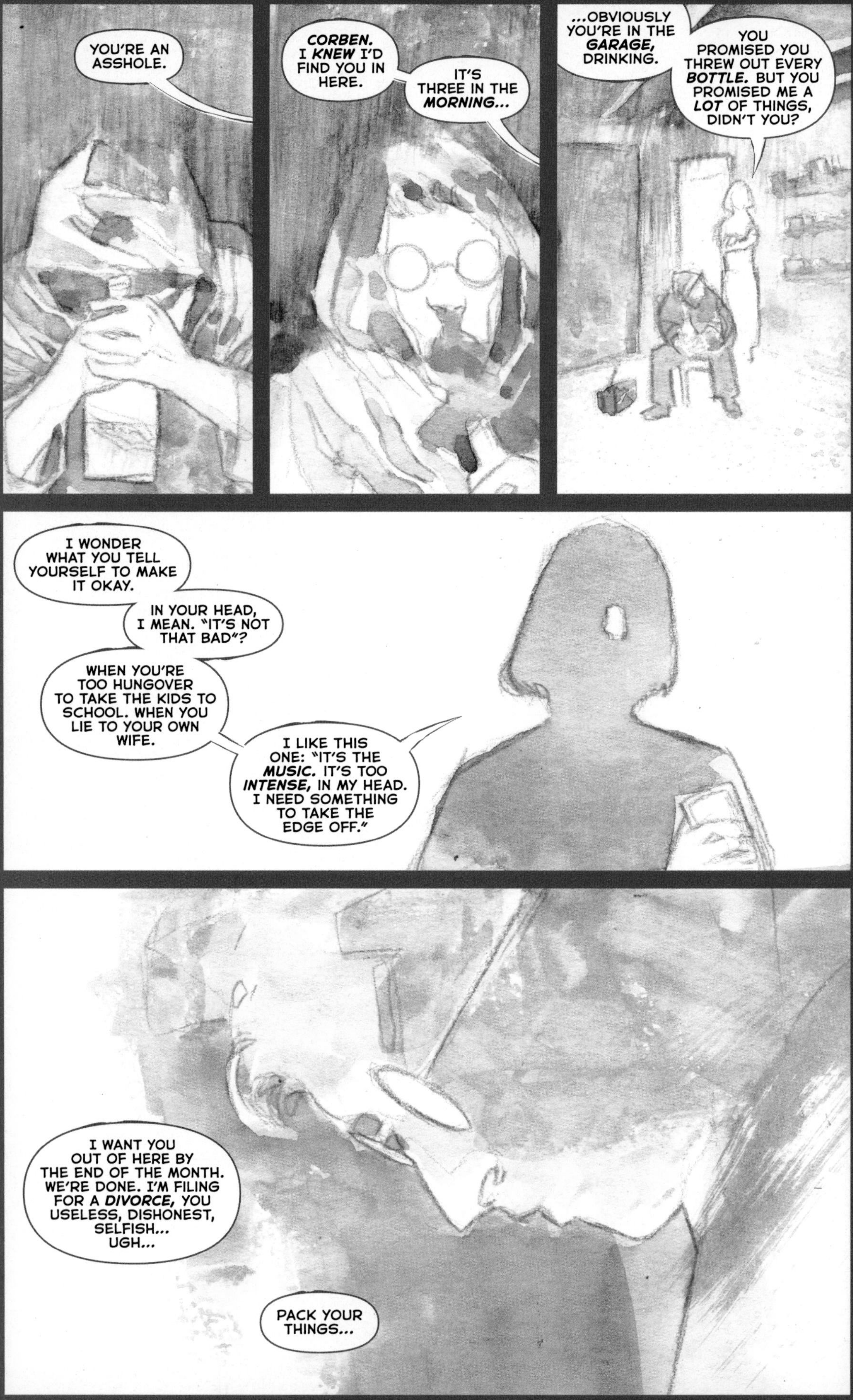
YOU'RE AN ASSHOLE.
CORBEN. I KNEW I'D FIND YOU IN HERE.
IT'S THREE IN THE MORNING...
...OBVIOUSLY YOU'RE IN THE GARAGE, DRINKING.
YOU PROMISED YOU THREW OUT EVERY BOTTLE. BUT YOU PROMISED ME A LOT OF THINGS, DIDN'T YOU?
I WONDER WHAT YOU TELL YOURSELF TO MAKE IT OKAY.
IN YOUR HEAD, I MEAN. "IT'S NOT THAT BAD"?
WHEN YOU'RE TOO HUNGOVER TO TAKE THE KIDS TO SCHOOL. WHEN YOU LIE TO YOUR OWN WIFE.
I LIKE THIS ONE: "IT'S THE MUSIC. IT'S TOO INTENSE, IN MY HEAD. I NEED SOMETHING TO TAKE THE EDGE OFF."
I WANT YOU OUT OF HERE BY THE END OF THE MONTH. WE'RE DONE. I'M FILING FOR A DIVORCE, YOU USELESS, DISHONEST, SELFISH... UGH...
PACK YOUR THINGS...

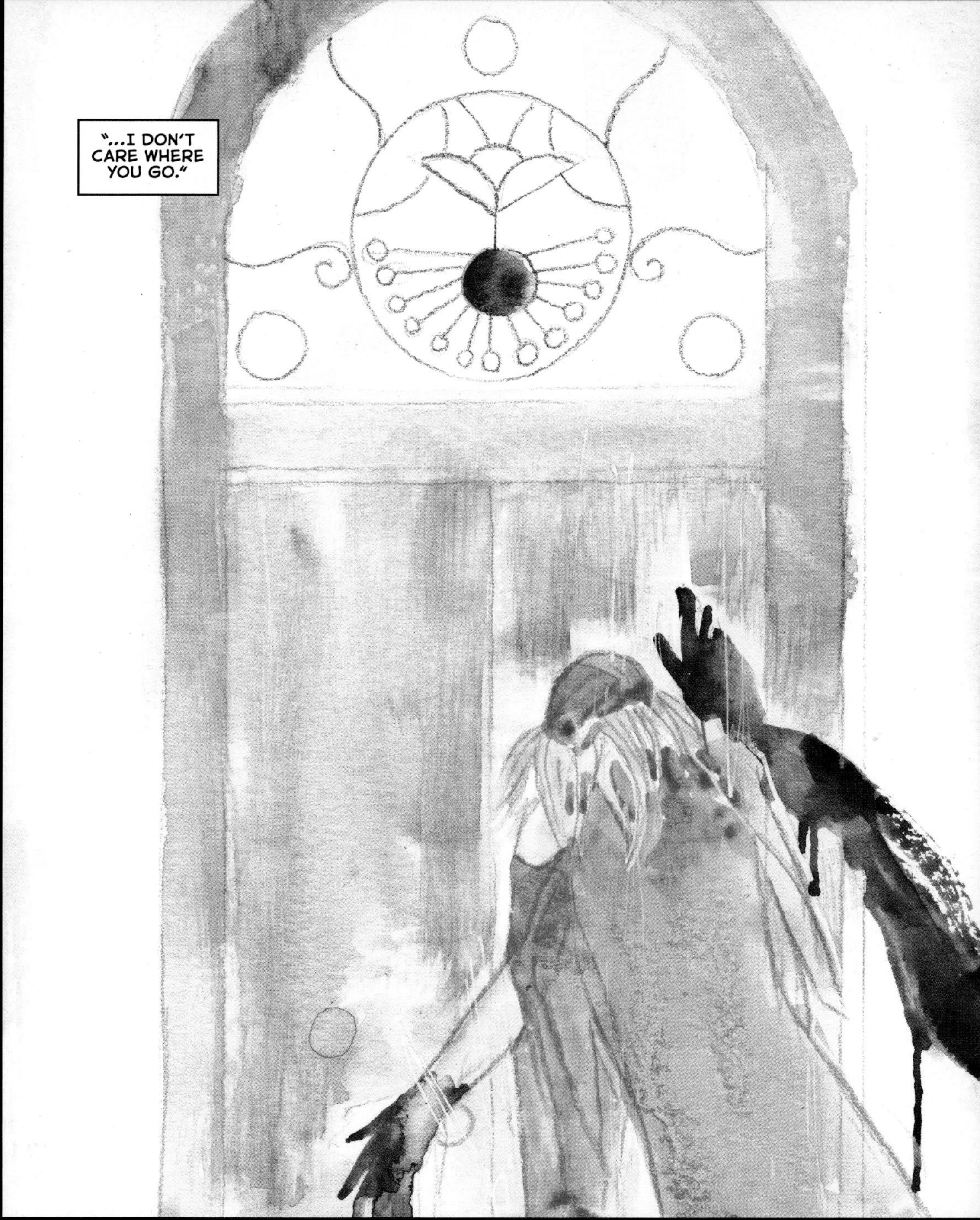
"...I DON'T CARE WHERE YOU GO."

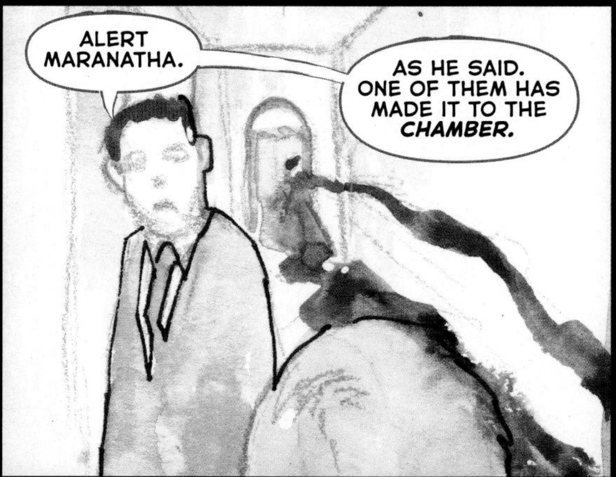
ALERT MARANATHA.
AS HE SAID. ONE OF THEM HAS MADE IT TO THE ***CHAMBER.***

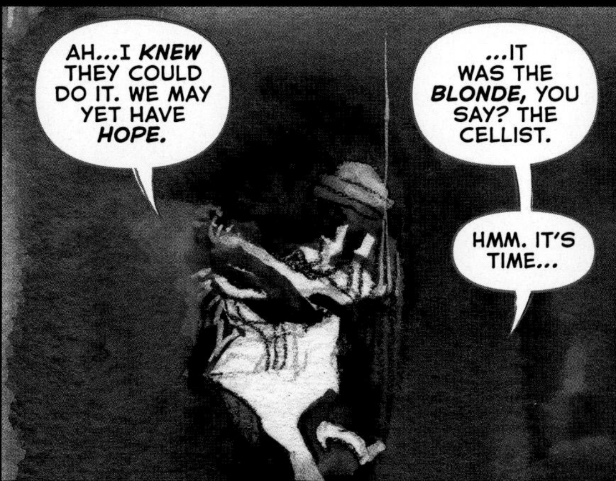
AH...I ***KNEW*** THEY COULD DO IT. WE MAY YET HAVE ***HOPE.***
...IT WAS THE ***BLONDE,*** YOU SAY? THE CELLIST.
HMM. IT'S TIME...

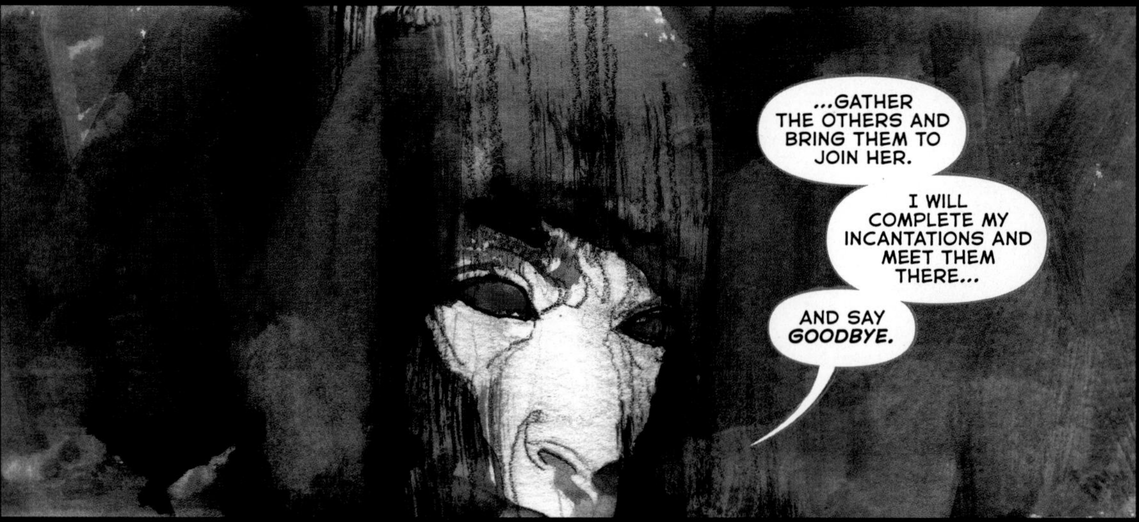
...GATHER THE OTHERS AND BRING THEM TO JOIN HER.
I WILL COMPLETE MY INCANTATIONS AND MEET THEM THERE...
AND SAY *GOODBYE.*

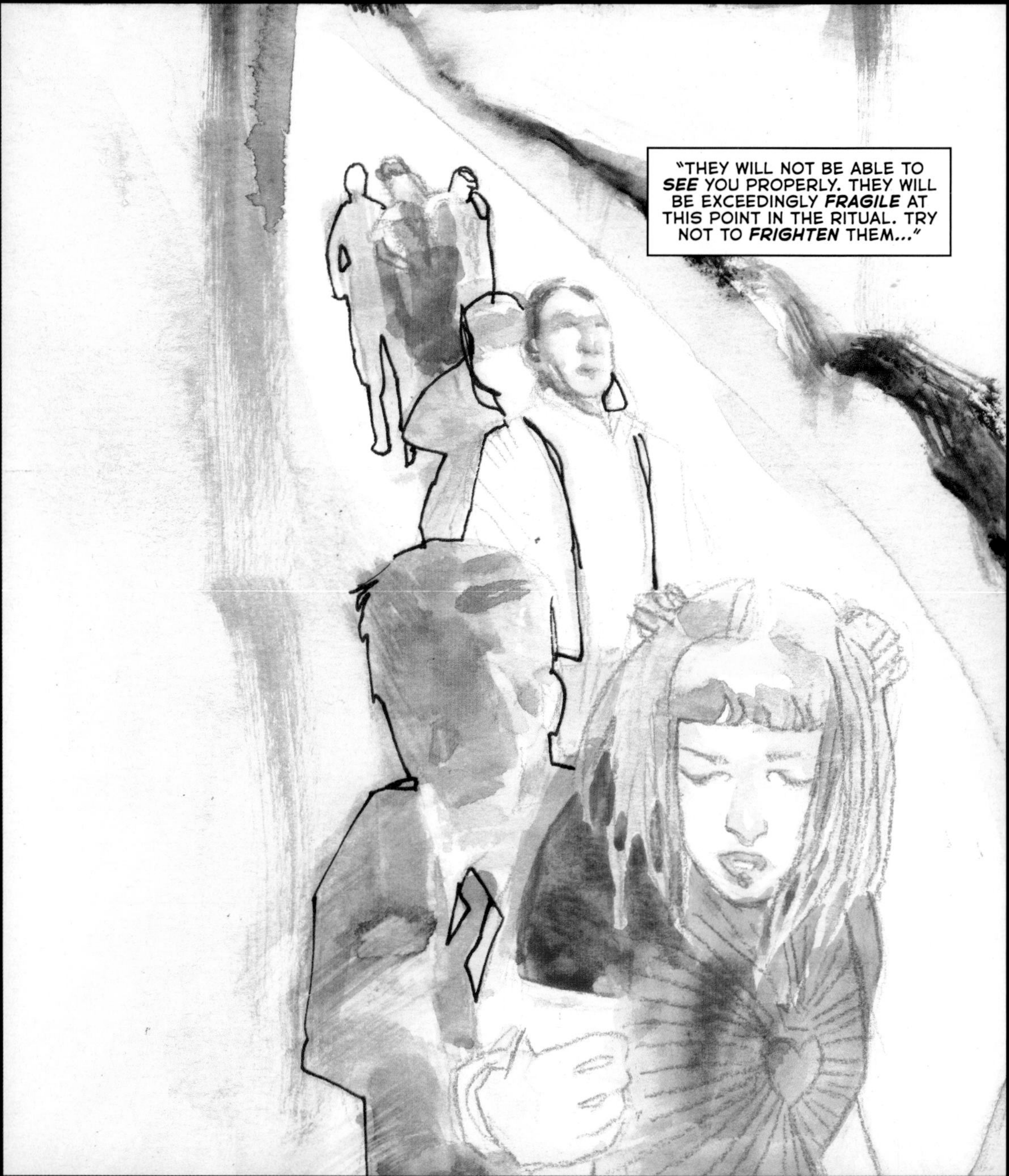
"THEY WILL NOT BE ABLE TO *SEE* YOU PROPERLY. THEY WILL BE EXCEEDINGLY *FRAGILE* AT THIS POINT IN THE RITUAL. TRY NOT TO *FRIGHTEN* THEM..."

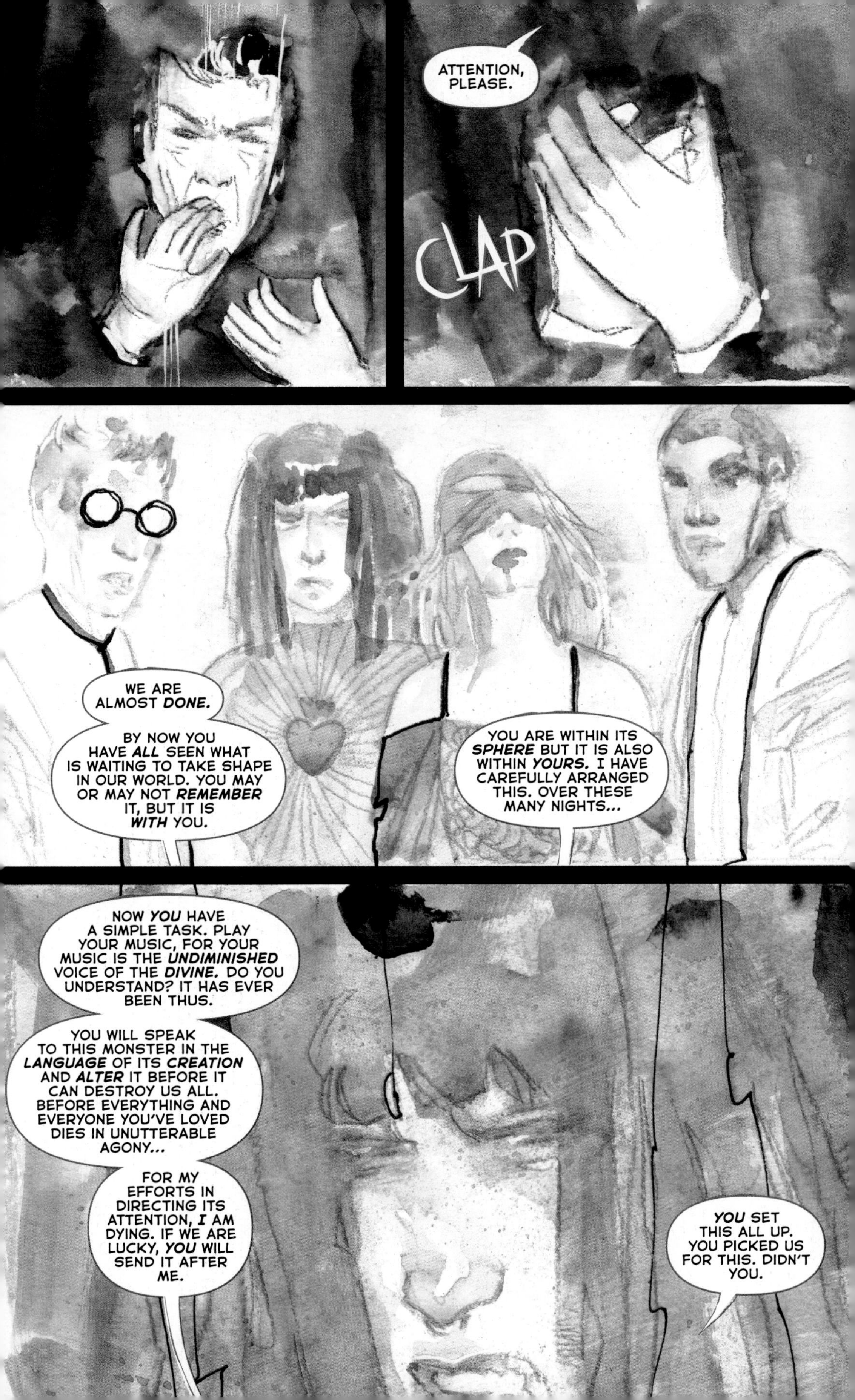
ATTENTION, PLEASE.
CLAP
WE ARE ALMOST DONE.
BY NOW YOU HAVE ALL SEEN WHAT IS WAITING TO TAKE SHAPE IN OUR WORLD. YOU MAY OR MAY NOT REMEMBER IT, BUT IT IS WITH YOU.
YOU ARE WITHIN ITS SPHERE BUT IT IS ALSO WITHIN YOURS. I HAVE CAREFULLY ARRANGED THIS. OVER THESE MANY NIGHTS...
NOW YOU HAVE A SIMPLE TASK. PLAY YOUR MUSIC, FOR YOUR MUSIC IS THE UNDIMINISHED VOICE OF THE DIVINE. DO YOU UNDERSTAND? IT HAS EVER BEEN THUS.
YOU WILL SPEAK TO THIS MONSTER IN THE LANGUAGE OF ITS CREATION AND ALTER IT BEFORE IT CAN DESTROY US ALL. BEFORE EVERYTHING AND EVERYONE YOU'VE LOVED DIES IN UNUTTERABLE AGONY...
FOR MY EFFORTS IN DIRECTING ITS ATTENTION, I AM DYING. IF WE ARE LUCKY, YOU WILL SEND IT AFTER ME.
YOU SET THIS ALL UP. YOU PICKED US FOR THIS. DIDN'T YOU.

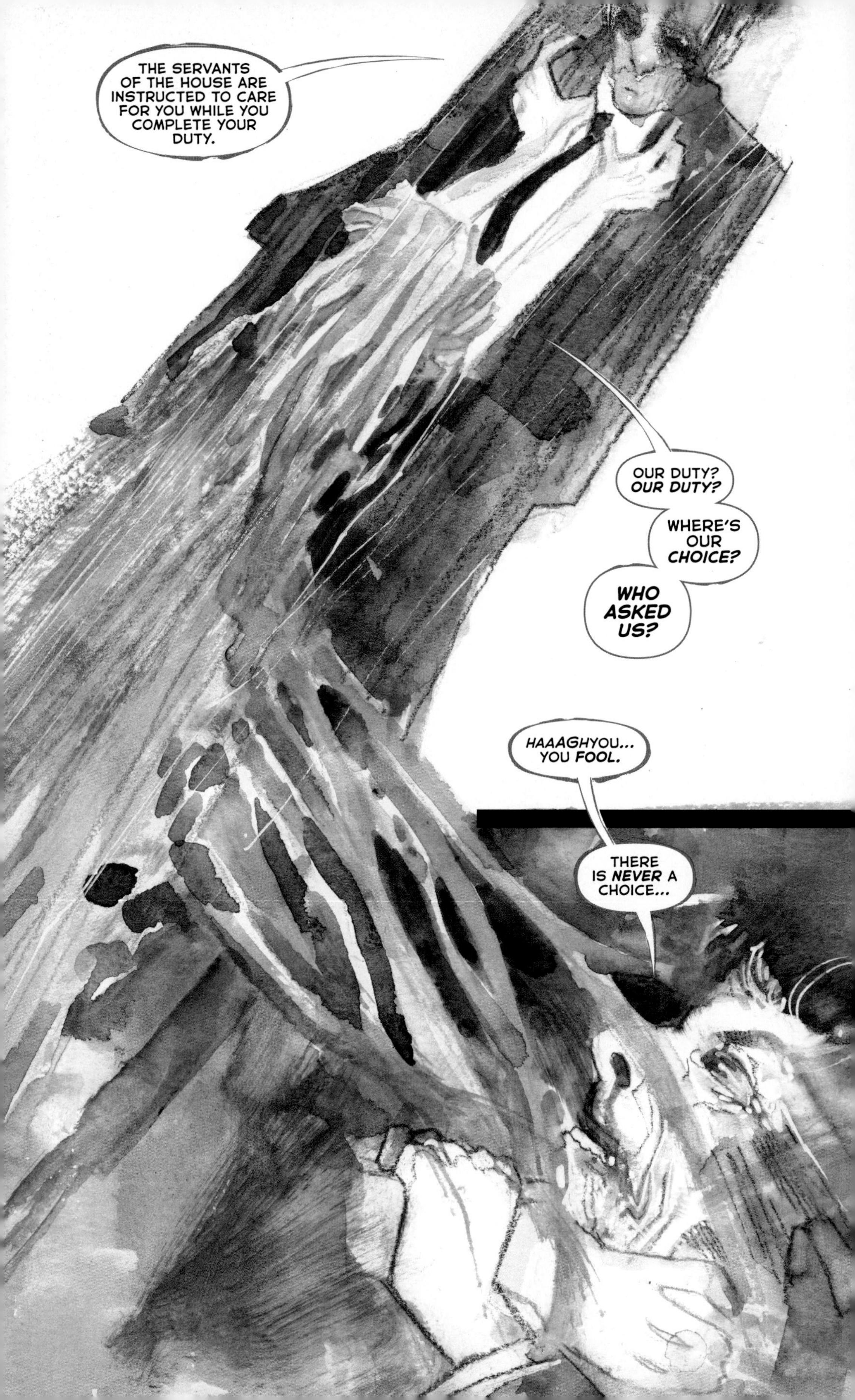
THE SERVANTS OF THE HOUSE ARE INSTRUCTED TO CARE FOR YOU WHILE YOU COMPLETE YOUR DUTY.
OUR DUTY? *OUR DUTY?*
WHERE'S OUR *CHOICE?*
WHO ASKED US?
HAAAGHYOU... YOU ***FOOL.***
THERE IS ***NEVER*** A CHOICE...

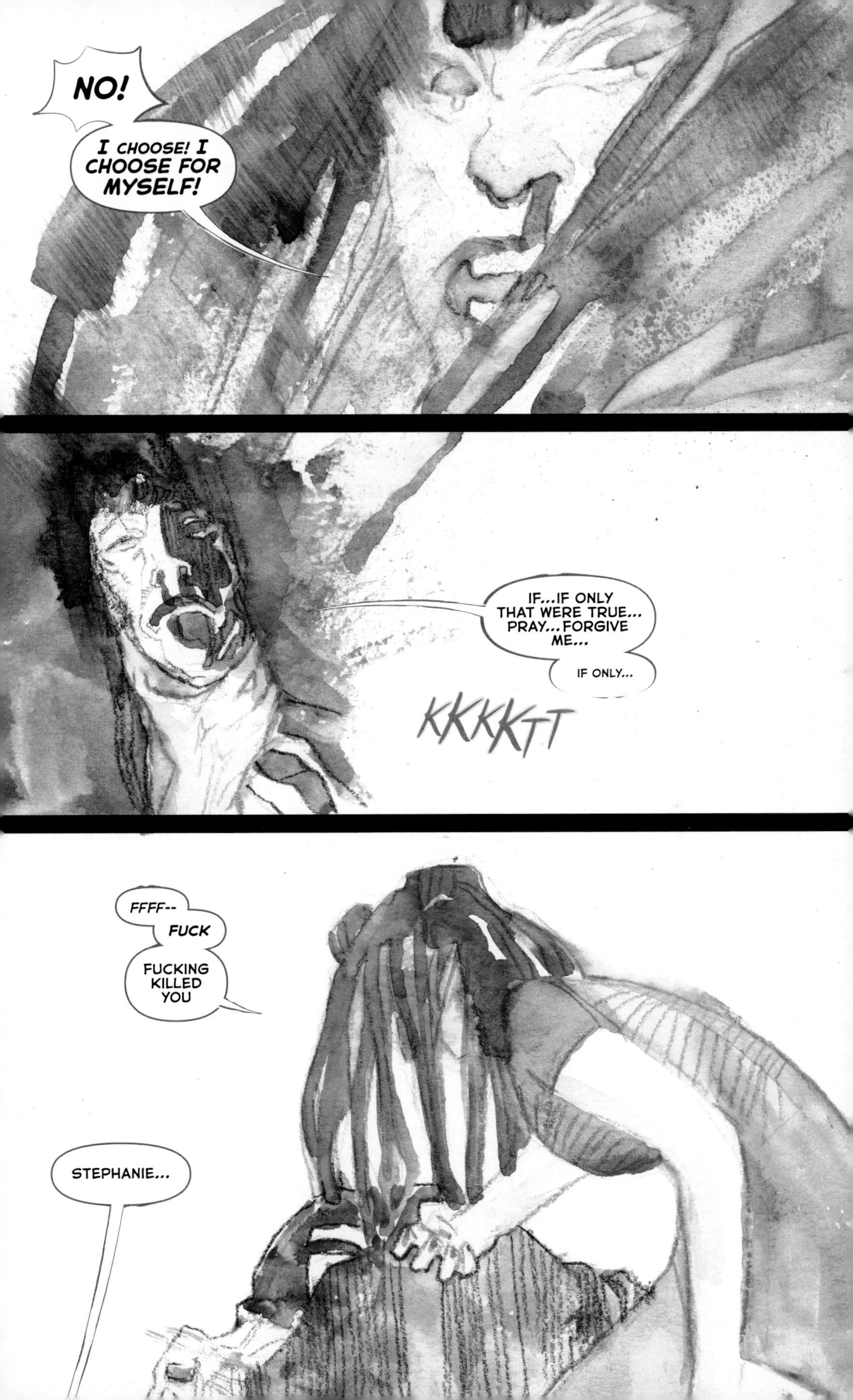
NO!
I CHOOSE! I CHOOSE FOR MYSELF!
IF...IF ONLY THAT WERE TRUE... PRAY...FORGIVE ME...
IF ONLY...
KKKKTT
FFFF--
FUCK
FUCKING KILLED YOU
STEPHANIE...

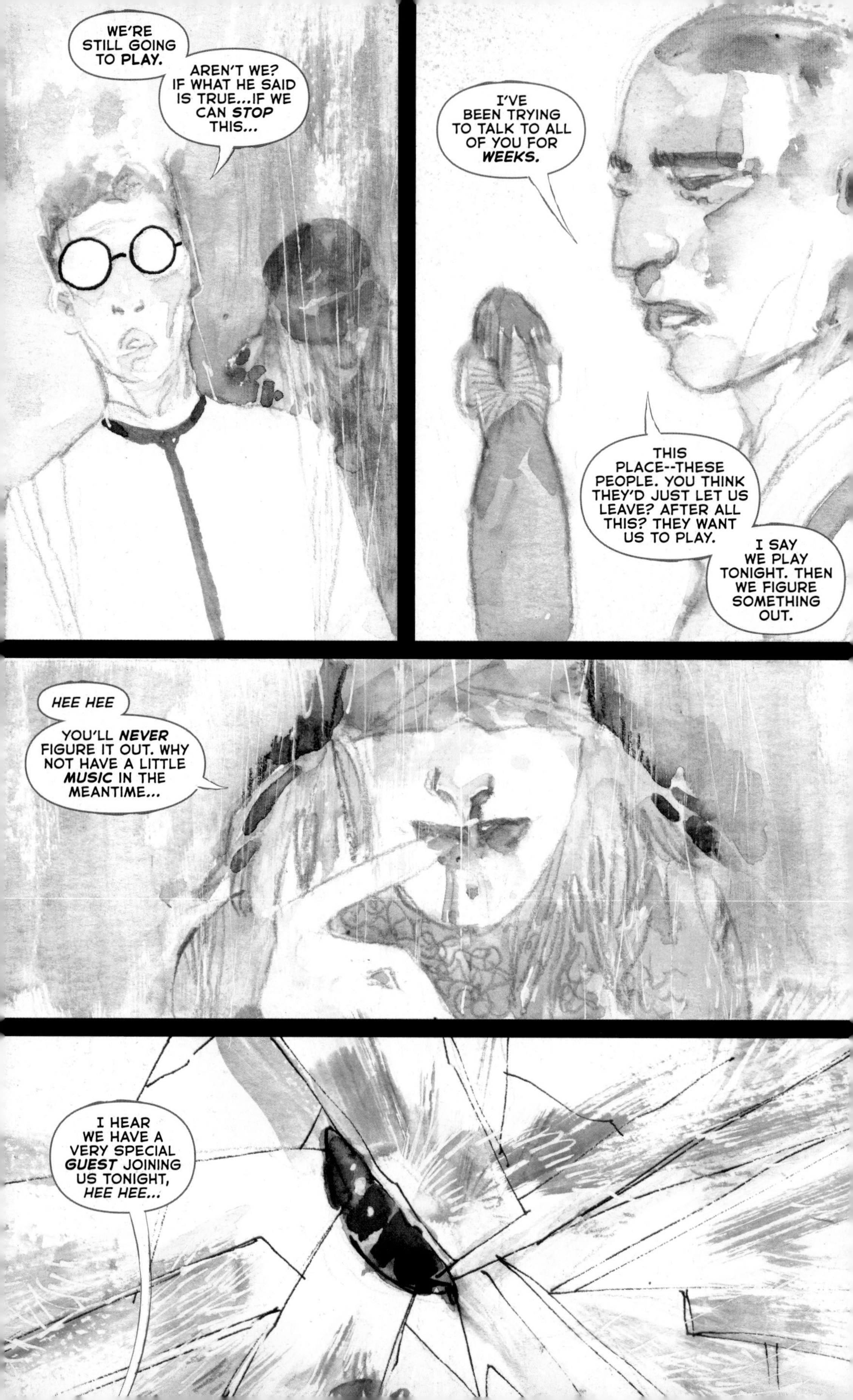
WE'RE STILL GOING TO PLAY.
AREN'T WE? IF WHAT HE SAID IS TRUE...IF WE CAN STOP THIS...
I'VE BEEN TRYING TO TALK TO ALL OF YOU FOR WEEKS.
THIS PLACE--THESE PEOPLE. YOU THINK THEY'D JUST LET US LEAVE? AFTER ALL THIS? THEY WANT US TO PLAY.
I SAY WE PLAY TONIGHT. THEN WE FIGURE SOMETHING OUT.
HEE HEE
YOU'LL NEVER FIGURE IT OUT. WHY NOT HAVE A LITTLE MUSIC IN THE MEANTIME...
I HEAR WE HAVE A VERY SPECIAL GUEST JOINING US TONIGHT, HEE HEE...

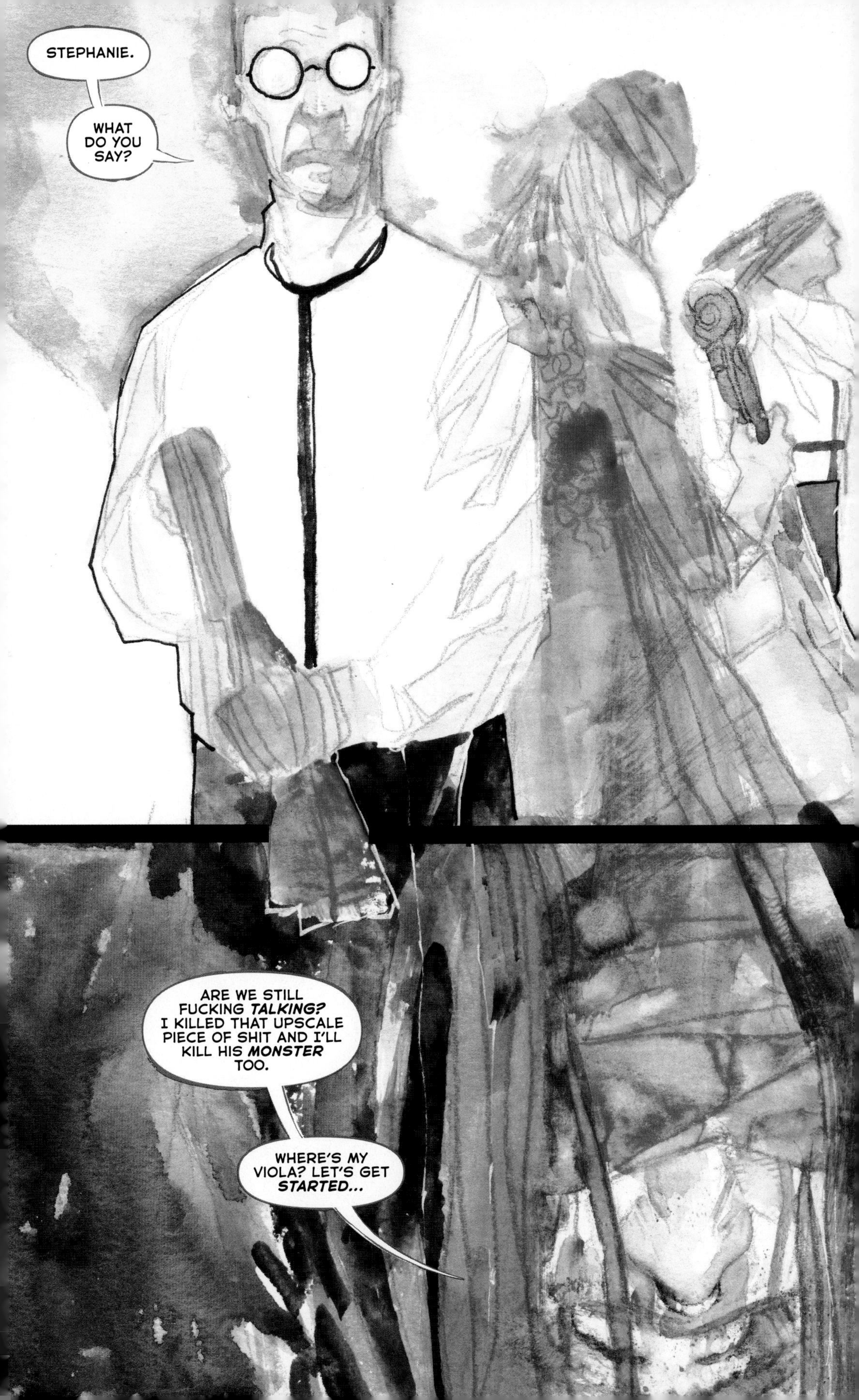
STEPHANIE.
WHAT DO YOU SAY?
ARE WE STILL FUCKING *TALKING?* I KILLED THAT UPSCALE PIECE OF SHIT AND I'LL KILL HIS *MONSTER* TOO.
WHERE'S MY VIOLA? LET'S GET *STARTED...*

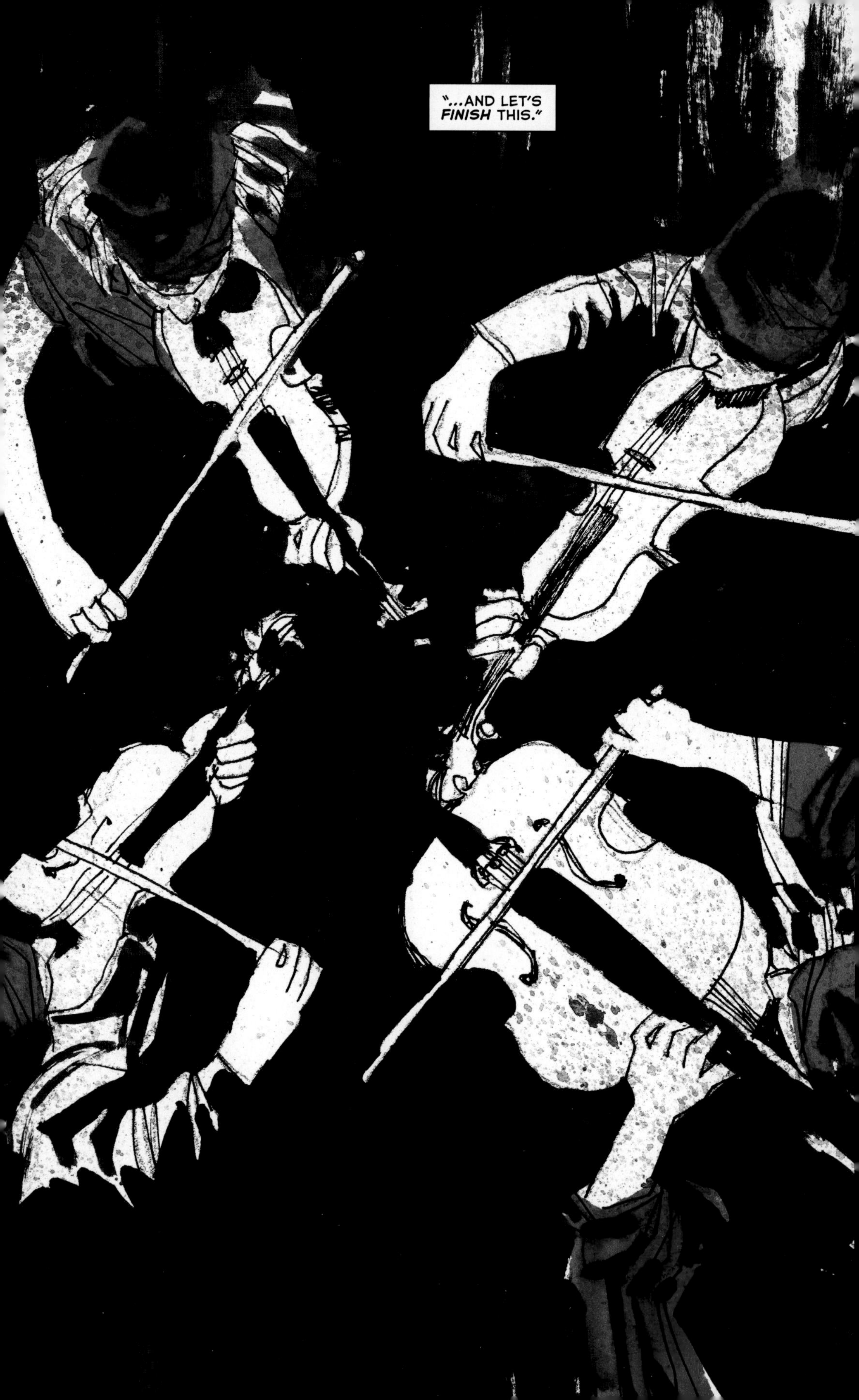
"...AND LET'S FINISH THIS."

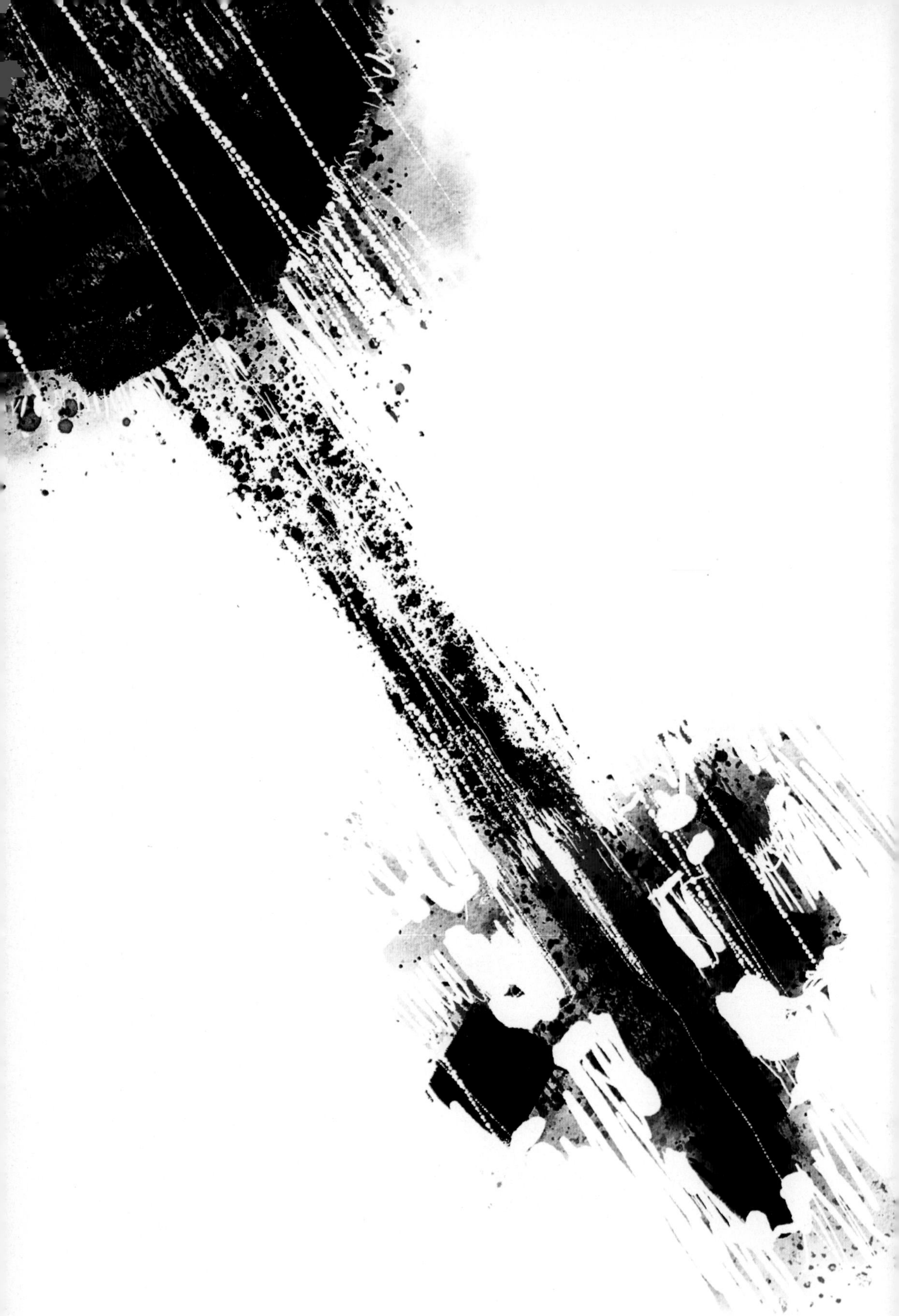

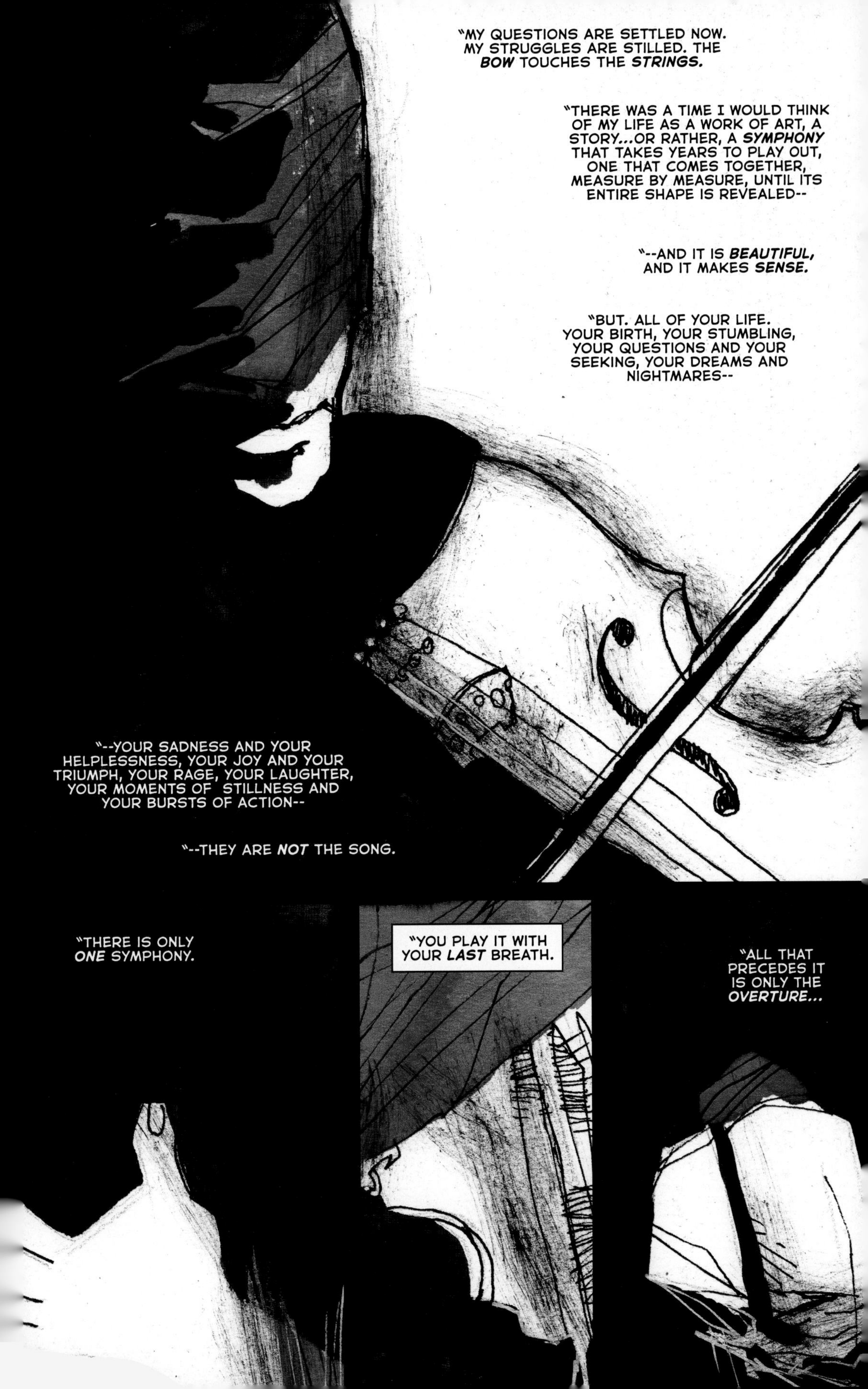
"MY QUESTIONS ARE SETTLED NOW. MY STRUGGLES ARE STILLED. THE BOW TOUCHES THE STRINGS.
"THERE WAS A TIME I WOULD THINK OF MY LIFE AS A WORK OF ART, A STORY...OR RATHER, A SYMPHONY THAT TAKES YEARS TO PLAY OUT, ONE THAT COMES TOGETHER, MEASURE BY MEASURE, UNTIL ITS ENTIRE SHAPE IS REVEALED--
"--AND IT IS BEAUTIFUL, AND IT MAKES SENSE.
"BUT. ALL OF YOUR LIFE. YOUR BIRTH, YOUR STUMBLING, YOUR QUESTIONS AND YOUR SEEKING, YOUR DREAMS AND NIGHTMARES--
"--YOUR SADNESS AND YOUR HELPLESSNESS, YOUR JOY AND YOUR TRIUMPH, YOUR RAGE, YOUR LAUGHTER, YOUR MOMENTS OF STILLNESS AND YOUR BURSTS OF ACTION--
"--THEY ARE NOT THE SONG.
"THERE IS ONLY ONE SYMPHONY.
"YOU PLAY IT WITH YOUR LAST BREATH.
"ALL THAT PRECEDES IT IS ONLY THE OVERTURE...

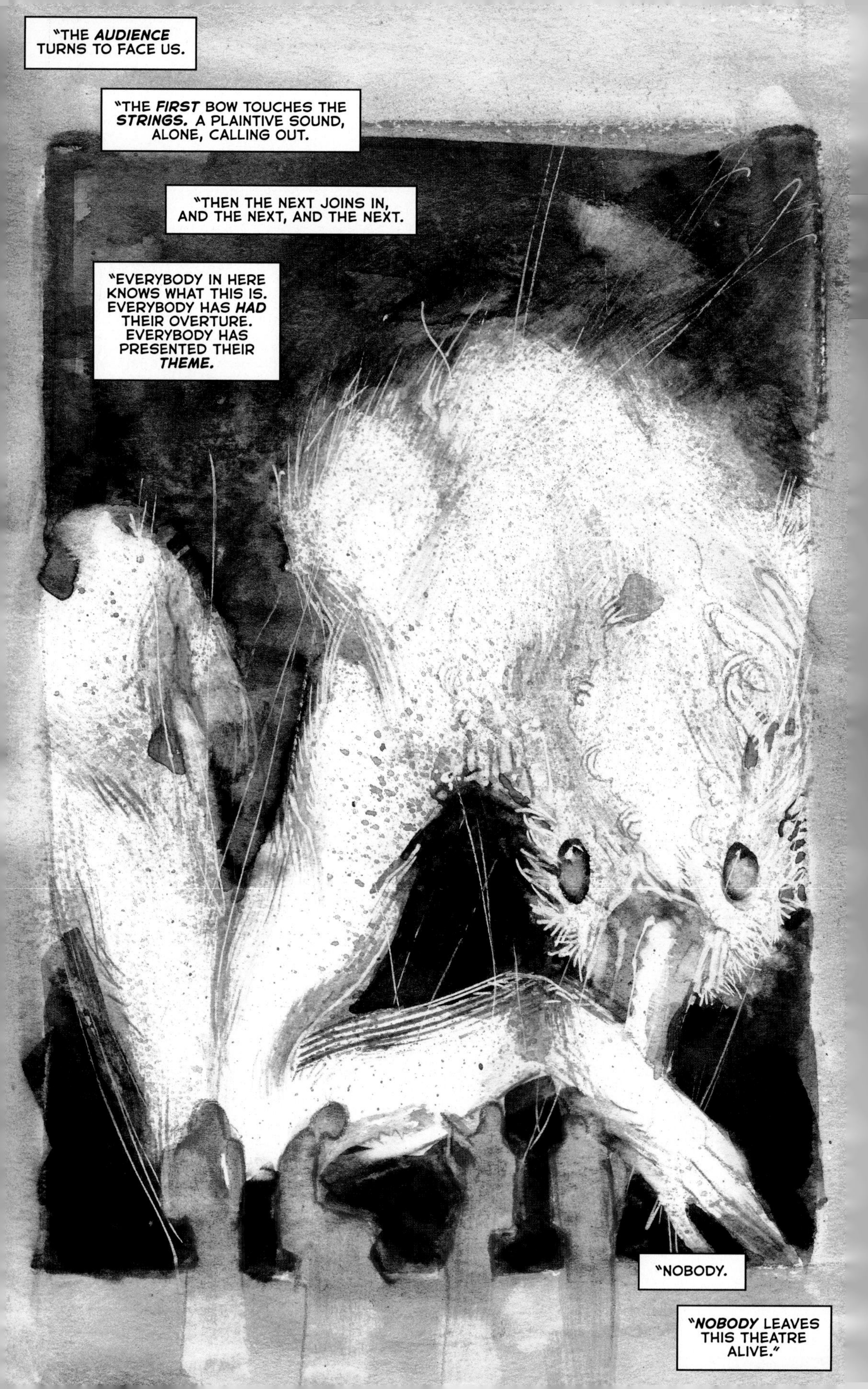
"THE *AUDIENCE* TURNS TO FACE US.
"THE *FIRST* BOW TOUCHES THE *STRINGS.* A PLAINTIVE SOUND, ALONE, CALLING OUT.
"THEN THE NEXT JOINS IN, AND THE NEXT, AND THE NEXT.
"EVERYBODY IN HERE KNOWS WHAT THIS IS. EVERYBODY HAS *HAD* THEIR OVERTURE. EVERYBODY HAS PRESENTED THEIR *THEME.*
"NOBODY.
"*NOBODY* LEAVES THIS THEATRE ALIVE."

SYMPHONY

PART SIX:
MARANA THA

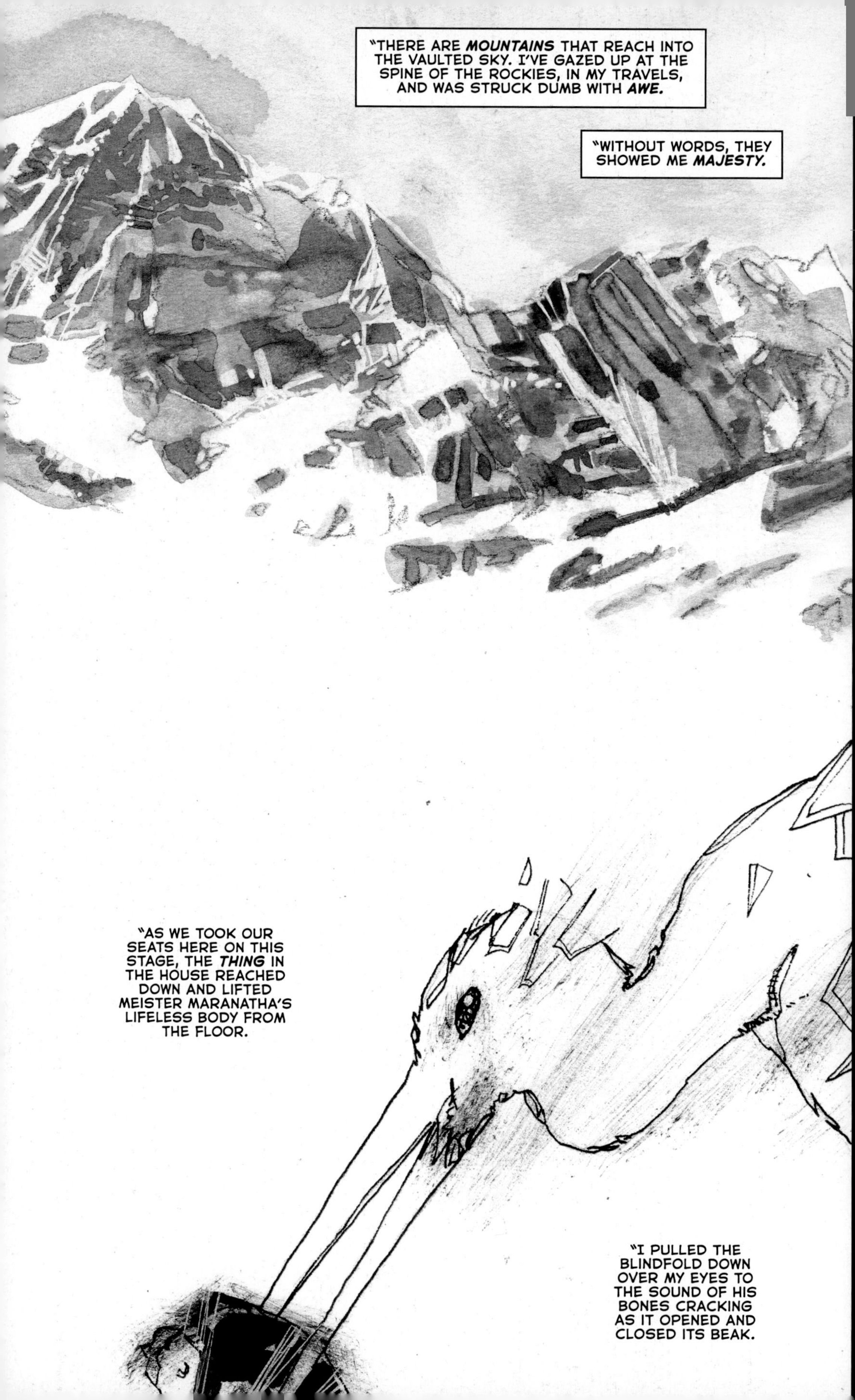
"THERE ARE MOUNTAINS THAT REACH INTO THE VAULTED SKY. I'VE GAZED UP AT THE SPINE OF THE ROCKIES, IN MY TRAVELS, AND WAS STRUCK DUMB WITH AWE.
"WITHOUT WORDS, THEY SHOWED ME MAJESTY.
"AS WE TOOK OUR SEATS HERE ON THIS STAGE, THE THING IN THE HOUSE REACHED DOWN AND LIFTED MEISTER MARANATHA'S LIFELESS BODY FROM THE FLOOR.
"I PULLED THE BLINDFOLD DOWN OVER MY EYES TO THE SOUND OF HIS BONES CRACKING AS IT OPENED AND CLOSED ITS BEAK.

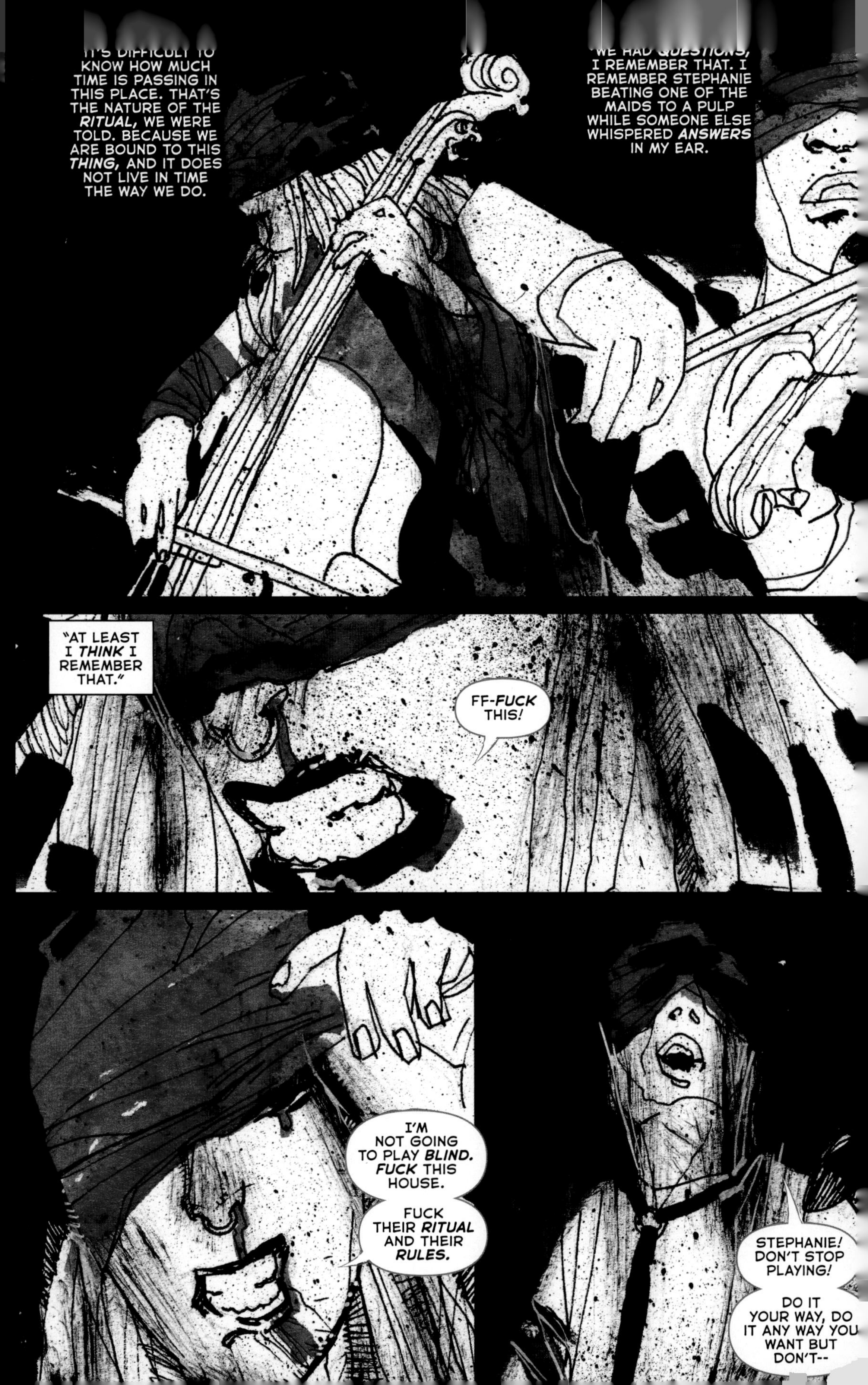
IT'S DIFFICULT TO KNOW HOW MUCH TIME IS PASSING IN THIS PLACE. THAT'S THE NATURE OF THE *RITUAL,* WE WERE TOLD. BECAUSE WE ARE BOUND TO THIS *THING,* AND IT DOES NOT LIVE IN TIME THE WAY WE DO.
"WE HAD *QUESTIONS,* I REMEMBER THAT. I REMEMBER STEPHANIE BEATING ONE OF THE MAIDS TO A PULP WHILE SOMEONE ELSE WHISPERED *ANSWERS* IN MY EAR.
"AT LEAST I *THINK* I REMEMBER THAT."
FF-*FUCK* THIS!
I'M NOT GOING TO PLAY *BLIND. FUCK* THIS HOUSE.
FUCK THEIR *RITUAL* AND THEIR *RULES.*
STEPHANIE! DON'T STOP PLAYING!
DO IT YOUR WAY, DO IT ANY WAY YOU WANT BUT DON'T--

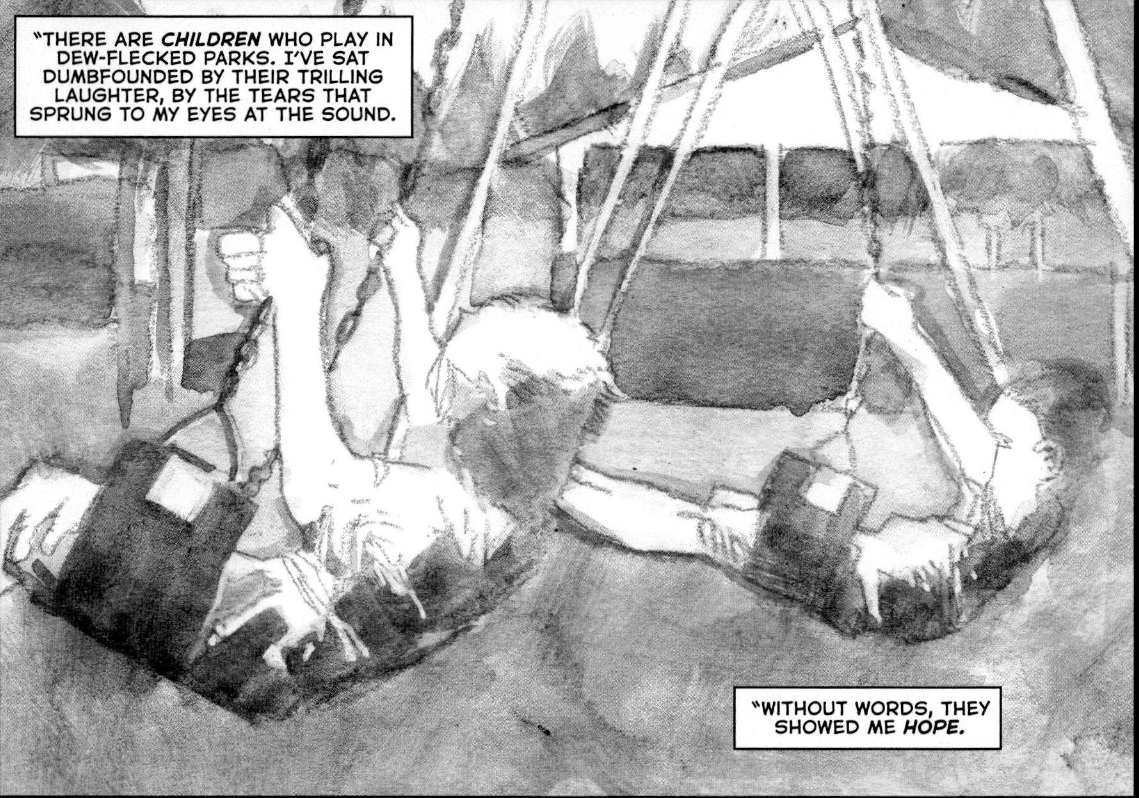
"THERE ARE *CHILDREN* WHO PLAY IN DEW-FLECKED PARKS. I'VE SAT DUMBFOUNDED BY THEIR TRILLING LAUGHTER, BY THE TEARS THAT SPRUNG TO MY EYES AT THE SOUND.
"WITHOUT WORDS, THEY SHOWED ME *HOPE.*

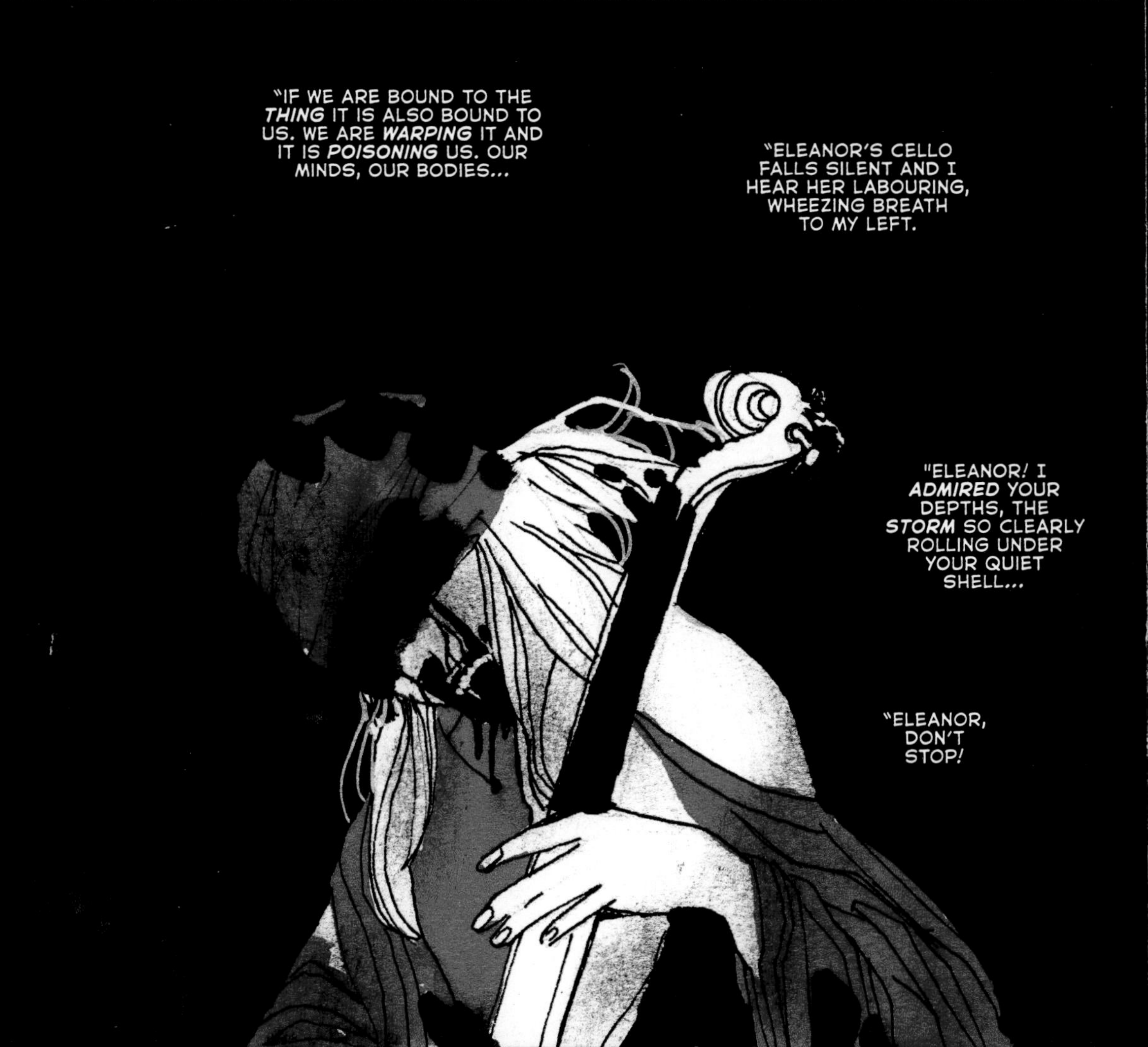
"IF WE ARE BOUND TO THE *THING* IT IS ALSO BOUND TO US. WE ARE *WARPING* IT AND IT IS *POISONING* US. OUR MINDS, OUR BODIES...
"ELEANOR'S CELLO FALLS SILENT AND I HEAR HER LABOURING, WHEEZING BREATH TO MY LEFT.
"ELEANOR! I *ADMIRED* YOUR DEPTHS, THE *STORM* SO CLEARLY ROLLING UNDER YOUR QUIET SHELL...
"ELEANOR, DON'T STOP!

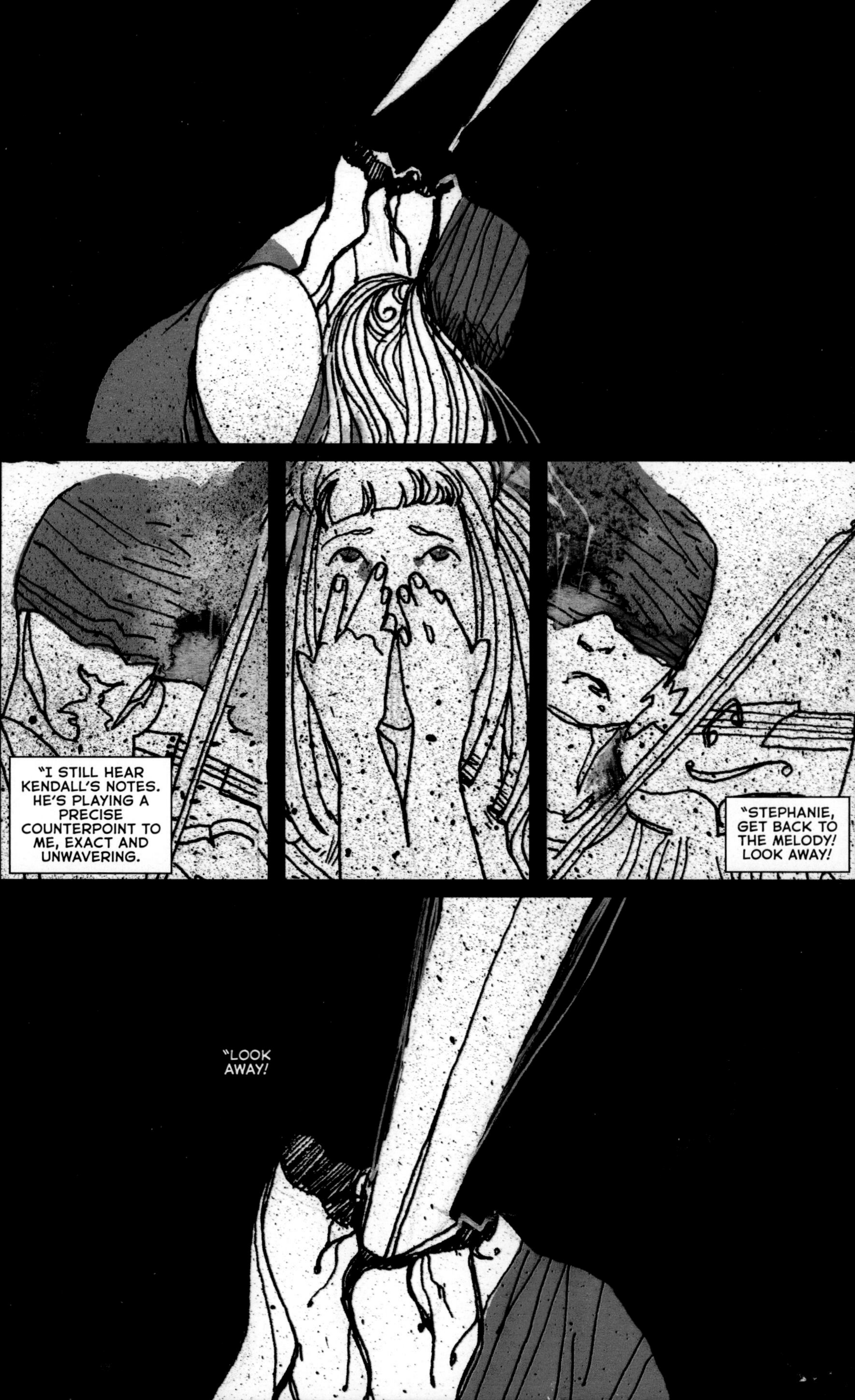
"I STILL HEAR KENDALL'S NOTES. HE'S PLAYING A PRECISE COUNTERPOINT TO ME, EXACT AND UNWAVERING.
"STEPHANIE, GET BACK TO THE MELODY! LOOK AWAY!
"LOOK AWAY!

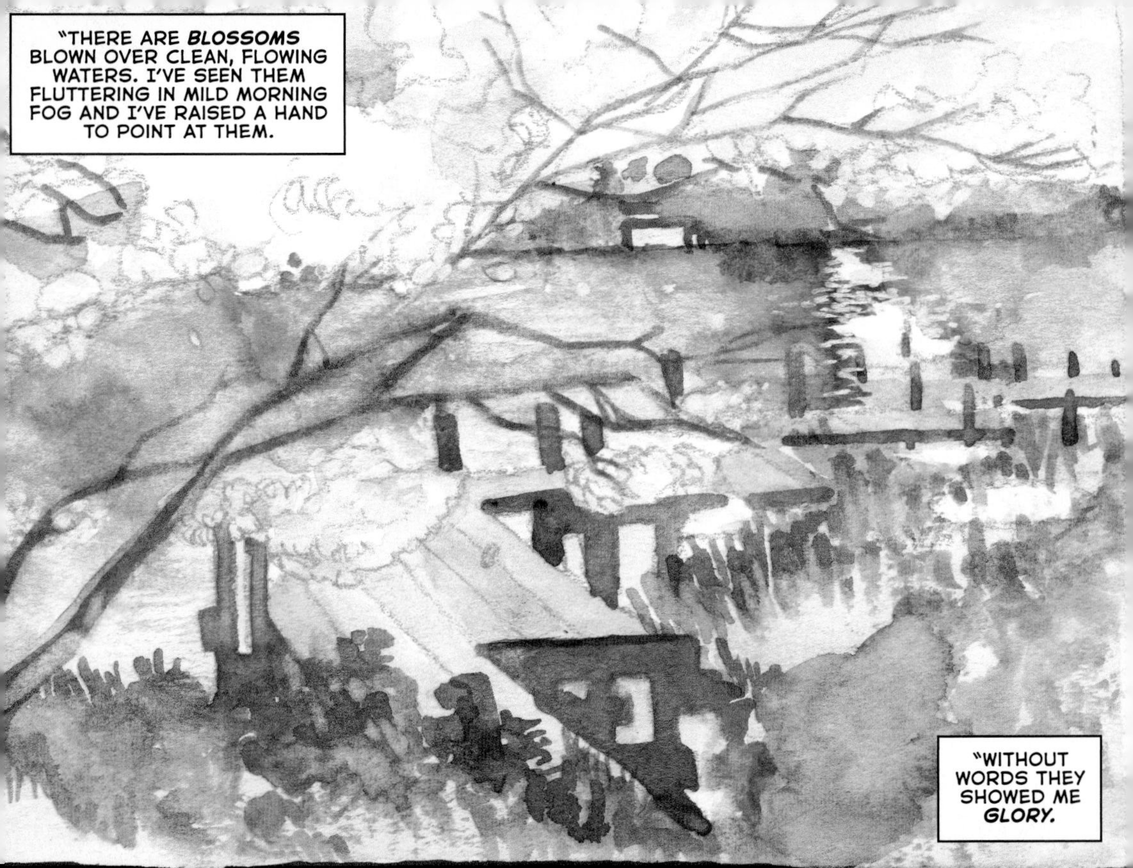
"THERE ARE *BLOSSOMS* BLOWN OVER CLEAN, FLOWING WATERS. I'VE SEEN THEM FLUTTERING IN MILD MORNING FOG AND I'VE RAISED A HAND TO POINT AT THEM.
"WITHOUT WORDS THEY SHOWED ME *GLORY.*

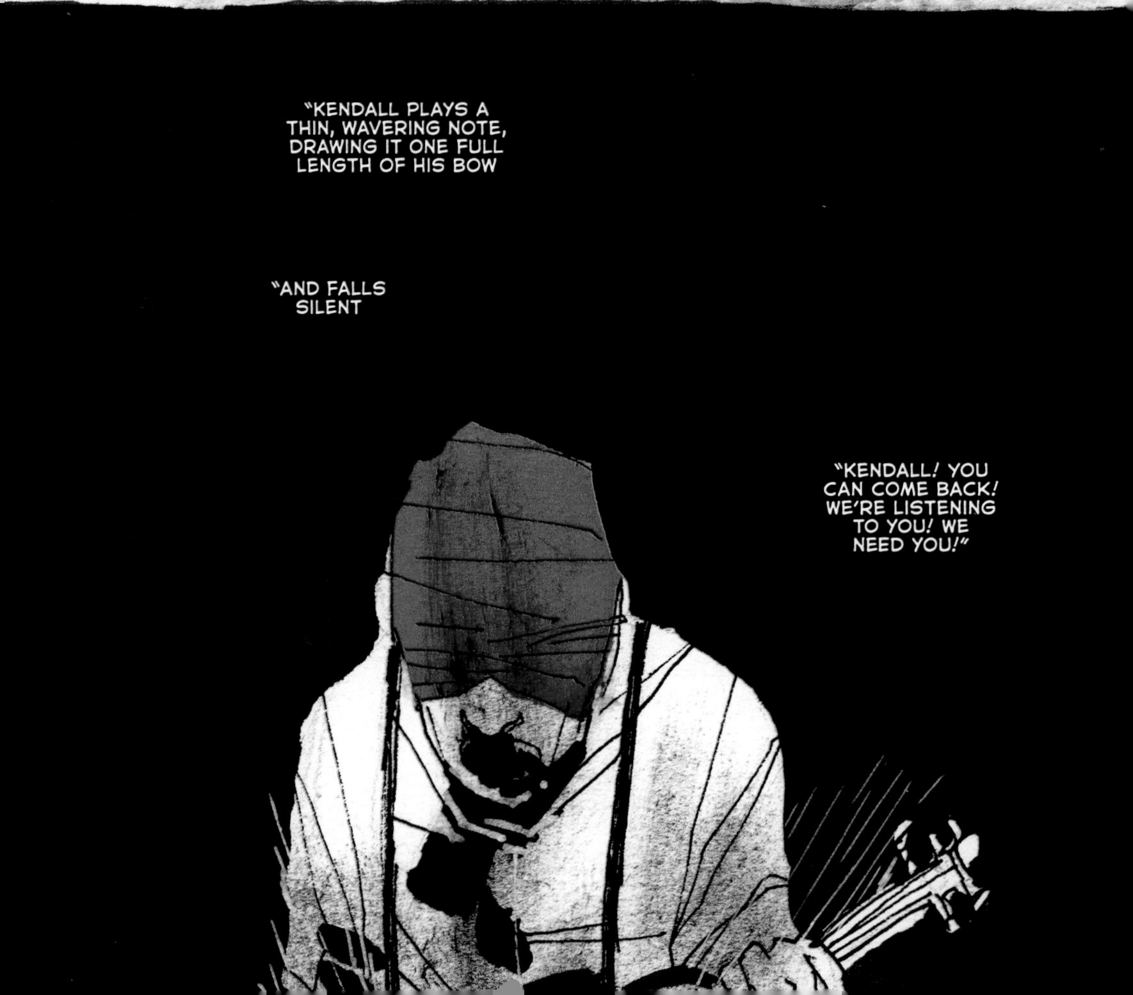
"KENDALL PLAYS A THIN, WAVERING NOTE, DRAWING IT ONE FULL LENGTH OF HIS BOW
"AND FALLS SILENT
"KENDALL! YOU CAN COME BACK! WE'RE LISTENING TO YOU! WE NEED YOU!"

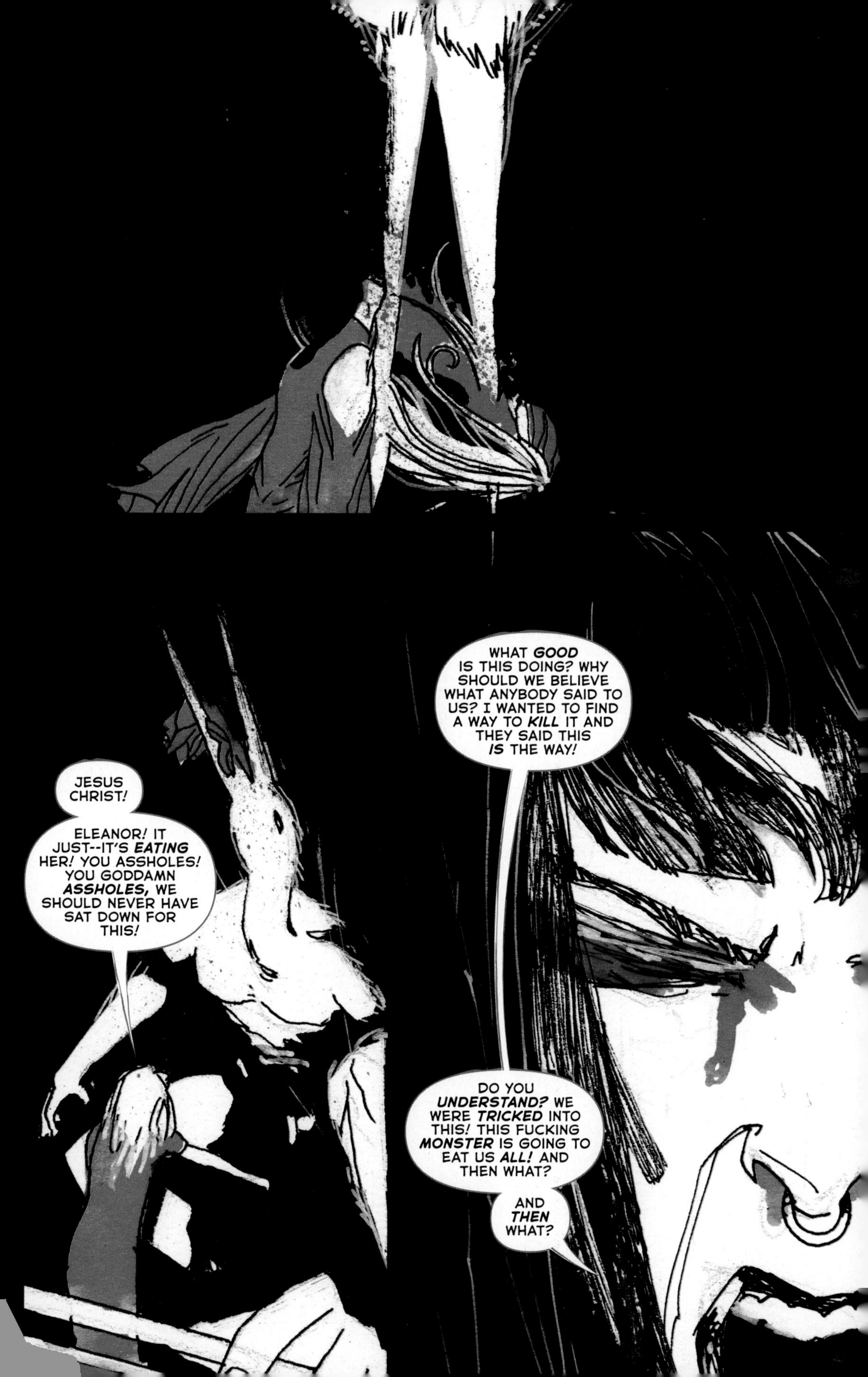
JESUS CHRIST!
ELEANOR! IT JUST--IT'S EATING HER! YOU ASSHOLES! YOU GODDAMN ASSHOLES, WE SHOULD NEVER HAVE SAT DOWN FOR THIS!
WHAT GOOD IS THIS DOING? WHY SHOULD WE BELIEVE WHAT ANYBODY SAID TO US? I WANTED TO FIND A WAY TO KILL IT AND THEY SAID THIS IS THE WAY!
DO YOU UNDERSTAND? WE WERE TRICKED INTO THIS! THIS FUCKING MONSTER IS GOING TO EAT US ALL! AND THEN WHAT?
AND THEN WHAT?

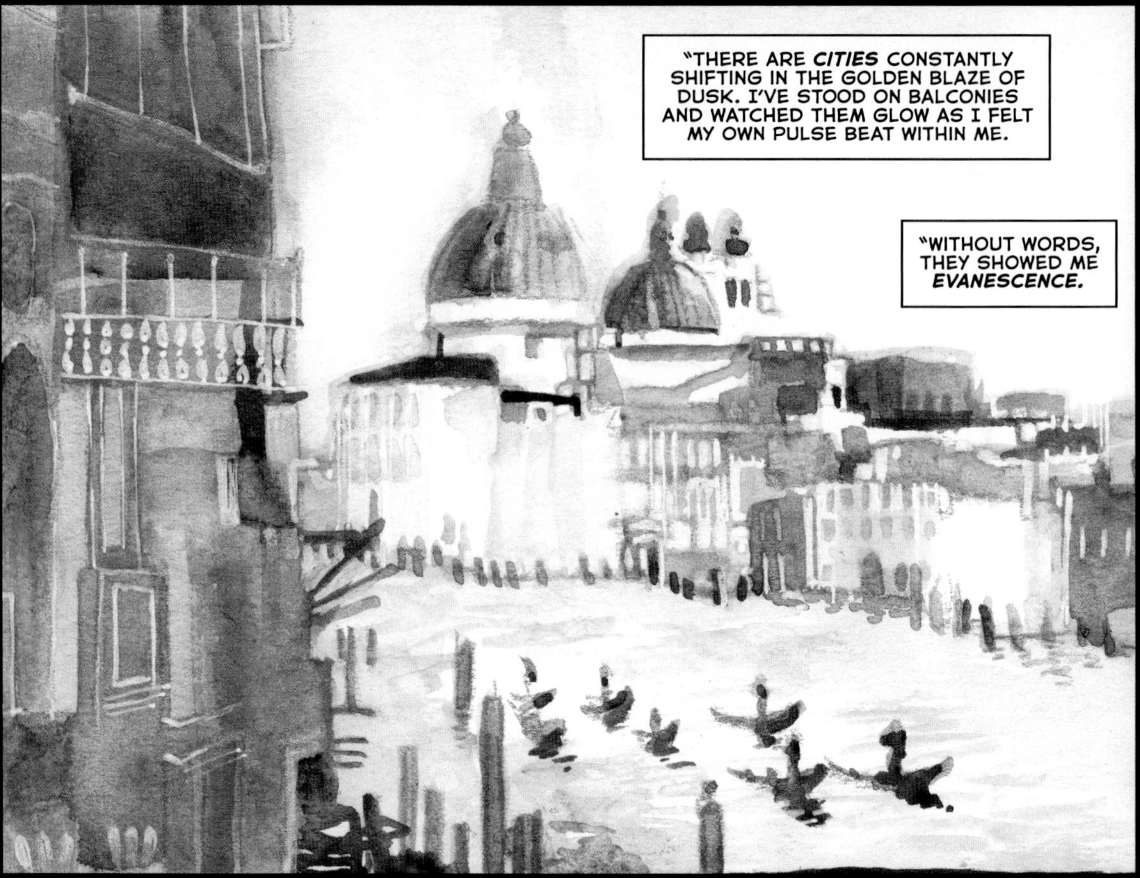
"THERE ARE *CITIES* CONSTANTLY SHIFTING IN THE GOLDEN BLAZE OF DUSK. I'VE STOOD ON BALCONIES AND WATCHED THEM GLOW AS I FELT MY OWN PULSE BEAT WITHIN ME.
"WITHOUT WORDS, THEY SHOWED ME *EVANESCENCE.*

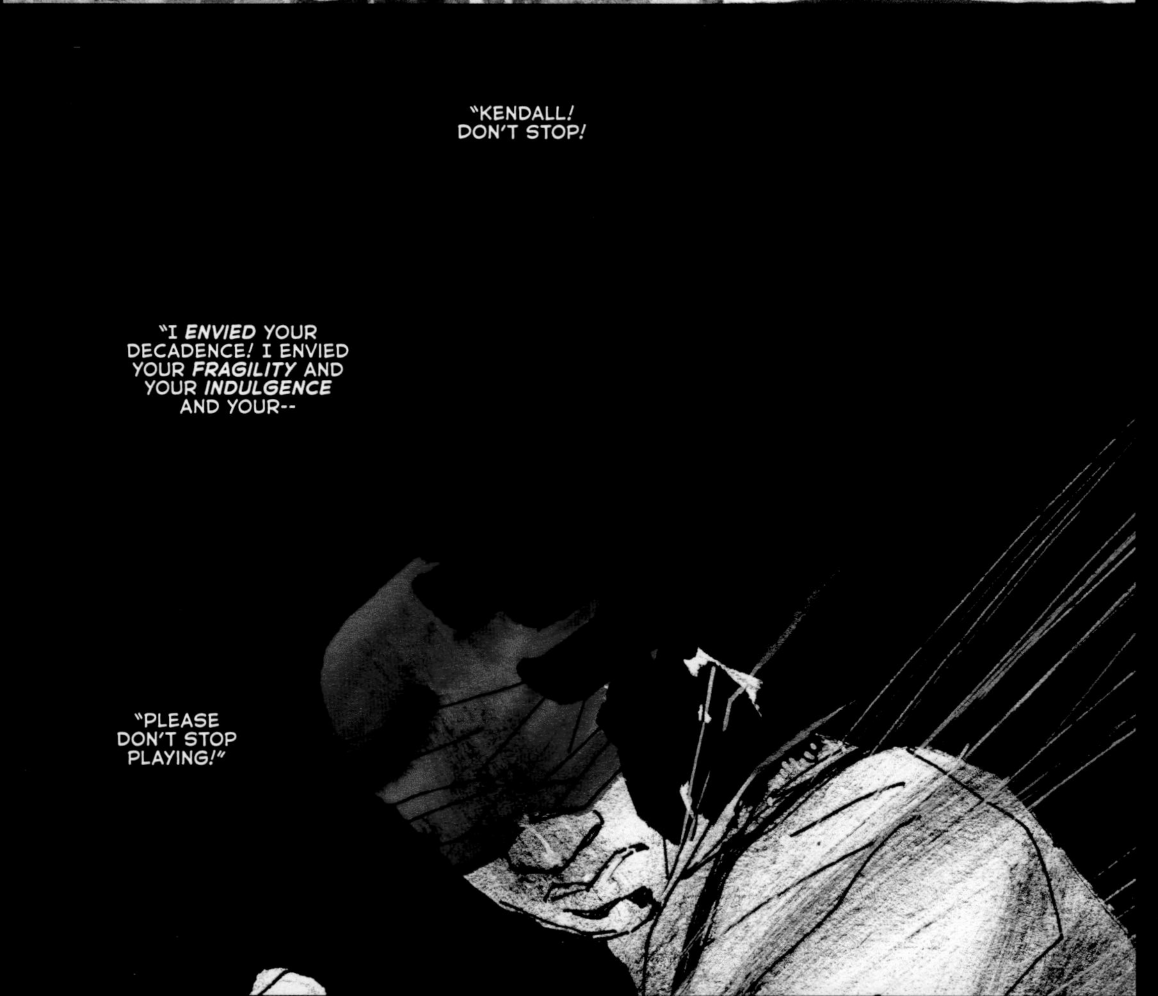
"KENDALL! DON'T STOP!
"I *ENVIED* YOUR DECADENCE! I ENVIED YOUR *FRAGILITY* AND YOUR *INDULGENCE* AND YOUR--
"PLEASE DON'T STOP PLAYING!"

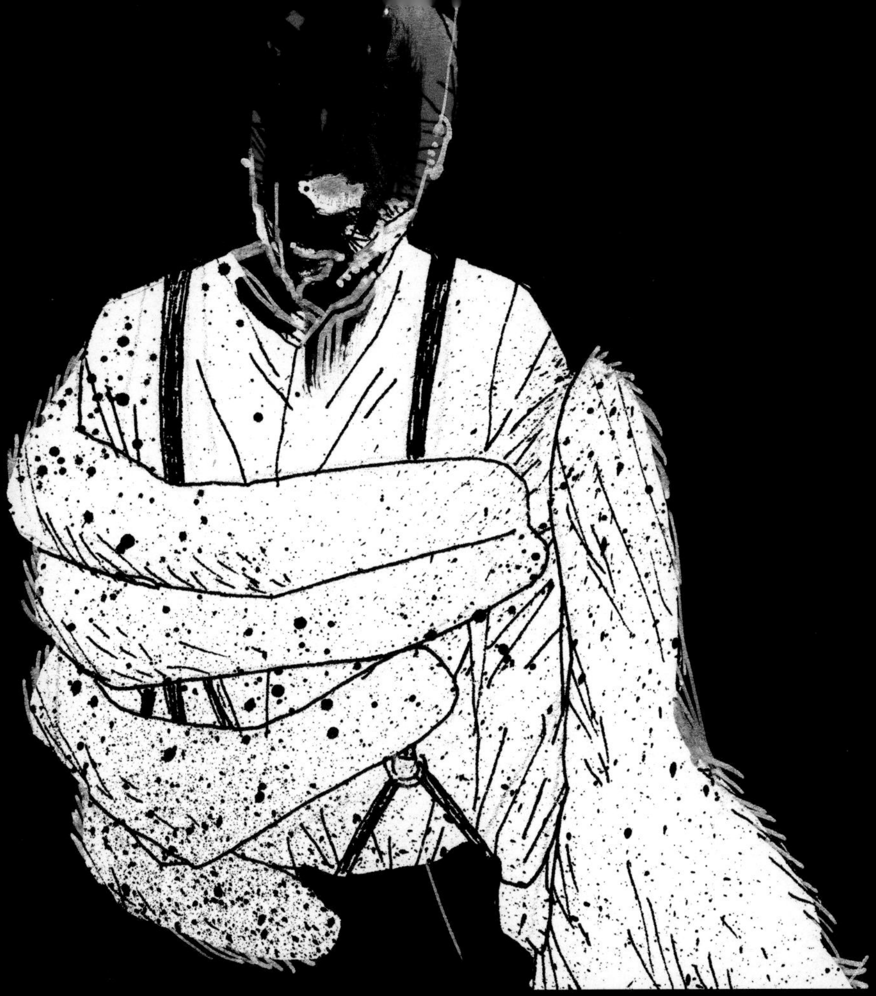

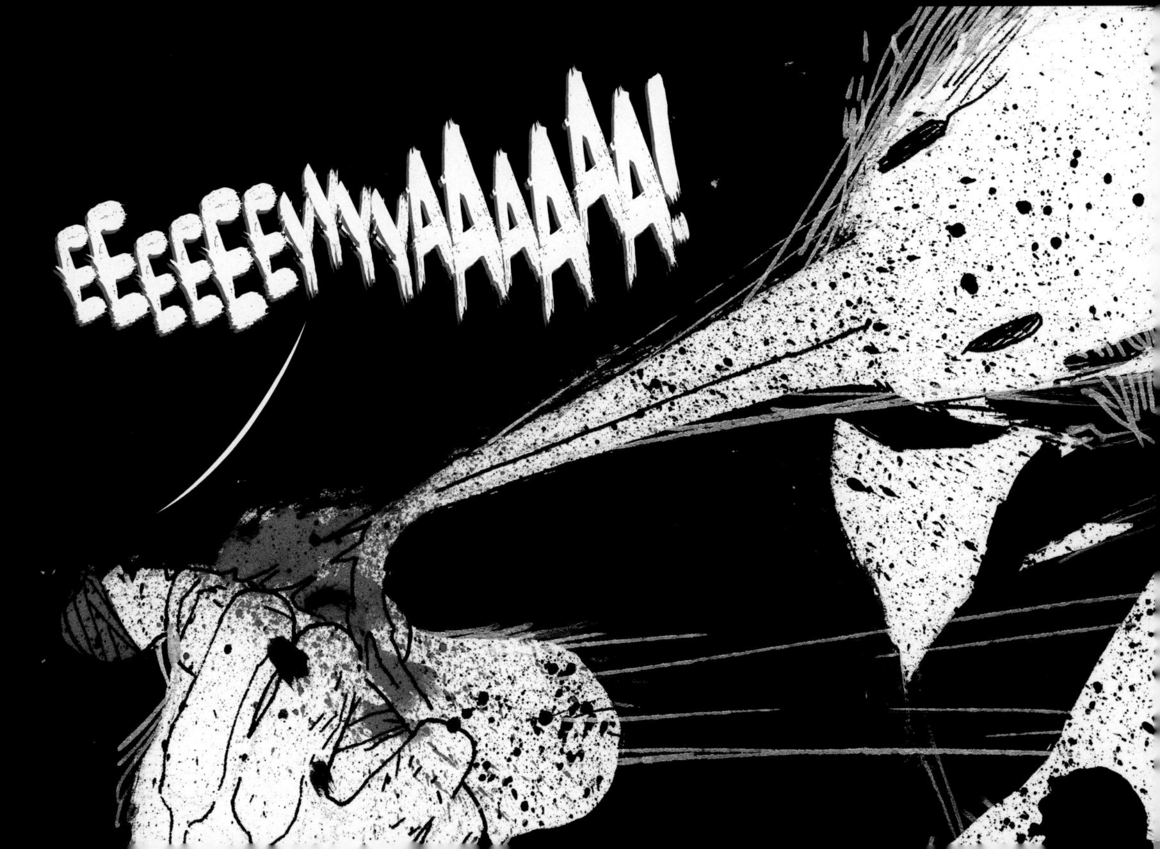
EEEEEEYYYAAAAAA!

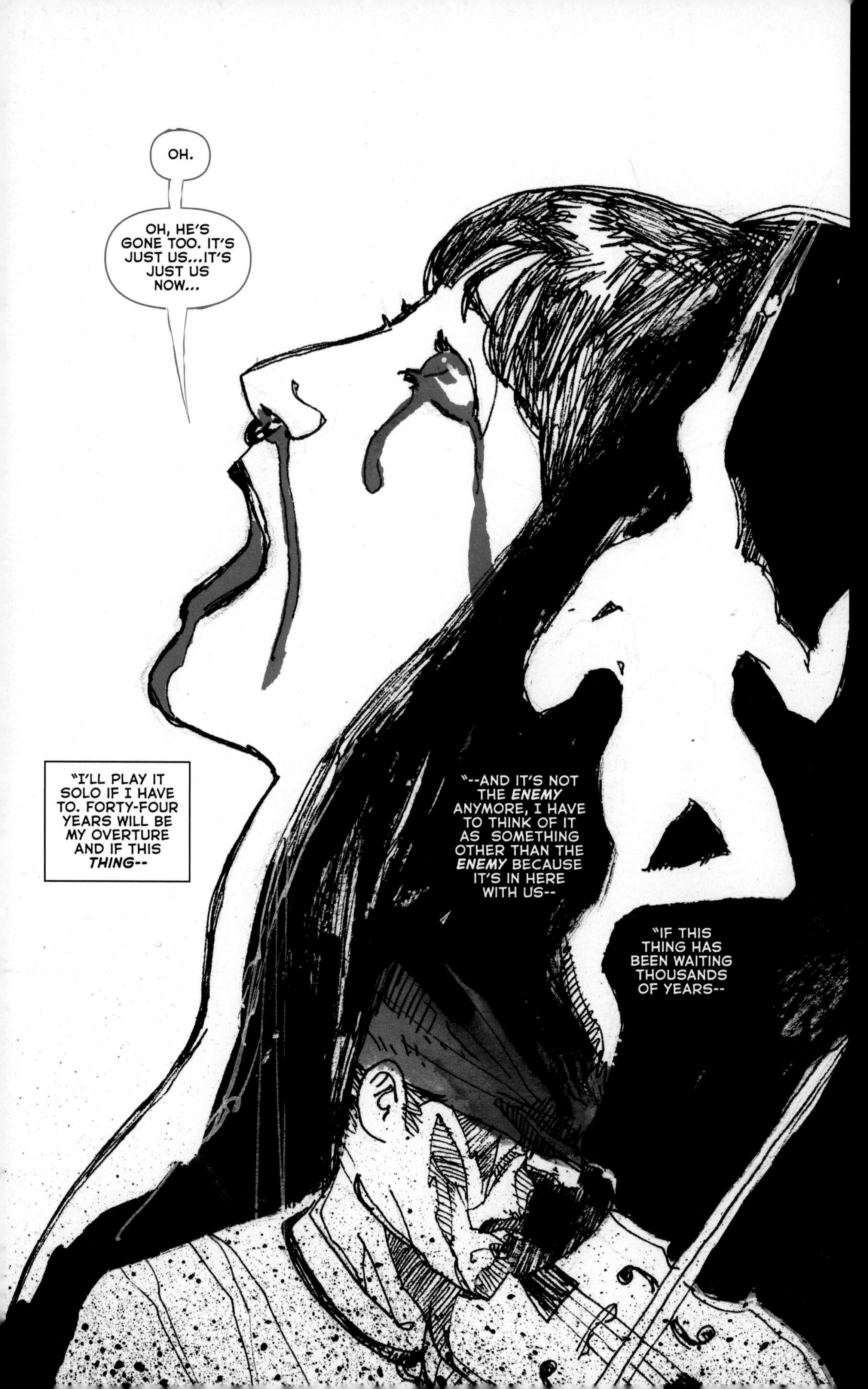
OH.
OH, HE'S GONE TOO. IT'S JUST US...IT'S JUST US NOW...
"I'LL PLAY IT SOLO IF I HAVE TO. FORTY-FOUR YEARS WILL BE MY OVERTURE AND IF THIS THING--
"--AND IT'S NOT THE ENEMY ANYMORE, I HAVE TO THINK OF IT AS SOMETHING OTHER THAN THE ENEMY BECAUSE IT'S IN HERE WITH US--
"IF THIS THING HAS BEEN WAITING THOUSANDS OF YEARS--

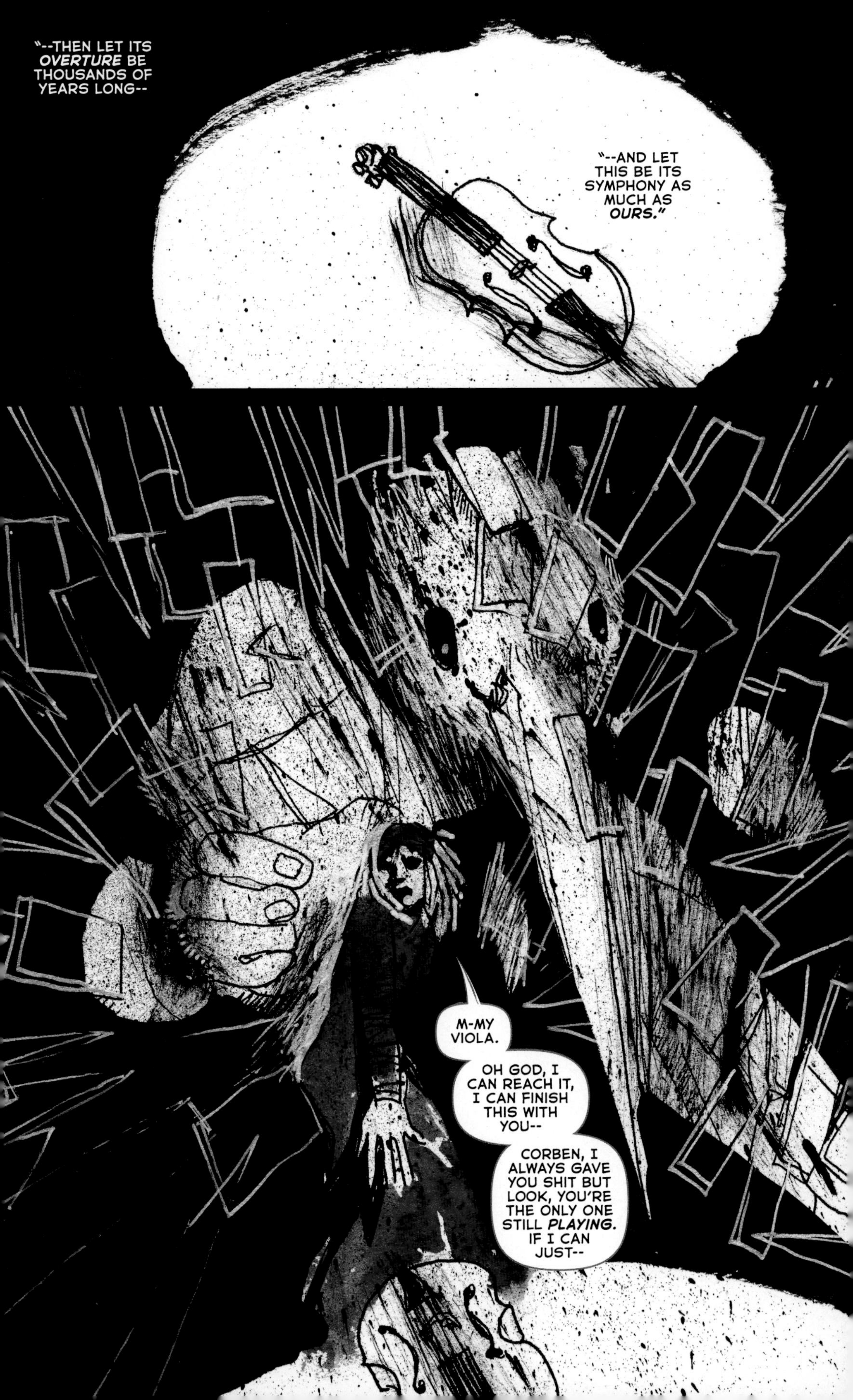
"--THEN LET ITS OVERTURE BE THOUSANDS OF YEARS LONG--
"--AND LET THIS BE ITS SYMPHONY AS MUCH AS OURS."
M-MY VIOLA.
OH GOD, I CAN REACH IT, I CAN FINISH THIS WITH YOU--
CORBEN, I ALWAYS GAVE YOU SHIT BUT LOOK, YOU'RE THE ONLY ONE STILL PLAYING. IF I CAN JUST--

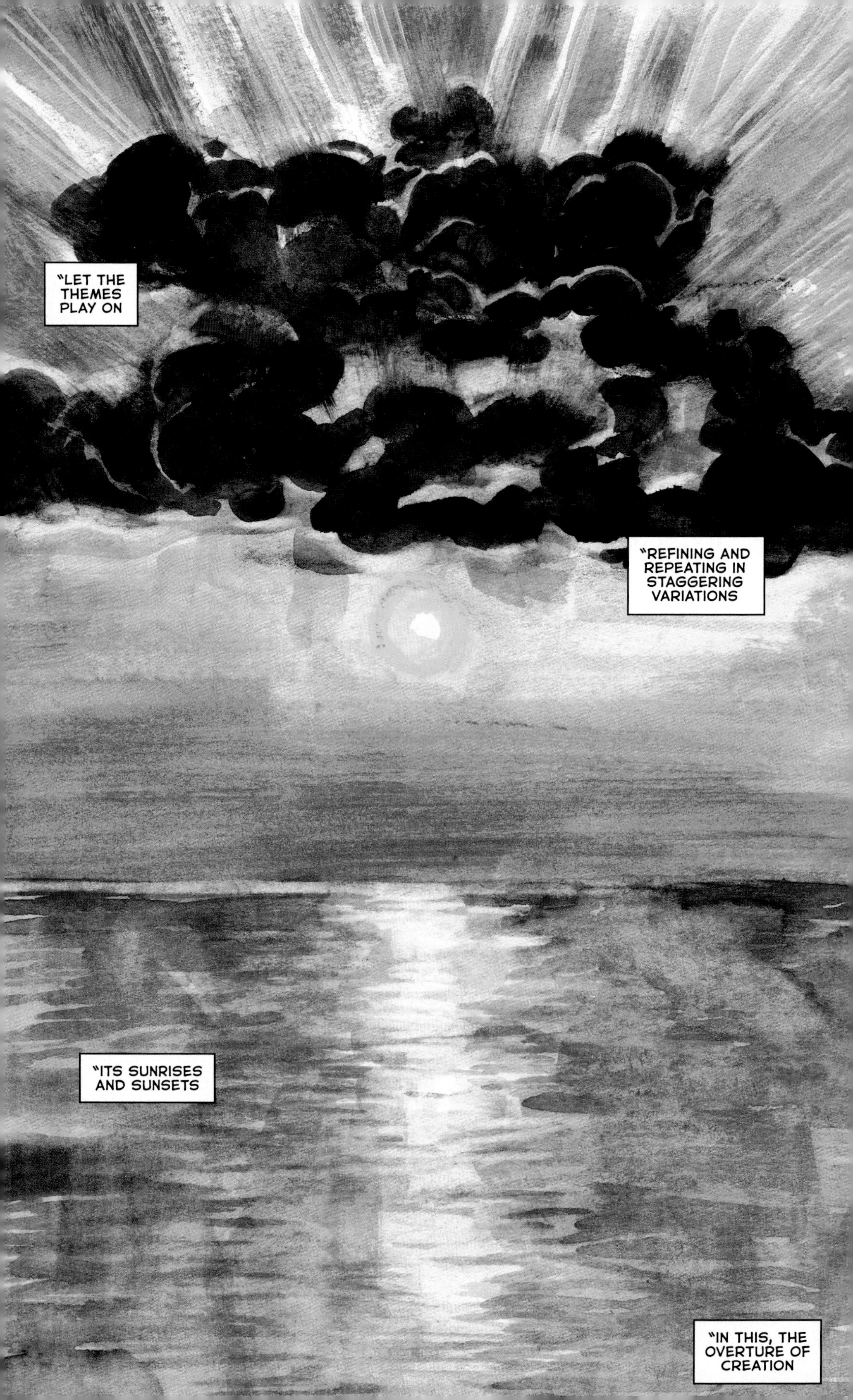
"LET THE THEMES PLAY ON
"REFINING AND REPEATING IN STAGGERING VARIATIONS
"ITS SUNRISES AND SUNSETS
"IN THIS, THE OVERTURE OF CREATION

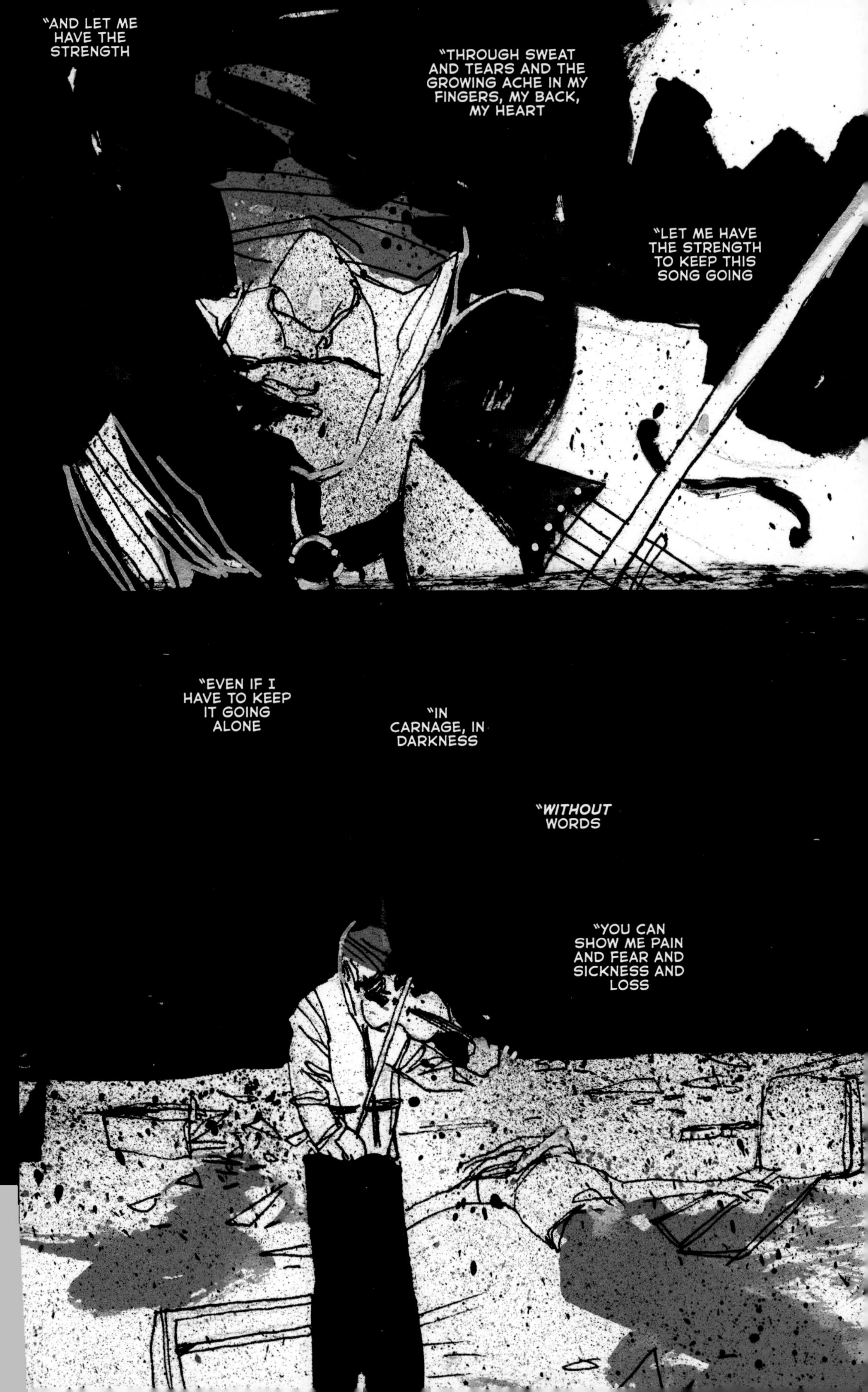
"AND LET ME HAVE THE STRENGTH
"THROUGH SWEAT AND TEARS AND THE GROWING ACHE IN MY FINGERS, MY BACK, MY HEART
"LET ME HAVE THE STRENGTH TO KEEP THIS SONG GOING
"EVEN IF I HAVE TO KEEP IT GOING ALONE
"IN CARNAGE, IN DARKNESS
"*WITHOUT* WORDS
"YOU CAN SHOW ME PAIN AND FEAR AND SICKNESS AND LOSS

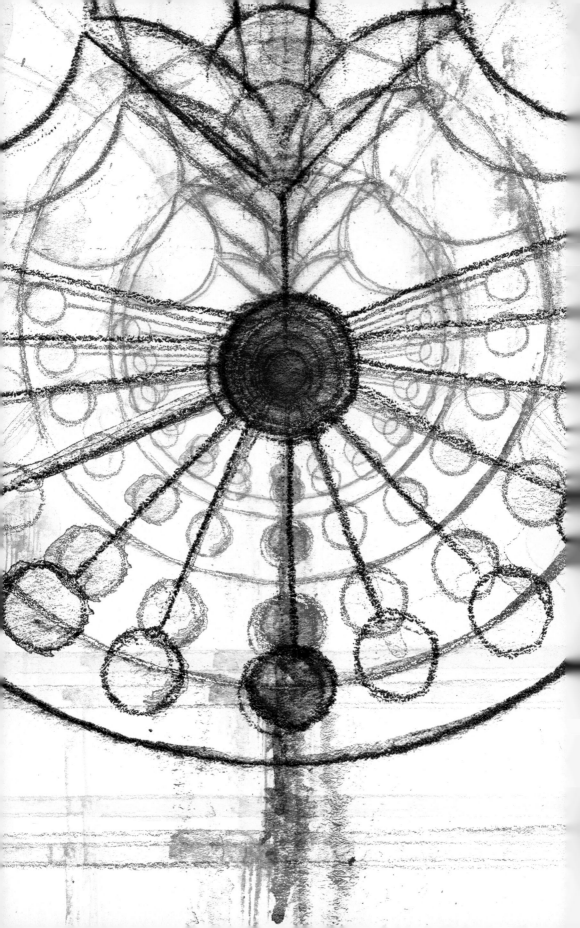

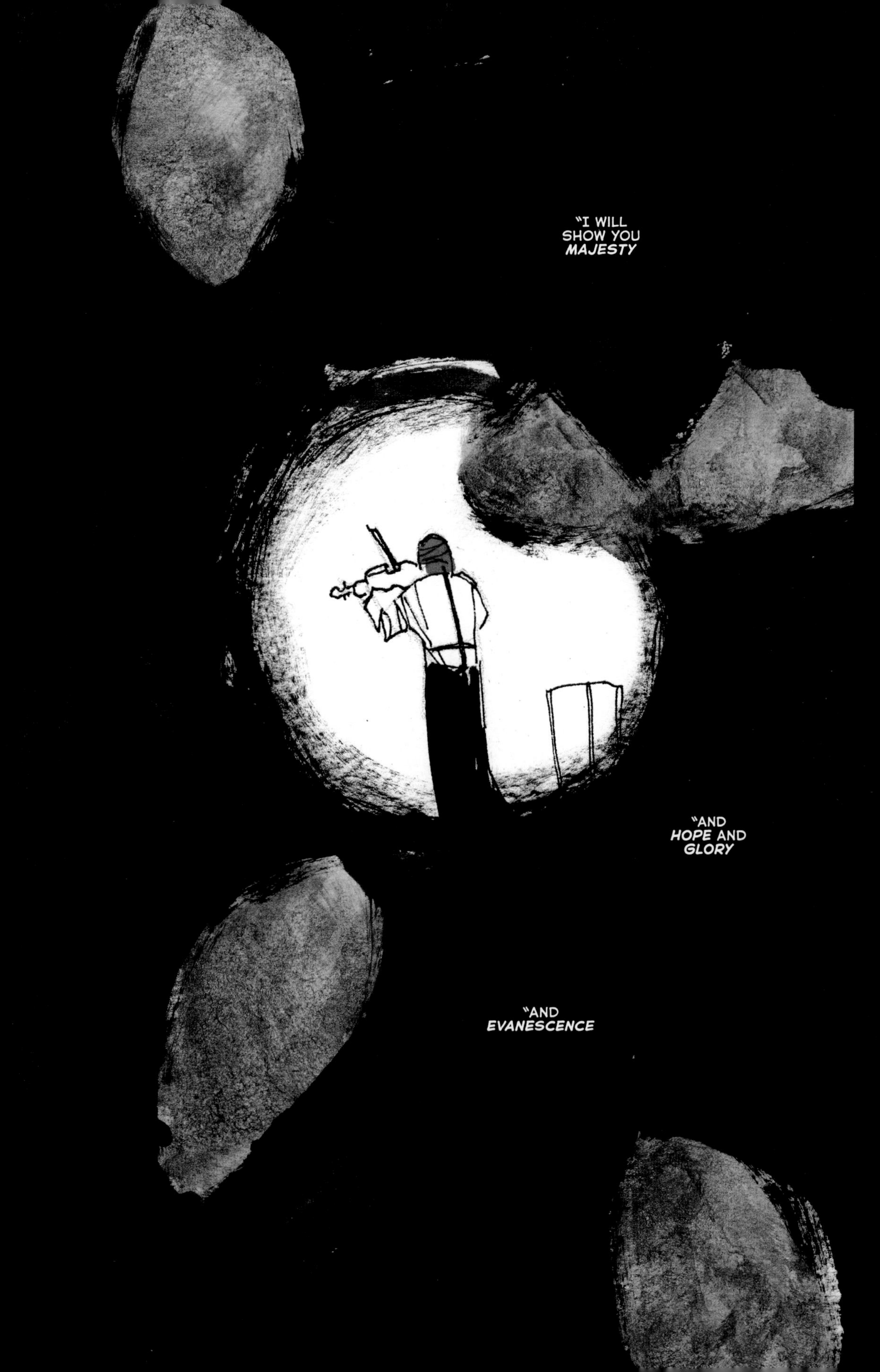
"I WILL SHOW YOU *MAJESTY*
"AND *HOPE* AND *GLORY*
"AND *EVANESCENCE*

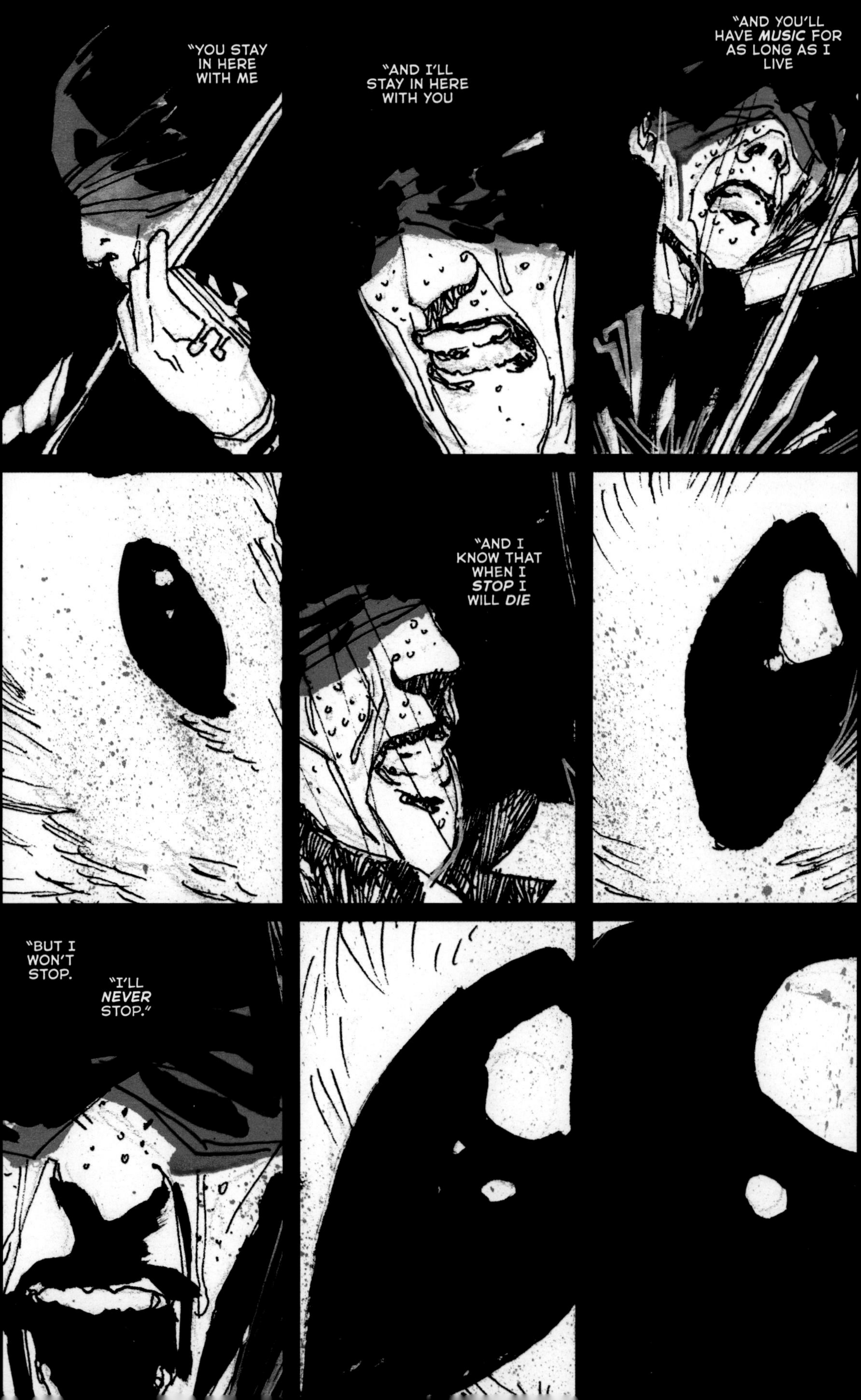
"YOU STAY IN HERE WITH ME
"AND I'LL STAY IN HERE WITH YOU
"AND YOU'LL HAVE *MUSIC* FOR AS LONG AS I LIVE
"AND I KNOW THAT WHEN I *STOP* I WILL *DIE*
"BUT I WON'T STOP.
"I'LL *NEVER* STOP."

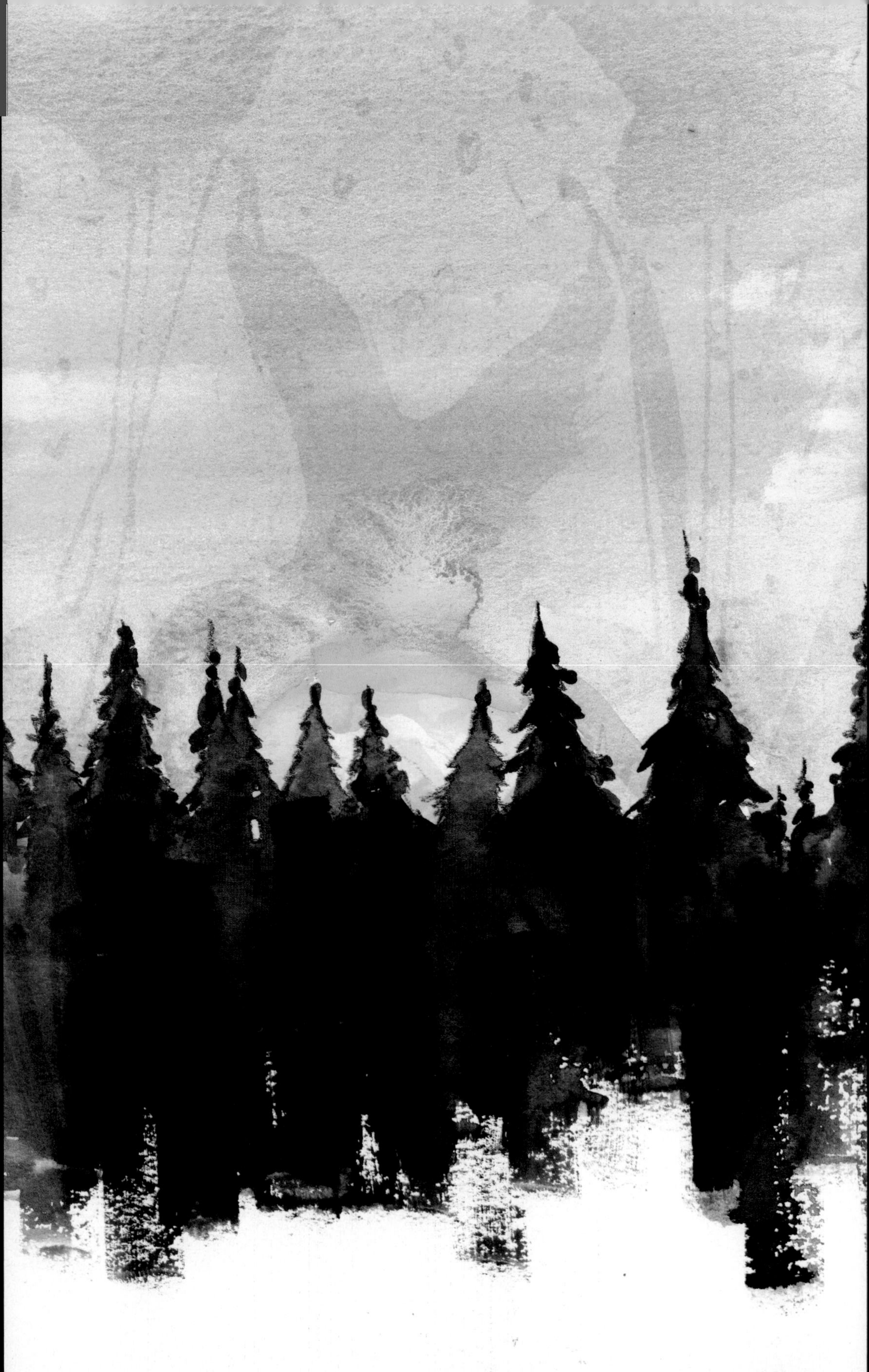

The End